FAR AS THE EYE CAN SEE

On the Way Home

The Lives of Riley Chance

Almighty Me!

The White Rooster and Other Stories

A Hole in the Earth

The Gypsy Man

Out of Season

Far as the Eye Can See

A NOVEL

Robert Bausch

BLOOMSBURY

NEW YORK • LONDON • NEW DELHI • SYDNEY

Published by Bloomsbury USA, New York

Bloomsbury is a trademark of Bloomsbury Publishing Plc

All papers used by Bloomsbury USA are natural, recyclable products made from wood grown in well-managed forests. The manufacturing processes conform to the environmental regulations of the country of origin.

LIBRARY OF CONGRESS CATALOGING-IN-PUBLICATION DATA

Bausch, Robert.
Far as the eye can see : a novel / Robert Bausch. — First U.S. edition.
pages cm
ISBN 978-1-62040-259-7 (alk. paper hardcover)
1. Military deserters—Fiction. 2. Swindlers and swindling—Fiction. I. Title.
PS3552.A847F38 2014
813'.54—dc23
2013044007

First U.S. Edition 2014

1 3 5 7 9 10 8 6 4 2

Typeset by Hewer Text UK Ltd., Edinburgh
Printed and bound in the U.S.A. by Thomson-Shore Inc., Dexter, Michigan

Bloomsbury books may be purchased for business or promotional use. For information on bulk purchases please contact Macmillan Corporate and Premium Sales Department at specialmarkets@macmillan.com.

Once again, for Denny—
I will study wry music for your sake . . .

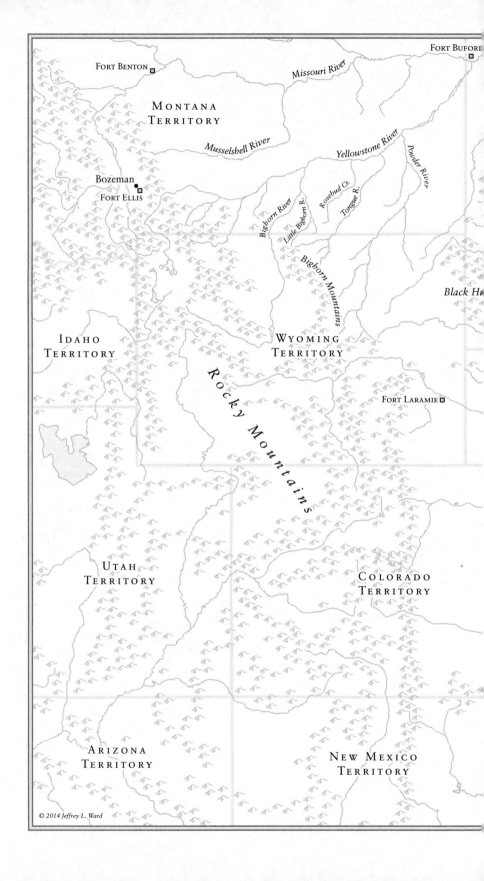

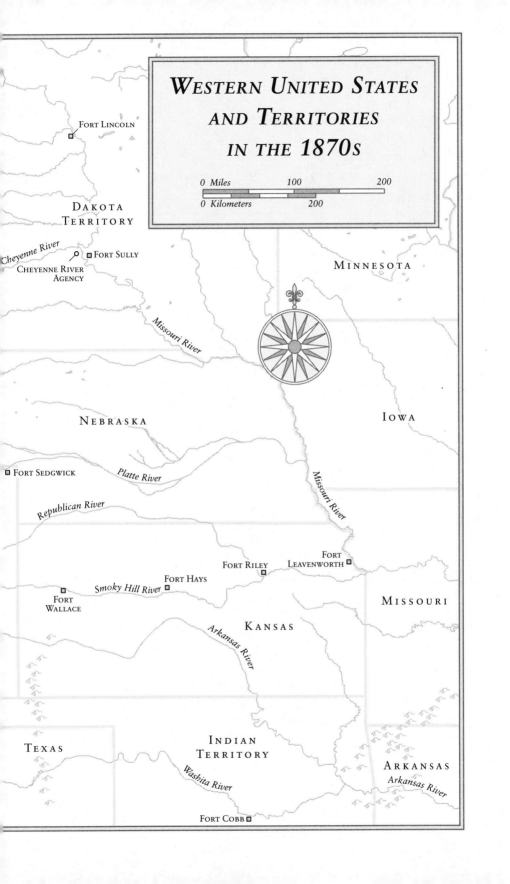

WESTERN UNITED STATES AND TERRITORIES IN THE 1870S

0 Miles   100   200

0 Kilometers   200

FORT LINCOLN

DAKOTA
TERRITORY

Cheyenne River

FORT SULLY

CHEYENNE RIVER
AGENCY

MINNESOTA

Missouri River

NEBRASKA

IOWA

FORT SEDGWICK

Platte River

Republican River

Missouri River

FORT
FORT RILEY   LEAVENWORTH

FORT HAYS

Smoky Hill River

FORT
WALLACE

MISSOURI

Arkansas River

KANSAS

TEXAS

INDIAN
TERRITORY

Washita River

ARKANSAS

Arkansas River

FORT COBB

PROLOGUE

Ink

March, 1876

FROM A BREAK in the rocks where I stand, the country is as big as any whole earth I ever dreamed of. When you're heading west, into this country, you don't get a sense of its size because you don't know where it ends. It's open and wide, of course, but you got this notion of finding the other side of it. Once you been here, and the years pass, you get used to it—to spaces surrounded by blue mountains that pile so high, you can't believe a man can walk in them. So when you find yourself feeling like you ought to skedaddle out of it as soon and fast as you can, it hits you how endless and gigantic it is.

And I feel like if I don't get out, I might get killed by either the army or the Indians. It may be both of them species of animal is after me. Until a few days ago, I was scouting for General Gibbon, coming from Fort Ellis in Bozeman, Montana Territory. He told me that soon Custer will come from the east and Reno from the south and we would settle the Indian question once and for all. But then I done something just by accident really and now I'm trying my damnedest to avoid Indians and Cavalry alike.

The trail stretches so far in front of me, everything in the distance fades to blue. You can barely see where the sky meets the ground. Some rolling purple clouds clamor in the farthest corner, light up with blue fire and a rumbling, and I know it's rain miles and miles from here, but it moves, like a train sometimes.

I got my horse, Cricket, next to me and she's lame. I'm tired, and sweat soaks through my clothing, so I would welcome a little rain. And I see something moving up the path in front of me, way up in front of me. Rocks rise up slightly on my right, and to the left is a great boulder that makes good shade and shelters me from the sun. The path is thick with brush and patches of thicket full of thorns and dry, twisted branches, but it's a path, and way beyond the two knobs of hill in front of me, I see him coming along on foot. A dark, thin shadow that might be a Indian or not. I can't tell. I stop moving, though. For my money, a soldier's just as dangerous as a Indian.

I don't make much of a shadow because the sun is in front of me. I've been standing here, trying to figure out how I can drag a lame horse up that path. I'm trying to go west, to Bozeman, where I hope the only woman I ever known that treated me like a important somebody, like I ain't a skunk, is waiting for me. Her name is Eveline and that particular appellation all by itself is music to me. I promised her I would be finished with this here expedition in the spring—June the latest—and then I'd leave the army here and head back to her. She said she would wait that long. She and her sister, Christine, want to go all the way to Oregon, and I signed on to take them there, if I can get back to Bozeman in time. Eveline said she would hope for me. You might say we are betrothed, even though we ain't said nothing about it out loud. With her, I might just find a way to save myself. Eventually I want to get away far enough that maybe I can live for a while in a house, near a ocean, and I won't wake up to the smell of horse manure, wet hay, and pigweed. I won't have to contend with the constant buzz-ing of blackflies, neither. But mostly now all I want is to go where nobody wants to kill me, and I'll have a fine good woman to take care of me.

Where the dark clouds hover it looks blue, and wet. And cool. I want to feel cool air again.

I don't feel like hiding, but I pull Cricket back and settle down in the curve of rock and high boulder just off the path. I figure I'll wait here and see who that is. Out in the middle of the whole world, not a buzzard or a jackrabbit in sight, and here walks this fellow. I set there for a while—watch the sun move above me and a bit down west. Then I get impatient. I move out into the path to see how far the fellow has to go, but now he ain't there no more. I can't see a damn thing except a few clumps of weed and juniper bush. He hides now, or he wants to creep up on me.

I move back to my horse and get my pistol and rifle. I carry a army-issue Colt .44 pistol and a carbine I bought a few years after the war ended. It's called a Evans repeater. It looks exactly like a Spencer repeating rifle, but it ain't. That specific breed of weapon only holds seven rounds. This here carbine holds thirty-four rounds of ammunition. When I fire it and then pull the curly cue handle on it, it ejects one shell and loads another, just like the Spencer, only faster. I can hold off a small army if I have to. I got a good strap on it so I can carry it over my shoulder.

I move around the other side of the rock. I can keep moving that way, but then it hits me I might do better to scale to the top of the boulder and look down on everything. So I take off my boots and socks, stick the pistol in my belt, sling the carbine over my shoulder, and start climbing. The stone is smooth and hot, but I get hold of a few small creases in it, and my bare feet and toes dig in on that flat surface a lot better than a pair of leather-soled boots. It takes a while but I get to the top, laying on my belly. From up there I can see a long way. The country curves up a little, but a lot less than I thought when I was standing on the flat ground looking at it. It's not really a hill at all but a long, gentle slope toward the west, with scrub grass, juniper bushes, and other brambles scattered like sleeping cattle on both sides of the path. To my left, the ground rises up slightly more, and the bushes give way to rocks and falling sand that empties at the foot of the boulder I'm laying on. I can't see a thing but I know he's somewhere out there, not moving. I make up my mind I'll lay here as long as it takes. He'll have to move sometime. Then I see him on my left, laying flat on the ground, moving between two bramble bushes as swiftly as a snake. He's coming for me, all right, trying to get around behind me.

He has to be a Indian. It makes my skin prickle watching how swiftly he can move on his belly. I take the carbine and aim it carefully. He stops moving, but I can still see a brown patch of what's got to be skin, above the lighter brown leggings he wears. I can hit him right in the middle if I don't waste no time, so I squeeze off a round. I see dirt kick up just where his body meets the ground, and he rolls over and disappears. It's like he dropped into the ground or something. I can't be sure I hit him. I stay low and get ready for another shot. The carbine made enough noise and left enough smoke in the air, he'll have no trouble seeing where the shot come from, so I'm ready for him. I get as flat and close to that rock as I can, still aiming the carbine in that direction. I hear Cricket shutter and stomp. I don't like it that she's down there where I can't see her, and my boots are there, my saddle. I remember, too, that Cricket pulled up limping, and I don't like that problem, neither. It's a bad time all over again and I am suddenly pretty exercised about it. "Damnation," I say to nobody but the air. Nothing moves in front of me. Except for the ringing in my ears from the damn carbine, there ain't no sound. I concentrate on the patch of ground where I seen the Indian roll into oblivion. I wonder if a dark spot there on the ground is blood or just the shadow of one of the juniper bushes.

I don't know how long I wait there looking for something to move, but finally I decide I have to get down off that rock and go looking. The first thing I do when I'm back on the ground is put my boots back on. My horse hangs her head low, looks at me. I untie her, remove the bridle and the saddle and all my gear. I do this without looking away from the dark side of that boulder, where I know the Indian will have to come if he's coming.

"Go on, Cricket," I say. "Eat what you can find, girl. We'll camp here for a while." She seems to nod, but she don't go nowhere. "Suit yourself," I say.

Then I pick up the carbine and sling it over my shoulder again. I hold the pistol in my hand, ready to shoot, and move around to the left of the boulder, into the shadow. I stay low as I can and keep my eyes ahead of me. I look for any movement. I'll shoot the first twitter of light or dark I see. I'm that wound up. It feels just like it always felt going into battle in the war. Like my whole body is cold with seeing and feeling, every square inch ready. My heart's a stuttering bag.

I don't get too far from my horse before I see him. He's crouched in a small ravine, behind a thick clump of grass, laying on his side, his legs drawed up, his back to me, not moving. From where I stand, he looks like a small, rectangular rock. It's no wonder I couldn't see him from the top of that boulder. If not for his black hair, I might of kept on toward him thinking he's a rock, but I stop in my tracks and wait.

I think to shoot him again, but then I want to see if he'll move. I hope I got him with the one shot. I learned in the army there ain't no use in wasting bullets. So I watch him for a while, and when he don't move, I step a little closer to him. I'm maybe ten feet away when I hear him groan. That's when I know. No man ever made a sound like that.

It's a woman, and she's crying to beat all, holding every breath of it, trying not to make no noise.

"Aw, Jesus," I say, and she screams. She didn't know how close I was. I crouch down and move to where I can see her face. She grimaces in pain and the whole front of her is covered in blood. She screams again when she sees me.

"Aw, Jesus," I say again. "I'm sorry." It's a young girl, scrawny and dark. Long strands of wet black hair cover her eyes and run down into her mouth. She wears leather pants and shirt, and beads around her neck. She clutches a heavy pouch. She has a big hunting knife sheathed in leather, tied to her waist. I put the carbine down and kneel next to her. I'm afraid to touch her, but I got to see the wound. "Here," I say, and I reach out and touch her on the shoulder. "Let me see."

She looks at me, still breathing heavy, still frightened so completely her eyes dart like a trapped animal's eyes, but she don't move when I touch her. There's something real fierce in her fear, if you know what I mean. Like she'll quiver and all, but if I make a wrong move I'll have that hunting knife to contend with. "You speak American?" I whisper. I smell urine. Her nose runs badly with mucus and her hair is all tangled in it. The eyes are dark, and yellow-rimmed. "Iisáakshi-m," I say. "I thought you was a young man." I know a little Crow and not much else of Indian languages. "Maybe you speak Crow?"

She closes her eyes, then whispers, "English."

"I'm glad of it," I say. Gently I try to unfold her, get her to lay on her back, but she won't budge.

"Let me see the wound."

She moves one of her arms down, then turns slightly, and I see where I got her. She's hit in the side, all right, but it went along the front of her abdomen. She was laying in such a way that the bullet come in low and skimmed under her skin in front and out the other side. I hit flesh and only flesh. It burned her—I can see the skin black and still smoking a bit—and she is bleeding, but if I clean it up a bit, it won't kill her.

"You'll be all right," I say. I am really glad I didn't take another shot when I first seen her. "What the hell are you doing out here all by yourself?"

She's stopped crying and sniffling but I can see she's still in a lot of pain. I move some of the hair out of her face, and she opens her eyes and maybe sees me for the first time. I mean, she studies my face real hard. Her dark skin and black eyebrows make her look almost unnaturally evil, but it don't scare me none. I never have believed in stuff I can't see or hear or taste or smell or touch. I don't believe in no devil nor demons. I think we're all bad enough here on earth—we don't need no outside help, if you know what I mean. I seen a lot of men praying and I seen them dying. Didn't seem to matter if they was believers or not. A bullet don't care what a fellow believes, and for sure folks don't give a damn, neither.

The woman is helpless and small, wounded and needful. I can leave her here and she might die, but I ain't gonna do that. Damn it, I know I ain't gonna do that. I say to her, "You'll be all right. I'll take care of you."

She watches me put the pistol in my belt and then put the sling on the carbine over my head so the gun is across my back. "I'm going to try and help you up," I say. "You got no broke bones and you should be able to walk." I lift her up, and she comes easily enough, though she lets out this little whimper of pain—or maybe it's fear. "I know you're hurt," I say.

She says nothing, she just looks at me. Now her eyes are sad and kind of pitiful looking. I feel sorry for her. "You're going to be all right," I say. We move along pretty slowly. She takes little baby steps but then starts to move a little better. She holds her arm and hand across where her belly is ripped and the blood still runs. It looks almost black on her leather pants. I know she's really hurting but she don't cry out no more, and I'm starting to think she's a lot tougher than she looks. "I'm sorry I shot you."

No response.

"You're so thin, it's a damn miracle the bullet skimmed under the skin like that."

She don't even look at me.

"Why was you trying to sneak around behind me?"

She shakes her head and says something so drowned in tears and heavy breathing, I can't understand it. I think she said she wasn't doing no such thing.

8

"I thought you was trying to get behind me."

"I just wanted to go around," she gasps. She speaks American clear as a bell.

"You speak real good American," I say. "Where you from?"

She coughs, then spits on the ground in front of us. I stop and check the little globule of spit close. "Ain't no blood in it," I say. "You're gonna be all right."

She wipes her nose, pulls some of the matted hair away from her face. She has wide cheekbones and a thin-lipped mouth. The skin around her top lip is so dark, it looks almost like a small mustache. Her lips are thin and pink.

We scoot back to where I'd let Cricket loose. She's not far off. I let the girl ease down on the ground again and rest her head on my saddle. "Just wait there," I tell her. Then I go to my saddlebag and get a clean piece of calico—I rip the back out of one of my shirts—and a ball of twine and a sewing needle. I got a bottle of whiskey in there and I grab that too. I don't think the calico is gonna be big enough to wrap her. I pour a little whiskey on both wounds, clean them up as best I can. She has a long bruise that runs from one hole across her abdomen just under her belly button and right up to where the bullet went out. The skin there is tore all to hell. I use the twine to sew it up. She don't move or bat a eye while I'm rooting around in that bloody thing. And right up to the second I close it up she was sure bleeding out of that hole. Much more than where the bullet gone in. It's a good thing my shot was low. If I'd aimed just a inch or two higher, she'd of sure died. The bullet would of cut her right in two. I tell her as much, but she's out cold by the time I finish wrapping the calico tightly around her middle. It fits better than I believed it would. I don't know if she's asleep or if she passed out.

She's just a thick ball of black hair and, hanging underneath that, a sad, round face and just a slip of a body. I guess she needs something to eat. All I have is a sack of dried beans, a little raw sowbelly, a bag of coffee and sugar cubes, a few strips of beef jerky, and some hardtack. I go back to where her pouch is and find some leather leggings, some more dried beans, and a piece of sowbelly that looks to be at least a half a year old. It stinks to high heaven, but it will cook up just fine. I take it all back and set it down at her feet.

9

In a little while, Cricket comes back, looking lame as ever and disappointed.

"What's the matter, old girl? Nothing much to eat around here, is there." The Indian girl thinks I was talking to her. She opens her eyes a little and frowns. "Not you," I say.

I think she might start crying again, but she reaches for my hand and tries to pull herself up. It's just too much pain.

"You're all bruised up down there," I say. "You won't be able to use them muscles for a spell."

She takes a deep breath, then looks at me like a hungry puppy. "Help me up," she says.

I try to be gentle but it hurts her to bend like that. I set her up against the saddle with her feet splayed out in front of her. She points to the blood on her moccasins.

"Dripped on them while we was walking," I say. "But you ain't bleeding no more."

It looks like the saddle is causing her sizable pain. "You want me to lay you back down again?"

"No."

"Looks like it's hard to get air. You having trouble breathing?"

"No."

"It must just be the pain, then." I set there looking at her, wondering what I might do next.

After a while she seems to settle down. I get up and put the bridle back on Cricket and tether her to the trunk of a pretty thick juniper. I get some of the sugar out of my pack and feed it to her. "There'll be plenty of grass up ahead, old girl," I whisper.

The sky above us is absolutely white. Not a cloud nowhere and no depth to it. The sun is behind us now, so it does no good to crouch in the lee of the boulder. The only place that looks like a sky is the deep blue distance where it rumbles and sparks.

"Somebody's getting wet," I say, taking a place next to my wounded companion. "March thunderstorms can be pretty bad. You feel up to a little talk?"

She seems to nod, but she looks at me like she hopes I'll change things somehow.

"What's your name?"

"Ink," she says. She don't look away from me.

"That a Indian name?"

"I am called Stand Alone Woman by the Sioux."

"What kind of name is Ink?"

"It is what my father called me when I was little. I am so dark. My real name is Diana."

"Your daddy a white man?"

"My mother was Indian."

"But he was white."

"Yes."

"So what the hell you doing out here?"

She grimaces a bit, seems to take in a little more air. "I am running away from my husband."

"You married?"

"To a Miniconjou brave."

"Really."

"I did not want to be. I was taken when I was sixteen. They killed my father. My mother . . ." She stops.

"What about your mother?"

"I don't know what happened to her. I never saw her after I got taken."

"They took her too?"

"She was Nez Perce, but she was living with the Crow when she took up with my father."

"Miniconjous don't like the Crow."

"Only white men like the Crow."

"And you been with the Miniconjous how long?"

"I lost track of years. Seven or eight. I do not know. I was sixteen when they got me."

"You don't look much older than sixteen now," I say.

She falls silent for a while. Maybe she wants to cry a little, but she don't.

"Diana," I say.

"I am Ink," she says. She's studied me all through this conversation, but now she looks away. She's made up her mind that I ain't gonna hurt her no more.

"You're a pretty tough little thing, ain't you," I say.

"I have never seen hair as red as yours," she says.

"Not even among the scalps your tribe taken?"

"Who are you?"

"I ain't nobody," I say.

"What is your name?"

I tell her I got lots of names but Bobby Hale will do.

"Why you got so many names?"

"I joined the Union army a few times during the war."

"The big war in the east?"

"That's the one."

"What is your real name?"

"It ain't nothing I want to tell," I say. She looks at me. There's something in her face now that surprises me—like she knows more than she lets on about a lot of things and she won't let me in on a bit of it unless I tell her my born name. So I say, "My first name was Charlie. I didn't like it. You're Ink. I'm Bobby Hale. I been Bobby Hale since the war. It don't matter what folks called me when I was growing up. I hated that name and was glad to get shed of it."

A smile works its way to the surface around her mouth. I think the pain has eased up some.

"You feeling better?"

"I'm hungry," she says.

"Well. You run away with nothing but that 'ere knife of yours, the leather on your back, and a pouch full of dried beans and rotten bacon, you're bound to be pretty hungry before long. And since you couldn't of come far that way, we must be pretty close to your village."

Her eyes get a little bigger.

"Ain't we?"

"I ran all night and most of today. We are a long way from there."

"Where'd you think you was going?"

"The last place I lived with my father. Fort Buford."

"Well, you was headed in the right direction, but it ain't straight east. It's way north of here too."

She don't say nothing.

"It's where the Missouri and Yellowstone Rivers meet."

"That is where I must go."

"I'm trying to get to Fort Ellis myself. It's a long way in the other direction, west of here."

"Are you a soldier?"

"I was with the army for a spell. A paid guide, kind of. I ain't enlisted nor nothing. Now I'm avoiding them if I can."

"But you go to Fort Ellis."

"Well, I'm trying to get back to Bozeman. I ain't going nowhere near the fort if I can help it."

"My village was near the Musselshell River."

"That's a good ways."

"I ran all night and most of the day. That is how far."

"And you thought you was going to run all the way to Fort Buford."

"I did not care," she says. "Maybe I wanted to die. I thought I might run until I died. Then I ran into you."

"Right about the time I seen you, I expect."

She tries to move a bit, and again her face shows real pain. But she don't make a sound. She reaches for her pouch and I hand it to her. She takes out the sowbelly and starts chewing on the end of it. It's white and slippery and she almost drops it, but she gets a good bit of it in her mouth.

"That will make you sick," I say.

She shakes her head, still chewing.

"You don't think so."

"It once made me sick. I'm used to it now."

"I'd rather eat raw buffalo."

We set there for a while without saying nothing. I watch her gnawing on the fat of that bacon like a small dog. I think it might make *me* sick. I could use it fried up in a pan, though. I could make fried dough with it.

"You really wanted to die?" I say.

"I was not worried about what was in front of me. Only behind me."

"Well, you brought along that hunting knife."

She looks away.

"And if you really wanted to die, I almost got the job done for you."

I hear the sky rumbling again, a bit louder this time. I stand up and look beyond the rock and, sure enough, the sky darkens a little closer this way. Lightning flashes a few times. Ink smells of piss, so I ain't all that unhappy about the rain. We could both use a good soaking. "I sure hope that rain is coming for us," I say, settling back down beside Ink. "I could use a good rinsing off."

It ain't just the rain, though. I suspect one hell of a lot more than rain is heading our way.

PART ONE

Theo

1869

{ CHAPTER 1 }

I STARTED OUT HERE by myself in 1869 on a damn train. Got to St. Louis riding in a coach. Then bought a big red mare—I named her Cricket—and a fairly new .44 Colt Dragoon sidearm. I bought a army pup tent, some blankets, and a few cooking utensils. I bought ten pounds of coffee, some dried beans, smoked ham, and five pounds each of sugar and salt. Sugar was near a dollar a pound back then, so I spent most all I had. I also got some sowbelly and molasses; stocked up with whiskey and two canteens of water. I figured I'd fill those canteens whenever I needed to. But the best investment I made was the Evans repeater. It's right difficult to load and takes a bit of time, but once you got all thirty-four of them shells in there, you can fight a long time. I picked up a hundred rounds of ammunition for the pistol and a box of two hundred for the carbine.

I was ready to strike out on my own, but of course I wouldn't head into this country by myself. Everybody said it was the place to be—with free land and open skies. Well, I'll tell you: it's beautiful. As pretty as anything you can find in your head, dreaming or awake. There ain't nothing more beautiful. What folks don't mention is the dry heat in summer, the long, cold, empty winters with snow falling and blowing sometimes for days at a stretch, and the ferocious storms all year-round. They don't mention the clouds of locusts or the work you'll do. Or who you'll do it with.

Anyway, it was in March of 1869 I followed a small wagon train, led by a man named Theo, north out of St. Louis, and rode along with them for about three or four hundred miles or so. He had a Crow Indian named Big Tree as his wagon master on the train, and one look at that fellow and you known where he got his name. He was more than six and a half feet tall and solid as stone. His face was smooth as a butcher block, with dark eyes hiding in the lee of his great forehead. Big Tree almost never smiled, but every now and then he would let out a loud sort of harrumph that was clearly the first notes in a pretty qualified laugh.

I wasn't with the train in no real sense, but I camped right in sight and helped hunt along the way sometimes. The women on the train cooked up what we killed and I shared in it when they invited me.

I was alone, but it wasn't something I wanted for myself. I mean, I didn't come all the way out here to be by myself. I thought I'd make it, though; maybe I'd have women and respect and land. Lots of land. I wanted a place I could name and it would be what I'd leave on the earth when I died. To tell the truth, I didn't never know what I wanted, but I was sure that I was a man of destiny.

During the War of the Rebellion I joined the Union army seven times. I'd collect the bonus, then when I could I'd slip away, go back to some Northern city and change my name, spend the bonus, then enlist again. But eventually I ended up in a few battles. One or two is a lot of battles, to tell the truth, but you only need to see one to know you don't want no part of no other.

The truth is, I lived through some of the worst fighting near the end of the war: I felt the heat of bullets slicing air and snapping right by my face. I seen men dropping next to me in rows like something cut down by a thresher in a wheat field. And I stood there a facing it.

I was a soldier off and on for almost three years. And when the war ended, I figured my future was going to be out in the open country where land was there for any fellow with the nerve to stake it out and call it his. That's what I thought I was going to do. In such a big country, what could stop me? The government passed a law that said if I could stake it out, I was entitled to one hundred and sixty acres of free land.

I had no kin to speak of. Just a aunt who was already in her late fifties and too old to even think about travel and change. She lived in Philadelphia and that's where she thought I would return after the war. My mother died of cholera and my father lit out in the same year. (You'd a thought he killed her.) I was nine years old. At the time we lived in Pittsburgh, but then I went to live with my aunt until the war broke out. She was a old maid that never married and I don't think she liked men very much. She never once looked upon me with anything but impatience and disparagement. I don't think she was sorry to see me go when the war took me away. I wrote her a few letters and got one or two back and that was that. When the war ended, I was stuck in Walter Peck's brigade just outside Petersburg, Virginia.

I turned in my uniform and bought a few linen shirts and a pair of denim pants, and I hung around Petersburg for a little while. Then I went with some fellows out to the ocean on the Virginia shore and swum for days in the salt water. It felt like I was washing the war right off of me. The dirty sweat of fear and uncertainty. I was going to live, by God. And that's when I got to thinking about going out to the big West. I thought about it a long time. Year after year I thought about it.

It was always something I planned to do, but I hung around Petersburg, working in a shop that made saddles and leather goods. I guess I did that kind of work for most of a year, then I spent some time working in the new ironworks in Richmond. I kept thinking about getting out, but I'd drink a lot of whiskey, work dawn to dark, have little of money in my pockets, and a warm place to sleep. Four years just went by with me living day by day. Then I got laid off at the ironworks. I didn't even have much money saved, but I just said the hell with it, I'm a-going.

Folks called it "the big West."

It's big, all right, but what they forget is, once you get near it, you realize how small you are. Small and unimportant, like something squeaky in the hay of a big barn. You don't know what might step on you.

It's how I felt anyway.

You notice the sky out here. And land so far in front and next to you and behind you—as far as the eye can see. Hills and ravines, mountains and long empty prairies; forests that give way to long, deeply green fields of wild grass. Rivers that run down between draws and meet at the tip of great divides of land; rocks that seem to reach all the way to the sky.

You can feel so alone, though. Even a little wisp of smoke in the distance can seem to have the glow of a big city, even though it might be a Indian fire. Indian fires have to be avoided because you never know. You might wander into a Piegan camp and they would greet you kindly and with true hospitality—then, when you're on your way, follow you so they can catch you. Then they'd have just as much fun cutting off small parts of your body and feeding it to you as they would chasing buffalo or hunting game. And you can't really trust a camp full of white men, neither, unless there's women amongst them. I had a friend when I first come out here that got tied upside down to a tree by white men who run off with his horse and saddle and all his belongings. It was Indians that saved him.

Towns and villages are scarce out here and nothing much to speak of when you find them. They're really outposts.

There ain't nothing luxurious or enlightening about this part of our country, and I don't know why folks get so rapturous about it. You'd think people out and about in a place as barren and hardscrabble as this would be more friendly, but they ain't. They don't much like folks in need. They see most kinds of needfulness as weakness. They're so all fired proud of their independence and strength, their will and endurance, they ain't got time to worry about how others are faring.

Like those folks in Theo's train that I traveled with when I first come out here. It was a small train—eight wagons. Twenty mules and nine horses. Seven families and two fellows, Joe Crane and Preston, with their own wagon. They said they was going to be men of destiny too. We crossed the Missouri River at Fort Leavenworth and started out on what they called the "Oregon Trail." There was supposed to be more water that way, better rivers, and fewer Indians. We would go across Kansas, into Nebraska, and then on to the Wyoming Territory. We'd avoid, too, much of the Dakotas, travel north to Montana, on to Utah Territory, Oregon, and then down to California. That was the plan anyway.

Theo was a big fellow, almost as tall as Big Tree. He had a great mane of hair on his head and his face, with only a little skin showing, a small red nose, and two black eyes peering out from all that hair like a bat from a cave. He had huge arms, a terrific boulder of a chest, and almost no waist at all. His legs was long and lean, so he looked like he ought to be a strong man in a circus. He had a wife and five little ones to contend with. He was short-tempered and had a stern disposition, but he took gentle care of them kids and his wife too. He known where he was going and you could follow along or not. I know he had a agreement with the others in that train—that he would get them there and they'd all stick together—but it really was like he decided he was going and the others tagged along, hoping he wouldn't notice they was there. In the first weeks on the trail, he didn't say much to me. I can't say he was even friendly in the beginning. His kids didn't say much, neither. Even the little ones only got to caterwauling when they was hungry. And he could shut them up with a look.

His wife was hard boned and thin, with a kind of chiseled face— like she was carved from rock. She never smiled or frowned or had no expression on her face at all. But she governed the other women and they did most of the cooking for the train. Theo's wife made the best biscuits I ever eaten in my life. Set them in a frying pan with a little salt pork and let them cook over a open fire until they was hot and crispy. It only took a few minutes per batch and she'd make several every morning—twenty biscuits in a big iron pan—and feed the whole camp with them.

The other women made soups and stews with the squirrels and wild fowl we killed along the way. Sometimes we'd get a doe or a elk but they'd stew that too. It wasn't like they was trying to please. Eating was what you had to do to keep alive and moving and that's how folks looked at it. We eat ourselves a few potatoes and carrots we found along the way now and then, but mostly it was just the biscuits, and the stewed meats with lots and lots of beans.

My first true introduction to the big West was a few days after we got into what folks said was Indian country. Theo kept us near water whenever he could. We followed a stream north for a while, then bent with it to the west until we found another one going straight west and we followed it until it turned north again. Theo took some time to find the best place to cross it so we could keep west. I didn't know the territory we was in when this happened, but we had just crossed the river when we passed a place called Atherton's Cut. Like I said, I was following along just a little to the side of the train, and we was riding along a slight rise of ground to the top of a green hill next to a small stuttering stream. At the top of that rise we'd been following, the terrain sloped gently down again and we come to a fork in two small rivers, and where the two rivers split we found a abandoned Indian village. I seen Theo jump from his wagon and walk down there. Big Tree rode over and got off his horse. The rest of the folks in the train had their rifles out and crouched by their wagons. I rode down to where Theo stood by a dying campfire. Big Tree was kicking the ground where lodgepoles had been. Fires still smoldered in several places. It stunk to high heaven.

"Probably Blackfeet," Theo said.

I said, "Looks like they just left."

"They stay until they can't stand the stink any longer, then they move on."

"What is that smell?"

"Over there." He pointed to a small bend in the stream on our left, where water seemed to dig into the embankment. "It's where they shit and piss. As long as the wind stays right, they tolerate it. When it shifts and it gets too bad, they move."

It was really bad. "Jesus," I said.

"Or if they're following buffalo. That gets 'em going too."

"I think it was the smell this time."

"If there's good hunting, they won't move far. They're probably a few miles up one fork of this river or the other."

"Which way we going?"

"Well, I'm going to see if I can't figure out where they went. I'd like to take the opposite way if I can." He looked at Big Tree. The big Indian nodded and got on his horse and rode on ahead until he was out of sight.

"Where's he going?" I asked.

"He'll let us know what's up ahead a long way."

I got back up on Cricket and Theo went to his wagon and spoke to the folks there. Theo come back on one of his horses. "There's probably only ten or twenty braves," he said. He talked real slow because we was in danger and he wanted to be absolutely clear about what we had to do. I thought I was done with war, but this was just like it. We was at war and moving in enemy country. And that ain't no first impression, neither. It's how it was the whole time I was in the big West except you never really known who the enemy was: it could be white men or any number of different kinds of Indian.

Theo rode by me, studying the ground. I said, "Mind if I tag along?"

He didn't say yes or no. I turned Cricket and followed him. We didn't get far. A few yards up the path by the river on our right, he stopped. He seemed to be smelling the air with that little button nose, but then he got down off his horse and walked a little further.

"No," he said. "They didn't come this way." This seemed to make him happy. He swung back up on his horse and started back to the wagons. I stayed right where I was and waited for them. Before long the wagons groaned and creaked down the hill toward me. Theo was up on his wagon again and one of his oldest boys was riding on the horse.

I realized Theo wanted to follow that arm of the river as quietly as we could, but eight wagons and all them horses and mules can make a hell of a lot of noise. The path was rocky in places and those wagons sounded like some great animal was pushing a house along the ground. Even so, I moved closer and closer to the wagons. I didn't want to be too far out there alone, and yet I found it hard to be in amongst all that noise too. It was getting dark. We'd have to stop soon.

Theo's wife spoke low to him. He nodded, staring straight ahead. Far ahead of us was nothing I could see. The path leveled out and moved along the gash of the river that wound its way a little to the northwest. We'd have to cross it eventually. Far to our left was the other arm of the river, which run in front of what looked like a great, dark forest. We was in the middle of what folks called "breaks," which is flat prairie marred every few hundred yards by twisted rivers and rolling hills and ravines.

When we finally stopped, on high ground about a half mile from the river, we circled the wagons and built a couple of campfires. Theo left the horses tied to the wagons, ready to roll if we had to. I tethered Cricket to one of the wagons and got my pack roll off and settled in by one of the fires.

Joe Crane and Preston, the two fellows who was traveling without a family, come along carrying their rifles and sat down next to me. Preston had a cup in his hand: I known both of them wanted some of my whiskey. I didn't mind sharing it. They was sure a odd pair. Joe Crane was bald and round, not more than five feet tall. His face looked like it was etched in wire—thin lips, thin brows, a long skinny nose. His friend Preston was a foot taller. He had hair only on the top of his head because he shaved all around his ears and on his face so he looked like he had a black bowl on top of his head. When he wore his hat, he looked as bald as Joe Crane. Preston was broad from shoulder to hip, with runt-like bowlegs. He chewed tobacco all the time, so I would not let him put them brown stained lips on my whiskey bottle. He had to bring that little cup with him.

We sat a good distance from the fire but I could still see their faces pretty good. Preston stared at the glare of the fire. Joe Crane said, "Where'd you get that repeater?" He pointed at my rifle.

"Richmond, Virginia."

"You a Yank?"

"I was."

"You get that in the army?" Preston said.

"No army ever give nobody a gun like this," I said.

They both had single-shot carbines.

"It ain't no Spencer, is it?" Joe Crane said.

"No. This holds a lot more bullets than a Spencer." I told him what it was.

"Evans," he said. "I ain't never heard of a gun like that. It just looks like a Spencer."

Theo strolled over to us. "A gun like what?" I handed it to him and he hefted it, then aimed down the barrel. "Kind of heavy, ain't it?"

"It's fully loaded," I said. "Thirty-four rounds."

He took his time examining every part of it. I explained how it worked. He held it up before his eyes and shook his head. "If we'd of had these at Vicksburg, the Yanks would still be trying to take it."

"And we'd still be at war," I said. "Who could want such a thing?"

He looked at me. "Make sure you're standing up front with me tonight if we have visitors."

"Sure," I said.

"You expecting trouble?" Joe Crane said.

Theo had no answer. He studied the rifle a bit more, then handed it back to me. "Handsome," he said. He poked at the fire with a small stick he took from it, then he said, "I thought I smelled whiskey." He was too proud to ask, so I handed him the bottle and he took a big gulp of it. He held the bottle for a while, watching the fire. "Good whiskey," he said, and took another swig.

"Help yourself."

"I want you to ride in front with me tomorrow," he said.

"I'll do that."

"Bring that 'ere gun." He handed the bottle back to me. "Good whiskey," he said again. Then he stood up and walked back to his own fire.

"You think he's expecting Indians?" Joe Crane said.

"Maybe he's always expecting them," I said.

Preston spit some tobacco juice. "This is the country. This is where Red Top got his start."

"Who's that?" I said.

"Red Top's Sioux. The Wahpekute variety. He's a real killer."

I never heard of Red Top and I said so.

"He had two sets of twins," Preston said. "Nine wives. He lived in this country and hunted every foot of it. He got along with most folks too. Some have said he was a good neighbor. Got along with white folks." He went on and told how the cavalry attacked another tribe of Sioux and his wife was among them. They killed her.

"I heard they killed his whole family," Joe Crane said.

"I don't know about that," said Preston. "But he's been on the warpath ever since."

"I hope it ain't Red Top in command of that band we come on today," Joe said.

"No, Theo thinks they was Blackfeet," I said.

"Them Wahpekutes follow Red Top and do what he says. He's like a general to them," Preston said.

"Ain't all the chiefs like generals?" I said.

"Indians don't have no generals or commanders or nothing like that," Preston said. "Not like you might think. They fight amongst themselves, and they follow any brave who has what they call 'good medicine.' Nobody's really in charge. It's the most democratic society you ever seen."

Joe Crane laughed. "Yeah," he said. "Savages every one and they're deemo-cratic. I bet Red Top's got so many wives, those folks following him might all be his family."

"They *are* democratic," Preston said. He spit more juice. "I been among them. I've traded with them and lived with them as neighbors."

It got quiet for a spell. I could hear the other fire crackling and folks talking low. The children was all asleep.

"Anyway," Preston said, "they killed his wife, and Red Top went on the warpath. He started killing white folks, and when he did, he never left the mutilation to the women. He and his braves did it themselves. They killed forty or fifty whites at Fort Buford, then rode on north to Canada. He's been raiding from there ever since. Killed hundreds in Minnesota, I heard."

"The army will get him," Joe Crane said.

"Red Top's a old man now," Preston said. "Probably in his seventies, and I heard tell that he's blind. But nobody ever caught him."

I picked up a small twig and stirred the fire with it. "Theo didn't say nothing about Red Top, nor Wahpekutes."

"I don't want nothing to do with Blackfeet, neither," Preston said. "They're like the Pawnee. They don't like nobody."

We talked like that for a while, and gradually the moon sank behind the distant trees. Joe Crane and Preston went back to their wagon, and I lay down with my head resting on my pack roll, and let the fire die. I fell asleep for a while.

It must have been near dawn when the Indians come. They was not interested in battle. Seemed like they only wanted to show how brave they was. I thought at the time maybe they was just trying to scare us away. They rode around us, yipping and cawing like hawks. Theo told all of us to hold our fire. "I'll clobber the first man who fires his gun," he said, and he meant it. He stood by his wagon, watching us, while the Indians danced and circled around screeching to beat all. I could hear children crying in one of the wagons. The Indians wasn't shooting, neither. Whenever one of them felt like it, he would ride right up to where we waited for him, guns at the ready, and touch one of us on the head or shoulder with his lance. Theo still would not let us fire a shot. His woman fed sticks into the campfire at the center of camp, and all of us watched the Indians riding around us in the orange morning sun and yellow firelight. Their horses was small and lean and very quick. It looked like each pony was a part of the Indian on his back, like one brain moved both of them.

I stood next to Cricket behind Theo's wagon, and I got hit twice on the top of the head with a Indian lance. I didn't even see who hit me until I felt it and then I'd hear the "Yip, yip" and feel the breath of the damn horse as the brave whirled around and rode away. One kept riding up into the firelight—just a few feet from Joe Crane's wagon—and he'd wave a long spear with a red bandana on the tip of it.

"That's Sioux," Theo said. "Red Top's bunch."

I heard him say that, and something broke down inside myself. I mean, I felt something give way in my gut. I only heard "Sioux" and "Red Top." As that fellow with the red bandana on his lance rode up the hill toward me, I aimed my rifle and shot him in the forehead. The Indian fell off his horse like a sack of meal. The rest of them broke and run down the hill.

Theo turned to me and stared with them small black eyes.

"I got him," I said.

"You got him, all right. You son of a bitch. Now we're in for it."

"You said it was Red Top. I thought the rules had changed."

"That wasn't Red Top, you damn fool."

"I heard you say it."

"Did I tell you to fire?"

"No. But you said Red Top and I figured . . ." The way he was looking at me made me stop.

He shook his head with disgust. "Well, now we're riding into trouble." He left me there and walked over to the fire. He threw a bearskin over the main campfire and herded all the women into the wagons. He got them to lay down as close to the floor as they could. Then he come back and got everybody in position to fight off the attack. He told me to stand in front—but not because he was mad at me. I had the Evans carbine and could lay down a pretty withering fire.

A little while later, a band of them Indians come charging up the hill, letting out that "Yip, yip" sort of war cry, but we started shooting and it looked like the noise alone driven them off. Somehow, during the confusion and all the shooting, they dragged the dead one away.

We waited a long time for them to come back, but they didn't. I thought when the sun come up full they'd over run us, but they was gone. There wasn't nothing there but a few pieces of feather, and a pretty big blood spore from the one I shot.

Theo got up on his wagon and started slapping the reins on the horses, and everybody followed him. He didn't look at me. I rode Cricket up next to him like he asked me the night before, but he said nothing to me and I wasn't gonna say I was sorry again nor nothing.

After a while Theo looked down at me sternly. "I know folks out east think what happened today was just a commonplace," he said. "We run into a spot of trouble and handled it. A few of us, situated well on high ground, drove off some marauders and killed one of them. But the truth is, we went into Indian country and murdered a brave. That's what we done. There ain't no other way to look at it."

"It's what I done," I said.

He didn't bother to notice I'd spoken at all.

{ CHAPTER 2 }

AFTER I KILLED my first Indian, Theo bade me ride in front of the lead wagon with Big Tree every day, so I guess you could say I become a part of the wagon train because I killed a man and proved I could be useful.

Theo thought it best to track north toward the Platte River and Wyoming Territory. We stopped at Fort Riley on the Smoky Hill River in Kansas, and he decided we'd wait for a few more wagons to join us. "I want to be a larger party," he said. "We're going up Nebraska way first, then to Wyoming. Lots of warriors between here and there."

"I didn't come out here to fight Indians," I said.

"You want to go to California or Oregon, you got to fight Indians at some point along the way. You already killed one. I hate to think what you might do with that gun of yours if you was *looking* for trouble."

We camped outside the fort, but we got to go in and buy things at the store any time we wanted. Those of us who was white anyway. Big Tree couldn't go in there, but he had his own thing going. He never stayed in a wagon. One of the packhorses carried his lodgepoles and the skin he used to build a Indian teepee just east of where we was camped. The whole time we was there, I hardly ever seen him. I seen some of the soldiers, though. Sometimes a few of them come out and set with us around the campfires. They talked about the war and fighting Indians. "Indians ain't like Rebs," one of them said.

"Or Yanks," said another. From what I could see, most of them was too young or too old to be talking about the war. A lot of them drunk too much and staggered back toward the fort like weak-kneed fawns. To a man they hated Indians.

But they was all good drinkers and talkers.

One night I was sitting by the fire with Preston and Joe Crane, sipping some more of my whiskey. Preston chewed his tobacco and spit it into the fire and Joe Crane puffed on a short stump of a cigar.

There was a young fellow with us named Treat. He come from Chicago on another train that had lately arrived. A big bearded trapper named Roman Turley strode out to our campfire and announced he was raising a militia to go fight Indians in Dakota Territory. The idea of being in a militia excited Treat. He said he'd missed the whole damn war because he was too young, and now that he was seventeen he thought he might be ready for a military career. He was traveling with his sister and her husband, and he said nobody had a hold on him. "I can go anyplace I want," he said. "Where's the Dakota Territory?"

"Up north a ways," Turley said. "The Black Hills, Sioux country." He had long, light-brown hair that he wore in braids, with leather thongs and single feathers hanging down each side of his face. The beard was full and darker than his hair. He wore a skunk skin hat and carried a long rifle, and his moccasins was knee-high. He had blue army trousers on and a checkered long-sleeved shirt. "We intend to protect folks in the country up that way," he said. "There ain't enough cavalry to do it without we help them some. You want war, I can give it to you."

"You don't want no part of no kind of war," I said.

"I can fight Indians," Treat said. "I heard they run away when you shoot at 'em half the time."

"Well, they have to be dressed for it," Turley said. "They don't like to fight if'n they don't have the right garments and such."

"You know what a coupstick is?" Preston asked.

"No," Treat said.

"It looks like a lance, but it's usually decorated with feathers and the tip ain't that sharp. Sometimes it's curved like a shepherd's stick."

"So?"

"What them folks try to do is count coup. Every time a brave touches somebody with the tip of that lance, he scores coup for himself and makes good medicine for his people." Preston turned to me. "That's what that brave was doing in that skirmish we had a few weeks ago—until you shot him in the face."

"That good medicine got him killed," I said.

"It's crazy," Preston said. "But a lot of them do it. The Cheyenne especially."

"That fellow tapped me with that lance pretty damn hard," I said. "They don't tap easy."

"What I wanted to say to you," Preston said to Treat, "is the Lakota Sioux don't often just count coup. They're more of the direct-attack variety. Some of 'em got rifles and they're the best cavalrymen you ever saw."

"They sure run away the other night," I said. "One volley and they turned tail." I really was kind of unimpressed at the time.

"You never heard of a retreat?" Preston said. "Ain't none of them cowards. You don't want to fight them if you can avoid it."

Treat was determined, though. He said he was going to join the militia even if it wasn't really part of the army. The Ninth Cavalry manned Fort Riley and I think they pretty much disapproved of the militia. Roman Turley looked more like a renegade than a soldier. He was missing his front teeth but it didn't matter much, because he didn't smile so often. He spit tobacco juice through that hole in his teeth and set by the fire and talked about the trek north and what he was planning against the Northern Cheyenne and Sioux. And Treat got more and more excited about it. "I can shoot. I learned to shoot when I was just a kid." His sister had come over to get him for supper, and she was standing right there in front of the fire. Treat looked up at her and said, "Ain't that so?" She owned that he could. "I wish it wasn't so," she said, "but he's sure good with a gun, I'll give him that."

The next day I was sipping coffee with Preston, Joe Crane, and Treat when Roman Turley come by looking for Treat. "Come on," he said. "I'll swear you in with some others I recruited this morning."

Joe Crane and Preston went along just to watch, but when they come back they was both swore in too. We was sitting at the back of Theo's wagon, watching his children play in the dirt, when they come prancing back. Preston wore a wide-brimmed hat with a long eagle feather in the band. The militia didn't have uniforms or even guns or horses half the time. What they had was the freedom to go anywhere they wanted to. They didn't have families, nor land, nor nothing to keep them.

"Looks like we're in the militia," Preston said. He was kind of sheepish.

"Why would you want to do that?" I asked. "I thought you was headed for California."

"I was," he said. "I changed my mind."

"You know how Indians fight," Theo said. "You're telling Treat he don't want no part of them, and then you go and join yourself. You know what you're getting into."

"I been among them," Preston said. "I know they ain't going to be easy."

"We'll see," Joe Crane said. "Maybe when we get there we won't have to fight nobody."

"The militia give you that hat?" Theo asked.

"Nah," Joe Crane said. "He bought it in the post store. I seen it first but he had to flip a gold piece over it."

"And you lost."

"Inkpaduta will sure like taking those feathers for himself," said Theo.

"Inkpaduta? Who's Inkpaduta?" Joe Crane said.

"Red Top."

"And that's why we joined the militia," Preston said. "There's gold in the Black Hills. If I'm going there, I want to do it with a lot of fellows with guns."

"So it's the gold," Theo said. "You think you'll have time to look for it?"

"I ain't no Indian fighter," Preston said. "I just want to see if it's like they say. Gold everywhere as far as the eye can see."

The Black Hills was sacred ground for the Sioux. It's where they buried their dead. That's what Theo said. "Those people won't like a lot of white folks poking around up there, digging holes and such."

"We'll take care of them," Joe Crane said.

The Indians around the fort was mostly just as fine as they could be. They was near all of them of the Crow tribe, but there was a few Arikaras, and even some Sioux. They was polite to folks and seemed to enjoy their children as much as anybody. I didn't like their chanting much, but at least they was quiet of a Sunday morning. Them folks in the wagon and at the fort got to singing early, and a mite loud.

"You going to keep that wagon and them horses?" Theo asked.

"I'll take it with me," Preston said. "Horses too. We're lighting out in a few days."

The night before they left I was feeling kind of rootless and solitary. I might of gone with them, but I didn't want to fight nobody. Still, they seemed kind of happy to be headed for some kind of adventure. What if there really was gold up that way?

We was sitting around a campfire behind Preston's wagon. It was me, Theo, Preston, and Joe Crane. I'd sipped a little bit of more whiskey. I shared some too. I got to be kind of curious and talkative. I wanted to know how Preston and Joe Crane come to be traveling together.

"Started out from East Tennessee," Joe Crane said. "We was both with Colonel Broward there."

"You was Confederate?"

He nodded.

Preston said, "One or two skirmishes can make brothers out of some folks."

"We fought together," Joe Crane said. "And after the war decided to pool our money and come on out this way."

"We was fur trappers for a while," Preston said. "Up and down the Missouri River. All the way north to where it bends to the west and heads out here. Never had such fun. We was just playing is all, trapping otter and beaver and selling the skins. Did that for half a decade, then decided to sell everything, buy the wagon and go on further west. Get some gold, maybe."

"I was all the way in California when I was a boy," Joe Crane said. He sat right across from me, his legs crossed in front of him. His round belly almost covered his boots. The fire seemed to glisten off his bald head. "My daddy went and took us out there in '49. He was looking for gold too. But he never found none. He went to work for the railroad and got hisself killed in a train wreck. I was fifteen and holding my momma up for a while before the war."

"What happened to her?" I said.

"We come back to Kansas, and then I went and joined the Confederate army and I ain't seen her since."

"You never went back?"

"Oh, I looked for her and all. One day her letters stopped coming, and then she was just gone."

"Died probably," Preston said.

"I like to think she married some rich fellow and moved to a bright, big house in Chicago, or St. Louis."

"And she wouldn't want to write you nor nothing after doing that?" I said.

"How would she know where to write me? It's what I like to think," he said. "It's better than a picture in my mind of her face rotting in the dirt someplace." He cleared his throat and looked away. Preston put his hand on his shoulder just briefly, but Joe Crane didn't say nothing. He stared at the fire for a spell, took a sip of my whiskey. He looked almost misty-eyed, but then he suddenly reached up and tried to grab the hat off Preston's head, but Preston was ready for him and jumped to his feet. "Nice try at it," he said.

"I ought to have that hat. It looks better on me, and it don't fit you worth nothing at all."

"It fits just fine."

"You look like a squaw with that thing on."

"It ain't so. Anyway, I don't care how I look."

"The hell you don't."

"I don't."

"Gimme the feather, then."

"What for?"

"Just let me have it. If you don't care how you look, what do you need the blasted feather for?"

"It's just part of the hat."

"Because you like how it looks, am I right?"

"You two ought to get married," Theo said.

Preston come around the fire and sat next to me. It got quiet for a spell, then I said, "You know, my ma died and my daddy couldn't abide it. He took off."

"And just left you?" Preston said.

34

"I must of reminded him of her."

"She have red hair like yours?" Joe Crane said.

"I stayed with my aunt," I said. "But she never liked me much, neither."

"Well, me and Joe was going to get rich after the war, but all we got is them two horses and that 'ere wagon."

"You got that hat too," Joe Crane said.

"A lot of folks wish they had a wagon like that," I said. "I seen them on this trip."

Theo said, "It ain't that good."

"Look," Preston said. "Theo had to set a axe handle in the thing for one of its spokes. The wheels creek and wobble. The damn thing's falling apart."

"It's a good wagon," said, Joe Crane. "It sure keeps us dry of a cold winter night."

We talked a long time. I begun to realize I'd miss laughing at them two fellows when they was gone. It amazed me how easy it was to talk to some folks and get to feeling like you known them all along. I was thinking I made a couple of good friends that I might see again someday and I drifted off to sleep a-hoping for just that.

Sometime in the middle of the night, a little while after I'd fell asleep, I heard what I thought was Indians circling around the camp and hollering to beat all. I jumped up quick and grabbed my carbine. The fire had banked pretty much, and I couldn't find nobody in the dark that resembled Theo, nor nobody else, neither. I think I could hear my heart a-beating like hell. Dark shadows run by me, and one of them nearly knocked me down.

I raised my carbine and got ready to shoot one of the shadows, when I heard Preston's voice coming from it. "Damn it all."

Joe Crane wasn't as much whooping as he was laughing. I seen him crouching forward when he run by the embers of the fire, and he was holding Preston's hat on his head. Preston was right behind him trying to get his hands on it. Leaning forward as he was, Joe Crane made it near impossible for Preston to get even a grab at the feather that stuck out of the band on the side.

They disappeared around behind Theo's wagon, then come out the other side, still howling and hollering. I think they both was laughing.

Theo poked his head out the back of his wagon. "What in hellfire is going on?" he said. He had his own rifle in his hands, and it looked like he was about to shoot the first shadow he seen and he didn't care none what he might hit, neither.

"It's Preston and Joe Crane," I said.

He pointed his rifle at me. I realized he didn't know I was standing so close to the back of his wagon and I scared him considerable.

"I almost put a bullet in your brain," he said.

Joe Crane come running back our way. Preston finally grabbed him around the waist and pulled him down. They wrastled to beat all, still laughing. Preston got the hat and held it up, trying to roll away.

"Is this my hat or not?" he said.

Joe Crane couldn't talk, he was so out of breath from running and laughing. He lay there on his back, in the moonlight, his belly rising and falling. Preston stood up and brushed his trousers off with the hat. "Dad-burned fool," he said.

They rode out early in the morning heading north—Preston and Joe Crane and Treat, with about twenty others that Turley recruited. Two of his recruits was Crow Indians who promised to lead the way and scout in advance of the column. They tried to get Big Tree to go with them, but he wouldn't have none of it. I watched them cross the Smoky Hill River and disappear over the horizon.

A few weeks later, Theo announced that he had joined our train with the one that Treat's family come in. That made twenty wagons. "They're going to Oregon, so they can travel that far with us, then we'll continue south to California," he said. "We'll be safer if we all travel together." So they spent most of that day loading provisions and getting ready to set off. I helped Theo shoe a couple of horses, then went to the post store and bought more coffee, sugar, ham, and hardtack. I bought beans, too, and a slab of sowbelly.

Theo still wanted me riding out front with Big Tree. I had to look up at him as we rode along because his horse was at least two hands taller than Cricket and he was so tall hisself. It was like riding next to a great moving statue. He wore yellow leggings and low-cut boots and a yellow leather jacket with fringe down each arm and across the back of it. His hair was black and long, tied back with a length of twine tangled around a single long, white feather with a black tip. He wore one of them fur hats with bull horns on it.

For the first day he didn't say a word. We crossed to the south side of the Smoky Hill and stayed alongside of it most of the day. We made about thirty miles and quit at dusk, setting up camp near the river. We was still close enough to the fort that it didn't feel like there could be much danger, but Theo had us circle the wagons when we stopped. He was still in charge. The other wagons joined us, in other words, and plighted their selves to our fate rather than the other way around.

We made about ten to fifteen miles a day. Each morning we set out just as the sun come leaking over the ground behind us. Eventually Theo turned us away from the river and we followed the trail further and further north and west. Then a few days after we turned directly west again, Big Tree said his first word to me. He suddenly pulled his horse up and said, "Death."

"What?"

He pointed off to the right a little. In the distance was a clump of trees with dark trunks and hanging branches, low and slightly moving in the breeze.

"Over there?" I said. Then I smelled it. The breeze was moving in our direction and the smell it carried was unmistakable. "Oh," I said. "Death."

Big Tree nodded, then he turned his horse in that direction and trotted off. I signaled to Theo what we was up to and then followed Big Tree.

It was a body hanging in a tree. The head was almost pure black from burning, but the hair piled only on top of it told the story. It was Preston. His hands was tied behind his back, and he wasn't wearing no boots. Big Tree got down off his horse and untied the rope at the base of the tree and then lowered the body down until it laid on the ground. He was almost gentle with it. Preston looked like he blew up to three hundred pounds, his body was so swollen, and the smell was so strong it cut into my nostrils.

When Theo got there, he said, "Indians don't hang folks."

"What's that mean?" I was kind of sick. I felt awful for Preston. I liked him and it didn't bode well for this trip that he ended up like that only a few weeks or so after he started out.

"Wasichus," Big Tree said.

"He must've done something to piss off those fellows he was traveling with," Theo said.

"What happened to Joe Crane? He wouldn't stand for this peaceably."

"You don't know," Theo said.

"Wasichus," Big Tree said again.

"What the hell does that mean?" I said.

Theo said, "White men."

I walked over and got back on my horse. "It's a hell of a thing," I said. Then I started circling around that place, looking for Joe Crane.

Maybe I should of seen Preston's death as one of them portents of things to come.

{ CHAPTER 3 }

ME AND BIG Tree buried Preston right next to that tree where we found him. We worked fast. The wagon train moseyed on by while we worked, and when we was done, it was almost ahead of us. I didn't find Joe Crane anywhere around there, but I did find one of Preston's boots. It had the sole ripped out of it, so it was useless. There wasn't no blood on it but it was sure his boot. Preston was a big man, and he wore them high-heeled pointy-toed things Texans wear.

When I got back to the train, I went right out front again, next to Big Tree. I talked as we rode along, trying to see if I could get him to say whatever thing. He didn't say a word the whole time we was a-digging that grave. Riding next to him, I hated looking up so high to see his eyes. I couldn't tell if he was listening to me or not. We rode most of the day, and Big Tree held that nose of his high in the air, looking for more "death," I guess. At one point I said, "Do you speak American?"

He nodded.

"When?"

He didn't look at me, just kept staring at the horizon. The sun begun to gleam off his eyeballs as the day wore on.

"You know," I said, "I sure hated to see Preston hung up there like that."

Nothing.

"I wonder how that happened."

"Wasichu," Big Tree said.

"But what could have caused it? I mean, you think he committed some sort of crime?"

He looked down at me and I felt like a small child.

"He must of committed a crime," I said.

Big Tree made that harrumphing sound. Then he said, "Wasichus kill for gladness." I couldn't tell from my position below him, but I thought he might of smiled a little.

*   *   *

Theo ordered a halt near dusk at a place on the Smoky Hill River in Kansas called Fort Hays. We had to get permission from a Colonel Harding to set up outside the fort for the night. Theo put the wagons in a big curving U around the front gate. We formed a good perimeter with the fort in the open end of our encampment. The colonel seemed to like that arrangement. He was a short, dark-haired, muscular fellow with great black whiskers that curled all the way down the side of his face and up over his nose. His eyes was dark as a cow's eyes and almost as big. His uniform was a little too tight, and with all them gold buttons and yellow striping down his legs and medals on his chest, he looked like he ought to be the emperor of something. He suggested a pig roast, and that was something everybody in the train was happy to take part in. Two of the Indians that lived around there butchered a hog in no time and then we got several fires going. Some Swedish fellows from one of the new wagons built these Y-shaped structures, then hung a spit in the middle of them and turned the meat as it cooked over the fire. You could tell the Indians never eat a whole pig, but they liked it enough.

When darkness come, with all the fires, and the children running wildly—with the smoking meat and pots of stew, and lots of whiskey and beer—we really had a high old time. But watching that pig meat turn black and crispy, I couldn't get the look on Preston's face out of my mind. That rope made his jowls stick out, but his eyes looked out in sightless wonder, and his mouth a little round hole—like he was getting ready to whistle a tune. He was just talking to me not more than a month ago. I seen guys drop next to me in the war, but you expect that because you're in battle and ain't nobody trying to do nothing but kill you, and you're trying to kill them. If I'd of seen Preston on the ground with a bunch of arrows sticking out of him, I'd of thought, *Well, he went looking for that.* But to see him hung up there in that tree, and not knowing what could of put him there . . . It was a mystery that made me sick.

Sometime near the end of the night, Theo come over to where I was getting ready to bed down.

He said something as he approached, but there was still enough noise from the revelers that I didn't hear him. When he got to me I said, "What?"

"Tomorrow."

"What's tomorrow?"

"A few of the families want to press on."

"How many wagons?"

"Nine."

I waited.

"So, can you take them out?"

"What? No. I mean, why me?" I was fairly shocked.

"You seem to know where you're going, and you got that repeater."

"I'm completely new in this country," I said. "I have no idea where I am half the time."

"You found your way back when you went looking for Joe Crane," he said. "Most new folks would've got lost."

"I know how to find north and south," I said. "East and west."

"Just take them west," Theo said. "Follow the river until you get to Fort Wallace. It's about a hundred miles directly west from here. They got somebody waiting for them there that will lead them the rest of the way. You can wait at Fort Wallace until we come along."

"How long?"

"We'll probably be leaving here in a week or less."

"Why don't we just all go now?"

"I want to buy more horses and a few more head of cattle," he said. "The army's bringing in rations for the Indians and the troops and there's plenty to be had for our trip."

I didn't like it a whole lot, but then I got just a little bit impressed with myself too. "Why can't you send Big Tree?"

"He stays with me."

"I don't know none of them folks," I said.

"Just keep the river on your left as you go along."

"And I ride out in front."

"It's not hard," he said. "You been doing it for us."

"I been doing it with Big Tree," I said. "Next to a target like that, I'm pretty invisible."

"You can pick whichever body you want from the train to ride with you. A few of them Swedish teamsters grown up a fair size."

He stood there waiting for me to say something. When I didn't, he turned and started back toward his wagon.

Two men, both bald, both carrying their wide-brimmed hats in their hands, passed him and approached me.

"You agree to take us out tomorrow, ya?" one said. I never heard nobody who sounded like him. I nodded.

The other one said, "Ve don't vish to be any *trobble.*"

"We'll gather in the morning," I said. "Have your wagons in a train and we'll cross to the south side of the river at dawn."

"You say the south side? Ve take the vagons across the river?"

"We do." They both nodded and bowed as they backed away from me. It was good to see that they would trust me and follow me. I figured I'd lead them the way Theo seemed to lead us—quietly, and like I had firm knowledge of both the terrain and our destination, even though I had no such thing.

What Theo said was "Keep the river on your left," but I remembered that he said I should stay to the left of the river, so the next morning, before the sun was above the horizon, I started out to find a place to ford the river. I rode for about a mile upstream and found where the water run only a few inches above a gravel bed. It was perfect. By the time the sun was fully up, I'd led the train across the river and we swung to the right and started our journey west to Fort Wallace. I had the river on my right.

I picked a man named General Cooney to ride with me. He was not a Swede, as it turned out, but most of the others was. Cooney was much older than me—probably in his forties. A great, drooping Confederate hat on his head shadowed his face and especially his eyes. He had a full head of dull brown hair that hung down both sides of his face, and a dark brown mustache under his nose. He was not as tall as Big Tree, but that part of his body above the waist seemed elongated and way too big for the short, bowed appendages he called legs. Riding a horse was painful to him. He complained a lot about his tailbone and he clutched the reins in one hand and held fast to the saddle horn with the other. He had a musket over his shoulder and wore a pistol on a belt around his waist.

He was proud of the way he could shoot his pistol. He'd been with Braxton Bragg in Tennessee, then Joe Johnston; commanded a infantry brigade. For most of the war he'd been on foot. "I guess now I'm cavalry," he said.

"You a general?"

"Not really. A brevetted brigadier general."

"Ain't that a general?"

"Only for a while," he said. "When the war's over, you go back to being a captain. But folks are kind enough to keep calling you 'General.' "

We rode along quietly for a while. It was a windy morning, but it come mostly from out of the east, so we had it at our backs. I don't mind wind if it ain't cold. This was pleasant and felt like it helped us along. The wagons squeaked and groaned, the horses and oxen rattled their bridles and clip-clopped along the flat ground like they was cobblestone streets, and the leather of my saddle creaked with every step.

To be twenty-nine years old and leading a entire wagon train, including a former Confederate general, made me more proud than I thought possible. I don't think I ever felt stronger in the big West. I resolved to let General Cooney do most of the talking and I would remain as quiet as I could until we got where we was going. One commands respect by their silent leadership is what I always say. And I intended to earn respect.

But events conspired against me.

The ground next to the river got to be marshy and too soft for horses, much less wagons. We had to veer south for what I hoped would be just a little while, until we could find solid ground. The marshland stretched a long way and it was almost dark by the time I figured we could turn the wagons back west. But now there was a different problem. The ground started rising, and the trees seemed to grow denser. We had the marsh on our right, and the angle of it seemed to bend more and more south, and further from the river.

General Cooney said, "There's no trail? Are you looking for a trail?"

"We just have to stay west," I said.

He looked over his right shoulder at the sun. "We seem to be going away from the river."

"Right. We can't take the wagons through that." I pointed at the green, waterlogged marsh.

He started to say something, but he stopped. His eyes fixed on something ahead of us. "Indians," he said. He fairly gulped out the word. I turned and seen a party of braves on horses coming toward us. I halted the train and set there watching them. It was about twenty braves. Women and children walked behind them. There were lodge-poles strapped to mules and they even had a wagon with them. I wondered where they got the wagon.

"What do we do?" General Cooney said.

"I believe we'll just wait a bit. But go back and tell each driver to be ready to put the wagons in a circle. Tell them to circle to the left, *away* from the marsh." As I said this, I noticed the Indians was not really moving along with that wagon. It was stuck and they had been trying to get it out when we come on them. I watched as they finally managed to get it moving and now they was turning it away from the marsh.

We was probably a full day's ride from Fort Hays, and maybe a third of the way to Fort Wallace. While General Cooney went around to each of the wagons and give my instructions, two of the braves broke off from the group and started toward me at a gallop. They carried lances with black and white feathers tied to the tips, and again I was amazed at how each of them looked on a horse, like horse and rider was one.

General Cooney come back next to me. His horse let out this loud shudder and shook its head. The bridle clinked. We watched the Indians coming at a slow walk now, their horses nodding their heads like they was saying yes to the world.

The Indians wore yellow leggings, and leather vests all draped with beads. They wasn't painted. One was a little bigger than the other, but both of them was tall. The only Crow brave I ever seen was Big Tree, and with that name I thought he was unusual. But both of these fellows was almost as high as Big Tree. One was pretty old but held

44

himself erect and proud. He raised his arm when he stopped his horse in front of us. General Cooney did the same. The older brave pointed at himself and said, "Chíischipaaliash."

I said, "Hello."

The younger one started speaking, "Hinnay cheesh eepaul eeash kook. Bineesh bach eetuah kook. Deelapaache beeluuk." I didn't understand a word he was saying and neither did Cooney. The older one smiled a bit, nodded his head as the other talked.

"You speak English?" I said. "American?"

The older one smiled broadly.

"Baamniawaawalakuk?" the young one said.

I shook my head to let him know I didn't get it.

"Hinnay baaniiummauak?"

"No understand," Cooney said.

The older one started trying to communicate through sign. He gestured with his arms, made circles, and pointed to invisible things in the air. Then he made a sweeping motion with his hand and pointed at us. "Baaniiummauak."

Then the smaller one reached into a scabbard at his side and pulled out a great hunting knife. It gleamed in the bright sun. I looked at the knife, but I had no time to think about what it meant. Cooney jerked his pistol out of his belt and shot the fellow in the breastbone. He fell over backward off his horse. "Jesus!" I screamed. The other Indian held on while his horse rose up, then turned and careened the other way. Cooney and me turned our horses and run back to the wagons. I could hear the Indians shouting behind us. We galloped up to the lead wagon that was already beginning to turn to make the circle, and I hollered, "Keep going! No circle! Just head back fast!"

The guy on the wagon slapped the reins hard on the backs of his horses and started yelling at them: "Heyaaa, heeyaaa!"

"Go, go, go!" I screamed, turning Cricket to face the wagons as they teetered and leaned, the horses and mules struggling in the traces; finally the whole train straightened out and got to running. I waited until the last wagon was headed in the right direction, told Cooney to stay at the rear, then raced to get on the lead. I didn't hear no other shots.

We raced over that terrain a long time. Didn't lose a wagon. Nobody got hurt. When it was dark, I halted the train and galloped back to Cooney. He was still on his horse, watching the trail behind us. Two boys in the last wagon was crouched down in the back of it, looking down the barrels of their muskets, at the ready.

"See anything, General?" I said.

"Nary a thing."

"Nothing at all?"

He shook his head, still staring back down the way we'd come.

"We could probably make it back to Fort Hays before dawn," I said. "You think we should try?"

He looked up at the sky. "Moon's pretty low right now. Why don't we give the horses a breather and then see if we can make it. I don't want to just sit here and wait for them."

So we let the horses calm down and get to breathing naturally and then we started off again, this time at a slower pace. I rode out front by myself and kept us going due east once we got back to the river. We got to Fort Hays just after sunrise, crossed back to the north side of the river and joined Theo's circle of wagons.

He was not happy to see us. And the Swedes we was leading wasn't too happy, neither, but they was glad to be alive. For a while there I was a kind of hero because I had led them out of the danger of them wild Indians.

Then those same wild Indians come riding up to the fort right behind us. They still had the wagon with them, the mules hauling lodgepoles and tepee skins, and the women and children. Colonel Harding, who spoke the language, rode out to meet them. He had Theo with him. They talked for a bit while the rest of us watched, our guns and rifles ready to fire. I stood next to one of the wagons with my carbine resting on the top of a wagon wheel, and I was aiming at the center of the big Indian who did all the talking. It was so quiet, all you could hear was a dog barking somewhere in the camp, and the wind whipping through the tops of the trees. Then Harding and Theo come back to where we was all waiting. Theo got off his horse and walked up to me, shaking his head. Harding stayed on his horse but he come over in front of me, too, right next to Theo. The Indians turned their horses

46

and trotted a few hundred feet to our left, near the river, and started dismounting and unpacking the mules.

"They're going to camp here for a while," Theo said.

"What's going on?" I said.

"Who did the shooting?" Harding wanted to know.

"General Cooney," I said, at the same time that he said, "I did."

"You killed a innocent man," Theo said.

"He pulled a knife," I said.

"He wanted to show it to you—he was offering it to you as a gesture of goodwill."

"It didn't look like goodwill to me," General Cooney said.

"He was just going to show it to you," Theo said. "He was proud of it. He wanted to trade it for something."

I wasn't feeling like a hero no more. It was damn hard to look Theo and Harding in the face. All I could say was "You really believe that?"

"I don't know many Indians that lie," Theo said. "That's the one thing you can count on. They don't bother to lie."

"Yeah, well," I said. "Just about everybody lies about something."

"That older gentleman over there is Chiischipaalia. That means 'Twines His Horse's Tail.' One of the great Crow medicine men."

"He didn't look like no chief," Cooney said.

"They all look like chiefs," Harding said. "These are Crow Indians. We ain't never had to fight them. They're on our side."

I had nothing to say to that.

"Well," Cooney said, "I sure am sorry about it."

"You're going to have to do better than that," Harding said. "You got to give them something."

"What?"

"You own more than one horse?" Harding said.

"No."

"They want something from you. You ought to make it pretty valuable."

"Can I buy another horse from you?"

Harding rubbed his white-gloved hand under his chin. "I'll sell you one, but you give them Indians that one you're riding. That's what the young fellow you killed wanted to trade the knife for."

I shook my head. "The devil take me."

The two Swedish gentlemen, again with hats off, come over and seemed like they wanted to ask something. "You may as well settle in here for a while," Theo said to them. "We'll all start out again soon." Then he turned and looked at me. "That okay with you?"

"Certainly," I said. My face felt hot and swollen. "I didn't want to lead no train anyway."

"You did all right getting them back here," Theo said.

It was later the next say that he found out I'd led them on the south side of the river. He didn't think much of that. "You would not of even run into Twines His Horse's Tail's bunch if you'd done what I said to do."

"Where'd they get that wagon?" I said.

"I don't know. They hunt all along this river and camp where they please," he said. "Sometimes for sociability and to be where they can trade for a few things, they camp near one of the forts. They're good neighbors."

I shook my head in shame. "I'm sorry," I said.

"Don't apologize to me."

"I mean I'm sorry I took the train on the wrong side of the river."

"That won't be the only mistake you make out here," he said.

He was sure right about that. I was still powerful curious to know what happened to Preston. What kind of mistake led to his death.

I felt so sorry for that poor Indian that Cooney shot. I thought I should at least apologize to them folks if I could.

I asked Theo if he and Big Tree would come with me and Cooney to apologize to Twines His Horse's Tail. It took a while to convince Big Tree, but he come along. "That your business," he said.

"We need you to translate."

"You need me to guard."

"It ain't nothing I thought of," I said. "But you're right."

It was a bright morning. We approached the village with a bit of caution. Cooney and me was walking out front. Theo told us to go at a steady pace, but not too fast.

"They'll kill me," Cooney whispered to me. He was sweating terribly, and although it was already pretty warm, and promised to be a very hot and humid day, there was a cool breeze drifting in and out of the trees around the fort. "I know they'll want to torture and kill me."

"No they won't, General," I said.

"Won't what?" Theo asked.

"Kill the general."

"They might want to. But if we walk in there and ask to speak to the old man, they won't. Indians tend to honor folks that ain't afraid."

When we got to the camp, a young brave come out to meet us. Big Tree went ahead and translated for us because the brave walked right up to him and begun speaking. All Crow Indians are pretty tall and stately; they have very nearly perfect bodies, every one of them. But Big Tree was aptly named. Even on foot, he towered over most folks, even the other Crow braves.

The young brave and Big Tree spoke very stiffly to each other, then the brave gestured with his arm that we should come into the camp. There was huge lodges all in a big kind of circle, with some inside the circle at various placements, but all around the center of the camp where the wagon stood. A few dogs barked. Children run about, circling us and hollering to beat the band. Like they was on a raid. When we got to the center of the camp, the brave stopped and turned around.

He said something sounded like "Hinnay, hay."

"He says we should wait here," Big Tree said.

Then Twines His Horse's Tail come out of the big tepee next to the wagon. He was dressed with a breastplate of colorful reeds of some kind, and bright beads around his neck. He wore yellow leggings and a black loincloth, and his moccasins was decorated on the top with beads. On his head was a huge skullcap of a buffalo, with the black horns arching toward each other over his dark eyes. He had a old man's craggy face, with lines that run from next to his deep-set eyes and down both sides of his mouth from his nose. His jet-black hair, twined with gray strands, draped his shoulders and hung way down his back. He was tall as well, and carried himself with absolute dignity. I felt like

I was in the presence of a personage as great as Lincoln. Four other younger, tall, decorated braves stood next to him.

He spoke in a deeply resonant voice.

Big Tree said, "He wants to smoke a pipe with us, then he will talk."

Inside the tepee, we all sat in a big semicircle, and the old man lit this long pipe with beads and feathers a-hanging off of it. He passed it to his right and each brave puffed a bit, then passed it to the next until it reached Theo, who sat across from me, all the way on the other side of the half circle. Theo puffed, then passed it back toward the chief. When it got to him, he puffed it again, then passed it to his left and eventually it got around to me. I held it briefly, wondering at the sweet aroma. It was tobacco, but there was something else in it too. I puffed gently, inhaled it, and then passed the pipe back. The smoke was hot and almost made me cough. If I believed in a God, I'd of been praying very hard not to cough. But then one of the braves on my right coughed a bit and nobody seemed to notice. When the pipe was finished, Twines His Horse's Tail spoke.

Big Tree looked gravely at General Cooney and me. "Women are grieving today," he said. "They are cutting off their own fingers in their grief."

Twines His Horse's Tail waited for Big Tree to tell us what he said, then went on. "The dead man had many fathers. Many mothers," Big Tree said.

Cooney looked puzzled but said nothing. I looked at Theo. He never took his eyes off the chief.

The chief glared at me when I turned back to him. I said nothing and there was a long pause that I thought I might of caused. But then I realized that the chief was waiting to see what Cooney had to say. Big Tree said to him, "What do you say?"

"I made a mistake," Cooney said, his voice shaking. He really did feel it, I think. "I am sorry."

Big Tree spoke those words in Crow and the chief nodded.

"What do you offer?" Big Tree said.

Cooney said, "I have two horses."

Big Tree said that in Crow.

There was no response. It was quiet for a long time, then Cooney realized he had to say more. "I have a Springfield rifle, and two Confederate pistols."

When Big Tree spoke, Twines His Horse's Tail said something emphatically, but his face was not angry. It was stern, maybe, but not angry.

"He says to keep your pistols," Big Tree said. "He will take the horses and the rifle."

There were nods and stern frowns all around. I know there was grieving somewhere in that camp but I didn't hear none. When we all of us stood up, the braves didn't want to look nobody in the eye. They kept their heads down and bowed out of the tepee, but I think they was proud of their leader and glad of the outcome.

As we got ready to depart, Theo said something to Twines His Horse's Tail. They spoke quietly for a while, then shook hands. Theo come up behind me as we walked back to the circle of wagons outside the fort. "I think I know what happened to Preston," he said.

I stopped, but he got up to me and said, "Keep walking."

When we got back to our camp, I went with Theo to get water. We walked in silence down to the riverbank, each carrying two buckets. We filled them both with water. We started back up the bank, and still Theo said nothing. I had my carbine slung over my shoulder but it kept slipping down because of the two heavy buckets I was hauling. I had to keep stopping and putting the thing back in place.

Finally I put the buckets down. Theo said, "Put the sling over your head and carry the rifle across your back."

I'd already had that idea and was in the process of doing just that. "I don't generally like it this way," I said. "I can't get it in hand and ready to shoot very fast if I got to pull it up over my head."

"I reckon you'd ought to've had enough of shooting fast."

"It wasn't me," I said.

"You won't need the gun here." He set his buckets down and waited for me.

When I had the rifle in place and was ready to start again, I said, "What'd you find out about Preston?"

"I just traded two army mules to Twines His Horse's Tail for his wagon."

"That was Preston's wagon?"

He nodded.

"How do you know that?"

"Didn't you see the back wheel? It was missing a spoke. I used a axe handle to repair it."

"It was the same one?"

"Unmistakable."

"So the Crow killed him?"

"No. I don't think so. Like I said, they're on our side. But Twines His Horse's Tail may know what happened." He leaned down and picked his buckets up again and so did I. With the rifle across my back, it was easier. When we got back to camp and handed the water over to the women, Theo invited me to set a spell by his wagon. Nobody else was there except me and him. He said he'd take the two mules over to the chief in the morning and then he'd find out what happened.

"Maybe he knows what happened to Joe Crane too," I said.

Theo had a pipe of his own and he filled it with tobacco and lit it. He offered me some of it but I didn't want it. He puffed awhile, watching the sun get swallowed by a great white mountain of a cloud.

"I think we'll start out again in the next day or so," he said.

"What did the old chief mean, the dead brave had many fathers and mothers?"

He shrugged. "The Indians don't keep their children like we do. They adopt."

"Adopt?"

"Young'uns are the business of the whole tribe," he said. "A young boy or girl can be taken on by grandparents or interested neighbors. Hell, among them folks almost every adoption is welcomed. The children live where it is most convenient for the tribe. And for the young folks. A couple only married for a year or two needs their privacy. So the children are adopted and taken care of. Later in life, that same couple will adopt and take care of a young'un. It might be their grandson or their closest neighbor's boy or girl. Things get took care of and it ain't done with no lawyers nor clergy, neither."

"That's sort of how it worked in my family," I said. "I was raised by my aunt."

He nodded.

"She was pretty indifferent to me."

"It ain't that way with Indians. Each one of them feels and acts like a child's parent. A kid is pretty lucky to be born among them folks."

"I guess so."

"And when one of them dies, he is grieved by all of his parents. The women will mutilate themselves. Cut off digits and such."

"Jesus Christ," I said.

"Maybe physical pain helps them forget the other kind."

"All through the war," I said, "the one thing I known for sure was that if I died, nobody would grieve a lick."

"Well. That may be a lucky way to go through this here business."

"As you say."

He smiled. "In the end, ain't none of us nothing but alone. And nobody gets out of here alive, neither."

"I know," I said. "I know that."

The next day Theo found out what happened to Preston. He'd gone as far as Fort Sully in the Dakota Territory, near the Cheyenne River Agency. He was so close he could almost see the Black Hills. Then he got in a fight with one of the Sioux scouts over a horse. Roman Turley ordered him to give one of his horses to this Indian named Small Knife. Preston said he wouldn't do it. Twines His Horse's Tail did not know why Preston owed the Sioux brave a horse, but whatever it was, Preston took the horse and his wagon and lit out for the southern trail, back toward where he come. He may of wanted to join up with our train again. "He almost made it," Theo said.

"Small Knife caught up with him?"

"No. Turley sent three of his new recruits after him."

"Why?"

"Probably to keep the peace," Theo said. "Folks don't like it when a Indian kills a white man, it don't matter what for. So Turley would've made sure white men took care of it. We may never know why Preston owed that fellow a horse. But it was the three who went after him that hung him up for a horse thief and then set fire to him."

"Big Tree was right. He said it was white men."

"The chief said one of them was just a kid."

"How's he know that?"

"They traded him the wagon for two horses, some buffalo meat, and a few skins."

I shook my head.

"Chief said the small young one wore a white hat with dark eagle feathers in the brim and had a white pony. He did all the talking and the others followed him around. He said he must have good medicine."

"Well, whoever they was, they was murderers."

"I expect they thought it was justice. Seeing as how Preston run off with that horse."

"But if he was ordered to give it up, that ain't really stealing, is it? He disobeyed a order, is all."

Theo puffed on his pipe and stared off at the white clouds. "It don't matter what you call it, now, does it? Preston's paid for it, whatever it was." It was early morning, but the sky was magnificent with all that mixture of clouds like white cliffs and mountains and the dark blue behind them. "I traded Twines His Horse's Tail a pistol and a mule for that old wagon and I'll let you have it if you trade me that repeater of yours."

"I'd rather have the rifle, thank you."

He tried to talk me into it. Finally I agreed that he could have it if something happened to me. I signed a piece of paper that said as much and he give it to his wife, then told me the wagon was mine. The next day I bought two horses from the army—used my last ten dollars—and hitched them to the wagon. I tied Cricket to the back of it.

We was getting ready to embark again. Some of the river Crows was going to ride along with us for a spell. They known we was headed into Sioux country and the Crow wanted to steal horses from the Sioux—their worst enemy. In fact, Theo told me that the word "Sioux" means "Enemy." The Sioux call themselves Lakota or Dakota. There's a lot of them—a lot more than the Crow—and they roam all around this part of the country, making war on just about everybody they please. Red Top was a Wahpekute Dakota, and all the trouble in Minnesota Territory, Iowa, and the plains was blamed on him. Theo said, "He ain't never had more than twenty or thirty braves with him, but he can fight like Sheridan or Forrest, and it would take a Sheridan or Forrest to run him down."

"I hope we don't run into him."

"The army will ride with us for a spell—until we get to Fort Wallace. Then we're going to turn north a bit, cross the Republican River, and head for Fort Sedgwick."

"Where we going after that?"

"Bozeman, Montana Territory—Fort Ellis."

"Think we'll make Bozeman before winter?"

"Absolutely. We'll be there by August, the latest."

"With or without trouble?"

"Oh," Theo said. "There's always some kind of trouble."

{ CHAPTER 4 }

WE TRAVELED A long way with the army right next to us, or never further than a couple miles away. The country was teeming with game. We killed deer, elk, rabbit, buffalo, and every kind of fowl. Big Tree killed a cougar, skinned it, and ate it, and nobody wanted no part of that meat. He offered it too. I was beginning to see that he wasn't a parsimonious fellow.

We seen things I didn't think was possible. One day a great big bald eagle swooped down and picked up a small dog. It carried the thing high up to its nest on the top of a slim, craggy rock formation which was flat on the top. Theo said that normally a eagle would fly up way in the sky and drop small prey like that to kill it, then they'd sweep down, pick it up, and carry it to the nest to eat. But this eagle took it all the way up to the top of that rock, and never dropped it. The great bird set the dog down in the nest and the damn pup stood there and wagged its tail, looking down at us, and eventually it commenced whimpering to beat all. We stopped the train to watch it. The eagle flew around over its head like some kind of winged death. And the dog started howling finally. We had no time to wait long enough to see what happened to it, but I couldn't help but think that maybe we're all a little bit like that dog. We occupy our little space of earth and wait for the damn bird to strike.

We seen a tornado drop down out of the sky like a twisting snake and rake the whole world for as far as we could see. It moved away from us, but the rain it sent back our way was sharp as coffin nails, and you had to lean down to let it bang against your hat or you'd come away with skin cut just as bad as if a warrior sliced at you with a hunting knife.

We seen a three-legged wild pig chase down a groundhog and kill it with one powerful bite. The pig seemed to yell something to us when it was done. Like it wanted us to come on over and see what he might do with that snout on one of us. Theo said, "There's a reason the Cheyenne call them things devil dogs."

We continued north and west, and left the army behind when we crossed the Republican River in Nebraska. In a few days we was into Colorado Territory, headed to Fort Sedgwick. By the time we got there I was feeling pretty well at home in the big West. I known what I was doing. Big Tree showed me how to clean the meat off a buffalo, then wrap it in the skin and make a big package that we could carry along with us. We did the same thing to most everything we killed except for the fowl. Them we pulled the feathers, gutted, and hung up on thongs to dry a little before we cooked them up the same day. The wrapped meat would last a long time. Wrapped up in the bloody skin and hung up on poles to dry out, it tasted fresh even several days after we killed it.

There was never a shortage of water. We crossed many streams and small rivers, and moved for miles and miles across open meadows and fields that stretched before us, with the great, loyal, blue-and-white Rocky Mountains always in sight—either in front of us or to one side or the other. I never dreamed there could be such a country.

Every now and then we'd come upon a village. Twenty or thirty lodges with good fires and children running and dogs barking, and women tanning skins or washing clothes, and the braves would come out and greet us. They'd sign to us if they didn't speak Crow or English. We come upon Arapahos, Northern Cheyenne, Arikaras, Blackfeet, and Sioux. They was always pretty friendly, even the Sioux. We didn't have one scrape. The worst thing that happened was that we almost killed two fellows that turned out to be scouts for the U.S. Army.

This was after the army from Fort Riley had left us. We had just crossed the Republican River and was still in Nebraska, but not far from Fort Sedgwick, when two men wearing leather leggings, buckskin vests, and not much else, rode up over the horizon in front of the lead wagon and stopped. They seemed shocked to see us, then turned around and skedaddled. Big Tree and me rode after them a-ways, but they disappeared. We stopped—I thought to wait for the train to catch up—but then Big Tree moved off the trail a bit and I followed him. He never got off his horse. He pulled the animal around to face the trail. He carried a Sharps rifle with feathers dangling off the front of it, and he kept it at the ready while he watched. He said nothing. I held my carbine across the front of my saddle and waited with him. Then, before the wagon come up over the rise, we heard them two fellows coming back. They rode along, crossing in front of us, slow and steady. They had another with them, a big man in blue cavalry pants, with a yellow stripe down the leg and a bright red shirt. He had long black hair that stuck out under a black hat. He wore a mustache that hung all the way down to the neck of his shirt. When they'd passed in front of us, Big Tree looked at me and then moved out in the trail behind them. I followed.

We all rode like that until the first wagon come into sight. I didn't know if them fellows known we was behind them or not. When the train come into full view, Theo stopped it. He sat there for a spell, waiting. Then he give the reins to his wife and climbed down out of his wagon. Big Tree made his presence known by trotting out a little to my right so them three fellows could see him. His Sharps was pointed right at the big black-haired man. The two others didn't seem to mind it much that they was staring down the barrel of Big Tree's gun. I rode out a little to my left and held my carbine on them. I had all thirty-four rounds loaded in the thing and I was ready, too, I guess. Them two fellows we first seen looked like some kind of Indian but I couldn't tell which ones. Without the army near, Theo took no chances. He had his own gun. He stood by the front wheel of his wagon. The horses in Theo's team stomped some and made a bit of noise. It was like a low growl that come from deep inside each animal.

Theo signed a "Hello" to the three men, which was always just a hand raised high above the shoulder. The big black-haired fellow moved forward between the other two. "Hello," he said. It was friendly enough. "Maybe you should tell us where you are going."

"Fort Sedgwick," Theo said.

"Well, I will tell you." He leaned forward a little in the saddle, his elbows on the saddle horn. "You ain't far from it."

"No sir," Theo said. "I expect we'll be there before dark."

"How many are you?" He looked around a little, like he was expecting company.

"You army?" Theo said.

"Fifth Cavalry. I am Major Eugene Carr. At your service."

The two fellows behind him now made no sign. They was both sweating in the July heat. Each carried a long-barreled Enfield rifle. If they wasn't Indians, they was former Confederate.

"We had a escort until the day before yesterday," Theo said.

"How many are you?" the major asked again. .

"We're enough. Twenty-three wagons."

"Well, there are some renegade Injuns around here."

"Dog soldiers," one of the other fellows said. "Tall Bull and many others."

"Sioux?" Theo said.

"Cheyenne," Major Carr said. "A big raiding party." The two other men got down off their horses and walked toward us.

"We'll camp at Fort Sedgwick," Theo said. Then he moved away from his wagon and approached the two men, who had stopped walking toward him. Both of them was small in stature, with brown faces and dirty black hair. When Theo got close enough, one of them said, "We would like some water." Theo must have sensed something, because he reached out and grabbed the weapon out of the fellow's hand and pointed it at both of them. "We got plenty of water," he said. The second one give some thought to running but then he put his gun down on the ground. I got down off of Cricket and picked up his weapon, then backed away a bit, still pointing my carbine.

Major Carr looked mighty surprised. "They are scouts, sir," he said. "They are with me."

"You don't look like any major in the army I ever seen," Theo said. "Get down off that horse."

He sat there staring at Theo. "You are making a big mistake," he said. Then he turned his horse and galloped off. Theo aimed his rifle at him but never fired.

Big Tree said, "I go after him?"

"We got these two," Theo said. "Stick around."

"What do we do now?" I said.

"These here are Pawnee," Theo said. "The worst of the worst. And I'm thinking that 'ere major is a renegade."

"We are not Pawnee," one of the little fellows said. "My name is Mitch Boyer. This here is Tom."

"You'd be white men," Theo said.

"That's right. We ride with the major."

"You don't look like white men. Why you dressed like that?"

"We scout for the major. We are not enlisted."

Theo looked at me. "They're Pawnee. Tie them to the wagon."

He held the gun on them and I got some rope and with the help of Big Tree tied one to the front wheel and the other to the back wheel. First we tied their arms. Then we pulled their legs apart and tied them so each man was spread-eagled across the wheel, feet and arms sticking out beyond the rim. With their knees on the ground and their lower legs bent back under the wheel, and their arms tied at the elbow, they commenced to breathing really hard. I could see the breastbone on each of them, protruding in the sunlight. When we was done, Theo said, "We're gonna find out some things and then maybe I'll get on this wagon and take them for a little ride."

I never seen it done, but there was always plenty of talk about it even when I was in the army. Tied to the wheels like that, if the wagon moved forward even one revolution, each man would break both arms and both legs. He could keep his head from getting crushed by holding his chin against his chest, but after that one revolution of the wheel, if the wagon kept moving, it would cause so much hurt, most men couldn't even do that. It would kill them pretty horribly and pretty fast.

The fellow who claimed to be Mitch said with some desperation, "At least give us a chance to prove who we are."

"What are Pawnee doing so far north?" Theo said.

"We scout for the army."

"You're stationed at Fort Sedgwick?"

"Yes."

"Where's your tribe?"

"I am half Sioux. My father is a white man," the one called Mitch said.

The other fellow, Tom, said, "I ain't no Indian at all. I am Italian."

Theo laughed. They both looked at him without fear, but you could see that he had their attention. "How is it you look so much like a Indian then? I don't know as I ever seen a Italian fellow out this way. I don't even know what a Italian looks like."

Both men looked at him as though he'd suddenly started singing a opera song.

"Why'd that other fellow run off?" Theo asked.

"Look," Mitch said. "That was Major Carr. He probably went for help."

"You think we . . ." Theo started to say, and then we heard a lot of horses coming down the trail. They was coming hard and they made pretty big cloud of dust. The horses on Theo's wagon started to snort and titter, and the wagon moved a little bit.

"Jesus Christ," Tom said. "Cut us loose."

Theo stood in front of the team and calmed them, but it was a risky thing to do because Theo had his back to whoever was coming down that trail. Big Tree got down off his horse and stood next to it, holding his rifle over the saddle, aiming toward the approaching horses. I did the same. It could of been Indians come to kill us all, but it was Major Carr again, this time with half the Fifth Cavalry. They trotted over the hill and fanned out around us. We watched them get into place, then Major Carr come forward again, this time with his sword drawn and resting against his shoulder. The dust swirled around us, and Theo's horses tried to pull back away from it. The wagon moved again, but only slightly.

"Cut those men loose," Major Carr said to Big Tree.

Big Tree put his rifle in the scabbard on his horse, walked over to the wagon, and did what he was told. Mitch and Tom stood there rubbing their wrists. Then Tom walked over to Theo and looked up at him, stared into his eyes with this fierce expression on his face for a long time without saying nothing. Then he spit at Theo's feet and walked past him. Theo looked properly scolded, but he didn't have nothing to say, neither. I think he was right embarrassed. I was just glad I didn't have to see them two broken to pieces by that wagon.

Major Carr announced who he was again. "I take it you can believe it this time."

"Yessir," Theo said.

"We are from Fort Sedgwick, and we will escort you there now."

"We don't need no escort," Theo said.

"Just the same. There are dog soldiers in this area and we are at war with them at the moment."

Dog soldiers was Cheyenne, as I was to learn later. The Cheyenne was among the most highly organized of all the Plains Indians. They had fighting teams of warriors each with its own name and leader: the Elk Warriors, or the Crazy Dog Soldiers, or the Red Bear Warriors, and so on. Each team had its own chief, and they took turns directing the entire tribe when they was all together. But a lot of the time they was independent of each other and traveled and hunted and raided by themselves. The chief of the dog soldiers was named Tall Bull. They had a huge camp west of Fort Sedgwick and they'd been threatening the fort and any travelers who might wander from there all summer. They had not killed nobody yet, but they'd raided a few trains, stolen some horses, and counted coups among the bands of soldiers who was sent out to keep the peace. They was, according to Major Carr, "a confounded nuisance." He said he was going to have to get them to go back to Fort Laramie, about a hundred fifty miles west and north of Fort Sedgwick. We was going to be headed that way, so Theo volunteered to leave the train at Fort Sedgwick and accompany the major on his mission. He wanted me to go with him.

"We'll get a look at the country between here and there," he said, "before we have to lead the wagons across it."

I hoped it would be a peace mission of some kind, or at least that we'd run them off without much of a fight. Theo said that happened a lot with the Indians because they was not too concerned with occupying a position, or land, or no place in particular. The Indians believed that land was like light, or air, or the weather: it belonged to everybody alike. They picked where they fought, and it was usually not so much a place as a good opportunity. It could be a decision any one or two of them might make.

"Tall Bull is probably a man with good medicine," Theo said, "and a lot of Indians follow him, but he ain't no 'general' in our sense of the word. There ain't never been a people anywhere in the world as free as Indians. I mean absolutely free. The braves running with Tall Bull don't belong to him, they ain't in his 'army.' They'll fight together, but Tall Bull won't operate with a strategy or a plan of battle. No Indian really ever does. One might start a fight and the others'll join in. Indians never want to defend something so fat or stupid as a fort."

"What about a village?" I said.

"Sometimes, if the hunting is good, they'll stake a place and defend it. But you'll see. They don't often bother to protect themselves even in the camps. They frequently don't even post a guard. And if they don't think it's a good day to fight, or if they ain't dressed for it, they won't bother, even if they got you outnumbered by hundreds."

"They don't need a guard with all them dogs," I said.

"Hell, a dog'll bark at anything."

"But *we* ain't fighting, are we?"

"We'll watch," he said.

We was riding close behind Major Carr's regiment. There was maybe three hundred of them in two columns in front of us. Sioux scouts—real Sioux, not just Mitch and Tom—fanned out to the left and right. There was twenty or twenty-five of them.

We left on a searing-hot Sunday afternoon while singing at Sunday service still rung out in the fort. The sky was white and empty. The sun felt like it was only a few feet above us.

We rode along in silence for what seemed like a hour or so, maybe more. We circled around the Indian camp, a long way around. I never seen even a wisp of smoke. But then we come to the village. It was at a place called Summit Springs. Up to that time I never seen so many lodges in one place. It seemed like hundreds of them spread out along the banks of the creek in a great, sprawling half circle. We come at it from the west, over a small rise of land that allowed us to survey the whole village. Indians always form their lodges in a big horseshoe with the opening facing east. The entrance of each lodge always faces east. So we was coming at them from behind. Major Carr raised his hand and we stopped. The air was absolutely still. We was only about fifty yards from the first lodge. I didn't hear a dog bark. The inhabitants was all inside the lodges, out of the heat; most of them was taking a afternoon nap. Carr raised his white gloved hand, then give the signal to charge. The whole troop raced down the slope and charged into the sleeping village. They threw ropes over the lodgepoles and pulled down the tepees, dragging the skins away. I seen folks getting up and

looking for weapons and running around, gathering children and helping old men and women. I don't think the Indians got off very many
shots, but the troops laid down a pretty withering fire as they rode
back and forth through the village. Major Carr said he didn't want to
kill a lot of folks, he wanted to gather everybody up and herd them
back to the fort without a lot of killing. Even so, Tall Bull was shot and
killed. So was his son and wife. Two children was maimed by lunging
horses. In all, more than fifty Cheyenne was killed, and maybe another
hundred or so wounded. There was five hundred of them in all. Only
one of Carr's troops could be counted as a casualty. One of the officers
sustained a pretty bad gash on his cheekbone—probably from a Indian
lance, or maybe from his own sword. All four of the officers in the regiment rode into the village with their swords held high in front of them.

Theo and I never even moved from the top of the rise. We watched
the whole thing without saying nothing. When it was over and the
Indians was all lined up, and the women busy taking down the lodges
and packing up their belongings and their dead and wounded, Theo
said, "Back east they'll call this 'the Battle of Summit Springs.'"

"Some battle," I said. The whole thing lasted maybe fifteen
minutes, but it took several hours to get the whole village rounded up.
I could hear women wailing the whole time. It almost sounded like
singing.

A week after Summit Springs, we headed west with the wagons. I rode
Cricket out in front of the first wagon with Big Tree. I had plenty of
chance to study the landscape and learn about the country from what
I could see, because Big Tree didn't say much. For a hundred miles he
scanned the horizon in front of us and scarcely let out a sound. He
sneezed once, and it seemed to shock him. He looked at me and I
smiled, but he said nothing. I said, "Bless you."

He frowned.

"That means God should protect you from whatever spirits you
just got shed of," I said.

He understood that, or seemed to. He nodded his head slightly. I
think he believed it was a spirit he expelled, too, but I wouldn't testify
to it.

Theo gradually depended more and more on me. We'd sit up at night and study where we was headed, what we'd face in the way of rivers, forests, mountains, and valleys. He taught me the country I couldn't yet see. All that time, I never once understood that was happening: that he was teaching me. It just seemed like talk even when he unfolded maps and pointed things out.

We led our train all the way to Bozeman. There was a little settlement there, and Fort Ellis and lots of people. Indians, Canadians, even some Mexicans. It was where everybody took off from on the trip to Oregon or northern California. I thought Theo would take the train the rest of the way, but once we got to Bozeman, he didn't seem to be in much of a hurry.

We camped outside the settlement for two days, and finally on the morning of the third day I walked over to his wagon. He was setting in front of a fire that his wife tended, smoking a stumpy pipe, watching his brood play in the dirt with a few of the Indian children. They was chasing after a jackrabbit leg that still had the fur on it. They each had a small lariat and the game seemed to be trying to catch the leg with the lariat and keep it from the others. They kicked the leg, and threw their ropes at it, but they couldn't touch it with their hands. Theo's wife looked up when she seen me and give a sort of half wave of her hand. "It's Bobby," she said.

Theo didn't even look my way. He patted the ground next to him as a way of telling me to sit down.

I set there watching the children too. Theo's wife offered me a cup of coffee and I took it. "Thank you kindly," I said.

She smiled at me and went back to tending the fire. Theo studied the bowl he was smoking, tamped the tobacco down with his forefinger, then put the pipe back in his mouth. It was cool and breezy, and white clouds bunched up in the east like a city you might see from the prow of a ship. The sky was deep blue against the white clouds.

"I like this country," he said finally. "These hills. It's a good place to raise horses."

"What about the rest of these folks?"

"It's a good place to raise kids too."

"No, I mean the train."

"It's already three weeks into August," he said. "Too late in the year to head for California now. They'd never make it before winter, so they'll stay here until spring. They got plenty of time to find somebody to take them."

I said nothing.

After a long time he said, "I expect you might take them."

"I can't do that."

"Of course you can. You are able."

"I don't want to."

"What will you do?" Theo said.

"I don't know. I guess I'll stay here awhile." I didn't want to go to California no more. Leading that train out the rest of the way was the furthest thing from my mind. I didn't say nothing to Theo about it, but there was no way in hell I'd try to do that. "I like it here too," I said.

He nodded, still puffing on his pipe.

"You know," I said, "maybe I'll do some trapping."

"There's lots of folks doing that south and east of here. In the Musselshell country. I think Big Tree's going down there to trap a few beaver. You can catch on with him."

"Maybe I'll just go by myself," I said.

"You could do that too."

"Even if I was with Big Tree, it'd feel like I was by myself."

"Well, he knows what he's doing. He'll be glad to have you along, I expect."

I didn't want to go on with the train, but it was kind of upsetting to be suddenly cut loose from it. I had no idea what I wanted now that the whole future was sort of thrust on me. I mean, Theo deciding to stay in Bozeman left me wondering what the hell I was doing all the way out there. When I set out from St. Louis, I had this foggy dream about destiny and finding good land and being somebody, but the last thing I wanted was to try and settle on a piece of ground in this place all by myself. I had nothing to buy land with anyway, and I could see Theo didn't want me hanging around, depending on him none. He was done with me and I known it from that minute a-setting by the fire while he puffed on his pipe.

Not long after that day I said my good-byes to Theo and his wife. It turned out that Big Tree *was* going to the Musselshell River country, south and east of Bozeman, to do some trapping. So I decided to throw in with him. I bought a bunch of traps and other things I'd need and made sure to thank Theo for all he taught me. The wife told me to take care of myself and it seemed as if she really meant it, although she never said a word to me the whole time I rode with them.

I traded Preston's wagon for two mules and fifty dollars. I bought twenty feet of trapline and a few pelt packs. I figured I made out pretty good even though the wagon was the biggest thing I ever owned and I known I'd miss it when it rained or snowed.

PART TWO

Big Tree

1870–75

{ CHAPTER 5 }

AROUND BOZEMAN THERE was a lot of Indians: Crow and Northern Cheyenne, Sioux, including Uncpapas, Miniconjous, Lakota, and Dakota. There was also Shoshone, and Piegan Blackfeet. Tribes like Pawnee and Nez Perce even showed up from time to time. Each had their own kinds of battle; they stole horses from each other regularly. The Crow especially fought a ongoing battle against the other tribes because they was outnumbered by all of them. They was always at trying to outwit the Sioux even though they had inner-marriages and families that crossed from one to the other tribe without much bitterness at all. They was hard to figure; they even worked together sometimes, hunting buffalo or fighting the Blackfeet. But they never forgot that they was always enemies. The Crow had to steal horses from the Sioux and Cheyenne just to ensure their own survival, and that's also why they stayed pretty close to the settlement and white folks. To get at the Crow, sometimes a fairly large war party would raid near the settlement; and if it was more than the army could handle, it would be up to the militia to chase them off or even capture some of them if possible.

Me and Big Tree had just set out for the Musselshell country, and was only about five or six miles from Bozeman, when a column of militia come upon us. We seen the dust they raised long before they come over the rise to our left and stopped for a second looking down on us.

No one in the militia ever looked very much like what I would call a good man. They was dirty, and had a look of bitter reproof in their eyes. They rode into a camp like they was chased there, jumped off their mounts, and went right for the water, or the whiskey. They was always looking for renegades or Indians that might be a irritation to the army. Like I said, the army didn't like them much but they always claimed to be a big help keeping the peace and all. They rode in packs, like wolves—twelve or twenty or so in a pack. You didn't look at them if you could help it because sometimes they'd take that for a throw down on them—a challenge. You had to ignore them unless they said words to you, especially if you was a Indian.

Now we had my two pack mules, and Big Tree had a mule of his own. I rode Cricket and Big Tree was on the same big horse he rode on the trail coming out here. We kept on heading south and east on the trail and then the militia galloped down the hill until they was right up next to us. They sort of fanned out around us as we moved along until finally we stopped. The man in front was a short, barrel-chested, ugly fellow with white hair and beard. He wore earrings and had trinkets dangling in his long hair, so I figured he was a Frenchman. The rest looked just as ugly. There was about twelve or thirteen of them.

"What do you think you're doing?" the Frenchman said to Big Tree.

Big Tree just stared at him. Sitting upright on his horse, his mane of black hair brushed high, he towered over the white-haired Frenchman. In fact, he towered over all of them. I was positioned a little bit behind Big Tree, and the way he looked rising out of the crowd like a statue in the middle of a fountain was almost comical.

"We're going to do some trapping," I said to nobody in particular.

"I'm talking to this big ape," the Frenchman said.

"He don't say much," I said. "Maybe it'd be better if you just talked to me."

We all sort of stared at each other.

"It might be wise not to call this fellow ape, neither," I said.

A few of the horses made some noise. I looked at the other men, who by now had pretty much surrounded us. One fellow was pulling back some of the covering on my pack mule.

"Leave that alone," I said.

"What you got here?"

"Traps and such."

"You got any pelts?"

"We're just going to get some," I said.

Big Tree's horse backed up a bit, bobbed his head up and down and shuddered loudly. Big Tree settled him. Then he said, "We will go now. On our way."

But he didn't move. Then I noticed that kid Treat from Fort Riley. The one that bragged he could shoot a gun and wanted to fight Indians. Next to him was Joe Crane. Treat wore a white hat with black eagle feathers, and he was setting on a white Indian pony. He had a Spencer rifle with a feather attached to the end of the barrel. He wore a light buckskin jacket and high-topped leather moccasins. All I seen on Joe Crane was Preston's hat.

"Well, if it ain't a small world," I said.

Treat looked at me.

Joe Crane said, "Well, I'll be hornswoggled. If it ain't Bobby Hale."

"I seen you somewhere before," Treat said.

I didn't think it wise to ask what happened to Preston. I couldn't take my eyes off his hat, though. It still had the feather.

Treat said he remembered me. "You was at Fort Riley. Where's the rest of your train?"

"They're at Bozeman. Ain't going on until next spring."

"What're you doing with this half-breed."

"He ain't no half-breed," I said. "He's Crow."

"He's a renegade," the Frenchman said.

Big Tree moved his horse up closer to the Frenchman, then he reached down with his left hand and placed it around the fellow's throat. "We go now," he said.

The Frenchman was not struggling at all. It was clear that Big Tree had his hand wrapped completely around his neck—his fingers may of touched in the back—but he was not squeezing. It looked like if he did squeeze, most of what was in the Frenchman's head would fly out of his eyes. I was worried Big Tree's horse would spook and pull him away with that grip still in place. The Frenchman only looked at him. "We go now," Big Tree said again.

It was probably only a few seconds, but it seemed like eternity. Big Tree still had the grip on the Frenchman's neck, and the Frenchman just kept glaring at him, even with his chin all bunched up above the meat of Big Tree's dark brown hand.

Finally Treat said, "Where'd you get them mules? They look like army."

"They are," I said. "I traded a Conestoga wagon for them. I got the receipt right here." I took it out of my vest pocket and put it in his outstretched hand. The Frenchman said, "Treat?" He still kept his gaze on Big Tree. Treat held the receipt up so the Frenchman could see it. "I can't read this," he said. "Is it a receipt?"

The Frenchman tried to nod his head. Then he said, "It's real."

Treat waved the receipt for me to take it back. Big Tree finally removed his hand and sat back in his saddle. "We go now," he said.

Treat had his Spencer raised, not aiming it, but ready to.

The Frenchman said, "Shoot the bloody bastard."

"No," Treat said. "You let him grab you like that. I'm of a mind that it was your fault."

The Frenchman rubbed his neck. He still didn't take his eyes away from Big Tree.

"You go on," Treat said to me.

We started moving and the others got out of the way. I nodded to Treat as we went by. He looked like a kind of viper to me. His dark brown, seedlike eyes followed us as we moved and his head didn't turn even a little bit. I wondered what had happened to him out here in less than a year to make him so cross looking and wore-out. I also wondered what he could of done to get folks like Joe Crane, folks twice his age, to follow him and take his orders. He didn't look so young no more even though he wasn't even eighteen, unless he had a birthday since I seen him last. I was sure he'd already killed his share of folks. Women and children too. I was also sure he let us go because Joe Crane known me; in a odd kind of way I felt grateful to him and I was for sure thinking Big Tree ought to of taken note. In my mind it was already a good thing he let me come along with him. I guess it was a few hours later when it hit me that I should of had the courage to ask Joe Crane what happened to Preston. I was kicking myself good for not having the spittle for it.

It wasn't nothing to militia or soldiers to shoot Indian women or children. For one thing, it was the women who mutilated bodies after a skirmish, and sometimes the children—at least the older female ones—would help. Theo said it was religion. A simple ritual to keep a enemy from populating the life after. Many of times he'd seen the women crying and wailing while they was doing it. He said he supposed they was mourning their own dead, but sometimes he felt like it was a mother's sadness at having to dismember a young soldier or brave. "You know, like one of their own is a certain age and this here fellow they was a cuttin' on the same age and all. But it's just their practice and their duty. They do it to any enemy, Indian or not."

"It'd be bad enough to die out here," I said. "But to be cut to pieces and scattered too . . ."

"When you're gone, you don't know it," Theo said. "And anyway, it ain't no good to die nowhere, ain't that right?"

I owned it was probably true, although I said as how I wouldn't mind it so much in a warm bed of a snowy night in my sleep. He agreed that was so.

Big Tree and me rode away from the militia without looking back again. Even though they moved their horses out of the way to let us pass. I didn't hear no movement at all behind us. They was just a setting there, watching us as we rode down the trail. I think I could feel their eyes on us. That Frenchman wouldn't forget Big Tree. I feared what might happen someday if we ever run into him again and Treat's gone off somewhere else.

Later that night, I had my first real conversation with Big Tree.

We'd left the trail after the run-in with Treat's militia. We was still headed for the Musselshell country, but now we went along a small stream, then cut up into higher ground and better cover from trees and rocks. They wasn't following us, Big Tree made sure of that.

We camped out just as the sun started to scuttle along the horizon. It sent yellow beams into the sky and lit the underside of great, blooming clouds. It didn't look like rain—in fact, it looked clear and clean like after a rain—but the crisp breeze that rose up every now and then smelled like ice, and green earth.

When we had a fire going, Big Tree settled himself in front of it, his legs crossed in front of him, his hands resting on his knees. In the smokeless firelight his hair hung down by his face like some sort of cape. I couldn't see his eyes right away. I known better than to chatter like I used to around him, trying to get him to say something. We done most everything without words, or much sound at all, except for our breathing and chuffing when we carried wood to the fire or tethered the horses and mules in some tall grass so they could feed.

I cooked some ham in a frying pan over the fire. We had set up a few yards away from the shade of a big cottonwood tree. Along with the ham I heated some water for coffee. Big Tree set there watching the water as it commenced to boil. Just when I thought I'd chew on some ham, drink some coffee, and then puff on a pipe for a while before going to sleep, he reached behind him and come out with a small leather pouch. Inside was a few small stones, four small white bones, a few planks of tobacco, a hank of hair, and a short, stubby pipe. He was careful with the pouch, holding it in both hands, his eyes so focused he probably didn't remember I was there.

"You gonna have a smoke?" I asked. "I was going to wait until after we eat something."

The corners of his mouth moved a bit. Then he said, "This good medicine."

Dumbly, I said, "Oh."

Now he looked at me. "Say your name."

"Bobby."

"Bubby."

"Bahbby," I said. "Bobby Hale."

"Bubby Hairle" was how he pronounced it.

"Yeah."

"It mean nothing?"

"Nothing."

He frowned.

"No, really. It don't have no meaning."

"I am Big Tree That Blocks the Sun."

"That means something," I said. "You folks give names that describe a activity, or a thing. We don't do that."

"When I am young boy," he said, "I was different name."

I waited. He sat there stuffing his pipe with tobacco and a few seeds from his pouch. It didn't look like he was gonna say another word, so I said, "You had another name?"

He nodded, looking directly at me, maybe for the first time. His eyes was dark black and the firelight sparkled in them.

"What was you called when you was a little one?" I said.

"My first father and mother name me Talking Boy."

I didn't want to but I laughed. His face changed and his eyes went even darker.

"I'm sorry," I said. "I'm not laughing at the name. It's just that . . ."

"I am Talking Boy when I am young man," he said. He was indignant, but I think my laughing may of loosened him up a bit. He didn't take it unkindly. It may of been some kind of opening for him to see me as a fellow, a human being, instead of just a wasichu.

He lit his pipe, then settled back to enjoy it, with the little pouch in his lap. He held the pipe with his left hand and let his other hand rest over the pouch like he was going to protect it from me. I asked him if I could have some of his tobacco and he took my pipe from me and put some of the tobacco in it. He tamped it down with his thumb, then handed it back. "Good medicine."

"Thank you kindly," I said. I didn't believe in none of that hocus-pocus, but I didn't see the point in telling him that. I wanted to know about his life. About how he come to know Theo, and work with him. But I'd have to ask questions to get those answers, and to tell the truth I was damn sick and tired of carrying the conversation.

But then he started drinking from a canteen that I soon learned was full of whiskey. After a while he offered me a sip and I thought it was water. I'd already eaten the ham and drunk my coffee and I was a mite thirsty, so I took a big gulp and it damn near choked me to death, and this made him laugh louder and harder than I ever seen a body laugh. His laugh was like a elk barking in a canyon. After that, he kept snickering off and on for a long time, remembering the look on my face when I commenced to choke. I didn't see as how it was so damn funny, but I liked it that he was laughing. It loosened him up a little more.

He drunk a fair bit of the whiskey, then held it out toward me to see if I wanted some, but I shook my head and he laughed again. I lit my pipe and commenced to smoke, so I had nothing to say. But then he started talking. He told me about his parents, the first pair, then the second. How all four of them raised him. "My parents gave me life at a young time," he said. "Their parents adopted me." He told me they always kept their lodges close together. His voice was smooth while he remembered. Like affection run deep in him and it somehow smoothed his spirit and shrunk a bit of his natural hostility.

At one point he said, "Where is your father?"

I shook my head. "He could be dead."

"He die?"

"I don't know where he is. I was raised by my aunt."

"Theo's father," he said, gesturing with his pipe, "live in big city. New Jersey."

"I don't think New Jersey is a city," I said. "But they got a few big cities there."

"Theo's father live there. In New Jersey."

I owned as it was probably so.

"All white men leave their fathers," he said. He looked at me with a kind of pity that could pretty fairly of been scorn. "You leave your father, or he leave you."

"I guess."

"It is different with my people. We never leave our fathers."

"Never?"

"We all live in same village. Where my fathers go, I go with them."

"And you have more than one."

"All my people have more than one. It is Indian way to adopt the young men and women as they grow."

"I've heard it was such," I said. "It's a good idea."

"Why do wasichus go away from their fathers and mothers?"

"I don't know," I said. "I guess it's the way the world is."

"No," he said. "It is wasichus. Not the world."

"Well, you ain't with your father now."

"No. I live on land of my fathers."

I could see I had better not argue the point. I wanted to know how it was any different from white folks; most can locate their daddy if they've a mind to, but they just don't necessarily hang around after a certain time of life. All I said was "Our villages don't ordinarily move nor nothing. So most can find their daddy if they need to." It was quiet for a while, except for the cicadas and tree frogs.

Big Tree said, "What is daddy?"

"It means father," I said.

He nodded. "I know where my people hunt. When I go with Theo, I leave my father like wasichu leave father."

That was a pretty revealing thing to say and it set me back a little. He didn't express it with regret nor nothing, but I sensed it anyway. I said. "I would like to of known my mother."

"You have not known your mother?" He tamped the tobacco down in his pipe.

"My mother died when I was very young," I said.

His eyes softened. He told me how he was adopted a third time by a medicine man with medicine so powerful he kept it in a pack and let it hang from a stand of three branches tied together at the top. He always did this so his medicine wouldn't never touch the ground. Touching the ground would rob his medicine of its power. "He was called Stone Hands," Big Tree said. "He fought the Sioux, the Southern Cheyenne. He counted many coups on the Sioux and they shoot at him. All try to kill him. He ride right in front of their eyes and then come back and no arrows touch him."

"I am a orphan," I said. "I was raised by my aunt."

He nodded, his eyes gleaming. Then he said, "I tell you about Stone Hands."

I said nothing.

"One day he put his medicine on his stand and a young brave, racing his horse through the village, knock down the stand and Stone Hands' medicine fall to earth." He looked at me with the most serious expression, like I should understand something a lot more than I did. I almost said, "So?" But then he said, "Very bad thing when medicine fall to earth. All its power gone. Now it is nothing but bones and thread, and feathers and tobacco ash." I remembered he'd told me that, and I felt bad for making him repeat it.

"I know," I said.

"Stone Hands hold his head high, he look in the face of white moon with the same strength and fire, but he know then he no longer have good medicine. He tell the women and children, 'I will die before new moon.' But none of the people believe him. One of his fathers tell him to take his pack to the top of the hill on the other side of the Yellowstone. To set it out again on the stand, high among the mists and clouds. 'You will get your medicine back,' his father say. 'You go on another vision quest with that medicine and it will be good again.' And the next day, when we hunt for buffalo, he ride out toward the top of the ridge. He leave his lodge and all of his wives and horses. He just ride out on one horse carrying a lance and the medicine pack."

"What's a vision quest?"

"You go out by yourself," he said, a mite annoyed to have to explain it to me. "You take no food. Only water. You stay long time—many days. You wait for dream. Vision. You see outside who you are."

"I don't much attend to spiritual things and such," I said. "It's enough to keep breathing out here." He stared at me for a long time, then I said, "Go on. Finish the story."

"A man must be worthy to hear about these things." He sat back against the cottonwood and puffed on his pipe. He seemed to be finished with me.

"No," I said. "Tell me. I'll try to be worthy."

He studied the bowl in his hands, then raised the canteen and drank a huge gulp of the whiskey. I asked him again to go on and tell me the story.

He said, "Stone Hands walk in mountains and in the hills. He follow the Yellowstone, he go across many rivers and climb to high clouds above water and earth." The whole time Big Tree spoke he waved the pipe around, took quick puffs on it, pointed with it. I never seen him so animated. I felt relaxed and kind of privileged, if you know what I mean—like I was being gifted with something pretty well valuable and unusual to boot. "Stone Hands follow the backbone of the earth," Big Tree went on, "and then go west a long, long way into evening. Then he make camp in highest place next to where white moon rises. He wait for a vision. Night and day. Nine days. Finally a raven come to him and speak."

"A bird," I said.

He nodded, but I could see he would not take a challenge to the facts. "The raven tell him to follow the trees along the big river until he see the blue tail of a cougar. The cougar will say to him what he must know."

I'm a pretty skeptical fellow, and I think some of my natural doubt must of showed on my face. He looked hard at me for a second, then he said, "Stone Hands told me this."

I didn't say nothing. I wanted to be worthy.

"Stone Hands do what bird tell him and he walk for many days, and then he see cougar with blue tail. It walk in front of his eyes. It move fast, and secret. Stone Hands follow it, with no spear or bow. Only his knife and small bag of medicine tied around him. He move like cougar, silent, and stalking, through leaves and thickets. The cougar know Stone Hands follow. The blue tail grow longer, until it drag on ground in front of Stone Hands. He can reach down and touch it. Then Stone Hands say the cougar stop. The great cat turn around, the long tail still on ground in front of Stone Hands. 'Pick up my tail,' the cougar tell him, and he did. The tail was like hemp, and cold. Stone Hands want to drop it. It frighten him."

"It would sure enough frighten me," I said.

"The cougar tell him that before a new moon he would walk among the dead ones, blue and cold like long tail." Now Big Tree took a stick and stirred the fire a little. I waited to see if the story was over. I got to admit it gave me a bit of a chill. He knocked the ash out of his pipe and took another swig of whiskey. Then he turned directly to me, leaning over so his hair almost draped over the fire. "Stone Hands come back to us on his horse. He was sad. A blue death is not a death in battle. It is from disease or freezing. He want to die in battle. He is a warrior." It was very quiet for a while. Even the crickets seemed to listen. The fire hissed a little. Smoke curled up in front of us. Big Tree shrugged and sat back. "After that, Stone Hands will not dance. He will not eat or drink. A few suns after that, we find him under water of a swift stream. He is blue. His eyes stare up out of ice water. Small black stones."

"How did he die?"

Big Tree shook his head. "The spirit leave him. He turn blue and fall in water. The water ice-cold."

Now the crickets come back. I swear, it was eerie the way they seemed to listen to Big Tree, seemed to know when his story needed the quiet.

A little later that night, I set my bedroll next to the fire and laid down to sleep. Big Tree sat up at the base of the tree, sipping his whiskey.

{ CHAPTER 6 }

I'D HEARD ALMOST nothing about Big Tree, and learned even less
for the first few months I known him. I rode next to him in Theo's
train for four hundred miles or more, and he maybe spoke four
words. I known from those words that he had no use for wasichus, and
since I was one of them, he had no use for me.

But once we was traveling together, just the two of us, once he
started sipping on that whiskey, he become a different fellow to me. It
wasn't no match at all between the man I known as Big Tree when I
first rode with him and the fellow he become once we was comrades.
We camped in the great collection of valleys and sagebrush-covered
plateaus in Wyoming and the Musselshell country. We trapped a little
and hunted a lot. We roamed on the open plains and rode up into the
white-tipped mountains that always seemed to surround us. We spent
so much time in them mountains, I begun to think of myself as a
mountain man. We spent some time in the Gallatin valley in the west,
and further east along the Powder and Tongue Rivers. I got to know
the country far better than I ever could of learned it studying Theo's
maps, even though I was grateful for all the time I'd spent doing that.
One season we went south as far as the Washita River just outside Fort
Cobb. I don't think we was too far from Fort Riley where I first come
to this country. But most of the time we ranged north to the Missouri
River in Montana, and all over Nebraska, and Dakota Territory, and
even Kansas and Colorado Territory. We hunted in the Bighorn
Mountains and the Black Hills. Folks have no idea how big and lonely
wide-open this damn country is. We went sometimes for weeks without ever seeing another human soul. Then we'd ride up on a Indian
camp and be honored guests for a night or two. We was always welcome
if we rode right on in. Theo taught me that. Maybe Big Tree taught it
to him. He rode in so natural and calm—like he belonged there. It is
just true that no Indian will fall on a man and kill him if the fellow just
rides on into a village, his arms at his side, a-smiling at the barking

dogs and squealing children. It ain't nothing but courtesy among them folks, pure and simple. They figure if you meant any harm you'd be coming in quiet and catlike, or hollering with war in your heart. Even the Sioux will leave a man alone if he just ignores the idea they might want to cut him up good.

Big Tree said the Sioux come from the north where there ain't nothing but ice and snow. They come down on horses into the country of the Cheyenne and the Crow, the Blackfeet and Arapaho and Piegan, and commenced to warring on them pretty particular and hard. They was great warriors and a lot of them too. Lakota, Brulé, Dakota, Miniconjou, Arrows All Gone, and Wahpekute; Yankton, Uncpapa, and Oglala, and half a dozen other names—but they all spoke pretty much the same language and they all got together once a year for what they called the "sun dance," and to hunt and share family histories and such.

"'Sioux' mean enemy," Big Tree said. "It is Crow word."

"Theo told me it was Cheyenne."

I didn't know whether he could know all he seemed to know about the Sioux, but it was easy to see that he admired them and in his own way I guess he feared them a bit too. He said he never wanted to be in a fight with the Sioux if he could help it. He said Theo felt the same way. "That is why Theo get angry that you shoot that Wahpekute when you are first in this land. Theo believe sure he will end up fighting not just Sioux but Red Top."

Anyway, me and Big Tree spent several seasons running on the same ground as the Sioux. Years went by without my noticing nary a one. I was just having the time of my life, I guess. I didn't think about much except where we might go next and what kind of game we'd hunt or trap.

I grew enough hair on my face that I could tuck it into my shirt and keep warm in the winter. And the winters in all of our wanderings was as tough as any I ever seen anywhere. Our first few winters was about fifty miles east of Bozeman, on the Musselshell River. That's where Big Tree said there was still plenty of beaver and otter and we'd get plenty of pelts in the cold months.

Some nights the weather would come up on us by surprise and we didn't have time to erect Big Tree's lodge. As quick as a squirrel he'd build a windbreak with pine branches and stones, and we'd crouch down under them small shelters while what seemed like a ocean of icy air passed high above us, dripping on us now and then and roaring constantly, and so cold it seemed to freeze the smoke of our fire and drive what heat it might give off back into the burning wood. For most of them winters I wore fur from four different animals and wrapped my feet with buffalo hide, sometimes still warm from the kill. Big Tree wore furs, too, but he never seemed to be cold. He'd build a fire in the center of his lodge and then we'd huddle there out of the dark, ice-filled wind, and cook our buffalo or venison or elk. The wind would slap the walls of that lodge and howl over the hole in the top where the smoke flew, but we'd be warm from the fire. The smell of them animal walls, and the woodsmoke with the cooking meat, always made me sleepy. Most times Big Tree had a large can of whiskey that he refilled his canteen from, and night after night in the cold months he'd sip that whiskey while I curled around the fire and drifted into warm sleep. I don't know if he ever slept, to tell the God's truth. I never seen him do it. He was awake when I got up in the morning and when I gone to sleep at night.

We wasn't failures nor nothing, but the pelts we was collecting wouldn't make us rich, neither. We had maybe forty or fifty after the first winter. I heard that trappers used to get pelts in the hundreds in one season, so we known it was the end of a kind of life—but I wanted to lead it anyway, as long as I could. The only thing I was sure I didn't want to do was work. At the end of our third winter we rode into Fort Benton, north of Bozeman, and sold what we had at a trading post there. Big Tree seemed happy. But I wanted to go on down to Bozeman and see what Theo was up to. It was getting down near the end of April that year—1873—and I wanted to read a newspaper and see what was new in the world.

I didn't find Theo, but I got myself a hotel room with some of my pelt money, and took a hot bath. I didn't cut my beard off, but I trimmed it a bit. It was full and covered my neck for sure. I thought I looked older and more rough-and-ready with it, but women shied away from me like I was a dog with foam at the mouth.

I spent a few weeks in Bozeman. Nobody could tell me what happened to Theo. One fellow told me he believed that Theo stayed for two winters, then packed up and set off leading a train for California. "If that's who I think it was, he got tired of the cold winters." But he didn't know for sure. It might of been somebody else. He didn't remember no children nor a wife, neither.

I went on back to Fort Benton. Big Tree was glad to see me, I think. He bought some more traps and other gear—including a buffalo rifle. He'd also traded one of the packhorses for a Colt pistol and two mules. I went ahead and bought another horse from the army. The fellows there tried to get me to scout for them, but I told them I wasn't interested. They was gonna be chasing a lot of Indians and I didn't want no part of that.

Folks told as how some Indians signed a treaty way back in 1865 that promised for all time that they would stay the cold winters at various forts that the whites called "agencies." The cavalry promised food and shelter if the Indians stayed put, and a few of them went ahead and took advantage of it for a while. They was always going to be free to hunt in the spring and summer in their usual hunting grounds, but in the cold long winters they could take shelter at a fort and protect their children and old people from hardship. The whites believed that the one Indian that signed that treaty spoke for all of them. No Indian ever spoke for nobody but hisself and his family and maybe his followers if'n he had good medicine and folks followed him. Then somebody found gold in the Rocky Mountains, and more and more wagon trains come through with white folks and settlers wanting to get rich quick. The agencies carried only so much food, so they'd feed the wagon trains as best they could and the Indians gone hungry. In the wintertime, lots of the tribes would leave the protection of the army and go back out into the rough country to hunt. The agency just could not feed everyone in the winter months and no man should be expected to watch his children starve just for a treaty signed by some elder in some other tribe years ago who he ain't never met and who certainly did not represent him nor his interests. So the Cheyenne and Sioux, the Arapahos and Blackfeet, the Shoshone and Pawnee, would raid and hunt all over the Powder and Tongue River country, the Black Hills and Bighorn Mountains, and the army would send troops out to round them up and try to get them to come back to a agency where, from the army's point of view, they had agreed to stay. The argument was that the Indians was in clear violation of that treaty. To the Indians, there was no treaty none of them was bound to respect, since almost all of them was not there when it was signed, did not know who signed it or why, and did not believe one man could make no decisions, ever, for all of them. There never was no leader in that sense among the Indians.

I said it before and I'll say it again: there wasn't never a man more free on earth than a Indian. They was even free from each other. They never had to learn to follow nobody's orders but their own. There never was a Indian general or a Indian army. They had fellows who was called "chief," but that was something the settlers agreed on. A man like Red Top or Sitting Bull might lead a band on the days his medicine was good, but his followers was welcome to leave any time. Sitting Bull wasn't no general—he was a medicine man, a shaman. People followed him for good medicine, not because he known how to fight a war or command a army. It ain't a wonder the Indians made such good soldiers: when they followed a man, they did so because he was a leader. Not because somebody tagged him with a piece of silver or sewn stripes on his sleeve. A Indian warrior led by the strength of his medicine and his character. Nothing else. A warrior in a Indian band might decide one day to just go to some other part of the country to hunt. The Cheyenne had bands of warriors in each camp, but they was more like clubs, and members could change from one to the other, and no Indian warrior was bound to no band if he didn't want to be. Each one was just his own self, even though he lived all his life with his mother and father and a half a dozen of other folks that adopted him.

And living among the Indians, a fellow can get to feel like he is free too. Truly free.

Big Tree didn't like the Sioux or the Cheyenne. His people was supposed to be the white man's ally, but he didn't like white men, neither. I think he finally got to like me. Or at least he come to trust me a little bit. He give me the pelts to sell at the post every year; he let me do all the negotiating when we was ready to set out again and needed supplies. At times like that, I felt like his assistant, but that didn't matter none to me. I didn't think I had to worry about much of anything as long as I was traveling with a giant like Big Tree.

Sometimes he'd act like that first Big Tree I come to know: he would remain silent for a whole day and barely notice that I was riding next to him. But then at night, by the fire, he'd tell me of a dream he had, or of some other adventure in his childhood. Or he'd give me more history of his people and the other Indians in his country. He was a gentle fellow, prone to misty remembering, especially of his family. He believed all of his dreams to be real experiences, and could not fathom the notion that something could only take place in his head while he was sleeping. He did not like waste or extravagance; he would of made a damn good banker. When we killed a animal that was too big to eat in one sitting, he'd clean the thing completely, keep a fur or two for us in the coldest months, and wrap and preserve the meat in tight sacks made from the rest of it. The skin under the fur would dry up eventually, but the meat would still be moist and ready to cook. He could keep meat fresh in the winter pretty much indefinitely. A pile of furs and skins packed solid with meat would hang heavy off of both mules sometimes. But Big Tree was also generous to a fault. He was always prepared to share our provender with folks that needed it.

In January or February of '75, we come upon a band of Sioux women and children and a few old men. These people had no food to speak of, and looked to be in a bad way. Their young men was out making trouble for somebody, but these folks was not in a fighting mood. If the warriors didn't return soon, some of the old men would die and the children was right puny too. We was just south of the Black Hills, in a part of the country that is full of gullies and draws, thick stands of pine and ash trees and plenty of game. We never did find out how long the men was gone, or where they went. The women seemed to be in charge, and they was not too friendly at first: they worried about the children and looked upon us with suspicion. The Sioux don't trust nobody, but they especially don't trust a Crow brave who's all of six feet seven or so and looks like he might be a perfect specimen of man ready for whatever he wants to take. The old men was not much good at hunting no more, and the kids didn't look old enough. All I wanted to do was get away from them before the men come back, but Big Tree got a pack of meat off one of the mules and stood there pointing at the ground. "We camp here," he said. So we set up camp right next to where them starving Indians had theirs, and then Big Tree took half our meat and just give it to one of the women—a fat, hard-nosed looking sheriff with a red scarf on her head and skin like leather. Her rocky face actually broke into something like a smile, then she carried the meat off and cooked it. Then the other women come one at a time and stood in front of Big Tree, just staring up at him, until he wrapped his arms around them and squeezed a bit. Then they'd run back to their camp, giggling like they'd been tickled or something. After a while, they come back around and seemed as if they wanted to touch the mane of hair around my face. It turned out to be a long night—me afraid to sleep for what deviltry they might get up to, and Big Tree standing watch with his buffalo gun, ignoring all of us. The next day, when we broke camp, they did the same.

"Now what do we do?" I said.

Big Tree said nothing.

"What if their men come back."

"We will not see them," he said.

"I know," I said. "That's what I'm afraid of. We'll be pincushioned with arrows before we see a damn thing."

They followed us the next day, and the day after that. And when a mealtime rolled around, Big Tree give them more meat. I don't mind telling you, I looked over my shoulder every second expecting we'd see their husbands and brothers coming back to find out what we might be up to with their women. We was heading north and west, generally, toward the Yellowstone River country. That big, ugly fat woman Big Tree first give the meat to started to warm up to him. The more food he let her have, the more she and the others wanted to be close to him. They even smiled a bit for him. And he'd feed them some more of our meat. But it didn't hurt none. Hell, there was always plenty of game wherever we went. I never gone to sleep hungry.

I think I was getting to the point of a kind of contentment. This was at the end of our fifth winter in the fur-trapping business. It was our last year, but I didn't know it. I didn't think much about it. I figured we could go on just hunting our food and living off the land like the

Indians did. It wasn't that I give up the idea of being a man of destiny, or getting some land, or finally going someplace else. Them things just never crossed my mind. Sometimes I got to feel like I was in a kind of perfect heaven. You never get used to the sky so close to the white frosty tips of the mountains, or the blue rivers running down in valleys and draws, washing over white stones and swirling in brown rushes over silver boulders in the moonlight. There are canyons of blue and rusty rock, wide meadows of green grass and blue and yellow wild-flowers. It was all just too colorful and wild and free to be nothing else but a paradise. For all that time with Big Tree I just about forgot what might happen to a fellow out in that wilderness.

After a week or so of them folks following us, we was a regular tribe. The women and old men and children camped right next to us, or just a little behind; when we stopped near water, they always camped downstream or behind us so they had to walk through where we was to get water. They hauled our water for us and then at night they'd come in—slowly at first, and one at a time—to sit around our fire. After a while, they helped make the fire, they fed it and kept it burning high and bright, and it seemed like it wasn't our camp no more.

They ate raw sowbelly and offered it to us regular, but I wouldn't touch it unless it was fried good and crisp. They made some boiled berries that was fine, and when they roasted a bird or a slab of buffalo meat over that fire, it was like we was all one big happy family.

Then, about the third week or so, a bit of trouble developed with Big Tree because he taken to hugging only the women he wanted to hug and leaving off the others. The women he give meat to come to expect it from him, and in the beginning he obliged. But then he developed preferences. Now we heard the women fighting pretty noisily at night and sometimes in the morning. It didn't bother Big Tree a lick, but I known things like that for a source of trouble—it was like a spark in dry grass. I feared the consequences.

I drew some interest from a tall, pretty woman named Morning Breeze. When I say she was pretty, I ain't exaggerating. She wasn't classic like some of them women in Virginia Beach, nor nothing like that—just real tall, and a mite wide in the hips, and not that chesty. In fact, it didn't appear that she had much a-going on in the chest area at all. In her buckskins, with her black hair all tied behind her, she looked like a young man. She had smooth, light skin—not nearly as dark as some of the others—and a wide, toothy smile. She had all her teeth and they was white as new snow. Anyway, Morning Breeze noticed the way Big Tree commenced to hugging some women and not the others, and she taken it to heart that the hugs meant something important.

Big Tree picked up the women he chosen and just squeezed for a little while. At first I think they liked it, but then after a time it begun to be clear that it wasn't such a good thing no more. I could see that, but they didn't want to let on, neither. As far as they could tell, it was Big Tree that killed every animal we skinned and ate in our travels. It was mostly true, I'll admit, but that didn't mean I wasn't good at it. Just that Big Tree known where to look better than I did.

Morning Breeze took to standing in front of me with that wide smile on her face. She was a head taller, so she looked down on my face. She didn't have no hope of Big Tree showing a interest because she was almost as big as he was, so she settled on me. The thing was, she had no hope of me hugging her, neither. I didn't think I could pick her up.

She would speak to me in Sioux, but I could only sign that I had no idea what she was saying. Then one day when we was camped near a pretty swift stream, she come up from the edge carrying a big trout. She caught the thing with her hands. It wriggled in her grip but she carried it over and offered it to me. I'd been eating some fairly heavy meat for a long time, and the idea of a light, delicate meal of fried trout just got to me. I whooped and hollered to Big Tree that we was going to eat like kings, then I took the fish from her and laid it on the ground and give her a big hug. In the process I stood on my tiptoes and kissed her on the cheek.

That was a mistake, of course. She come back in less than a hour with her father and her younger brother. The old man was probably sixty or seventy. Her brother may of been ten or eleven. He wore paint and carried a bow and arrow.

"I think he wants to stick me good," I said to Big Tree.

"She think you will marry her," Big Tree said.

"No, no." I said. I backed away a little. The old man said something to Big Tree.

"He wants to trade," Big Tree said.

"So now I'm gonna get a wife," I said. "What if I don't want one?"

"Why not? She will set up every camp for you, cook, tan hides, and wash you. She will carry water for you."

"You been hugging these women since they took up with us, and not one of them expects you to marry."

"They are afraid of me."

"And not me."

"You more their size." Big Tree said these things without a hint of a smile, but I could tell he thought it was damn funny.

"Why couldn't one of them shorter ones with more womanly features be interested?"

"This one like you. Not others. Others already married."

"It'd be nice to have somebody settin' the fire every night, wouldn't it," I said.

Big Tree nodded.

"But I don't want no wife."

He said something to the old man, who looked at me.

"Tell him I am honored but I can't do it," I said.

Big Tree spoke to him again.

The old man smiled. Morning Breeze averted her eyes and sort of bowed to me.

"What'd you tell him?"

"I said you'd give him your gun for her."

"No I ain't," I said. "Ain't nobody getting that carbine from me."

"That is what he wants."

"I don't care," I said. "You tell him he can have anything else, but not my gun."

Big Tree spoke to the old man again, then he looked at me. "You trade one of your pistols?"

I was so relieved not to have to part with my Evans repeater, I agreed about the pistol. Then it hit me what else I was agreeing to. Morning Breeze come over and stood next to me and the old man pronounced us man and wife. Then all the other women come out of hiding and surrounded us. They took Morning Breeze off to mess with her hair and get her cleaned up, I guess. I got my old army tent off the pack mule and set it up, and then some of them women crawled in there and started to clean up.

"No," I said. "Get the hell out of there."

They lay down a blanket and then poured some kind of oil on it. "Go on," I said. "Get the hell out of there." The oil smelled like feet. It was some kind of musk oil from otters or something. "Hellfire and damnation," I said. The old tent was small—a regulation army two-man tent, white and leaky—and now I had that damn smell in it.

Well, it was a week of celebration, it seemed like. Morning Breeze went about taking care of me, and that meant I didn't have to do a durn thing about our camp. I could hunt and fish, but that's all I had to do. She cooked, set the fire, cleaned and tanned the hides, and cut up the meat. She laid down next to me at night, and if I wanted her to, she'd be ready for me to have a little pleasure of her body. The thing was, she ain't never seen a bar of soap. Every day she wore leggings up to her knees, and a leather dress that hung down around there, and underneath was nature's portal. I finally took her down to that stream and made her set in it a while. I went up the hill to give her privacy, but I left a fine cotton shirt of mine that was longer than her leather dress. She come up the hill with the shirt on, and I sent her back down to wash the damned leather dress and them leggings. She only had the one outfit, so I give her a bunch of my shirts and a few pair of breeches in case she got cold.

Now when she come into the tent, she smelled right clean and fresh as a daisy. It didn't help the smell of that oil in there, but that wore off after a spell and it become fairly pleasant at night when it got cold, having Morning Breeze next to me.

I didn't want to take advantage of her or nothing, but on some of them nights I have to admit I did some powerful inside debating about it. After a while, I got to thinking it don't matter how tall she is. I had no truck with women since I first left them whores of Virginia, and the idea got me breathing fairly heavy. But I was afraid of what would happen to me when the men come back. And Morning Breeze always looked at me with a kind of smile that I just didn't want to sully, if you know what I mean. She did for me, cared for me, and waited. I resisted a powerful urge to just take her and forget what might happen to both of us.

Big Tree said to me once, "She like you. That is always good with women."

"I don't want a wife," I said.

"You sit by fire, look wise. Smoke. Eat. Hunt. She will do rest of it."

"I never minded taking care of my own things," I said.

It was just luck that I ended up spending those months with her. We traveled further west, toward the Bighorn Mountains, and didn't see nothing of the rest of the men in her tribe. It was just me and Big Tree and nineteen other souls—seven women, four old men, and eight children. And the funny thing was, once I had myself a wife, I noticed a more powerful desire to take care of everybody. We really was a small tribe. The women set up their lodges—four of them—and then they'd set up a new one they made for Big Tree, and I'd set there and smoke while Morning Breeze laid out my old U.S. Army tent.

You know she liked being clean too. It was a feeling that grown on her. Or maybe she seen how much it pleased me. She kept herself real nice. I got to where I could sign to her and she'd pretty much know what I wanted. And she could let me know too. We was married, but we done well never doing nothing like married folks do except in the daily living. We got used to it. I wouldn't have her in that way, and she didn't seem to mind it much. Oh, one night or the other she might smile at me a certain way, and move over closer and all, and I'd begin to think about having a go at her—like I said, she wasn't bad to look at. I had the devil on my shoulder every night with her, but I managed to say no, fretting what would happen if the men come back and seen us together or, if she got so attached in that way, what trouble I'd have leaving her with the tribe when the men did come back. And I known they would be back. I told Big Tree to let her know it was a temporary arrangement, sort of as recompense for us feeding her and her people and all, and taking care of them. He never said nothing back to me. He just stared at me for a spell, then turned away and puffed on his pipe.

And then early one spring day, maybe eight or nine weeks or so after our band of Sioux had commenced to follow us, the men come back, mostly naked and covered in war paint. We was in the foothills of the Bighorn Mountains, camped by a small stream that run off the Powder River. Them tired, wore-out braves was not happy to see Big Tree and me.

It wasn't like they was suspicious of our intentions; it wasn't jealousy that made them so unfriendly to see us there. It was plain rage at their own selves for letting the army surround and capture them. It took them a while to escape and then they had to go in search of their families because we had been on the move. They was also angry because their women and children got so hungry they had to depend on a Crow brave and a wasichu.

In the first nervous minutes when the men rode in on us, the women kept raising their arms high and letting them down in a sweeping bow before the men and they chattered to beat all. Luckily, Morning Breeze had gone down to the stream to get some water, so it wasn't like nobody could guess she was with me. And when she come back up with the water, I looked at her very sternly, so she carried it over to the side of the camp where the other women was a praising the high heavens that the men had come back.

Big Tree got up on his horse. He was still as a stone mountain just setting there with his rifle across his saddle. I got my carbine and mounted up myself. If we had to ride hard, we'd sure get away because the returning braves was clearly exhausted. Their horses was breathing hard and heavy, and they had white lather between their legs and all down their sides. The men got down and the whole group commenced to hugging each other. I watched Morning Breeze carefully, hoping she had somebody to hug, but she didn't. She set the water down and praised with her arms like the others, but nobody went to her. I have to say that even though I'd only been with her a few weeks, and never had spoken to her without using my hands, I felt right sorry for her. She didn't look sad nor nothing—she was happy as any of the others—but I felt like she must be alone.

I didn't feel bad for long, though, because it hit me we'd probably have much less trouble with them braves if I wasn't stealing one of their women. That's how I looked at it, never mind that her father and brother was there and the old man performed the ceremony. It just didn't seem like nothing but stealing, and every white man I ever seen out there that had a Indian wife called her a squaw and always acted like she was some kind of booty from a raid. Like a squaw was no wife at all but more like a captured horse or dog. How could them braves let me get away with one of their own? Not that I'd take her with me anyway. But you know what I mean. Even among the folks that don't have churches to marry them, it don't look right sharing your tent with a woman who ain't rightly yours. You'd think after almost six years in the big West I'd of figured it all out, but I didn't. When Morning Breeze walked back over to me carrying the water, I realized nobody seemed to care. Big Tree give a short laugh and got down off his horse. "Dismount," he said. "We stay awhile."

"What's so funny?" I said.

"She your wife," he said.

"She told them?"

"She is very happy and proud. You are good catch."

"For Christ's sake," I said.

She set the water down for me and then scooted into the tent.

We stayed in camp right next to them Sioux braves. Big Tree didn't want to move on yet, and it was okay with me, because I had not figured a way to leave Morning Breeze behind. We hunted a bit with the Sioux and both them and us got a good-sized elk. Ours had the better rack on it, but they both provided a lot of meat. The Indians did a little dance in front of the firelight before we ate what turned out to be really good broiled meat. I went back to my tent and found Morning Breeze a-laying there with her leggings off, and when I laid down next to her, thinking I'd pretend I didn't notice, she pulled at my drawers and before long we was doing the very thing I'd been trying to avoid. She got up on all fours when she was ready, and I went ahead and give it to her. I wasn't that experienced with it, to tell you the truth, and it wasn't never long before the whole thing was over. But it was powerful good. It made me sleepy and feeling all right about just about every-thing in the world. Morning Breeze held on to me then, all damn night. It was like she didn't want me to get a inch away from her.

When I woke up in the morning she was outside, tending the fire, heating me some coffee, and frying up some sowbelly and biscuits.

She didn't know the first thing about making no biscuits, but there she was, giving it her all. Big Tree sat by the fire watching her. She looked at me when I come up out of the tent and give a kind of smile, but I could see she had tears in her eyes. I swear a Indian woman is the damnedest thing.

"Are you okay?" I said.

"Beech-i-lack," she said, nodding her head.

Big Tree said, "She speak Crow. She think you will understand."

"What'd she say."

"She is grateful. Now she is your wife."

"Really."

"You have not been her husband until now."

"Beech-i-lack," she said again.

"What should I say?" I asked Big Tree.

"Just don't look away. Say yes."

I smiled at her, and then she jumped up, and before I could stop her she had her arms around my neck. She rested her head on top of mine.

"Okay," I said. "Okay."

"You do okay last night," Big Tree said.

"She say something to you?"

He got to his feet, a kind of half smile on his face.

"What?" I said.

"She don't speak," he said.

"Beech-i-lack," I said.

We only stayed put a couple more days. Then nothing I said would of kept Big Tree still. So we packed up our extra meat and broke camp. The Sioux remained where they was. I'd of had to hit her with a flat stone and left her for dead to keep Morning Breeze from coming with us. So I let her ride behind me on Cricket. She didn't seem to be too sad about leaving her people. They watched us heading out north toward the Tongue River. Morning Breeze kept looking back at them, but they only stood there watching until we couldn't see them no more. The country opened up a bit in front of us, and we followed a small stream for a while, then turned a little more toward the west. The weather was cooling off during the day and damn cold at night. Big Tree wanted to stay out of the Bighorn Mountains with winter coming on, but we was headed for a trading post in Wyoming Territory called Redbird.

The first day out, Big Tree started drinking from his keg before we stopped for the night. He'd never done that before.

"Why you hitting that so early?" I asked him.

He didn't even look at me.

We set up camp near the Tongue River in a stand of trees that looked down toward the bank of the river. We still had plenty of meat, and Morning Breeze set about cooking some over a fire. While I waited, I ate what was left of the oily biscuits she'd made that morning. I offered one to Big Tree and he waved it away. He was drunk and a goner for that night, and I could only hope he wouldn't pull the same thing the next day. He had plenty of whiskey.

Morning Breeze come to me that night again, and this time I did a fair job of it. Having a woman to lay next to at night and the bonuses that come with that was downright pleasing, and I was no longer capable of saying no to it.

I didn't sleep at all, though. I lay there most of the night listening to Morning Breeze and Big Tree snore. Sounded like a couple of elks going at it in a mud bog. I figured in the morning, before either one of them waked up, I'd try to find Big Tree's store of whiskey and deplete it a little bit. I'd heard tales of Indians once they started on the juice. I missed his company in the evenings, and I didn't like it that he'd started sipping the stuff before the sun went down.

{ CHAPTER 7 }

WEEKS PASSED. WE kept to the plains mostly, and I never did manage to diminish Big Tree's whiskey. He did that. Each day, he'd start a little earlier than the next. He never got to where being drunk made him mean, but he sure commenced to talk a little more before he passed out. All during that time, I didn't sleep the best I ever have. Things between Morning Breeze and me had started to cool somewhat. Gradually I noticed that she didn't look at me like she used to or as often. I didn't mind it that much, but I wondered what I had done to shift her eyes away from me.

Finally, one very early morning when I give up sleep, I decided to get outside and start feeding the fire. Morning Breeze was already up, so I rolled out of the tent and set there for a while breathing the cold air, trying to get my eyes to focus. The sky was dark still, and I could see the moon behind a thick bank of clouds in the south. It looked like there wouldn't be no sun at all on this day.

I don't know how long I set there before I realized I wasn't hearing no snoring from Big Tree's lodge and Morning Breeze was nowhere in sight. I got to my feet and walked over to the horses and they was still where they should be. I found my Evans carbine and put my boots on.

"Hey," I hollered. "Big Tree."

He come back down a little rise above our camp, walking stiffly. He wore his buffalo hat and had a odd look on his face. Morning Breeze was behind him. I realized she was almost as tall as he was.

"Where'd you go?" I said.

He signed that I should be quiet. Then he let me know that he was looking for trouble from the Sioux.

"Her band?" I said.

He shook his head.

I whispered, "They was grateful to us. Beech-i-lack." I looked at Morning Breeze, but she was bending her head in a shy way and did not meet my eye. "What's wrong with her?" I said.

"I am Crow," he said. "Sioux pay me beech-i-lack when they do not kill me." He paused and looked out toward the moon. In the dim light his face looked like the carved figure of a ancient god on the bow of a ship. "Morning Breeze go for water," he said. "I follow her."

I didn't see no water. He looked at me and noticed that the water wasn't going to back up his story. "She leave water when she see her people coming."

"I thought you said it wasn't her people?"

"They are Sioux. All Sioux her people."

I said nothing. I might of turned a deep shade of red, though. Morning Breeze would not look at me.

Big Tree said, "They come to kill Big Tree."

"They ain't," I said. "Not as long as I got this here." I held out my carbine.

"They don't kill you," he said. "They take our horses and kill me."

I got pretty irritable thinking about that. "Damnation," I said. "You feed their folks—their women and children and old men—and keep them alive for more than two months, and now they come after you?"

"These are not her people. They are different band. Still Sioux." He glared at me for a second. His face did not change, but I think he was embarrassed by what neither one of us was saying—with Morning Breeze standing there, looking kind of sheepish, and me knowing what they'd probably been up to. If I had of taken the time I would of finally come to see that he was a Crow brave; that meant he was like a statue of what God wanted when he dreamed up the creature he would call "man"—and he could speak her language. I was right puny in her eyes before long. But if the Sioux really were coming, it was just the wrong time for either one of us to even begin to mention what was going on between him and Morning Breeze. I didn't understand, but I'd like to say I did.

He looked at my carbine.

I think I known his thinking. Maybe I did, but anyway I lifted it and slung it over my shoulder. "We just going to wait here for them?"

"No." He turned from me and started taking down his lodge. I went ahead and started to fold my tent, but Morning Breeze pushed me away. She tried really hard to do it all herself. She could see I known what she'd been up to. She run around like if she got the whole thing wrapped up fast, without no effort at all from me, that would erase what she done with Big Tree. By the time we got everything packed, the sun had begun to leak a bit under the clouds. I still could barely see for the dim light.

Big Tree got up on his horse. In the gray light, he looked like a dark, towering shadow of death, with steam coming out of his mouth and his horse stomping the ground and a-moving his head up and down.

We'd gathered all the other animals and the two pack mules. We would be a slow train, but Big Tree wanted to get out of the open country. He had a feather attached to the end of his rifle. He raised the rifle a little and nodded at me, then he turned his horse and started out heading east, the pack animals following slowly behind. I got up on Cricket and begun to follow, dragging a line with my own animals, including the one Morning Breeze was riding on. Her legs dangled down both sides of that mule and practically touched the ground. The country was hilly and covered in saw grass, dandelions, and wildflowers. We moved at a trot sometimes, but mostly a slow walk up and down small hills and shallow ravines while the sun lit up the world on the other side of the dark clouds. When I could see the round white outline of the sun, it commenced to rain. A cold, steady rain that come on like a thing dumped from a bucket. I only had my leather breeches and a cotton shirt on, so it wasn't long before I was soaked and shaking pretty bad. I stopped Cricket and got down in a stand of thick grass and pulled a buffalo robe out of my pack. Up in front of me, I could see Big Tree a-setting there, his head down, letting the water run off of him.

"Don't you want something to keep warm?" I said, and then I seen him tilt his head back. He was drinking some of that whiskey.

"Well, I guess that will do the trick," I said.

He did not turn back to me, he just waited there. The water beaded up and dripped in the thick buffalo hair of the hat he wore, and it made the horns glisten like black knives. I took another heavy buffalo robe out of one of the packs and give it to Morning Breeze. She still did not look at me. I said, "You may as well keep dry."

I couldn't stand the look of sad guilt on her face, the way she cast her eyes down. I wanted to tell her I figured it out. I known what probably happened. They run into each other in the cold morning. It was talk, maybe, at first between them. She understood him, and he was a god to her and he spoke her language. They was human. It wasn't nobody's fault and I would not blame no one. It was not okay with me. I did not want to accept it. But I understood it and it seemed like I should find a way to make her see that. So she wouldn't feel so bad and mortified around me.

She covered herself with the buffalo robe and, without looking at me, she said, "Beech-i-lack."

"It's okay," I said. "Don't fret about it."

I don't know if she known what I was talking about.

In a little while we was off again. I could see the land rising in front of us and off to the left, toward the northeast. It was a path up there and it led to a thick stand of black trees. Big Tree kicked his horse into a trot again, and I did the same. I didn't look back and I had no idea if the Sioux was following us or not.

What I seen in front of us was a kind of mirage, because the land dipped way down into a bare ravine that stood between us and the trees. We wound around in the shadow of high walls on either side of us until we come to a place where things leveled out a little and heavy tree branches covered the whole sky above us. It was like a deep cave and the rain only dripped through the leaves. The path got too thin to keep riding on it, so we gathered all the horses and mules into a good-sized gulch that bent off the ravine. We strung the leather up in the low-hanging branches to tie the animals in place. They was all breathing so loud, I couldn't hear nothing behind us. Big Tree scurried up out of the gulch and lay down at the base of one of the trees that leaned over the edge of the ravine. I followed him, not even thinking about Morning Breeze. When I got up next to him, he was wiping the barrel of his Sharps carbine with a piece of linen. When he was done, he handed it to me and I wiped mine down. I figured with his seven rounds and my thirty-four, we'd be fairly redoubtable. I could keep shooting while he reloaded, and when mine was spent he could time his load so he'd be able to keep firing while I done the same.

I couldn't see nothing for the sheets of rain. Water dripped out of the tree above us onto our backs. It dripped pretty steadily off the brim of my hat. Big Tree was as silent as ever, just watching in front of us. When I thought of Morning Breeze, I looked over there in the gulch and seen her crouching down next to one of the mules, holding on to the tether for dear life. It was hard to find her at first because she was covered in that buffalo robe and hunched down so close to the animals, she just looked like one of them.

Big Tree noticed me looking over there at her. I said, "She ain't my wife. Not among my people."

He didn't say nothing, but I heard a sound come from deep in his throat.

"It ain't nothing to me," I said.

Well, we laid there half a day or so and never seen no Indians. The rain begun to settle into something that felt permanent, like it would just drip like that steady, all the rest of time. There wasn't no wind nor nothing, just the rain.

"Are you sure you seen her people a-coming?" I said.

Big Tree didn't look at me. He got to his feet and crouching under the branches, started back down to where we'd left the animals. I followed him, but I wondered what the hell he was thinking; it even occurred to me that he made the whole thing up about the Sioux because he was embarrassed about me waking up too soon and finding him with Morning Breeze.

But I was wrong about that. We rode on, wet and miserable, for most of the rest of that day. We had to ride back out of the ravine the way we gone into it, then skirt around it to the east for a hour or so before we could make for the trees. The rain finally quit, but it was still no sun, soggy, and cold. We rode in silence except for the constant breathing and coughing of the animals. Their breath and ours sent vapors in front of us as we moved along. I don't know if I've ever been so cold, even with one of them buffalo robes over my head and shoulders. Big Tree never put nothing on himself. He was half naked, with just his warrior's vest, his leather breeches, and that huge buffalo hat with the two black horns curling over his head. I couldn't wait to stop somewhere under them trees and build a fire.

We rode a long way, and just when we was leaving a long stretch of flat ground crowded with small black bushes and a few rocks, I seen the Sioux to our left, coming down from the far hills. They rode along in the same direction we was going for a while, then disappeared behind the rise. There was maybe twenty of them. If they started riding hard behind that hill, we'd have no time to do much of anything but take them on from horseback. Big Tree turned his horse and at a gallop rode back toward me. I pulled up on Cricket and turned her to the side a bit, and Big Tree come up on my right and grabbed my carbine right out of my hands.

"Go into the trees," he said.

I hollered for him to stop, but he never even looked back at me. He turned his horse and galloped off toward where we last seen them Indians. His pack animals stayed put, so I went and got the rope that held them and started for the trees as fast as I could. It was a shocker to see them Sioux coming along like that—like they was a-stalking us. I guess I was wrong not to believe Big Tree from the beginning. My suspicion got the better of me. Morning Breeze and me made it to the trees and rode up into the thickest part of them until we could see down below to where Big Tree was. It took a while but then I seen him, sitting up high on his horse and moving at a walk up along the side of the hill the Sioux was coming down. By that time he was behind them and down the hill a ways. They didn't see him. They worked to hold their animals back, as the horses now scuffled down the hill, curling their front legs and turning their bodies to the side a bit as they pranced down. The hill was slick and it was real work for them folks to keep from slipping and falling. Some of them Indian horses did fall, but they rolled right back up with their rider still in place, both of them covered in mud. Big Tree was about thirty feet from them when he started running at them, this time firing my carbine. I seen two braves fall from their horses after the first two shots. They never seen him or known he was back there even when his horse begun thumping after them. I seen the other braves twisting their horses around. Then all hell broke loose.

"God save us," I said to nobody in particular, even though Morning Breeze looked at me as if she understood. I thought I was going to see Big Tree get slaughtered. I wasn't even thinking about the fact that he had my gun and I'd lose that too.

It was hard to see in the misty damp air, but he rode right into them fellows, firing my carbine the whole time, and it seemed like every time he fired it one of them Indians dropped off his horse. There was six or seven of them on the ground when Big Tree got through the whole bunch, wheeled his horse around, and started back in. He come at them from the side, so they was just getting their horses swung around when he wheeled his and started back in amongst them. He held the gun up against his shoulder and fired it with one hand. It was strange to see the smoke and fire come from the end of the gun, and hear nothing at all for a few seconds, and then the sound it made. I could barely hear the Indians a screaming their war whoops. Big Tree got four more of them, then swung down the hill away from them. He got to the bottom of the hill, turned his horse around, and started back up, but now the others was a-running from him. They had all they wanted of him. I don't think one of them even fired a shot from a gun. They may not of had guns. But it wasn't enough firepower in wood arrows or knives to face that Evans repeater in the hands of a crazy man the size of Big Tree, a-riding and shooting like a one-man army. He didn't chase them long up that hill. Their horses dug in deep in mud and started sliding back down toward him, but he'd already turned and started over the barren ground to where we waited for him. The Indians that was fleeing up the side a that hill stopped finally and watched Big Tree as he rode over to the edge of the trees and disappeared in the forest. They was waving lances with spears high in the air and singing as loud as they could. One of them, a tall fellow with a red sash around his neck and a long feathered lance, started after Big Tree, hollering "Yip, yip, yip." Big Tree didn't even look back at him. The brave stopped short and his horse reared up into the air. He raised the lance high, still hollering. The others seemed to be singing with him.

"They praise him," I said to Morning Breeze. "Right?"

She didn't understand. I tried to sign to her that Big Tree was some kind of big deal now among her people. "Like king," I said. "Like God among the Sioux."

I looked back to the battleground and seen the Sioux coming back down to their dead and wounded. Big Tree was deep in the trees to our left, and I sent Morning Breeze to go get him. I tied all the pack animals up and started to set up a camp.

Big Tree come in riding that big horse, towering over me. He had Morning Breeze on the back of the animal. I pointed to the clear sight I had through the trees. "We watched you," I said. "You had good medicine." The hot, heavy breathing and huffing of that horse steamed the air.

He handed me the carbine. "This good medicine."

"You're giving it back to me?"

He nodded.

I slung it over my shoulder. It was still warm from firing. I was glad to have it against my side as we set up camp.

That night, under a clear sky and a bright moon that scuttled high over the black trees and scattered a frozen kind of light over our camp, I sat right close to a hot fire and reloaded the Evans repeater. There was eighteen rounds left in the magazine.

"How many left?" he wanted to know.

"You fired sixteen shots," I said.

It was quiet for a spell. I was finally warm and dry—at least in the front—and the crackling fire made me a little sleepy. Morning Breeze had worked hard setting up my tent, but now she sat in front of Big Tree's lodge. It took her a long time to settle there, and I watched her the whole time. It looked like she was getting down into ice-cold water, but she only wanted me to know what I already guessed.

"You can sit closer to the fire if you want," I said. I signed for her to join us, but she only bowed her head and stayed put.

I finished loading my carbine and set it down next to me. Big Tree sat on the other side of the fire looking at me with no expression on his face. Finally I said, "How many you kill?"

"I shoot plenty," he said.

"Think they'll come back?"

"No."

He stared at the fire. His bronze skin glistened in the light and I could see his breath. It seemed clear to me what I had to do. I couldn't stay with them no more. I realized I was miserable now and embarrassed and feeling like I didn't belong there. Winter was coming and we was a long way from Bozeman, but that's where I figured I should go, so I told him.

"Why?" he said.

"It seems like the next thing we should do. I'm done with this here." I meant our trapping adventure, but he took it to mean something a lot more.

"I just want to go on back very soon," I said. "I don't want to spend another winter out here." There was no way I could make my departure about anything else but what he and Morning Breeze had done, but I wanted to.

He looked at Morning Breeze, who lowered her head. Then he picked up a stick and stuck the end of it in the fire.

"Beech-i-lack," I said. "You probably saved us from that Sioux war party."

He said nothing.

"Was it her people?" I pointed to Morning Breeze.

"It was Sioux. Some were among her people."

"I saw a fellow with a long spear and a lot of eagle feathers dangling from the end of it. He wore a red sash around his neck. Was that Red Top?"'

"Red Top is old man. That was White Dog."

"How do you know about him?"

"I know."

"He was singing pretty loud when you was done."

"He want me to come back. Fight him."

"He'll be out to get you now." I pointed to Morning Breeze. "Probably any other time she'd be grieving some of them folks you killed."

He looked at me briefly, a smile slowly beginning to grow on his face. "We should not let woman come between brothers," he said.

I only stared at him, nodding my head like a fool. Then I picked up my carbine, strode over to my tent, and crawled inside. I let the flap down once I was in there. It was my way of letting him know that I was okay with the new situation between us. To tell you the truth, I was kind of glad not to have to worry about Morning Breeze no more. I was glad to be shed of her. That's what I kept telling myself anyway.

PART THREE

Eveline

1875–76

{ CHAPTER 8 }

A FEW WEEKS AFTER Big Tree's battle with the Sioux, I left him and Morning Breeze and went out on my own. Big Tree said he was going to the Cheyenne River country to find his fathers, and of course Morning Breeze was going with him. I was headed west, maybe toward Bozeman, and I planned to enjoy the time alone and go on a long hunt. I took my own horses, but I traded the two pack mules to Big Tree for some hides and a skin packed with buffalo and deer meat. He also give me some tobacco and a small pipe to smoke it. I thought it was a fine gift, because he give it to me after we done our trade. It was his way of saying good-bye, or maybe he wanted to apologize for Morning Breeze. I thanked him and got on my way. I can't say I was brokehearted about Morning Breeze. I thought about her some—I admit it. I missed the friendly way she greeted me of a morning. You get to like having smiles to look at and sometimes to offer up. I don't like talking about it. Morning Breeze wasn't just a help to me. I'll say that, and no more.

I seen no one for the most of that trip. I found all kinds of game on the hunt. I didn't shoot no buffalo, but I got a antelope late one day—and there was always wildfowl and small game, rabbits and groundhogs and such. I never went hungry and I'd learned from Big Tree how to clean, cook, and eat almost any kind of meat. By now it was late fall and the weather was turning, so I finally set my sights on Bozeman. Once I made up my mind I was going there, it took eleven days of steady riding, the last few days in wind and cold rain. I'd lost the touch of putting my tent up with any sort of speed, and begun to hate doing all that work by myself. I talked to no one, not even Cricket. The first human beings I seen was just outside Bozeman, a lone wagon heading along the trail in front of me. I didn't want to catch up with it, to tell you the truth, but I did. The thing was being pulled by one ox, its head bowed heavy, bobbing up and down as it walked, breath a puffing from its nostrils. It was tired and cross and was still dripping water even though the rain had stopped finally. The sky was still bruised and surly looking.

My hair hung down over my shoulders and I had a thick beard, so that I don't reckon a body could see much of my face. I took off my hat because it was two women a-setting on the wagon. "Afternoon," I said. It was the first time I looked at Eveline and her sister. They didn't want to speak much. They granted me the afternoon, then stared straight ahead. I rode along next to them for a spell, not saying nothing. When I put my hat back on and started to scoot Cricket on ahead, one of them said, "Are you a mountain man?"

I pulled Cricket back a little. "No," I said. "If I have a name at all by this time, I'm just a squaw man."

"What's that?"

"I was married to a Indian woman for a short time. A very short time. A lot shorter than I been up in them mountains, but I reckon that's what folks would call me."

"Is that a bad thing?" the other one wanted to know.

"Not to me. It's just what I am." I calculated they should know that I had been with women and was married to one and I ain't a bad fellow. They both was wearing white bonnets and had leather-tough faces. They didn't wear no powder nor eye paint. Eveline had brown hair a-sticking out from under the bonnet. She held on to what looked like a Sharps rifle across her lap. The other one was younger. She held the reins and was nearest to me, and I couldn't see no hair at all, but her eyebrows was substantial and dark brown. I seen a Colt Dragoon in her lap. They both wore thick cotton dresses with long sleeves. The younger one holding the reins said, "What's your name?"

I told her.

"Well, Bobby Hale," she said, "this is my older sister, Mrs. Eveline Barkley. And I am Mrs. Christine Howard." She smiled and I seen that she had all her teeth. They was broad and white and in comparison to her dark eyebrows made her look right smart. Eveline said, "We are going all the way to Oregon." Even though it was the first time I looked at Eveline's face, it wasn't no big deal right then. I don't think I'd remember it except for the way her eyes looked at me—fierce and gleeful at the same time; I felt like prey. I looked at what I could see behind them sisters in the wagon and I didn't see no man.

"Where'd you come from?"

"Fort Buford," Eveline said. She seemed right proud.

"I know where that is."

"Where the Yellowstone meets the Missouri." Her teeth wasn't so white. She had one missing on the side and another that was crooked and stained a bit.

"We have come a very long way and we have seen this country is truly God's," Christine said.

"God's country. Indeed," said Eveline. They both sounded like they was from up north and way east—like Boston, maybe, or some-place up around there.

They whispered something between them. Then Eveline said, "Most men lose their hair as they get older, but you have a full head of it. And bright red."

"There's other ways to lose your hair in these parts. But I aim to keep mine."

"It sure is darker red than most."

"It's a mite wet too."

Christine snapped the reins a bit to keep the oxen moving.

"How'd you two get all the way to Fort Buford?"

"That is a story to tell," Eveline said, and they both laughed. "We are from Rochester, New York. We came out here with our husbands to find a home and get rich."

"You come a long way."

"That we did."

They wasn't, neither one, bad to look at.

Cricket snorted, shook her head, and the bridle rattled. Then she nodded her head up and down the way horses do.

"Where'd your husbands get off to?"

Eveline made a short, snuffling sound like Cricket. Christine said, "They took off from Buford with the other wagon."

"They wanted to go south to the Black Hills and search for gold," Eveline said.

"And they let you take this here wagon on your own?"

"They left us at Buford," said Christine. "They thought we should—"

"They *instructed* us—"

"Yes, they *instructed* us that we should remain at Fort Buford until they came back."

"And you didn't want to wait."

"We waited a year," Eveline said. "A whole year. We grieved them. We believe they are dead. We are going on to Oregon."

"By yourselves."

"We got a fellow with us," Christine said. "He is just a little under the weather right now." She turned slightly and looked behind her in the wagon. I seen a shadow move, and then a head come up behind her, swaying with the movement of the wagon. It was General Cooney, the fellow who shot that poor Crow brave all them years ago, and then had to apologize for it.

"I know this gentleman," Cooney said. He neither smiled nor looked happy nor sad. He wore no hat. His hair was high in thin white curls on his head, and he'd shaved off his mustache. He looked like he was wearing some kind of woman's dress or something.

I saluted. "Right strange to see you thisaway, General," I said.

"What way's that?"

"A-setting behind two women with a dressing gown on."

"It ain't no dressing gown. It's a linen sleeping jacket."

"You sick?"

"I been peaked as a crow's beak," he said. "I need a fogmatic as soon as possible, or I fear the consequences."

Christine said, "The way he squalled, rolled, puked, and kicked the last few days was a caution to any woman that might be tempted by corn. And now he's asking for more of it."

"I'm feeling a mite better now," he said. "And I wasn't on no combustibles. I don't even have no whiskey."

"You taking these ladies all the way to Oregon?"

"Just to Bozeman. They'll hook up with a train of wagons there, I expect."

I looked at Eveline. "You ladies know you're in the company of a Rebel general?"

They both nodded. "The war has been over for a decade," Eveline said. "And we are not afraid of Border Ruffians."

"It don't seem like no decade," I said.

"Nosir," Cooney said. "It sure don't."

I rode on into Bozeman with them. Far as folks could tell, we was together. I hoped I'd see Theo and didn't walk nowhere in Bozeman without looking for him a little bit. Just about every big fellow I seen from behind looked like him for a spell at first, before I recognized it wasn't.

General Cooney stayed with the women and their wagon. He was trying to get his hands on another oxen for them. "Just one won't make it," he said. I only had a few pelts, and the money I got for them was barely enough to buy me a room at a place called Miss Pound's Rooming House.

I never seen nobody named Miss Pound. It was a fellow named Robert who met me at the door. He had the longest face I ever seen on a human being and eyes that he didn't seem capable of opening all the way, like he couldn't stay awake long enough to cut a smile. He was tall and lean and would of scared the hell out of me in a dark hallway. He showed me a back room full of boots, a mop, a old broom, lots of dust, and a small cot. "This here's all we got left," he said. "Take it or leave it."

"How much?"

"Six bits a night."

"That's right dear for a stink hole like this. Do I get to keep the broom or the boots?"

"Take it or leave it. It's a mite breezy outside."

"And if I want a bath?"

"It ain't here," Robert said. "There's a public house down the street a ways."

Bozeman was one street, a long mud bog when it wasn't covered in snow, and it was one or the other most of the time I was there. It was a long stretch between Miss Pound's place and the army post at the other end. There was two trading posts, and a small place called Beaver Richard's that you might call a saloon where some travelers stopped for a bit of mead or beer. Whiskey, too, sometimes. They sold whiskey in barrels to the army and to most of the wagon trains that come through. If a body wanted a small barrel to travel with, they'd sell it like that too. But they didn't serve whiskey to the folks that hung around Bozeman unless one of them barrels broke or commenced to rot.

There was also a few shacks that folks lived in. Above a stable near the army post was another kind of stable. It was four rooms each with a woman in there if you needed some paid-for company. When a fellow said he was going to the "upper stables," folks known what he was talking about.

The bathhouse was right next to the stables, and that's where I went on my first day in Bozeman. I went to the real stable first and put up the horses and hung a special bag of oats on Cricket's neck so she could eat any time she wanted. I paid for the other horses and stored my gear in a rented stall, then I went next door and checked into the bathhouse. I hadn't been in a tub of hot water in almost a year. I cut my beard off and trimmed my hair and then relaxed for a spell in the heat of it. The steam was almost like food to me, and cupping my hands in that water and splashing it gently on my face was like some kind of angel's wing a-soothing me. I took my time and shaved my face smooth and clean.

When I come out of that place, it had commenced to snow. I felt like I'd changed my skin. I walked up the street toward where the sisters had parked their wagon. I figured they might like to see a cleaned-up and right smartly trimmed version of the squaw man.

The snow was a long and sweepy kind of dropping down of nothing but white, coming hard in the wind and then falling as softly as a feather—as millions of feathers. When I got to the wagon, General Cooney was setting outside in front of a new fire. This time he was dressed, but the catarrh that gripped him didn't seem to be no better. He puffed on a pipe and stared at the flames, and the snow had just begun to come down, so he wasn't covered in it yet.

"Why you setting out here in the cold?" I said. "Wouldn't it be a touch warmer in the wagon?"

"I got me some corn," he said. I seen a canteen in his lap. "It's gonna be one hell of a winter," he said.

I took a seat by the fire and lit my own pipe. He offered me a sip of the drink in the canteen—a elixir that forced him to wince something awful whenever he sipped out of it—but I said I'd had enough of discomfort for a while. I only wanted a cup of water if I could get it. That bath had dried me out.

He called for Eveline and she come out of the wagon and jumped to the ground. "What do you want?" She wasn't wearing her bonnet, and her hair stuck up all wiry looking in the front and it hung down by her ears like a thicket of cut hay.

"Would you mind getting my friend here some water?" Cooney said.

She looked hard at me while she went to a barrel that hung off the side of the wagon. Next to it was a hook with a long-stemmed cup dangling from it. She lifted the cup, knocked it through a layer of ice, and filled it, then brought it over to me. When she handed it to me, I said, "Thank you."

The water was cold and very fine to drink. As soon as I was done, I wanted another cup. She stood there looking at me. "That was too good," I said. "Mind if I get another?"

"By God," she said. "You're Bobby Hale."

I smiled. I was wearing a big buffalo robe, but she could see my clean face in the firelight. She took the cup from me. Then she patted the hair by the side of her head. "You clean up very nicely."

Cooney said, "Uh-oh."

She turned to him and swatted him across the nose with the bottom end of the cup. It was really just a tap, but it knocked his pipe to the ground next to him. His fingers curled in front of him like he was looking for something to grab before he fell off a high bluff. His face was all scrunched up. "Damn it," he said.

"You mind your manners," Eveline said.

He shook his head. He couldn't find his pipe for a spell, but then he located it, patting the ground around it like he couldn't see or nothing.

"Are you okay?" I said.

"You see now why I'm a-setting out here," he said. "Never take up with women."

She started like she might hit him again, and he jumped back and covered his face with both arms.

I could see he wasn't no general in this camp.

We sat up and talked most of the night. I told him about all my travels with Big Tree. I told him we never did have a very good year trapping, but it was good enough having something to do every blessed day, and being in that paradise beyond all the cities and towns and church steeples.

He'd spent the last four years working for the army, first at Fort Riley, then at Buford. He'd seen every wagon train that gone out toward California and Oregon, and was always tempted to go there himself one day.

"Why didn't you go?" I asked.

"I don't know. I didn't have no money. I thought I might run into a woman that I could make a go of it with."

"Is that how you ended up with these two?"

"Well, sort of." He turned around to be sure they wasn't anywhere near. They'd both turned in a long time ago. I could hear the snoring from the wagon. "The truth is, there's some question about who owns that 'ere wagon."

"You don't say."

"I won half of it in a poker game with Eveline."

"She plays poker?"

"Like a Mississippi riverboat scalawag. Don't you get into a game with her."

"Why only half?"

"Well, sir"—he paused—"I was only in the game with the one sister. She couldn't lose the whole wagon because the other'n owned herself a half of it." The snow still silently swirled and collected around us—a kind of sneaky amendment in the general thickness and color of the landscape. A ordinary broomstick, leaning against the wagon, begun to look like the barrel of a white cannon. The snow piled up on Cooney's hat, and I guessed on mine. I had no beard for it to collect in, though, and the heat of the fire kept the front of us dry and warm. My shoulders and back commenced to feel right icy, but I didn't mind it. A buffalo skin is a fine shelter all its own. Before long, I was sipping on the hot liquid in Cooney's canteen.

It made me cough near about every time I took a sip of it. "What is this stuff?"

"In Tennessee we called it 'rotgut.' It's homemade. I bought it from one of the troops over to Fort Ellis."

"Tastes like something you'd get out of the roots of a rotted tree."

"It will do," he said.

It tasted awful, but the harder it snowed, the more of it I figured I could tolerate.

Cooney had the idea that we should team up and work for the army. Every year the Indians was getting to be a bigger problem. More and more white folks had come to the big West, and the Indians was just in the way. The army did not want them hunting on land owned by whites. They could not roam free no more because too much of the land was off-limits. Still, a lot of Indians stayed out to hunt because the army didn't never have enough food for the whole bunch of them. Some among the Sioux and Cheyenne was especial trouble, because they had not agreed to come into the reservation at all. Cooney thought we could get a good set of boots and winter in a good place if we offered to scout for the army.

"It's a General Gibbon in charge at Fort Ellis," Cooney said. "He's got to round up the renegade Sioux that ain't come in to the reservation between here and the Black Hills."

"What's a renegade Sioux?"

"Any Injun that ain't at the reservation near Fort Ellis."

"That's a lot of Indians."

"Yes, it is."

"A lot of warriors."

"This is something big a-coming up," he said. "The army ain't gonna be patient with them no more."

"Ain't gonna be easy work," I said.

"They'll pay us a dollar a week. And we'll spend at least half the winter in a warm place if we offer to be guide and scout."

"We'll be out with them," I said. "A-riding under the cold sky."

"Not the whole time, you see," he said. "I worked for them over at Fort Buford last winter, and I spent most of the time in the fort, sleeping in a warm barracks."

"You don't say."

"We chased some Pend d'Orielles all the way to the Snake River. That took about most of January." He took another swig of the rotgut. "That was about it. When we got back, they put us up in the fort and we never went out again until April."

"I've had about enough of them winters out on the plains, under them mountains, but I don't know if I'd like sleeping in a dry, smelly room all winter, neither."

"Didn't you start out in the Musselshell to trap beaver?"

"We did a little sum of it," I said. "Fat beaver ended up in our traps now and then. But folks don't want beaver skins no more, and we carried around a lot of pelts but hardly sold nary a one. We traded with the Indians for certain. But a Indian don't have much."

"You still got all your traps?"

"I left them with Big Tree."

"So you spent five winters out there in them mountains."

"I guess. We did all right."

"What happened that you ended up here?"

"It was a woman," I said. "I got married." I told him all about Morning Breeze and Big Tree. I said it didn't bother me all that much, but it was damn uncomfortable traveling with them after everything was settled. I realized while I was talking that it was how I really felt. It was a discovery.

"I expect they was glad I decided to go out on my own," I said. It seemed like all those seasons with Big Tree was a long, swift dream. You know what I mean? Like it went on for my whole life, and happened too quick to register. Only time it went slow was when I was miserable cold or hot. That's how it was anyway until Morning Breeze come along. After that, I remember some long, slow nights with her, when it was cold and we had a fire outside, right in front of the flap on my tent, and she'd take a stick and burn the end of it and then make drawings for me on the inside walls. It was the only way she could talk to me, besides having Big Tree translate. She could draw with the best of them, and even for the small canvas, before she finally went over to Big Tree. I had a right smart group of hunters and animals a-staring at me of a morning when the sun broke out and lighted up everything.

I got kind of misty remembering it but I didn't say nothing to Cooney about it. He took a big swig from the canteen. The snow had piled so high in the brim of his hat, when he threw his head back to sip the rotgut, some snow slid off down on his neck. He shuddered and shook himself like a wet dog. "Damnation," he said. "I wish we had a fire behind us too."

I wore a beaver skin hat and I had to take it off once in a while and shake the snow out of the fur, then put it back on. He held the canteen against his chest and leaned toward the fire. Then he looked at me. "You want to spend the winter out in the open? Like this?"

"I didn't say that. I just don't know how free I'd feel with four walls a-creeping up on me."

He scrunched down and hunched his collar up over his neck. "Hell, being free ain't nothing but a attitude."

"It's more than that. It's for every day, no matter what you've a mind to do. It's being your own general and army too."

"You can be free in a barracks same as anywhere else."

"Maybe so," I said.

"It's better than this." He scrunched up under his thick robes.

We drunk most of the rotgut that night, and when I found my way back to my little room at Miss Pound's place, the sun was already starting to find its way behind the white clouds that continued to empty down white and soft all over everything. I had to walk in deep snow to get back, and my boots was pretty wet and full of ice when I peeled them off. I put on a dry pair of wool socks and then I stretched out on that small cot and fell asleep. I didn't wake up until it was dark again. The place was too warm, and wearing all my clothes I felt wet in my skin and I didn't like my smell, neither. My head was full of rocks, and heavy. It was a little bit of work just to sit up.

I got my boots back on and my heavy buffalo robe, and strolled up the street toward the stables, intending to see if Cooney and his harem was eating something. I didn't see no fire as I got closer to it, but the wagon looked to be buried in the snow. The air was clear and cold, with no breeze, and the stars glittered all over above me. My boots crunched in the snow, and enough traffic had passed down this street that it wasn't too deep, neither. It was crushed down and squeaky and hard.

When I got to the wagon I said, "General, you in there?"

Christine pushed the flap back and set there staring at me. "Eveline was right. You clean up rather smartly."

"Is General Cooney available?"

"He is down again. I fear the worst for him."

Eveline stuck her head out next to her sister's. "He's got a fever again. This time he talks to himself and will not lay still."

"We have applied ice," said Christine. "We have got plenty of ice."

"Can I see him?"

She set back and let the small ladder down from the back of the wagon. I climbed up. It was close and smelled awful in there, but there was a small woodstove on the side, near the fifth bow, right behind the driver's bench. It warmed the air more than a little bit. It was the damnedest thing I ever seen. It had a pipe stuck up out of the back of it that bent at a right angle, and where it went through the canvas they had put a thick, flat metal plate with holes on its edges and rings that run through them and attached to other rings they'd sewed into the canvas.

"Is that what I think it is?" I said.

"It was Christine's idea," Eveline said. "She sewed the canvas to the rings and all. It works."

"Where'd you ever get a stove that small?" I said.

"We brought it along," Eveline said. "My husband bought it from the railroad. It used to sit in a caboose on a train. Christine just did the sewing."

"It looks a mite heavy for hauling across the country."

"That is what Mr. Cooney said." Eveline looked at Christine. "My husband said this wagon would hold eight tons. And we made it this far."

"It is bolted to the floor," Christine said. "And it gives off all the heat we need."

I put my hand on the side of Cooney's cheek and felt it. "Well," I said, "he's heating it up in here some hisself."

"Whatever it might be," Eveline said, "I hope it's not contagious."

"He seemed to be better last night," said Christine.

Cooney stirred a mite, then said, "It's misty down here, sir. Right misty."

"He's been talking to some officer," Christine said. "Giving situation reports and commenting on terrain. He was an artilleryman, you know."

"I didn't know that," I said. "He said he was in the infantry." I heard his stomach growl. "You might try to feed him."

Christine looked away. Eveline said, "He does not keep any food down."

"What about water?"

They both said "No" at the same time.

"Well, it's kind of you two taking care of him like this."

"I fear the worst," Eveline said.

Cooney died a few days later. Even as sick as he was, I didn't see it coming. Christine and her sister was sad for a while, but when they took him to the army for burial, they was told the ground was frozen solid and they'd have to wait until spring. In the meantime, the army gone through his belongings and the pockets of his trousers and they found a piece of paper he wrote on sometime before he died. He might of written the damn thing right after that night in front of the wagon when we was drinking his liquor and planning our future while the snow slowly buried us. It said:

This must serve as my last will and testament. If the present ailment should kill me, I am of sound mind although I think it is safe to say my body gave out on me. I leave, twenty two yards of calico to Christine Howard and Eveline Barkley because they did

*the best they could to take care of me when I got sick. It is my
intention and personal wish that Bobby Hale inherit my spencer
rifle, all the cartridges for it—which last amounted to seven
boxes, twenty five cartridges a box. Also, my horse, and saddle
and bridle and blankets and my fifty foot rope. I leave my hunting knife to Bobby Hale and whatever else he may want of my
personal effects including my watch and chain and my straight
razor with a good strop only if he wants it. I leave my portion of
the wagon that I won fair and square from Miss Eveline Barkley
to Bobby Hale. It is my hope that these articles may be of some
use to Mr. Hale, who has, of late, been my only real friend in this
world.*

   I am respectfully,
   General Ernest J. Cooney
   CSA, Retired.

I didn't want none of his things except the horse and the watch
and chain. Maybe the rifle—that was good to trade with the Indians. I
didn't know what I'd do with half a wagon. I wanted to know what
killed him and if'n it might get me. Neither Christine or Eveline seemed
no worse for having been taking care of him. I wondered how a man
his age could die like that. He wasn't no more than forty-five or so, if
that. He didn't have very thick hair at the end, and he was sure sickly.
I thought it might be consumption, but Eveline said it wasn't that nor
nothing he ate, neither. She said, "He just dried up. Could not get the
sickness out of his stomach."

"So he starved to death?"

"No. He died of thirst."

"Me and him drunk a whole canteen of moonshine the night we
got here."

She shrugged. "I am just telling you what the doctor said."

"He seen a doctor?"

She pointed at the fort, kind of impatiently. "An army surgeon.
General Cooney got a sickness in his stomach that made it impossible
for him to take in water or food. It killed him."

"Well, shit," I said.

"The doctor said it was probably infection from a cancer."

"He sure was unlucky," I said.

What General Cooney also left me was the idea of working for the army. I didn't want to be hunting on the prairies all winter long by myself, and I had to eat. I figured if Cooney was right about having a warm barracks to sleep in most of the winter, it would be a good move. I give the Spencer rifle and the cartridges to Eveline and Christine, just because I thought they might need it if they was to continue their journey west. I didn't say nothing about the wagon but I reckoned they'd need it too. I figured it was too early to try and make arrangements about it, but I guess fair to say I hoped they might find a way to get me to part with it.

General Cooney's body was wrapped in muslin and laying in a box on the ground next to it. I was getting ready to put the lid on and nail it down so they could keep him stored until spring.

"The army will help you out when you're ready to move on," I said. "They got horses to spare, I wager. And they might not like the idea of two women traveling with that old ox on the Bloody Bozeman."

"What is that?" Eveline wanted to know.

"What's what?"

"The Bloody Bozeman."

"That's what they call the trail you're going to have to take to go any further west."

Eveline said, "My husband called it the Gold Trail."

"It's been called that. Lots of folks still pan for gold all along the trail."

"But not you," she said. "You have no interest in gold?"

"I'm as interested as anybody else, I guess. But I don't like working down on my knees. Nor staying in one place too long." I put the lid down just right and started hammering the nails in. When I was done, I stood up and looked at the two of them. "Want me to help you push this under the wagon?"

They both looked at me kind of funny.

"It don't matter to me," I said. "We can leave it here, but if you have a day or two above freezing, and this sits in the sun, it might start to ripen a bit."

"Go ahead," Eveline said.

I started trying to shove the box under the wagon, but in the snow I couldn't get a good purchase with my feet and I kept slipping down to my knees. The thing would not even slide very well on the ice. When it become clear I wouldn't move the box by myself, the women helped me. We shoved it well under the shade of the wagon. The sun was high and dead in the sky and didn't give off a lick of heat.

"It is hard to believe it will ever be warm again," Christine said.

We stood there looking at the ground for a while, breathing steam. Then Eveline said, "What did you mean about working on your knees?"

I didn't know what she was talking about.

"You said you did not want to work on your knees."

"Oh," I said. "That's what you got to do to find gold. I don't want to spend my life looking through dirt nor digging holes, neither. I ain't no miner."

Eveline suddenly took my arm and leaned into me. "What if we can't find a train in the spring? If you travel with us, we will treat you very kindly." Her voice was husky, and by God it was clear what she was suggesting.

"How far would I have to go?" I said.

She smiled. "You want to go to Oregon?"

"Well, I guess not," I said. "I might go as far as Utah."

"That might be all we shall need," Christine said. "For now anyway." They both smelled like jasmine and maybe a little coffee mixed in. There wasn't nothing soft about them, neither. Their faces, though pleasant to look at, was chiseled, skin hard as calluses. And they didn't have no trouble when it come to shoving that casket under the wagon.

"Why don't you try and sell that ox," I said. "Or trade him for another horse. You can use the general's horse and my packhorse to pull the wagon along the trail."

"So you will go with us?"

"Let's put it this way," I said. "You got until spring to replace the general. June the latest. If'n you can't, I'll think about traveling a spell with you. But you got to join a train. I ain't traveling with only one wagon."

I don't know why, but it made me feel grand to see how happy that made both of them women. I even thought I might actually do it. I did own half the wagon, even though I was willing to part with it for the right stock-in-trade.

{ CHAPTER 9 }

I SIGNED ON AT Fort Ellis, just outside Bozeman. Both Eveline and Christine was real sad when I stopped in to say I was going out.

"Your dead friend is here," Eveline said. "You must come back for him."

"I'll be back here before Christmas," I said. "Come December."

"Where are you going?" Christine asked.

"General Gibbon is sending a scouting expedition to find Indians that ain't where they're supposed to be."

Christine wiped her eyes with a bit of white linen, but I didn't believe she was really crying. It was a show. And Eveline? She turned away and didn't even look at me.

When the expedition got started, the weather wasn't changed none: it was still cold as frozen steel and the air like to hurt inside when you got it in there. A whole lot of steam left my mouth every time I tried to speak or just walk along. Counting me, there was twenty-eight of us, mostly just fresh troops right off the farm or out of the dirty cities east of the Mississippi. They was green as crab apples and ain't none of them seen a real Indian, nor had to fight one except the fellow in charge, a officer named Bellows. He may of known what he was doing, by God. He said he'd been with Fetterman before that gentleman and all his troops got massacred by the Sioux back in 1866.

Bellows was under orders from a cavalry officer named Brisbin, who told him to go east until he found the Indians—Lakota, Cheyenne, Shoshone, he didn't care. They was all occupying land that was no longer theirs and they was in violation of the treaty of 1865. General Gibbon, who was in command at Fort Ellis, wanted to know where the Indians was so he could take his army and go get them in the spring.

I led the small detachment southeast, toward the two Bighorn rivers. We kept the mountains to our right and on the left was hills and valleys to beat all, and every now and then flat prairie as far as we could see. And everywhere snow with reeds of grass poking up like whiskers. We crossed frozen streams that still had water trickling under solid ice. I took them where I known the buffalo had been, or the elk. Traveling with Big Tree all those years, I learned about the movement of the herds and where to look for them. Once you found the herds, you found the Indians. It wasn't too long before I found snow beaten down until the brown earth showed through. I followed what looked like a long, winding scar in the whiteness, and by the time we got into Wyoming Territorry, we seen where other prints scattered up near the trail, and then we found blood and the spare carcasses of killed game. After that, you're only looking for smoke.

Twice in our travels, we come upon a fair group of braves. When they spotted us they whooped and hollered a bit, but then, not being dressed for no battle, they skedaddled.

"Man," one of the young troops said. "This is going to be easy. They're afraid of us."

"They ain't afraid of nothing," I said.

"Really."

"There's a reason they're called braves. They believe a man is supposed to be brave and they learn to conquer fear pretty early in life. I don't think they remember much about fear."

Bellows said, "When they're ready to fight, they'll fight."

"Do they know we're looking for a fight?" the young trooper said.

"I don't expect they do," I said.

"I ain't looking for a fight, neither," Bellows said. He had a long, pointed nose and thick eyebrows. He was bald, and didn't wear much more than a day or two's growth of beard. It just looked like his face was dirty. He always had a fat jaw full of chewing tobacco that he'd spit, even in the cold. The black juice run down his chin and sometimes looked like a thin-cut goatee. I asked him how he avoided getting killed with Fetterman.

He said, "That was the year after the war, not far from here."

"Where was you?" I asked.

"I was on a steamboat up the Bighorn River, getting a bad tooth cut out, when Fetterman and his men got killed. That was the war with

Red Cloud." He told me Fetterman was lured by a small party of warriors away from Fort Phil Kearny, and when he was far enough out in the open, the Indians attacked. "His entire command was massacred. Eighty-one men fell upon by fifteen hundred Sioux, Cheyenne, and Arapahos. That's the only battle these Indians ever won against the U.S. Army. And it was right over yonder, a few days' ride north and east of this very spot."

We was riding along the trail south of the Tongue River, bent over to keep our faces out of the cold wind. I looked back and seen the young troopers looking kind of dejected. I said, "I don't think the young fellows in our little army like to hear you talk like that about a massacre."

"Those fellows want to be famous. They wish they was riding with the Seventh Cavalry and Custer."

"I heard tell of that general," I said. "He's a Indian fighter to beat all, ain't he?"

"He ain't no general. He's a bloody colonel. He was a brevetted general in the war. Folks do him a favor calling him 'general.' "

"I known a fellow who got a brevet rank. A Captain Cooney."

"U.S.?"

"Confederate. He's in a pine box right now, under a Conestoga wagon, waiting for spring so we can put him in the ground."

We rode along for a spell, then Bellows said, "What happened to him? Injuns?"

"No, he got sick."

"There's a million ways to die out here," Bellows said.

"I guess there is."

On our tenth day out, late in the afternoon, we finally come upon a small canyon between two high ridges of ground. A stream run through there in summer, but now it was a white ribbon that snaked its way out of the canyon and further up into the hills. Next to the stream, on the north side of it, was nineteen or twenty lodges, and about thirty horses tethered behind them. Smoke from their campfires rose up from the tops of the lodges into the white sky. Dogs barked. I didn't see no people.

"They might be having supper," Bellows said. "Or they're keeping warm."

"It ain't like they didn't want to be found," I said. "If they known we was after them, we wouldn't find them that easy."

The troopers behind us was real excited. The hardware in the bridles of the horses rattled and I heard several magazines click with new ammunition. I said, "Wasn't we just supposed to find them? We ain't just gonna ride down there and start shooting, are we?"

"We'll be ready," Bellows said. "But I don't want to shoot nobody. I think we can talk them into going with us."

"All the way back to Bozeman?"

"No, we don't need to do that. We'll escort them to Fort Laramie. That's only three or four days from here."

"I thought the order was to find out where they are. We done that."

"We are going to transport these Indians to Laramie. I hear there's a Indian village there. It will save them. You don't know what's coming."

"You think they'll go?"

"I intend to ask them polite."

"I was at Summit Springs," I said. "I seen how it can go. Them Indians was taking a nap and the cavalry just rode right down on them. I'd like it to be different here."

"Like I said, I don't want to shoot nobody."

Bellows and me just rode down the hill and walked our horses steady into the middle of the half circle of lodges. We got to the center, and a tall brave poked hisself from a lodge to our right. Bellows raised his white-gloved hand and said, "How."

Then some other braves come out. They moved to our left and behind us, but nobody said nothing. The first Indian that come out raised his hand and then he motioned for us to dismount.

We got down and handed the reins to the fellows standing around. It was a handsome bunch. They was Cheyenne and not from nowhere near Bozeman, so they wasn't in violation of no treaty with the army up that way as far as I could see. The big fellow that first greeted us stood to the side of the entrance to his lodge and motioned for us to go in. It was warm inside, and there was lots of room. Drawings was painted on the walls, which reminded me of Morning Breeze. A hot fire blazed in the center. There was blankets all around, and two women and four children huddled in the back. It smelled like leather and smoke in there, close with sweat too.

We removed our hats and took a seat by the fire and our host sat down across from us. He signed that we was welcome. To show he meant it, he offered us his pipe and some tobacco. We all smoked silently, sort of staring at each other, then two other braves come in. One of them was tall and wore a long red scarf around his neck. He carried a long spear with white feathers hanging off of it and I didn't see how it wasn't the same Indian I seen chasing after Big Tree that time when he rode in amongst them. I tried to remember his name. He had to be a Sioux, but those two tribes traveled together a lot, so it wasn't no surprise. Our host wore a single white feather in his hair, and when everybody was seated, he spoke.

"Netawnyay," he said. "I am Saw-set."

Bellows and I nodded. Then Bellows told him our names. "You speak English?"

"I can some," Saw-set answered. He went on in Cheyenne, though. He signed that we were welcome again and wondered what we wanted.

Bellows told him in English that the treaty his people signed meant he must come with us to the Fort at Laramie.

"I signed no treaty," Saw-set said.

"Your people signed a treaty that you have mostly honored until now. You know of the treaty."

"We hunt," Saw-set said, speaking very clear English. He pointed to the tall Sioux with the red scarf. "This is White Dog." That was it. White Dog. I wondered if he seen me close enough to remember. I caught him looking at me. Saw-set said, "His people hunt with us. We feed and put skins on the people. We have no idea of war against the whites."

White Dog said, "You make war on the people."

"No," Bellows said. "I come to offer you a place to keep warm and to be fed during the cold winter."

"Are you not warm here?" Saw-set said. "There is plenty of game. We do not need your help, but we are grateful that you come to us and offer it."

Bellows looked down at his boots that was facing sole to sole in front of him. He had his hands on his knees. He rubbed his knees for a bit, then he said, "I am sorry, but you must go with us to Laramie."

It got quiet.

The tobacco was good, and when it was near finished, the pipe come to me and I smoked some and then offered it like it was a infant to Saw-set. He took it and just as gently set it down next to him. Then he looked at us. I seen real sadness in his eyes. He said, "Saw-set mean War Eagle in English. If you will make war, we will fight."

The other braves got up and went out. Saw-set, or War Eagle, remained where he was seated for a while, watching us with those sad eyes. "You may go in peace," he said. "But if you come back, it will be for fighting and not peace."

"I don't want to fight nobody," Bellows said. "We have many guns."

"You offer peace, then talk of guns," War Eagle said.

Bellows got to his feet. I looked up at him, then glanced back at War Eagle. He had no more to say. I known what was coming.

{ CHAPTER 10 }

IT TOOK US a while to get back to the men. We had to walk real slow, paying no attention to the warriors who was right behind us, watching everything we did. I felt sorry for Cricket, struggling to get up that snow-piled hill, with me a-pulling on her reins to hold her steady and at a walk. There was a huge commotion behind us, but we didn't dare look back. The Indians had yipped and hollered all the way back down the hill. When we reached the men, Bellows commenced ordering them into position for a fight. He formed them up in a column of two, rifles held to the right shoulder with the leather sling strap around the arms and wrist. In less than fifteen minutes he had his troops ready to go down amongst them. He had his sword out glistening in the winter sun. He was a different man—like a boy made free of school.

"You was hoping for this," I said.

"No," he said, looking me sternly in the eyes. "I hoped we could avoid it. But I won't sit around here wondering what to do. I have my orders."

"We was just supposed to locate them. Ain't this for General Gibbon?"

"Who knows where they'll be when Gibbon comes this way? There ain't that many of them. We'll take care of this here and now."

"And you think you can just ride down there and round them up like they was sheep or something?"

"Mr. Hale," he said. "We may have to kill a few."

"And that will save them," I said. I got up on Cricket and turned her away.

"Where you going?"

"I ain't going to be no part of this." I pulled back a little on Cricket's reins and she turned back some, her head bobbing up and down, steam blowing from her nostrils. "This ain't nothing but murder, Captain."

"You don't respect them braves very much, do you?" he said. He sat atop his horse like a falcon on a fellow's arm, ready to take flight. He held his sword up against his right shoulder. The blade gleamed. He turned the horse away from me and took his place in front of the men.

"You're going down there without me," I said.

"It ain't no obligation on you," he told me. Not one of his men even glanced my way. He smiled a bit. "You done what you had to do. You put us on them. Now I got to do what I been hired to do."

I almost told him that if I'd of known it would lead to this, I wouldn't of done it. But I known it wasn't true. I thought it might end up in a fight, and I signed on anyway. I needed the pay, and a fellow would have to be a durn fool not to know what would happen when troops went out to collect Indians off their own land and bring them into a fort to be fed like pet animals.

"You just wait right here," Bellows said. "We'll be back directly."

He hollered the command, and his men went behind him at a gallop down the hill toward the Indian camp.

I rode a little further down myself so I could see what happened. The women had already commenced taking down the lodges. A party of braves on horseback come out of the timber just to the left of where the camp was and started yipping and hollering as they galloped toward the column behind Bellows. I seen Bellows turn and fire his pistol, waving the sword now as he tried to get his men to turn and start firing. A few executed the right kind of cavalry move, I suppose, but once the arrows started flying, most of his men scattered and started running away from the charging Indians. Bellows run right at them, firing his pistol. He probably had no idea he was pretty much alone and there wasn't nobody at all a-charging with him. He took a arrow in what looked like his neck and rolled back off his horse and landed on his side, the sword flying away from him. He must of been dead before he hit the ground because he didn't move none once he settled. Another group of warriors come from the camp, riding across the stream in a single line, then scattering around the soldiers, who was still trying to figure out where to turn and what to do. It was a sorry thing to witness. The Indians chased after individuals, shooting arrows at them as they run, and when one fell, the other warriors circled him on their horses and shot arrow after arrow into the poor fellow. I think they got most of the men that rode down that hill. Without Bellows to lead them, they was as helpless as rats trapped in a dry well. A few got away. I seen them riding hard over the hills toward the Bighorn River. I figured they'd get lost and die if I didn't go after them, so I turned Cricket toward the north to cut them off.

I rode her pretty hard for a spell, but then I could tell Cricket was winded, so I stopped and let her walk a bit. I was in tall grass, still pretty high on the ridge that looked down at the Indian camp, about two miles upriver from it. Below me I seen three of Bellows's troops dragging along on foot, their horses trailing behind them. I could see they'd run the animals into a white, foaming sweat, and there was no run left in them. You can do that to a horse—you run him too hard and keep him on it too long, and he'll finally quit. Then it's hard to get him to run again for a long time. If you do, he'll flat-out die. Oh, you can kick one into a good gallop for a short while, but even with a solid whip, you ain't gonna get one to run long.

At first, when they seen me coming down the hill, they wasn't sure what sort of foe I might be. I was in my leather jacket and buffalo robes, with only the hat on my head to tell them I was a white man. But then one of them recognized me.

"Jesus," he said. "The captain's dead."

"I seen it," I said.

"Jake here is wounded."

Sure enough, the fellow behind him was sagging a little, and I could see he had a arrow sticking out of his side.

I said. "I guess they outnumbered you."

"There was so many of them. And the arrows was everywhere."

"I see. But they had no guns, right?"

"What do you mean?"

"I got to report all this back at Fort Ellis."

The third fellow, the youngest one there, said, "They had guns."

"Well, I watched it from up yonder," I said. "At the top of the ridge where we was before you rode down amongst them. I can't say I seen a single gun fired except for the captain's pistol."

He hung his head down.

Jake said, "Can you help us?"

"That's what I run down here for."

"I'm not doing so good here." Jake tugged on the arrow a bit and gritted his teeth. "I got to get this thing out of me."

"Yes, you surely do," I said. The youngest fellow was called Nate. He was from Illinois and he had red hair, and teeth that bent outward in the front like the cowcatcher on a train engine. His face was hairless, and from the way he was always looking at me, I'd say he did not like me very much at all. I probably wounded his dignity when I made that comment about the guns that didn't get fired in his first great Indian battle.

The first fellow, a tall, kind of craggy hillbilly from Georgia—too young to fight in the big war, but now glad to be in any kind of army— was called Daniel. He was Jake's best friend, as they come to let me know. Jake, who had the arrow deep in his side, told me that Daniel would one day be a officer. "He can already speak some of them Indian languages."

I set Jake down against a small embankment. Nate and Daniel was watching back from where they come just in case the Indians was still following them. They had their carbines out now and aimed at the horizon behind us. I thought, *God help the poor soul that comes over that hill.* But nobody come. Those Indians was a long way gone in the other direction.

Jake's wound was worse than I thought it would be. At first glance, it looked like the arrow had passed through the side of his body where there ain't that much in the way of internals, but it went in at more of a angle and pierced his lung. I could hear blood gurgling behind the wound. He didn't know it yet, but once we pulled the thing out of there, he'd probably bleed to death pretty quick. I seen this kind of wound in the war. Even pouring a gallon of whiskey into it wouldn't help it none.

When I seen how bad it was, he was watching my face. "What?" he said. "Tell me."

"It ain't good," I said.

"Tell me."

"You're shot through the lower part of your lung."

"I thought it might be such."

"It just went in at the wrong angle."

"I was hoping it would be low so it missed."

"Maybe," I said. "But I don't think so."

"Well, shit," he said.

"You want me to go ahead and pull it out of you?"

"I guess so. There ain't nothing else for it."

"Turn over a bit and let me break it off the other end."

He rolled a little to the side, and I reached that part of the arrow that went through and broke it off so when I pulled it out I'd be pulling the shaft and not the point back through the path of the wound. The whole time he didn't let out a sound. He was shivering, though. It was freezing cold on that hard, icy ground. I started to turn him back over and he said, "Thank you kindly."

When I settled him back again and got ready to pull the arrow out, he looked at me with the fiercest eyes I think I ever seen. Like a mountain lion's eyes. "Go ahead."

"This is gonna hurt like hellfire," I said.

"I know it."

"You want some whiskey first? I got some."

"I would like that very much," he said.

I went to my pack and got a bottle. A gust of wind come up behind me and sliced through me like a broad knife. I hunched up and stood there for a spell until it slowed down again. Then I took the bottle back to Jake. "It's probably a good thing it's so cold," I said. "You ain't lost much blood."

He was a-setting there, looking right at me, but his eyes didn't see nothing at all. He was dead. It wasn't no wind that hit me, it was his soul. I got down next to him and jerked the damn arrow out anyway. Then I sipped the whiskey, looking directly in his eyes. They was clear as marbles, not glazed over nor nothing, but you could tell there wasn't no life behind them; they wasn't eyes no more. They was only two green, polished stones. He was just a young boy, no older than twenty, and he didn't get to see very much of this earth. I took another sip of the whiskey, trying to settle my mind a little. "I'll be damned to hell," I said. It shocked me that the suddenness and surprise of this fellow's passing bothered me more than just a little bit.

I called Daniel over, and when he seen what happened to his friend, he couldn't take it. He fell to his knees and started praying over him, tears running down his face.

"He was bleeding real bad inside," I said.

Nate looked at me like I done it—like I killed him. I stood up in the wind that commenced to howling around us. The sky was low and gray, moving over us like thick smoke. "It's gonna snow again, fellows," I said. "We better get him situated and head back to Fort Ellis."

"What about the others?" Daniel said.

"What others?"

"The captain, the other troops."

"They're two or three miles back that away," I said, pointing to where they had come from. "You want to go looking for them, be my guest. I'm heading back." I took another sip of the whiskey—it warmed me all the way down—then I handed the bottle to Daniel. "You can have the rest of this. You're going to need it."

"You can't leave us here," he said.

"I'm going back. Right now. I hope to keep ahead of this here snowstorm heading our way. Why don't you strap that poor fellow to his horse and you two can follow along."

They seen it was the only thing to do. Before long we was all heading north and west, with the wind at our backs. By the time it begun to snow, we'd covered some ground, but not far enough that we wasn't soon buried in it. We was crossing some pretty big hills, west of the Bighorn River, when we finally had to stop and carve out some kind of shelter. We found a place where a rock jutted out over a ravine, and so we tethered the horses to a small tree and crawled under the stone, where it was mainly dry. There was a stand of pine trees nearby, so we dug up under them and found some branches and sticks and such. Daniel collected handfuls of pine needles and leaves and piled some of the sticks on top of it. It took a while with that wind, but I finally got a fire going. Every now and then the wind would shift a bit and the smoke would blow right into our faces, but mostly the fire burned in front of us under the stone, and it kept us warm. We left Jake draped over his horse out in the blowing snow. I watched him turning white, a-laying over the saddle, his legs sticking out like he was trying to get comfortable.

It was going to be one hell of a long night.

CHAPTER 11

THE WIND JUST wouldn't quit. We was scrunched up under that stone, trying to keep the fire going. We took turns going back across to the timber to gather up and collect branches and tree limbs to burn. Sometimes that took a long time, and with the blowing wind the fire almost banked.

Finally I got the idea that we should all three get it burning really high, then go into the pine forest and stock up for the night. We filled one entire side of our shelter with piled wood. A pine branch burns really quick, so we had to have a whole lot of it. Around midnight the wind finally begun to calm down. The fire crackled and spit, and we could settle in a bit and commence to feel warm. The front edge of the stone itself begun to heat up a little, and that helped.

Daniel said, "I wish I had some tobacco."

I poked the fire with a stick. "Me too."

Nate was on the other side of Daniel, sitting with his arms wrapped around his knees. He shivered a lot, but he had nothing to say.

A breath of wind come back in on us and smoke swirled in our faces and all three of us commenced coughing and spitting. It ain't nothing on earth like pine smoke and ash blowing right at you. I'd rather put my head in the smokestack of a damn train. Daniel covered his face with his hat, and when the wind died down again, he looked at me with watery eyes so it looked like he was crying. "Lordy, I'm hungry," he said.

Nate looked pretty well done in too. "I could eat a living buffalo."

"I got some sowbelly in my pack," I said.

They both looked at me. Daniel said like he was sorry for it, "All we got is some hardtack and coffee."

It took a while, but with some hard work back and forth from the horses to our shelter, we got some food in our bellies. The hardtack went well with the sowbelly. Even though I swore when I got out of the army I'd never eat that stuff again, I been eating it pretty regular ever since. The juice from the sowbelly softened it, and it almost took on the character of bread. I think Nate didn't hate me so much after we'd eaten some and could sip hot coffee while we fed the fire. "Was you a Reb?" he asked me.

I told him which side I was on. I didn't see the point of mentioning how many bonuses I collected before it was over.

"I was too young," he said. "I wish I hadn't missed it."

Daniel seemed to nod in agreement.

"You know what you seen today?" I said.

Neither one could look me in the eye.

"That little skirmish today was nothing at all," I said. "Not a blink of a gnat's eye to even the smallest named engagement of the war."

"I know that was no battle," Daniel said.

"You seen all of two minutes of ordered drill. Then you all took off. The only gun fired was the captain's pistol."

"There was gunfire," Nate said, and I could see he was beginning to dislike me all over again. "The Injuns had rifles."

"Nary a one," I said. "They did their fighting with lances and bow and arrow."

"I heard their fire," Nate said.

"Did you fire *your* rifle?"

He stared at me with real hatred for a second, then looked away.

Daniel shook his head. "Maybe we didn't," he said.

"There wasn't no rifle fire," I said. "Indians don't have so many guns as everybody thinks. They ain't allowed to have them at the fort. When they go out on their own to hunt without permission, you think the army gives them rifles? Where you think they got all them rifles you heard? There some kind of magazine or store out here we don't know about?"

"Okay, they didn't have guns," Nate said, and his face was red as his hair and his eyes looked little and mean, like a bat's eyes. "And we're cowards."

Daniel said, "I did run with the others. I couldn't do anything else. It all happened so fast."

"As it does in battle," I said. I seen a hopeless look in Daniel's eyes. He'd lost his best friend and he was trying damn hard not to let it get to him. It was beginning to hit him that if he'd of fought a little bit—if he'd fired his carbine in the direction of them Indians—it might of turned out differently. Jake took a arrow in the front, so he was facing the enemy. Daniel must of figured out that if a arrow had found him, it would most likely of hit him in the ass. That's a real bad thing to realize about yourself, and I seen it take ahold of him. "It ain't nothing but a mess of confusion when the fighting starts," I told him. "Them Indians that come at you on horseback fight better with a bow and arrow than most men can with guns and pistols. They are great cavalrymen, and they got the best of your outfit today."

"We'll kill our share someday," Nate said.

"You go ahead and plan for that," I said.

We tried to sleep in shifts. It was almost impossible in that cold air. The fire would bank every twenty minutes or so and we'd feed it with snow-covered wood that hissed and steamed loud enough to wake a body that did fall asleep.

By morning it was clear and calm—but so cold even the fire struggled to give off heat. We was running out of fuel and I didn't see the point of trying to build it back up. "We better be moving on," I said.

We didn't get far before we run into three more stragglers. None of them had wounds to speak of and none had fired their carbines, neither. I refrained from pointing that out, but we trekked fairly directly north and west back toward Bozeman. The ground rose and fell like a great white ocean. We trudged up and down those hills and along ravines and valleys, trying to stay warm and keep moving. It was hard for the horses to walk steady in the snow, but we kept on, our heads bowed to the cold air. The damn sun wasn't no source of heat at all. It just hung up in the blue sky, with nary a cloud to block it, and the white snow reflecting the sun made it hard to keep your eyes open.

Even heading directly back, with no side diversions, we trudged through that rough country for six days. We shot a few groundhogs for something to eat and we finished all the rest of the rations the men had with them. The weather let up enough that it wasn't bad camping at night the rest of the way back.

By the time we got back to Fort Ellis, the weather had broke loose again, only this time it started a freezing rain. You couldn't stay dry for even a few seconds out in the open. Daniel, Nate, and the others was near dead with exhaustion. Jake's body was soaked, and hung over the back of his horse with his head dripping water like a man just coming up out of a cool swim in a creek. He was a sight to see, with purple skin and bulging eyes. It was too cold for him to start to bloat, so I guess that was a good thing.

I watched some clean, fresh troops take his body down off his horse and carry him off. The fellows I was with all got taken to warm quarters, but General Gibbon hisself wanted to talk to me about what happened. I sat in a wood chair across from a small desk in his office. There was a fireplace in the corner that kept the room warm. He leaned back in a high-backed leather chair. He was puffing on a long black cigar. He was a fairly slim fellow, with a short, clipped reddish-brown beard, a great handlebar mustache that hung down along the sides of his mouth, and fierce-looking blue eyes. He didn't mind silence. He set there puffing that long cigar while icy water dripped off of me onto the floor and the chair. I had it in my hair and beard, which had got started growing again. I started to shiver a bit, even in that warm room, and I realized there was a competent odor dripping off me too. I think I smelled like rotted buffalo meat.

General Gibbon said he wanted to know everything that happened. I didn't see no reason to get nobody in trouble, so I left out the fact none of them boys fired a single shot once the Indians started charging them, but I told him the truth for the most part. I described how Captain Bellows died a-charging right in amongst them, shooting his weapon, with his sword raised. "He had no fear," I said.

"Well," the general said, "he was a fool."

"I thought he was brave."

"What the hell was Bellows doing all the way down in Wyoming Territory?" he said.

"We was following a certain band."

"I told him to go east to the Yellowstone River."

"I took him where there was Indians. That was my job."

"And six of you make it back."

"There may be others," I said.

"I've got five companies of infantry and four cavalry troops," Gibbon said. "And come January I'm going east. We're going to find and engage every single non-treaty Indian camp in the Yellowstone River region of Montana. Wyoming is not our problem."

I said nothing.

"I wanted Bellows to find the Indian encampments, not go charging into them."

"I mentioned it to him. He said it was a small group and he could do it hisself."

He wanted to know how many Cheyenne was in Saw-set's camp.

I really didn't know. "Could of been thirty or forty or more," I said. "Maybe less."

"How many lodges?"

"I didn't count them," I said. "What I seen, maybe twenty."

He nodded, smoke clouding around his head. I think there was steam coming off me.

I said, "A band of them come out of the timber on our left—away from the camp. I don't think they was braves from Saw-set's village alone."

"You don't."

"They looked like Sioux."

He twisted the cigar in his mouth. Behind him the fire had started to bank a little. I was shivering again. The kerosene lantern on his desk made the buttons on his uniform glisten like hot coals. All I wanted to do was get warm.

General Gibbon said, "I want you to go dry off and have something to eat. Get a good night's sleep. Then come back here. I've got something in mind for you."

I stood up. He seemed to be waiting there for me to say something, or do something. I hesitated, then I said, "I'll be back in the morning, first thing."

He nodded and saluted, so I did the same and then I backed out of his office.

{ CHAPTER 12 }

OTH WOMEN LOOKED pretty good when I got back to the wagon. I went to the bathhouse first and got cleaned up a bit. The hot water felt really good and it was only my empty belly that got me out of there. I had put Cricket up in the stable and when I was all cleaned up I considered a visit to the upper floors there, but was too hungry to give it a try. It would be untruthful of me not to admit that I wondered what might be in store for me in that wagon with them two women.

It had pretty much stopped raining, and the sun peeked through the gray clouds and made shadows on what snow was left. When I reached the wagon I stood just on the outside and called to Eveline. She thrown the flap back and both of them stood in the opening looking down at me.

"You have returned early," Christine said.

"Not for long, I fear."

"You look a little worn-out."

"I'm okay." We didn't none of us speak for a moment, then I said, "You got that 'ere stove fired up in there?"

They welcomed me inside. They'd made biscuits and coffee that afternoon for supper and there was some left over for me. They watched me eat in silence. I might of gorged myself, but there was only three biscuits left and the coffee was at the bottom and full of grounds. It was wonderful to be dry and warm again.

"So," Eveline said. "Tell of your adventures."

I told them all that happened. When I talked about Jake, Christine needed to wipe her eyes. "He was just a boy," I said. "Like a lot of them. He ain't never seen a Indian come at him like that, firing arrows so quick you don't have time to aim your gun and shoot. They just come at you."

"Why couldn't he shoot?" Eveline said.

"It ain't easy against arrows a-flying through the air," I said. "You can't never see bullets in a battle. Hell, there's always too much smoke to really see nothing at all in front of you. So you can face bullets and pretty much concentrate on what you're doing until one of them hits into you. But a arrow's a big thing flying through the clear air coming right for your eyes. It makes it a mite hard to concentrate."

"It must be horrible," Christine said.

"You don't never get used to it," I said, like I known what I was talking about.

They was pretty sad when I said that old General Gibbon ordered me to come back to his office in the morning. "He's got something he wants me to do."

"I hope you will stay here tonight," Eveline said.

"Of course you are welcome," her sister said. I could see she didn't mean it.

Now, the truth is, I was interested in Christine. She was younger and had good teeth and was just plain better looking than Eveline. But it was Eveline that flirted with me and I known I'd have to deal with her first. In the lamplight, in front of that small stove, she didn't look all that bad, to tell the truth.

Christine started moving folds of her dress around, and then she come up with this heavy-looking book.

"Is that a Bible?" I said.

"You might say so," she said.

Eveline said, "Oh, not now, Christine."

"What sort of Bible is it?" I wanted to know.

Christine opened it and run her fingers over some of the pages, real soft-like, like she was brushing some kind of sweet oil on it. "Do you know how to read, Mr. Hale?"

"Sure."

"Have you ever heard of Shakespeare?"

"I heard tell of him."

"And have you ever heard of King Lear?"

"He was one of them English kings, right?"

Christine laughed. I didn't see what was so funny.

Eveline said, "She wants to impress you."

" 'I heard myself proclaim'd,' " Christine read out loud. " 'And by the happy hollow of a tree, escaped the hunt. No port is free; no place, that guard and most unusual vigilance does not attend my taking. Whiles I may 'scape I will preserve myself . . .' "

"Okay," Eveline said. "That's all we need of *Lear* tonight."

"King Lear wrote that?" I said.

Now both of them was laughing.

"It don't make no sense to me," I said.

"What doesn't make sense?" Christine said.

"That business about a happy hollow in a tree escaping a hunt and all. It don't make sense."

"It is poetry, Mr. Hale."

"What's it about?"

"It's about being an outlaw. About being pursued by everyone."

"Will you stay the night?" Eveline asked again. "I'll brew some more coffee."

"If I don't have to listen to no more of that Lear fellow, sure," I said.

They started giggling again. I settled myself back against a pile of blankets in the corner of that wagon and waited for my supper. Christine went on reading from that Bible in her lap. She let her voice rise and fall with it, and after a while it did sound right musical. I didn't pay no attention to the words—it was hard to keep up with it when so many of them I never heard before begun to pile up and all, but her voice was sweet, high and womanly. It reminded me of something I couldn't fully remember; like it come from someplace in another life I may of lived a long, long time ago.

And I was hoping we might find our way to a natural kind of relation, just the two of us. Or three, if Eveline insisted on it, but then I wondered how damned natural that kind of thing would be.

I don't think I was ever so warm nor comfortable nor safe in my life. I lay my head back on a good soft pile of buffalo robes and blankets, stretched out, and breathed easy, letting my eyes close; and before long, I dozed off.

I waked up from somebody a-fumbling with my pants. It was dark, and the stove give off almost no light at all. All the lanterns was out, and I could hear somebody snoring on the other side of the wagon. I started to jump up, but a hand on my chest pressed me down. I felt the belt go free and the buttons on the front of my breeches opening. I was a-stirring, and then this cold hand got ahold of me and just held on there. It tickled and I give a short laugh.

"Shhh," a voice said. I couldn't tell if it was Eveline or Christine. She whispered, "A man should not sleep with his trousers on." Then she yanked hard and pulled them off me. I come with them for a bit, and my head left the pile of robes and blankets it rested on and hit the floor of the wagon. It made a pretty loud sound.

"You okay?" she whispered.

"I bumped my head."

"Sorry."

"Don't be so rough," I said.

Then she got up on top of me and I felt myself inside of her. Just like that, and I wasn't even wide-awake yet. While it was going on, I realized I was powerful hungry again, and thirsty. I breathed hard and worked myself to where I needed to be, but it was no satisfying her. She wouldn't quit. She just kept on a-moving on me and making these quiet noises like a dreaming dog.

"Are you all right?" I whispered.

"Shhhh."

"I'd at least like to let you know I'm a-feeling it," I said, almost out loud.

"Be quiet."

She moved a little quicker, and I think I got more excited, because after a while she was really finding it hard to keep quiet herself. Then she grabbed my shirt just under the neck and started pulling on me, like she wanted me to sit up. I tried to oblige, but then she let go and I bumped my head again. She leaned over me and put her face right next to my ear, still moving now, but slow and warm. I felt her hot breath on the side of my face. It smelled of apples.

"Sorry," she said again. "I didn't mean to drop you like that."

"Are you almost done?" I said. She stopped. I heard her take in breath, then hold it in. Somehow I known she did not like the question. "I'm just wondering," I said. "I can go on as long as you like, but I'm afraid we might wake ..." I paused. I was never much of a gambler, but I figured I had a fifty-fifty chance of being right, and I didn't want to leave that blank a-sitting there to fill in, so I said, "Christine."

"We won't wake her. She sleeps like a dead person," Eveline whispered.

So now I known who it was a-riding me. I wasn't no bucking bronco. More like a tired old mule, but she sure had a good time. She finally stiffened and give a great shudder from her shoulders to her hips, and then she fell down on top of me, breathing so hard she couldn't whisper no more. "Did you finish?" she said.

"I guess I did," I told her. But to tell the truth, I never did. Once I known it was Eveline, it was just the feeling of it that kept me in the business of the whole thing. I wasn't going to get nowhere. Not that Eveline wasn't a fine woman and all. I just never had a notion of her that way, and was disappointed more than just a little bit that it turned out to be her a-riding me and not Christine.

I was sure relaxed, though. For a second time as settled as I ever did feel in my whole life up to that point. I forgot how hungry I was and never even got a drink. I just turned on my side. Eveline got up, whispered, "Thank you," and crawled to her side of the wagon, and before I could begin to figure out how I was going to remember this night, I was dead asleep.

I don't know as I dreamed it or not, but I think I had that fellow Lear being read to me right before I waked up in the morning. It was Christine's voice swirling in my head when I finally opened my eyes and stared out at the frozen morning light. But she was asleep and so was Eveline.

I got myself together and walked on over to the general's office, but he wasn't there. He left a cavalry officer to talk to me in his place. He was a lean fellow, tall and sour. He didn't smile at all. "Major Brisbin," he said. "At your service."

I took his hand when he offered it. He had a look on his face that told me he didn't trust me. He wore a great handlebar mustache, too, and had a pointed chin beard under it, so that it looked as if the mustache had dripped down on his face. "General Gibbon instructed me to make a request of you, sir."

He waited for me to say something, but I had nothing. I known when I signed on there wasn't no such thing as a request as long as they was paying me.

"Well," he said, kind of flustered. "No doubt you'd like to be back out in the field. The general wishes you to go with a detachment he will lead soon east into the Yellowstone River country."

"He wants me to show the way?"

"He can find it, sir. We will be operating along that river until spring."

"Doing what?" I said.

"Finding non-treaty Indians."

"If they ain't signed a treaty, what do we want to chase them for?"

"We have been ordered to go directly east and that is what we're going to do. The government and the army wants to protect the white settlers in that region."

"Why?" I wanted to know. "Is there war?"

"This campaign will put an end to the Indian problems in this part of the country," he said. "General Custer is marching out from Fort Lincoln on the Missouri River. General Crook has ordered General Terry to come up from Wyoming Territory. General Gibbon will drive east from here to meet them. Our main goal is to find the Indians and drive them out of the territory before they scatter to the four winds."

"Indians start out scattered. You think they're all gathering in one place?"

"There will be no more Indian attacks in the Yellowstone valley or anywhere else in this territory. We are going to clear them out once and for all."

It was getting kind of close in that little room with the fire going good. I seen sweat dripping down the side of Brisbin's face. I told him I would do what the general wanted. "I'll help him find them. I won't fight no Indians."

"You will lead a detachment of twenty white scouts," he said. "The general will have five companies of infantry and I will lead—"

"The general told me about his infantry and cavalry," I said. "That's a lot of folks all at once."

"We will drive out every tribe. All of them. Clear out of eastern Montana."

"So it's our war," I said.

"What do you mean?"

"We're making war on the Indians."

"We tried to buy the land from them. It can't be done."

"But if they ain't bothering nobody . . ."

"There's gold under the pine trees in those hills. We have to open that country and make it safe for folks to . . ." He stopped. "The Indians will kill white settlers who go into the Black Hills. They're the ones going to war." He stared at me for a second. Then he got up, walked around to the front of the desk, and leaned back on it, facing me. It looked like he was trying to remember something important, but then I realized he was looking at me to see if he should trust that I'd understand what he was about to say. He said, "Did you know there's a railroad from one end of this country to the other?"

"I guess I heard we done that, or was trying to."

"We are building a nation. We have to make the future safe."

I didn't know what I should say to that. It seemed like his big idea.

Then he said, "The general wants to leave at first light, day after the new year. Can you be ready?"

"I'll be here," I said.

"You don't look very certain about our assignment, sir."

"I said I'll be here," I told him. "It's the weather I ain't sure about. I don't much like folks shooting at me, neither."

"The general's orders are Manlian orders. Do you understand that, sir?"

I looked at him blankly.

"You don't know Livy's *History of Rome*?"

I had nothing to say to that. He known I ain't read nobody about the Romans. So I had him marked from that minute on as a truly stupid man. He was very happy about something in hisself—satisfied the way a man is when he knows he's sold a bad horse to a fool and got a Thoroughbred's price for it. "Livy," he said again.

I said, "I been reading that fellow King Lear."

Something happened to his mouth under that mustache. I had the feeling he was trying to hold back from laughing at me. Then he said, "Titus Manlius. Ever heard of him?"

"No, I ain't."

"Manlius was a military man, a Roman consul. To preserve discipline in his army, he killed his own son for disobeying orders. That is the kind of thing General Gibbon would do."

"Gibbon's son in this here army?"

"No." Now he was impatient. "Do you understand that if you are not here there will be consequences?"

"I'm in your employ, sir," I said. "Manly orders or no, I can leave any time I've a mind to."

He just looked at me. I don't think folks he seen as underlings ever talked to him like that.

"But I'll be here," I said. "I'll do the job I been hired for."

"Then we are in agreement," Brisbin said.

{ CHAPTER 13 }

EVELINE WAS NONE too happy that I was going off again so soon. I was told not to think of going back to my little room next to the stables. So I went and got all my things and moved into the wagon. I still used the bathhouse on occasion, and I made sure Cricket was well fed. That night I lay down in the same place with the pile of blankets under my head and Christine read me some more of *Lear*. When she finally quit and blew out the lantern, I lay awake a long time just in case Eveline got another notion, but nothing happened.

I can't say I was disappointed, but maybe I was. I waked up the next day to hot coffee and warm biscuits and even a little fried sowbelly. Christine did all the cooking. Eveline sat by the stove and stared at me like she was a-waiting for me to say something.

Finally she said, "Did you sleep well?"

"I did, thank you kindly."

Christine put a plate in front of me and I started eating the biscuits.

The next night things went pretty much the same. During the reading I let on I was ready for something else, so Christine said she'd read me some *Hamlet*. It sounded exactly the same to me, so I ain't sure she wasn't just humoring me and still reading from *Lear*. "You got anything else?" I said.

"I have some Dickens."

"Okay." I pointed to the other books. "He sound any different than these two?"

"Yes, he will sound different." She picked up a big black book that also looked like a Bible and started reading from it. " 'Chapter one. I am born. Whether I shall turn out to be the hero of my own life, or whether that station will be held by anybody else, these pages must show. To begin my life with the beginning of my life, I record that I was born (as I have been informed and believe) on a Friday, at twelve o'clock at night. It was remarked that the clock began to strike, and I began to cry, simultaneously.'" She stopped. "You know what 'simultaneously' means?"

"I think so."

"What does it mean?"

"It means the fellow cried like a simpleton," I said, not exactly sure. She smiled for a short spell, looking at me in surprise and shock I think, because I got it right. Then she went on reading. I could mostly understand it all, so I stayed awake longer. The truth is I liked her voice and it was especially pleasant to be able to understand most of the words she was reading. I liked the way she sounded when she said, " 'I am born.' " I could tell both them ladies was born to a higher station in life than me. Anyway, I listened for the better part of a hour or so, but eventually I found it easy enough to drift off to sleep in the warmth of that wagon.

The weather got a bit closer to thawing out for a while as Christmas approached, but then it froze up again good and solid. Sometimes the wind cut through you like a sword. To prepare for the long trip, I got myself a pack of buffalo skins and seven long poles for my own lodge. The old army tent had give out completely, and anyway, you couldn't have a fire in the middle of it like you could with a good Indian tepee. Big Tree had showed me how to make one and so I had a good-sized Indian lodge. I'd use three of the poles for the tepee to make a travois to carry all of it and a whole lot more. Since it all dragged on the ground, I didn't need but one other horse to drag the travois and my supplies and then on Cricket I only carried a bedroll and my guns, a few canteens of water, and a little whiskey.

Two days before Christmas, near the end of the day, the wind calmed down enough that I decided to put all my things together and assemble the travois next to the wagon. Christine come down out of the thing and stood there watching me for a spell. She was wrapped in a buffalo robe over a red dress, and I could see steam coming out of her mouth, but with no wind, it really wasn't so cold.

I tied three long poles together near the top and set them down on the ground, then I spread them apart at the place where they would drag along the ground. Crossways on the poles, I tied a wood frame with all my skins and a pack where I'd put food and ammunition and other supplies. I set the rest of the poles on top. It was all tied together with leather and she watched me while I cinched each knot to be sure it would hold.

"What is that contraption?"

"It will soon be my home," I said. "See, I'll lift this end at the top and tie it over a horse's back, and then it all comes along with me."

"I thought you did not have to go anywhere until after Christmas."

"I'm just getting ready. I ain't going nowhere yet."

"Have you thought about what you will give Eveline for Christmas?"

"I'll be leaving just a few days after Christmas, so . . ." I had nothing more to say, because I believed it would be understood that Christmas shouldn't be no fuss.

"But you will be here." She was smiling, but I could see she was ready to jump me if I said the wrong thing. Sometimes I think women have a way of tilting their head a bit to the side while they study your eyes as you talk. They're watching for it, even expecting it: the wrong thing. And if you say the wrong thing, they pounce on it like a cougar on a foal. "It will be Christmas Eve tomorrow," she whispered.

"Well, what do you think she wants?"

"A nice perfume would be just the thing."

I cinched the last knot and then stood there blowing out steam. "What if I give her my share of the wagon," I said. "She'd make a mite better use of that, wouldn't she?"

"I would very much like it if you did that. It would be a good gift for me. But it is not what you give a person who is . . ." She stopped.

"Who is what?"

"In a manner of speaking, your intended."

"Oh, she ain't my intended," I said a little too fast.

She moved her head back a little and her mouth went flat and straight across the front of her face. "I said, 'in a manner of speaking.'"

"There ain't no kind of speaking where I ever said nothing like that," I said.

"You have misled her." Now she was whispering a mite loud.

"It ain't true. If she told you that, she wasn't telling *you* the truth."

She stood there staring into my eyes. I could feel my heart beating under my leather shirt. "Damnation," I whispered. "I ain't lying. I don't believe she told you nothing like that, neither."

"What have you been doing with her on these nights?"

"One time," I said. "It wasn't my idea."

"So you just had your fun, is that it?"

"We both had fun," I said. "Nobody mentioned nothing about being intended."

"What did you say?"

"I believe you heard me," I said out loud.

She leaned back and hit me hard on my jaw with her fist. I almost fell over backwards. I stood there looking at her. I didn't know what I was supposed to do. She leaned back to give me another one, and I stepped aside and covered up so she only caught me on my forearm. "Christ Almighty," I said. I was glad she wasn't Eveline's brother. She could hit hard.

She moved closer in, like she was going to give me something under my arms and in the belly. I lowered my arms to protect myself, and she caught me again on the jaw with her right hand.

"Are you going to quit this?" I said. Now I had both fists up and was dancing around like a boxer. I made up my mind if she hit me again, I'd pretend she *was* Eveline's brother and give her nose a try. "You better quit," I said. "I ain't about to take no more."

Then she started crying. "You . . . you . . ." She couldn't get out what she wanted to say.

"I'll get her the perfume," I said. "Jesus."

She turned around so fast her long dress belled out a bit and I seen her black stockings. She stomped off and got back up in the wagon. I tried to get out of there, but while I was pulling the travois up in the shade next to old General Cooney, Eveline come down out of the wagon.

"I suppose you heard it," I said.

"Heard what?"

"You know what."

157

"I wondered what you two were whispering about. I was asleep for most of it."

"You was."

"I do not want any perfume," she said. She looked pretty good in that light. The sun was weak, as usual, but it made her skin look kind of golden, and with no smile on her face, she looked right pretty. She'd pulled her dark hair over her forehead, and her eyes kind of glistened in a lively way. "I do not want anything from you at all," she said.

"I'm glad to hear it."

"Except that one other thing you mentioned." Now she did smile a bit, and again the gaps in her teeth was kind of distracting. Still, something stirred in me, looking into her eyes. She was a woman that known life for all its splendor and taken what she wanted out of it, and I admired her for it.

"What other thing did I mention?"

"General Cooney's part of the wagon."

"If I'm here at Christmas morning, why don't we hang a few of stockings and see what any of us finds there."

"Will you come back to this wagon tonight?"

"I'll be here until I leave," I said. "If you'll take me."

Now I had to find a damn bottle of perfume. I known the store'd have nothing for women, so I rode over to Fort Ellis and tried to get in to see General Gibbon. I figured if he had his wife with him she might be able to help out. I wasn't going to find no perfume among the Indians or the troops, although a sizable portion of them fellows could sure use it. General Gibbon had gone back to his home in St. Louis for Christmas, so I went to the quartermaster's store and found some toilet water but it wasn't no real perfume. When I asked the fellow in there if he had something more sweet smelling, he laughed at me, and I got to laughing too. "I know it sounds pretty silly," I said. "But I live with two women."

"Oh, so you're the fellow living up the street a way in that Conestoga with them two ladies."

I nodded, holding the toilet water in my hand.

"I heard about you."

"You did."

"Living with two women. Chief of scouts, am I right? Why, you're famous."

"I guess."

The fellow was bald except for a beard that started in front of his ears and wrapped around his lower chin. "A lot of the soldiers talk about you and them women in that wagon."

"It's a blessing," I said. "They got a little stove in there that vents out the side and it stays mighty warm on these cold nights."

"Well, I guess it does. You don't need the stove, am I right?" He nudged me with his elbow and laughed again.

I laughed, too, a bit, but then I said, "It ain't nothing like that."

"Nooo, I guess it's not." Now he laughed really hard, like he was in on something together with me and we both was sharing in it.

"It ain't what you think," I said. Even if he had the right idea, I didn't want him to have it. It wasn't none of his business, and I didn't like it that he was talking about me and my friends in that way. I didn't care if he guessed my position exactly. I wanted him to shut up about it. So I tried to distract him with a question I really wanted to know the answer to. "What's that you heard about me and the chief of scouts?"

"You're leading the scout troop. Colonel Brisbin said so. You'll be his eyes and ears out there in the field."

I threw a half a dollar on the counter for the toilet water. "Any way I can sweeten this water a bit?"

"I wouldn't do that," he said, now in a soft voice. "My advice, sir? She's a woman and she'll know what that is no matter how you sweeten it."

"I guess so."

"Don't you want another one?" He stared at me, his face about to break into a smile, but he froze it like that, waiting for me to say something.

"I guess so," I said.

And then I seen this hanger with three white linen gowns hanging off it—the kind of undergarment a man ain't supposed to see. "Where'd you get them?"

"St. Louis. They was on their way to California, but no one ever come to get them."

"I'll take two of them."

"Well, you do have plans, don't you?"

"It ain't nothing like that," I said. "How much?"

"Four dollars each."

I looked at him hard.

"They are expensive."

"I'll take two for six dollars."

"You'll take one for six and I'll give you two dollars change. They're four dollars each."

"I'll give you a fine buffalo robe and six dollars."

"I got to see the robe first."

"Ah, the hell with it," I said.

It would be the first Christmas I'd spend under a roof in almost six years. I didn't want to look forward to it, but I did. The side of my face where Christine had clipped me was swelled up and it throbbed to beat all. And I was scared to death of what would happen that night in the wagon, so I figured it would be a good thing to come with more than one gift of a little toilet water.

{ CHAPTER 14 }

WELL, THEY HAD a little celebration with red candles and a little pine tree set up in the back of the wagon. They wrapped it in red ribbons with a few gold ribbons mixed in. They served boiled wine and fried up a piece of buffalo meat on top of the stove. They made gravy from the drippings and had fresh biscuits to dip in it. I ate like a king.

Then Eveline suggested we pray. I listened to them going on and on about the birth of Jesus and sacrifice and all. I was full of good food and a little sleepy, but I behaved myself. I ain't never placed much faith in all that hocus-pocus about a God and angels and all. I don't know how anybody that's been to a war can conceive of such a thing as a merciful Lord. It ain't nothing but the last thing a damn fool would invent if he seen the carnage of a battlefield. If there was no God, nor a idea of a God, and a fellow wanted to imagine something bigger than hisself, and he seen a battlefield, he would not ever come up with the idea of this old fellow in the sky with a white beard who gives a damn about what goes on down here. But some folks believe it. The Indians got their own version of it. Ain't nobody exempt from the temptation to believe it, I guess. But I don't. I ain't never and that's just the way it is. Sometimes I wish I *did* believe it.

I would not challenge them two women, though. I went right along and pretended to believe everything.

It was powerful warm and so comfortable, I started thinking about what was in my near future: marching around in the Yellowstone River valley and on out to eastern Montana and the empty plains. There ain't no shelter from the wind out there. The whole idea made me sick to my stomach and like to ruined the night. There ain't no use in thinking about the future too much because of what it does to what's going on here and now. If you think too much about a dark future, you ruin what's going on today. You got to take the future out of the equation's what I always say.

"Ladies," I said. "I'm feeling a mite sentimental right about now, and would like to give out the presents."

First come the toilet water. I'd wrapped both little bottles in brown paper and tied them at the top with yellow ribbon. The gowns I put in a single box—it's all the quartermaster had—and again wrapped it in brown paper. I wrote on the top, "For the Both of You."

They was pretty happy with the toilet water, but when Eveline opened the box with the gowns in it, they both started weeping and carrying on. They each give me a kiss on the cheek. "I wonder if this will fit me," Eveline said, holding hers up.

"Of course it will," Christine said. "They are just exactly the right size."

They was long gowns, and would cover them from neck to feet, but maybe Eveline's would be a bit tight. She was more ample in the middle than Christine, and the gown looked like it hung down without any kind of blossoming in the midsection. But it didn't dampen the mood none that she wondered about how it might fit. She was so happy when she kissed me, there was tears in her eyes.

"We have something for you," Christine said. She handed me a box that was pretty heavy. I hoped it was cartridges for my Evans repeater, or maybe a new pistol. The weight fooled me. When I got it open, I found another leather-bound volume that looked like a Bible—this one said *The Complete Works of Shakespeare.*

"Well, I'll be damned," I said.

"I know you loved to hear me read from this," Christine said. "So we wanted you to have it so you can read it any time you want, no matter where you might be in your travels."

"Thank you kindly." I didn't know what to do with it. It was the heaviest book I ever lifted. "I will read this wherever I go."

"And when you do, you will hear Christine's voice."

"I expect I will."

"Read it in remembrance."

"In what?"

"In remembrance of us and our time together."

"Oh, yes," I said. "Of course." I opened it and looked at the pages. There was a lot of space on most of them, but the print was so small I could barely make it out, and it was bunched up in such a way I didn't see how a body could read it. I was happy to see that it did have some pictures, but mostly they was far apart and there wasn't enough of them.

Later that night, the wind kicked up and froze the air again. It come from the north and blew on the side of the wagon where the vent for the stove was, so it kept banking down the fire and causing smoke to leak back into where we was sitting. We sipped coffee and tried to keep warm by the stove for a while, but I known we'd have to turn the wagon around out of the wind if we was going to be warm on this night. I didn't want to go out there yet and get started on it. I figured I'd have to drag Cooney out from under first, then hitch at least one horse to get the whole thing turned. Eveline got all bundled up with buffalo robes so she could help me.

"Well?" she said.

I got up and climbed down in the cold wind. Eveline said there was no need to hitch up a damn horse. "Just you and I can pull the tongue and it will move."

"We gotta get Cooney out of there."

"Leave him where he is. We only have to pull it a little bit, turn it some out of the wind."

I shrugged. If she wanted to lead the way, I figured I'd go along. If she was right, we wouldn't have much to do, and if she was wrong, then we had the horse. I walked around in front, kicking snow out of my way as best I could. Eveline come behind me. I picked up the one side of the trace and she picked up the other. We straddled each side, and when I give the signal, we started pulling as hard as we could. The wheels of the wagon didn't budge.

"We gotta get Christine out of there. Maybe a few other things to lighten it."

Eveline laughed. "You think Christine weighs that much?"

I could barely hear her in the wind. Christine, inside the wagon, heard her plain as day. She come to the opening in front. "What did he say?"

"I didn't say nothing."

"He wants you to come down out of there so we can pull this thing."

"Oh, get the horse," she said.

"I didn't say you was that heavy," I said.

"Get the horse."

"That's what I thought I'd have to do," I said.

I trudged to the stable and got my packhorse. He didn't want to go. I had to drag him out and put him in front of the wagon and hitch him up, The whole time he's doing everything to discourage me. I finally got him in the trace and hitched to the wagon, but then he wouldn't move. I started cursing to beat all, and Eveline didn't like it.

"On the Lord's birthday and you say things like that."

"I ain't addressing the Lord." I pulled harder on the reins, standing in front of the horse, and he kept bobbing his head and moving back away from me.

"Please don't curse like that."

"Just leave me alone right now," I said.

Finally the horse begun to move with me. He pulled and his hooves slipped a little in the snow, but he got it moving and I turned it around so that the wind was blowing at the back corner and I seen smoke beginning to billow out of the pipe that vented from the stove. "That ought to do it," I said. "You might ought to put a elbow on that pipe so it sticks straight up at the end. Then it don't matter which way the wind blows."

Eveline come up to me, put her hands on my face, and leaned in real close. "Tonight I will come to you again," she whispered. She waited there, looking into my eyes. In the cold moonlight, with steam coming out of her nose and mouth, her eyes gleaming, she didn't look like just a woman. She looked like a kind of spirit—beautiful and free. But I known she was a woman, a capable, strong woman. She made herself frail in a sad kind of way. I looked in her eyes and it was like the first time I really seen her. I was looking in the face of something that hit me like music, like a fine song, and I known for sure I was never going to forget it. Them eyes softened something in me I didn't like to think about. She was warm and alive and I come to see I had formed a attachment and that surprised the hell out of me.

I didn't know what to say. I put my arms around her and smiled.

"Do you want me?" she said.

"I guess I do."

She looked away, and I put my hands on hers, which was still up against either side of my face. "Eveline," I said.

"What?"

"I'm right taken by surprise here."

I think I was still smiling. I hope I was still smiling. Her face changed when she looked at me again. "I wish . . ." I started to say, and she put her head on my chest and said, "No. Please do not say it."

"This is something I ain't ready for."

"I know it."

"But listen," I said. "I don't mean that like you think I mean it. I just mean I'm taken by surprise here."

She didn't say nothing. I heard a little sound from her voice, but it was not clear to me if she was trying not to cry or laugh.

"I ain't never felt like I'm feeling right now," I said.

"Please."

"Please what?"

"Do not wish for anything." She let go my face and turned and climbed back up in the wagon, and I think a part of my soul went on up there with her. I unhitched the horse and walked him back to the stable, thinking about what I might be getting myself into. I guess it pleased me to think Eveline would be riding me again once I remembered it. When I thought about it, I felt kind of sorry for thinking of her in that way. On the walk back to the stable, and while I was putting the packhorse back in his stall, the only thing I could see in my mind was her eyes in that frozen moonlight and the sound of her name. Eveline. It rhymed with "fine" and "wine."

When I got back to the wagon and climbed up inside, they had fed the stove some and the heat hit me like sunlight at first. I took off my coat and settled back a ways from the heat, then eventually I bunched up the blankets and laid down again like I'd been doing. Eveline settled herself right at my feet but she didn't touch me none. We both just set there looking at each other, wishing Christine would leave off that Dickens fellow. She just kept on a-reading and feeding the stove and outside the wind wouldn't quit.

Both me and Eveline fell asleep finally, with Christine reading on into David Copperfield's adulthood.

I waked up the next morning in a pretty foul mood. Bright sunlight broke through the back flap of the wagon, but the wind had not settled yet. It was still cold air flying in and the fire in the stove had banked. I thought I'd go on over to the bathhouse and get cleaned up, but Eveline come over to me, real quiet, like, and started trying to get me to take off my breeches.

"Not now," I said.

"She is asleep still. We have time," she whispered.

"I don't know."

"Shhhh. This is your Christmas present from me."

Now my back ached something fierce, and it was Christmas morning, for Lord's sake. She was pawing at me, and I grabbed her hands. "Listen," I said. "It's too late for this now."

"You will be gone soon. You will be out on that prairie, in this weather. You want to have something fine to remember me."

"I already got that," I said.

"I never met a man like you. General Cooney was an animal compared to you, and he was older and a lot sicker."

"You was with General Cooney?"

"I had to say no to him a hundred times, as sick as he was."

"I ain't sick at all."

"Well, what's wrong, then?"

Christine snorted in her sleep, but she didn't move none. I nodded in her direction and said, "She punched me good yesterday. She don't like us doing this."

"It is not her business."

We was both whispering pretty loud. "She thinks you're my intended. Since we been—"

"It is not her business. Do you remember holding me last night outside in the cold?"

"What if she wakes up?"

"I will handle her."

"You'll keep her off of me?"

She wrapped her arms around my middle. "You have nothing to fear from her."

I'd of rather wrastled a big Indian than Miss Eveline Barkley. Before long she was on top of me again, trying not to make too much noise. The air in the wagon was cold enough that we was chuffing out a lot of steam with every quick breath and we was sure breathing fast. Christine was snoring on the other side of the stove, near the front of the wagon.

Strange as it may seem, that early in the morning I was ready, and I finished a long time before Eveline did. When she commenced to shuddering and thrashing and all, I held her close. I can't explain it, but I felt as sad as I ever did in my life at that moment. I'd lost a friend or two in the war, and it was sad leaving Theo and then Big Tree. I sometimes felt bad that I didn't have Morning Breeze with me. But at that moment, with Eveline a hunched down over me, slowly falling back to normal breathing and all, I felt like I might just start crying. I ain't felt like that since I was a little boy.

"That was a nice gift of a Christmas morning," I whispered.

Then I noticed she was crying—just a-snuffling in the crook of my neck. "Hey," I said. "Are you okay?"

She said, "I miss my husband."

I didn't know what I should say to that.

"I am not the kind of woman you think I am."

"I think you're a fine woman."

This made her cry even harder. I was afraid she'd wake Christine and she'd know what we was up to. There was something damn sweet about how sad I felt, and it was good enough I didn't want nothing nor nobody to make me feel no different. Eveline kept a-squeezing me.

"I'm sorry," I whispered. She snuffled her head against me some more. "Should I be sorry?"

"No," she said out loud. She sat back up a little and looked at me. "You should not be sorry." Her face was wet, and her hair stuck to it in crazy patterns. Her nose wasn't too dry, neither, but by God she was a beautiful woman.

She moved off me and got herself proper. She wiped her face clean with a piece of linen. I pulled up my britches and set there looking at her. "What if something happens now," I said.

"I won't get pregnant," she said. "It's not the right time of month for that."

"No, I mean what if something happens to me?"

"Don't say it."

"Are we intended now?"

It was quiet for a while. Christine stirred a little, and when she opened her eyes, Eveline offered to make some coffee. "You go get some wood for the stove, honey," she said to me. She was back to her normal self.

I climbed out into the frosty sun. It was early in the morning, and not a lot of folks was up and about. I started pulling small pieces of wood out from under the back side of the wagon. I piled it high in the back just inside the flap. Christine got up and brushed her hair. I noticed while I was placing one handful inside that she and Eveline sprinkled on a little of that toilet water. It hit me that I would soon be back out with the army. I'd have my lodge and a fire in it and maybe I'd be alone and wouldn't suffer no sadness over a little minute of animal pleasure with a person I come to care for. Maybe you think I was feeling guilty, but I really wasn't. It ain't guilt if you don't think you done nothing wrong, and I wasn't feeling that way. Hell, I was fairly certain I'd do it again if I was given half the chance. It was a pleasure, after all. It ain't fair, but what made me sad was affection. I liked Eveline. I couldn't get her out of my mind, and I known I wasn't going to be with her much longer and I didn't have no way of thanking her or Christine for making me feel comfortable and warm during those short days and long nights in the Bozeman winter. Maybe I was grateful for the time of peace and comfort. I never did feel so warm and sheltered. Like sleep was a peaceful retreat from life, instead of a temporary quest for a little rest before you got to open your eyes and look out for trouble again. It was restful as death almost, but it was alive and feeling good, feeling real good. Maybe I was sad that life don't ever stay that way for long. Those two women give me respite from strife and struggle. And they didn't even know it.

When we got the fire blazing in the stove again, I got all my things together.

"Where are you going?" Eveline said.

"I'm going to feed my horse and get ready to go."

"You don't have to leave right away, do you?"

"First light after new year," I said. "But I got a lot of things to get done beforehand, and there ain't much of the days left." I told them I'd be back in the evening and took the last sip of my coffee. "I thank you kindly," I said. "Both of you been very good to me."

Eveline looked at me and our eyes froze for a second. I think she known what I was thinking. I said, so only she could hear it, "You especially."

She got this look on her face like I slapped her or something.

"I don't mean about that," I said.

"About what?" Christine asked.

Both Eveline and me said, "Nothing." Then Eveline turned her face up to mine and give me a kiss on the lips. Just a soft touch of it. "You are better than any of the men I have known, including my husband," she said.

Christine set there staring at us. I nodded. I swear my chest felt empty just then, like there was nothing under the bones.

They watched me climb down out of the wagon, but neither said nothing.

The rest of that week it was just me and Eveline in the dark. Christine would read from that Dickens fellow, and then she'd settle herself and go to sleep and Eveline and me would commence to holding each other and loving when we could. It was not animal pleasure after all. It was a frantic attempt to hold back time and what was ahead of us.

On the last day before the New Year, I went and settled up on Cricket and made sure she was well fed and ready. I put the saddle and bridle on her so she'd be used to it by morning and so I wouldn't have to try and do it in the dark. I went back to the commissary at the fort and bought some sugar, coffee, tobacco, and dried beef. I packed the new supplies on the travois and tied it all down again. I worked right next to the wagon, in the cold, and around four in the afternoon—just before dark—Christine come down out of the wagon with a cup of hot coffee.

"You must be freezing out here," she said.

"Tell you the truth, I didn't notice it much until you mentioned it."
I sipped the coffee. It was hot and felt very good going down. When I
was done with it, I handed her the cup. "Much obliged."

"I am sorry about the other day," she said. Her eyes glistened a
little in the cold air.

I rubbed the side of my face. "You pack a wallop."

"I'm truly sorry." She bowed her head, like she was looking for
something in the cup.

"It don't matter," I said.

"My sister—" She paused, looking at me again. "She is a lusty
woman. Not to say lustful, but definitely lusty. She is hearty and vigor-
ous. She wants to enjoy life, and out here . . . she understands the life
out here better than most women."

"I guess she does."

"I expected her to have the decency we were accustomed to in the
East. I know now that is impossible."

"Decency?" I said.

"Maybe I mean decorum."

"What's that?"

"I just wanted you to be aware—I wanted you to know—that Eveline
may wish for certain things, but she has no expectations or demands
where you are concerned regarding matrimony, and neither do I."

"I guess that's okay," I said.

"But you should know she has found it in her heart to abide with
you—she has found a place in her heart only for you. She is devoted
and will not allow recriminations or reproach to come between the two
of you."

"Sometimes," I said, "you sound like that fellow Dickens, or Lear."

"Are you saying you don't understand me?"

"No, I understand. It just takes a concentrated mind to do it. I got
to listen real good."

She smiled a little. "You know what I'm saying."

"I do," I said. "It's enough that *you* understand all that. I would of
liked to hear it from Eveline, though."

*   *   *

On my last night in the wagon, we all three sat in front of the stove and enjoyed hot brandy. I calculated I'd be leaving before the fire banked in that stove, and every time the wind kicked up a little I wanted to scrunch a little closer to it. Eveline talked about how she figured I wished I was already back out with the army. I told her it damn sure wasn't no wish but it was going to come true right soon anyway. Now that Christine had said she understood things better, it didn't seem like such a bad thing to be warm and cozy in front of that stove. It was a mite strange to be a-wondering if Eveline really had no expectations or not. I didn't even think about my own wishes at first. But then I said, "You know, I guess this here is my home fire. My very own hearth."

Eveline smiled and Christine nodded slightly, then averted her eyes.

"I have one more Christmas gift," I said. "I think you will both appreciate it."

Now they was both looking at me. Eveline's eyes really seemed to glow.

"I make a gift of Cooney's part a this here wagon," I said. "I disavow it."

Eveline started crying again. But Christine didn't like it one bit. "Does that mean what I think it means?" she said.

"What?"

"You give us the wagon now. Why?"

"I want to be nice."

Eveline said, "Christine, what is it?"

"He's not coming back here in the spring to help us get to Oregon."

"Now, I didn't say that."

"Of course he will," Eveline said.

"He won't."

"I don't know what would keep me from it," I said. "Didn't I just say this here is my own hearth and home? And I'm a-leaving my leather-bound book here for you to keep for me."

"We will not ever see him again," Christine said. "Even if he wants to. He shall not come back, I just know it."

"I will too. And I don't want you, either one of you, trying to find nobody else to take you, neither. That's the only part of the promise I *do* want to take back."

"Something will happen to you. Something awful." Then she narrowed her eyes and really give me a Indian look. Like she could see my soul and there wasn't no place for it to hide. "You want to come back now. But will you? Will you?"

"Well, I guess I don't know," I said. "All I can say is I'm planning on it. Ain't that all any of us can say?"

I watched Eveline brush tears from her face. It would of been nice if she'd said something about it all, but she said nothing. After a while she seemed to find it hard to look at me.

"Damnation," I said. "I'm coming back. I hope I'll be welcome."

Now she met my eyes and smiled.

"I just hope I'll be welcome," I said again. "Look for me come June. You just look for me. I'll be here to bury the general and retrieve my copy of Shakespeare."

I wanted to run my fingers through Eveline's hair, but I figured under the current circumstances it might be a bit awkward.

{ CHAPTER 15 }

MAJOR BRISBIN DID not like my travois. That was the first problem. "You can't travel with us dragging that thing. You'll just slow us down."

"Indians move pretty quick when they have to."

"You'll be the only one out there with a packhorse."

"A Indian lodge beats the hell out of them army tents you're carrying."

"How?"

"A squaw could put this thing up in half the time one a your men takes to assemble a two-man tent. And she can take it down even faster."

"I don't believe it."

"I've seen it with my own eyes."

"You don't have a squaw with you."

"I don't need one. I learned how to do it."

He known I was right. "I guess if you want to be a damn fool, I can't stop you."

That first day, as we rode along heading east, he tried not to look at me, because every time he did, he'd lose his temper a little bit.

We was the vanguard of a pretty big force. The biggest I'd been with since the war. Since I known the terrain, my job was to lead them on the best trails while we searched for what Brisbin called "hostiles." To him, all Indians was hostiles, except for the Crow scouts in my troop. When we located a Indian encampment, we was to leave a detachment of scouts to watch and track them, and then get back to Gibbon to let him know where they was. Brisbin had about sixty cavalrymen with him, and Gibbon was coming behind us with the infantry. He had twelve wagons and four hundred troops, all walking in the wet snow on the trail. I had twenty scouts in my troop. It was a regular campaign. Brisbin said we was to keep moving east until we run into General Custer and General Reno coming up from the south. We was all going to collect every hostile in the whole territory. Brisbin said we'd stay out there until spring and even the summer if we had to. When he said that about the summer I almost said, "I ain't staying out here beyond the month of May," but I kept quiet. Working as a scout for the cavalry was a job, and I known I could quit any time I wanted to.

The first night I missed Eveline. Soon as I finished putting up my tepee and had time to sit in front of the fire, I heard her name in my head like a song.

It took me a while to set up the tepee. I had no trouble with the poles, but once I had them all arranged, I had to wrap the buffalo skin from the top by attaching it to one of the poles, then hefting it up and hitching it there. Once that was done, I'd just walk around the thing, unfolding the skin as I went and securing it to each pole. The problem was, I couldn't get it to hitch at the top. Morning Breeze done it with no trouble at all, and quick too. I known Brisbin was paying attention, so I hated having the problem.

When I was done, I collected a bunch of buffalo chips and built a fire in the middle of it and commenced to fix things to eat. I cooked up some cornmeal in a pan and made a pot of beans. I heated a piece of sowbelly on the tip of a stick and eat some of that too. When I was done I smoked a pipe and watched the fire for a while. I got kind of sad thinking about Eveline, in that wagon with her sister, missing me. I sipped a little of the whiskey, then curled up by the fire and went to sleep. In the dark of morning I made coffee and cooked some more sowbelly in a pan on the fire. I eat the meal real slow, wishing I had a biscuit, and watched the sun rise in a cold mist over the mountains before us. I had faced the opening of my lodge east, as the Indians always did. I was warm in that tepee, sitting there watching the light curl around everything dark and start to lighten it. The weather was warmer, and when I heard the camp beginning to stir, I packed up and was ready to go by the time the sun come up full.

We'd only been on the trail about a day and a half when I got into a little bit more of trouble. We'd traveled about thirty miles, and was getting far enough from Fort Ellis that Colonel Brisbin wanted me and my scouts to start fanning out and searching for signs of Indians. I sent five of my scouts south and five north, and I went east with the other nine. While I was gone, Gibbon's top sergeant come riding up to talk about where the general expected the colonel to be during the first days of the campaign. Turns out the top sergeant was a fellow named Garrison who was in the Union army during the war. We both served under General Thomas in the second half of the war. When I come riding back to let Brisbin know there wasn't nothing in front of us, I was shocked to see Garrison a-setting there on his horse, waving his white-gloved hands in a friendly conversation with the colonel. I wasn't sure he remembered me at first, but then he stopped talking and got to studying me a mite and then he said, "I'd know this red head anywhere. James. Christopher James."

This was right when Brisbin was getting ready to introduce me. "James?" Brisbin said.

"I been called that," I said.

"This fellow is Bobby Hale," Brisbin said.

"That's my name now. I changed it a few times."

Both of them known what for right away. They looked at me like I just murdered a child right in front of them. "So, a bounty jumper," Brisbin said with contempt.

"It was your army," I said. "Your war."

"Do you have no convictions, sir?"

"No. I was never tried for no crime."

"That's not what I meant," Brisbin said. "You are a deserter."

"Multiple times," I said. "But I fought too. I was at Fredericksburg. I fought in Tennessee, at Chickamauga with General Thomas."

"I suppose you can prove that," Brisbin said.

"I don't have to." I looked at Garrison. "Not now."

"He was there," Garrison said. He looked down at his saddle horn, seemed to grimace in pain. Then he said, "At Chickamauga. Fought bravely too."

I nodded. Brisbin give a little kick to his horse and started off. Garrison and I followed. We was all three riding in front of the troops. Cricket was a little taller than the other horses so I found myself looking down at the other two as we rode along. It was a windless, damp afternoon. I didn't look at Brisbin directly. I waited to see what he would do. I wasn't worried about being punished for my crimes. The war was long over, and anyway, I was a good soldier when I was forced to take that occupation on full steam.

Finally Brisbin said, "I wonder what the army's coming to."

"I ain't in the army no more," I said.

"You keep two women in Bozeman," he said. "You collected multiple enlisted bonuses, and skedaddled as soon as the opportunity presented itself." I started to take him up on that last, but he said, "I know. You fought at Fredericksburg and Chickamauga. You got trapped in it before you could run, am I right?"

I said nothing.

"And now you've sold your services to us."

"In a manner of speaking," I said. "I ain't been paid no bonus and I ain't enlisted."

"It's a good thing," Brisbin said. "You'd skedaddle on us too."

"Bonus or not," I said. "I didn't come along on this here expedition to fight nobody."

Garrison laughed. "Yes," he said. "It's a different army."

"You want to know what I seen up ahead?" I asked.

He looked hard at me.

"What'd you see?" Garrison wanted to know.

"Nothing," I said, still staring at Brisbin. "Not a dad-burned thing all the way to the Musselshell."

Brisbin half smiled, but he didn't say nothing to me. He sent Garrison on back to let General Gibbon know we didn't find no hostiles yet.

{ CHAPTER 16 }

IT WAS ONE hell of a campaign. We roamed all over the Yellowstone valley and down that river and the two Bighorns and in and out of small forests. We climbed hills and rode into snow-filled valleys beginning to turn green with heavy spring rain. By the time the weather commenced to get warmer, and the rain let up a bit, I had all my scouts camped together west of the Black Hills near the Powder River and I was really starting to worry about getting back in time to go to Oregon with Eveline. It didn't seem like we was nowhere near finished what we come out to do, and it was already getting on into March.

General Gibbon and his infantry was somewhere back west of us, on the other side of the Yellowstone, and Colonel Brisbin was camped out on the Tongue River. So far we'd chased a few straggling Indians off their campground—some Piegans made a little noise but there wasn't no shooting. We run into a "tribe" of half-breeds, mostly hunters with squaws traveling with them and plenty of whiskey, but they was not hostile and we even spent one day having horse races and cooking enough elk and venison to feed just about everybody.

I lost my travois betting in one of the horse races, so I was laying on a blanket under the spring sun, a little drunk from the whiskey, letting all the meat and corn bread I eat settle in my stomach, when a courier come up with the news that Brisbin wanted to see me. It was a long ride to where he was camped, and I said so. But the next day I rode on back to see what he wanted. He told me things was going to heat up pretty soon around there—that Reno and Custer was coming and we was going to round up all the Indians we could find.

"Well, ain't that what we been trying to do?" I said.

"We're going to turn south, to the Bighorn valley, and meet Custer and Reno there. General Gibbon wants to know what's between us and the other two."

Brisbin wanted me and my scouts to ride ahead in a kind of scattergun pattern, looking for signs of Indians. If we seen any kind of encampment, we was to move in close and get as good a look as we could and then double back and let Brisbin know what there was. He wanted us to count horses and tepees.

I spent the rest of that day riding slow along the trail back to my men. Near dark, I decided to set up camp and wait until morning to report back. I was regretting the loss of my travois. All I had now was a small army tent I got from Brisbin's supply wagon. While I was looking for a place to camp, I killed a couple of rabbits and tied them to my saddle for dinner.

I found a place near a pretty swift stream and started to get things set up. I was putting up the blasted tent poles when it started to rain. It was steady, cold, needle kind of prickly rain. By the time I had everything set up, I was soaking wet. The buffalo chips I needed for the fire was wet, too, so I cut some brambles and branches from the dogberry and sagebrush near the river and brought them inside until they could dry out a little. In the meantime, I huddled in that damn tent sipping whiskey and shivering to beat all. I got so tired for the shivering, I lay down and before long fell asleep. I guess I kept my own self warm from being out of the rain and cold air. I never did eat nothing or build a fire. I dreamed I was running down a mountainside, racing a waterfall or some such, and then I heard something. When I opened my eyes, I realized it was the yipping of Indians in the distance. I opened the flap of the tent and looked out. The sun was just under a dark shelf of clouds, shining bright, and I could see my breath again. It got colder overnight. The rain had stopped. I heard the yipping again, so I got my carbine and my pistol and went out low to the ground, scurrying up to Cricket and the packhorse. They was looking off nervously to the east, but no one tampered with their ropes. I started walking toward the sound, cutting through sagebrush, down toward the river. Then I seen what it was.

The sun was bright behind me, so I could not be seen, and in front of me was a pack of Sioux braves, maybe six or seven of them, prancing on horseback around a huge animal of some kind. They was circling around it, blocking my sight, and yip-yipping like crazy. Every now and then one of them would fire a arrow into it. I crept a little closer, my carbine loaded and ready, and then I realized it wasn't no animal at all. It was Big Tree. He had four or five arrows sticking out of him and he was down on all fours. They kept shooting more wood into him. He refused to go all the way down. He got to his feet at one point, staggered there, blood all over him, and then I seen his face. I think he looked right at me.

He tried to fire his carbine at one of the braves, but the shot only went off high above everybody. He stood tall for a minute, seemed to draw in air to scream, then he fell to his knees again and dropped the rifle. He still held a sheath knife, and I seen him take a pistol out of his belt. Several warriors was dead on the ground around him. But he was done for. I watched him struggle and spit, and with every short, icy breath I took, I known there wasn't nothing I could do for him. Even if I started shooting and got all of them, he was already dead. I don't know what it was in him that kept fighting. I hated myself because I couldn't save him. Hell, I hated the whole damn world and everybody in it.

Finally Big Tree raised up a little bit, then crashed down like a great oak. The Sioux jumped from their ponies and stood over him, some of them still putting arrows into him. Then one of them got down and scalped him. It was White Dog. I recognized him by his red scarf and scowling face. I remembered that day Morning Breeze and me crouched in the rain and watched Big Tree riding into White Dog's band with my Evans repeater. Now he held Big Tree's scalp up like he'd triumphed over something grand, something monstrous. He yipped for all of them. It was the third time I'd seen him, and I known as I watched him wave Big Tree's scalp over his head and then climb back up on his horse that I was going to by God see him one more time in this life. He rode off with the others howling like a wild banshee. He raised Big Tree's Spencer high in the air. I watched him disappear to the east, still yipping and carrying on, all the others howling after him.

I waited until I was sure they was gone, and then I looked around for Morning Breeze. I think I was fairly desperate to find her, but she wasn't among all the bodies laying in the grass. They was Sioux braves, seven of them, and I calculated that White Dog would come back here with his women and the whole tribe to take up their dead. I had to get the hell out of there but I couldn't leave Big Tree in that field. I known the Sioux women would cut him all to pieces so he couldn't be a enemy in the afterlife, and I figured I owed him a decent burial, even if I couldn't put him up on a scaffold high off the ground the way his people done with their dead. He wore only his leggings, a loincloth, and a leather vest. His arms was bare. His black eyes, rimmed with blood and spent fury, seemed to look coldly at me, like he could curse me from the other side of this life. I counted sixteen arrows in him. I took out the ones I could remove, and broke off those in his trunk, legs, and arms that had hit bone. I worked steady without thinking of nothing except the next arrow to get. I worked fast, as though pulling the arrows out somehow eased his pain. When I was done, I hauled his huge frame back to my tent. I laid him down in the rain-soaked snow and commenced to digging a grave. I had no shovel, so I used my hunting knife. The ground was still fairly thawed from the rain, but it took most of the day to scratch out a ditch about a foot deep and three foot wide and seven foot long. I ain't never gonna forget the damp smell of that dirt. Twice while I was working I seen something over by where Big Tree was laying move in the corner of my eye and I turned quick and looked hard at him. I was damned sure he was dead, but still he seemed to move when I wasn't looking over that way. Like he might sneak back from death and jump on me. I started talking to him. I told him I was sorry and I wish I got there sooner. "I might of shot a few of them," I said. "I guess I never was too much good for you." I hated the way he looked a-laying over there on his back, those spent black eyes looking at nothing and the high sun gleaming in them, like in still water. "God damn it all to hell," I whispered. I am not ashamed to admit I found it hard to take. While I worked I kept hearing his voice in my mind saying "Wasichu" and "Death." Those might of been the first words I ever heard him say.

I don't know why it was such a shock, but I never dreamed a force as big and able as Big Tree could actually die. He seemed so permanent and all. Like a feature of life and earth.

When I had the ditch deep and wide enough, I rolled him up in one of my best buffalo robes and shoved him into it. I said I was sorry again, then piled the dirt and the sagebrush and snow on top of him. I stood over the scar in the white snow, the pile of dirt and branches and leaves, and said a few words of praise. I told him I admired him and I didn't mind that he took my woman. I said I was grateful for him teaching me how to live in this country.

When he was alive I never thanked him, never said nothing to him about it, but he did teach me most of everything I come to know outside what I learned from Theo. He was probably younger than me by a couple of years, but he was big and wise and kind of like a father to me for all he taught me. I had affection for him, and I always thought our paths would for sure cross again and we would not have the embarrassment of Morning Breeze between us.

I admit I was in a kind of state when she went to him. If I convinced him I didn't really care, and I didn't, then he'd see her as devalued and he might even be insulted. He might take it to mean he had won nothing from me. But if I pretended to be angry and jealous, he'd be done with me and I didn't want that, neither. I thought the safest thing to do was to go off on my own for a while. I never dreamed I'd have to bury him.

Pretty soon I wasn't thinking about the army, or Colonel Brisbin, or even Eveline. I felt tightly wound and something sharp burned and festered behind my eyes. I can't explain the feeling, the sharpness that come down behind my brow and occupied my brain like a hot and mechanical device. It wasn't nothing I wanted more than sweet revenge. I wanted to look down the barrel of my Evans repeater and shoot White Dog with all thirty-four rounds. I didn't want nothing else, by God.

CHAPTER 17

I PACKED EVERYTHING UP and rode back to Brisbin's camp. Two men serving as pickets was glad to see I wasn't no Indian. I thrown them the two rabbits I'd killed the day before, and went on to Brisbin's tent.

I told him about the Indians I seen. "White Dog seemed to be the one they was following," I said.

"Why didn't you go after them to see where they went?"

"They're a day on horse from here," I said. "I can find them."

"How many were with him?"

"I don't know. Maybe seven or eight."

"That's it?"

"It was a war party. There was more of them in the beginning, but when the killing was done, only seven or eight was left standing." I told him about Big Tree, but I didn't let on about how much I owed him or what kind of friends we was to each other. I just said I'd witnessed it and that he killed about half White Dog's number. "Unless it's a big war, the Sioux don't send too many on a raid."

"So it was maybe fifteen of them to start with. And you saw these people where?"

"Southeast of here. Near the east fork of the Powder River."

"Seven or eight of them got away."

"If they've got women and children with them, it may be twenty or so in the whole damn group."

"Well, we'll send a detachment to find them. And if it's a smaller group, the general wants me to negotiate with them first. He doesn't want any shooting until he's sure we've got Crazy Horse or Sitting Bull in the main party. So we'll talk first. You can take the lead on that."

"I don't speak the language. I never did learn it."

"I'll send somebody with you who can."

*   *   *

What I got for my translator was Daniel, the young trooper that was Jake's friend. I asked him what happened to Nate and he said his buck-toothed pal was back at Fort Ellis.

"He got a distemper of some kind. Had to put him in hospital."

"It wasn't that he couldn't drink or eat nothing, was it?"

"No. He was down with a infection in his nose. Couldn't breathe worth a damn."

I mentioned General Cooney's illness, but he said Nate was not going to die. "The doctor told him to rest and drink a lot of water, so that's what he's doing."

I decided not to tell Daniel nothing about Big Tree. I bided my time and focused on my hatred of White Dog. I think I may of been a bit like old Big Tree hisself, since I had nothing much to say as we rode along.

Daniel had got over his first battle, but I could see he had a few dreams to contend with. He looked much older and his hair was now snow white. He wasn't no more than thirty. This turned out to be a advantage, because when we got to the Sioux camp, they was all goggly-eyed to look at him. Without the packhorses we made fairly good time, so it took us only three quarters of a day sidling along at a pretty fast clip, with long rest periods for our horses along the way, before we found the Indian camp. It was nestled in a gulch by a small stream near the Powder River. There was maybe twenty-five lodges, and a huge passle of horses. We rode in from the east, with the wind in our faces, so not a single dog barked. We was suddenly there at the front edge of camp, letting our mounts take one slow step at a time into the center of the thing. It was cold even for that time in March. The wind wasn't strong but it was steady and never slowed for a instant.

I didn't see White Dog or any braves I recognized. We was greeted by a elderly gentleman named Little Knife. He was a Lakota Sioux. He wore no feathers, but he had a necklace made out of bear claws around his neck and a long tan leather coat with long fringe hanging from each sleeve and across the back. He wore a loincloth and leather breeches and beautifully decorated moccasins on his small feet. He was not tall, and seemed to of rode a horse all his life, because he was bowlegged. He spoke no English.

I sat on Cricket and watched Daniel and Little Knife talking. I couldn't tell from the way they sounded if what they said was making a difference to neither one nor the other. After a short conversation, Daniel looked at me. "Do you speak any of the Sioux language at all?"

"I picked up a little of Crow traveling with a friend, but I don't know nothing about the Sioux language."

"Well, he wants us to go back to Colonel Brisbin and tell him they won't talk to us. They want to meet with the white man chief."

"Who would that be?"

"I think he wants to talk to the chief of all white men. He's saying 'dahn kah' which means 'big' and 'wah shee chue lah ay kdah.' It's something about the white man, or the white man's province or world."

I nodded. But I didn't know. I said, "Big Tree always called the white men 'wasichu.' But that's Crow."

"No, I think most of them call us that now. But he said 'wah shee chue lah ay kdah.' It's that 'lah ay kdah' part I don't get."

He looked at Little Knife, then back at me. "I think it means 'world.' He also said, 'Wee chah yah dah pee.' "

"Wee chah yah dah pee," Little Knife repeated.

"That means chief," Daniel said. "He wants to speak to the chief of all the white men."

"Did you tell him there ain't none?"

"U. S. Grant'll fit that bill, I wager."

"He wants to have a powwow with General Grant."

"Not General Grant. President Grant. He's president of the United States now."

It was news to me who the president was. I hadn't read no newspaper in half a decade, and it was too far away from me and this place to matter much.

"What should I tell him," Daniel said.

Little Knife spoke. He said, "Wee chah yah dah pee, wa shee chue lah ay kdah."

"He can talk to General Gibbon, I guess."

"You think I should tell him Gibbon is chief of all white men?" Daniel asked.

"He ain't dumb because he don't speak American. Tell him the best we can do is the chief of all the white soldiers in this part of the country." While I was talking, Little Knife watched me closely. I had the feeling he had seen me before somewhere. Maybe he was one of the Indians Big Tree and me traded with over the years. The wind blew his long hair and made him squint a little, but he stood there as erect as a poplar. I wondered why we was having this powwow and we wasn't invited to sit down for a smoke. We never got off our mounts. Unlike most of the Indians I had dealt with over the years, this fellow made no gestures with his hands. He stood there looking up at us, high in our saddles, and it didn't seem to bother him that we was looking down on him from up there.

Daniel spoke a bit more, and Little Knife did not look away from me. His expression didn't change much, neither.

Daniel stopped talking and Little Knife nodded, finally meeting Daniel's eyes. There was a long silence. I heard some squaw back in the camp, singing or wailing like a dead soul. I looked back among the lodges for White Dog. I don't know what I would of done if I seen him. It was getting near the end of the day, and smoke swirled in the sky above the tepees as the squaws stoked dinner fires. I smelled crispy, broiled buffalo meat, in the wisps of white smoke, and my stomach commenced to growling.

Daniel made Little Knife understand that he could have a powwow with the chief of all the soldiers and they talked about that business between them. By the time they was done, a few of the braves had come back from hunting and crowded around to see the white man with the silver hair. I looked for White Dog, or for any of them wearing a red bandana, which told me they was originally with Red Top. They was all young and dark and silent as cats as they moved around us and stared with blazing black eyes. I felt like a field mouse trapped in a corncrib. Then I seen one of them moving among the people, talking in a low voice to the younger braves. Daniel didn't seem to notice him, but I never took my eyes off him. He was stirring things up, I could see that.

Little Knife finished what he had to say and raised his hand to Daniel, and he did the same.

"Start backing out of here," Daniel said. He was being very cautious, so I known he could hear some of what that rabble-rouser was saying.

I pulled back on Cricket, and she bowed her head at first, then made a loud shudder from her nose and bobbed her head up and down furiously, but she backed up like I wanted her to, one step at a time. Daniel's horse was so well trained, he hardly moved his head at all. He just took backward steps easy and slow, with no display of indignity or reluctance.

We got clear of the camp and turned our mounts and headed back toward the column. About halfway there, Daniel told me he was going on without me. "I want you to stay here and take good cover."

"I'll make sure they don't get off nowhere without us knowing it," I said.

"They won't be going anywhere," he said. "I've arranged a powwow."

I said nothing, and he stared off up the trail behind us for a spell. Then he said, "I didn't like what that one hothead was saying."

"I figured it wasn't no good."

"I don't think he wants to negotiate with anybody. He kept talking about 'white devils.' "

I said nothing. We both set there looking at the horizon.

"Well," I said finally. "What's next?"

"You better stay here, off the trail and out of sight. If you see Little Knife coming, you can just take your time getting back to the column. But if you spot any of them renegades striking out on their own, come a-running so we can send a detachment to meet them on good ground."

I saluted him, and he turned and went on. I rode up to the top of a little ridge, where there was a small stand of timber, and disappeared in amongst them. I set up camp on a fine bed of pine needles and waited to watch the trail for a while. It was still pretty cold, but I didn't think it was safe to build a fire or even set up the tent, so I hunkered down under a couple of thick buffalo robes and smoked my pipe. I was sure hungry. All I had was some dried venison. It was good enough to make my mouth water and my stomach howl for something else. It chewed like the billet strap on a saddle, and had as much flavor.

About a hour later, I seen them coming. They was a long way off, a small party. Six braves on horseback.

I got up slowly. I figured it had to be Little Knife and his folks coming to negotiate. It was such a small party, it couldn't be nothing else. It took me a while to get the robes put away and tied to the back of my saddle in the pack, but the whole time I worked, I watched them coming along. They was moving at a pretty good clip. I seen them go down in a bit of a gulch and disappear for a spell, but then they come back up out of it and they was even closer. Something happened to my heart when I seen White Dog, with that red cloth around his neck, riding along in the lead. The five other braves rode a little behind him, three to his right and two to his left. They made a formation like birds on the wing, with White Dog out front.

This was a damn war party, moving fast and with a purpose. I figured maybe they was headed to find me and Daniel and kill us if they could. What I done next come as a surprise to me. I known and felt the rage—Big Tree laying there with all that wood in him—and not just what he looked like but what it sounded like to break off them arrows I couldn't pull out. Every hour since, I dreamed of having White Dog in my sights. It seemed like my whole life up to that time—everything else I remembered—just went away. I wasn't no veteran of the War of the Rebellion, I wasn't a fur trapper or a mountain man, a scout for the U.S. Army, or even Eveline's man. It ain't possible to tell how empty everything in my mind was except for one thing. And I don't believe I was thinking at all for what happened next.

I tied Cricket to one of the trees and moved over to the edge of the timber where I could see better. I had my carbine, fully loaded. White Dog rode high on his horse, like every Indian I ever seen did. He looked like he was the top half of the horse. His horse seemed to prance.

I laid down on the ground at the top of the ridge, set the barrel of my carbine on the edge of a small boulder to steady it, aimed very carefully at the middle of White Dog's chest, and fired. He fell backward off his horse. The others scattered a bit until they seen my smoke and where the shot come from. I fired again and hit one of the others, then fired once more and got a horse. White Dog's horse run with his tail between his legs like a scared dog. I heard one of the braves a-yipping and hollering, and then I seen White Dog get up and try to get on one of the other horses. I shot that horse, then hit White Dog again. He fell down. Two of the braves was now charging up the hill. I let them come for a spell, then shot both of them as high in the chest as my sights would allow. White Dog was dead, one other brave was wounded and running around after his horse, and two others was on the ground in front of me, also dead. I seen the last two a-setting there, holding their horses steady and watching for me. One of them had a carbine, and he aimed it my way and fired. I didn't feel no wind nor nothing from it, so he missed a long way over my head. I shot him before he could fire another shot. He held on to his horse for a while as it run away, but then he fell off. The other helped the wounded fellow that was chasing his horse, and both of them disappeared behind a clump of trees on my side of the gulch.

It took me longer to tell of it than for it to happen.

I stayed where I was for a while, watching for the two braves that got away from me. They come into sight a little ways beyond where the others was. I seen the one run to catch his horse, which galloped in my direction. The fellow was behind the animal, so I couldn't get a clear shot. His horse come to a stop a few yards away from me and the brave come up from behind him and grabbed the tail. He swung up onto his mount, then turned and looked at me. I raised my rifle, and he just sat there, staring—like he was waiting for it. I could see he known who I was. His eyes registered the shock and it stopped me. I didn't fire at him. He rode over to where the other fellow was and I seen him point and say something. Then they galloped off back where they come from. I watched them go, noticed the little cloud of dust their horses raised as they disappeared into the gulch again and then come up on the other side and kept on getting smaller and smaller in the dull light. I waited a little longer just to make sure there wasn't no movement. Then I got up and, while there was still some sunlight, walked over to the two dead Indians who was laying in front of me. I didn't recognize the first one. I got him in the neck and he laid there staring up at the darkening sky, like he was searching for the first star. "I wish you didn't rush at me like that," I said. The other one was hit just below the right eye. That whole side of his face was a mess, but I seen it was Little Knife I killed. He had a white truce flag tied to the sash around his waist.

I squatted down next to his body. I couldn't believe it. White Dog was riding with them, but this was the peace party after all. And I known right then that I had to get out of that country. As far away as I could. I had done the one thing that made a man a total renegade and outcast: I'd attacked a peace party. Daniel known he left me here, and that Sioux brave recognized me, so now the army would be after me and so would every Indian. It didn't matter that it was a mistake or that I really believed those folks was intent on no good. It didn't matter what I thought at all. Now everybody would want to kill me.

I stood up walked down the hill to where White Dog's body lay twisted in the grass where he fell. I felt my head begin to spin a bit. The dizziness turned something in my heart that felt like a stab of fear, and to forestall it I started howling, high and loud, at the gray sky. I wailed and yipped like a Indian, staring up at the thickening stars and the rising moon.

When I couldn't yell no longer, I sat down again. A few birds flown overhead and I seen their shadows cross over the glistening stones that was once White Dog's eyes. I didn't know what I might do or where I'd go. Then I thought of Eveline. My Eveline. I couldn't go directly west. The whole army was a-coming that way. But I had to get back to her. She would understand. When I remembered her—when I seen her eyes in my memory—it like to made me cry. I ain't ashamed of it. I howled again, only this time I was shouting her name. I figured I'd go northeast toward the Missouri River, then turn west once I was well beyond the Yellowstone country. I intended to take Eveline out of that part of the world. I didn't know where I was going for sure; maybe all the way to Oregon.

I had to keep a eye out for folks in front of me or behind me or to either side. I had to steer clear of every living soul all the way back to Bozeman. It was me and Cricket and only the gear I had tied to the back of my saddle. I needed to kill something pretty quick so I could eat. The winter was dying, sure enough, and it would be spring before long.

I was north of the Yellowstone River, and well south of the Missouri. I rode most of the day in the wide country along the Yellowstone valley, looking all the time for any sign of human life. I looked for any kind of timber so I could ride in shadow and out of sight.

The whole time I was hunting for game. Near nightfall, with no luck and nothing to eat, I pitched my tent and made camp a few paces from the Yellowstone River, back among the trees and underbrush where I could tie Cricket and keep her out of sight. I hunched in the tent under the buffalo robes and slept with the moist night air dripping out of my hair and down my face. I did not hear a single thing except the murmuring water and the toads singing to beat all.

In the morning, going further up the trail, I seen a lot of smoke up ahead of me. I turned north, toward a high ridge that looked out over the whole country. Cricket climbed steadily up a rocky slope, and sometime during that climb she come up lame. I didn't notice it right away because near the top I got down on foot and she walked behind me. When I could see the broad land before me—when I could see as far as any human eye can ever see—I realized I had gone around one of the biggest encampments of Indians I ever seen. Maybe a hundred tepees, and smoke curling from every one of them.

I had no way of knowing if those fellows in the peace party who got away was in amongst them, so I couldn't trust my luck enough to let them see me. I watched them for a spell, then walked due north along the ridge with Cricket behind me. I known from what I seen on top of that ridge that I wasn't never going to find no stand of pines, and I'd have to eat nothing but bitterroot and dried venison for the next few days because I wasn't going to be firing no gun where any of them Indians could hear it. What's worse, Colonel Brisbin told me that Benteen was coming up from the south, and Custer was coming from the east into this country to meet up with Gibbon. I felt trapped. And all I wanted to do was get back to Eveline.

The ground started to break downward on the north side and I got up on Cricket and tried to sidle down onto more level ground.

That's when I noticed she was lame. I didn't say nothing out loud, but she could tell I was feeling like the unluckiest bastard in the world. She looked so ashamed of herself.

Near the bottom of the ridge I found a trail that headed due west, so I got on it and walked into a stiff breeze. I was walking that a way for two days, and then I run into Ink and shot her.

PART FOUR

Ink

1876

{ CHAPTER 18 }

WHEN I SHOT Ink she was scared to death, her heart beating like a drum. Now she's asleep and the sky is turning purple. Wind begins to move through the bushes and rocks. Cricket frets and turns around her tether, stamping and shuttering.

I take the opportunity to move Ink to the lee of the boulder, where she'll at least be able to keep her head dry. She don't even stir. It's like dragging a small stump across the ground. I push the saddle way back under the base of the stone, set the stirrup up so she can have something to rest her head on. The wind is strong enough now that trying to pitch the tent would be foolish. I check to be sure she ain't bleeding no more, then I scrunch up under the stone with her, holding the rifle across my lap. The pistol digs into my abdomen, but I leave it there so it will remain dry when the rain comes.

The wind whistles in the bushes and dry branches. Ink opens her eyes and looks at me with a fierce expression. I don't think she knows who I am just yet. Then she remembers.

"Did you shoot me?"

"Yeah, I did. I'm sorry about it."

"My stomach is on fire."

"It will be for a while," I say. "Pray that lasts a bit, because once it starts itching, you'll wish you had the pain again."

"Am I bleeding?"

"I just checked it. It's fine."

"I am hungry."

"Once this rain passes," I say, "I'll set us up for the night."

"You got food?"

I reach into my saddlebag stuffed next to the saddle and get her another piece of raw sowbelly. "Chew on this awhile. It'll settle the hunger some."

She gives me a look.

"You already eat what's left of yours. It's all I got now, unless you want some hardtack."

"I don't want more of this," she says. But she gnaws on it for a spell. Cold wind gusts in circles around us, then the rain starts. Big, heavy drops at first that raise little puffs of dust on the ground when they hit. But then it comes down like something poured from a railroad water tank, so hard you can't believe it's only drops of water. It falls like curtains, one wave after another, and before a minute passes, both Ink and me are soaked through. But it don't matter: it's cool rain that washes the air and makes you forget sweat and exhaustion.

The rain begins to form little streams and pools and it splashes around us. I move to cover the stock on my carbine. I think to bury it under my shirt, but that's sopping wet, so I end up laying it down behind the saddle. I have to move Ink's head and force her to expose more of herself to the rain.

"You don't care if I get wet," she says.

"It's cool rain. It will feel good and you could use the cleanup." I make some room for the rifle behind the saddle, then push it back again so she can put her head down. "That gun cost me near a month's wages, and it ain't no good to get it wet. Especially the metal parts."

I settle on the ground next to her with my head on my pack roll. She's on her back, but she's got her head turned my way, watching me.

I stare into her eyes for a while, see how long it will take her to look away. She lets it last just long enough, but then she looks up to the rock above her head. I close my eyes and try to drift off. It ain't easy with the rain. She makes a little sound in her throat and I say, "You all right?" I keep my eyes closed.

"I have to sleep."

"I guess we both do."

"If my husband finds us, he will kill you."

"I expect," I say. "Wouldn't be the first to try it."

She's quiet for a while, and I think that she must of fallen asleep finally; but when I open my eyes to look, she's staring at me again. "I am so cold," she says.

"Where'd you learn to speak American?" I say.

"I went to Catholic school in St. Louis until I was ten. And it is not 'American.' It is English."

"Ain't it the same thing?"

"I don't think it is."

"Well, look at you now. All the way out here, and the bride of a Indian. Ain't no need for English with them folks, is there?"

"I am cold," she says again.

"Well, Jesus," I say. I turn over and get a blanket out of my roll. "This here will be wet as hell in five minutes, and heavy too." It takes a little effort to get it out, but when I do, she reaches for it.

"Wait a minute," I say.

"Just put it up here, under my head," she says. "I don't want it to get wet."

I stuff it up behind her head so it's on top of the saddle and balled up around her head and face. She actually smiles at me. "That feels warm," she says.

"I'm glad of it. When the rain stops, you can use it to cover up and keep from freezing to death." I see her lower teeth chattering. "I'm sorry," I say. "By Jesus, I'm sorry."

She don't say nothing.

It's quiet for what seems like a long time, and when I look over at her she's got her eyes closed. The high cheekbones look bronze in the returning sunlight. Her eyebrows are dark and thick over her eyes. They stretch over her nose a bit and meet in the middle, but they're real thin there so you'd hardly notice it. Everything about her is dark. The eyes when they're open look fierce—like she's made up her mind to hurt you and is just about to launch whatever it is that will do it. Her thin pink lips curve a little downward in the middle, and she's got a small dent in her chin. She's right nice to look at.

Not that I'm interested. Except for my aunt in Pittsburgh, the women on the wagon train coming out here, and Morning Breeze—which don't really count, since she forsaken me and went with another—I don't have what you'd call wide experience with the opposite sex. I ain't talking about amorous time with women—I tried a few of the whores in Petersburg after the war; I mean I just never had much to do with women, ever, until I met Eveline. I intend to keep my promise and get back before June. I still got time to do it. I know Christine is a-telling Eveline right now that I ain't coming back. It's already almost April, and the closer I get to June, the more I worry about Eveline doing exactly what she said she would do: she will go on west with her sister and forget about me. She'll just assume I was lying when I said I'd come back, or I went and got myself killed. And she don't even know how much I come to feel about her.

The only worries I have about my new companion is she might slow me down. I still got lots of ground to cover between here and Fort Ellis. And I got to cover this ground when both Indians and white men probably want to find me and kill me. I don't tell Ink none of this, but I expect I'll have to take her with me. It won't matter what she wants— I got to get her to a safe place and leave her there. It's the only thing I can do to make up for putting a bullet through her.

So I decide we got to go straight north to get away from whoever is chasing her. I know we're at least four or five days south of the Missouri River, and if we keep heading north we'll run into it. I hate to be going sideways from where I want to go, but I don't see no other way. If I head further south, I run into many of rivers, big and small, and the Black Hills. There's lots of tribes down that way I'd like to avoid, not to mention the damned U.S. Army. If I go straight west, the way I was going when I run into Ink, we'll have her husband in our path. The only way we can go is north. Once we find the Missouri, I figure we can follow it along as it winds east. Fort Buford can't be too far from where we'll be when we get to the river. The fort is at the point where the Missouri turns directly south. I might lose a day or two, but not much more than that. I figure I can leave her there and make better time getting back to Bozeman. But right now she can't walk, and I think I might open her wounds again if I try and lift her into the saddle.

When the rain is completely stopped and we can see the sun, I leave her sleeping and carry my gear and everything a ways off the trail and set up camp near a small stream that runs down out of the hills on our left. The water is clear and moves fast over white stones. Where it falls down a little over the rocks it makes a trickling sound that relaxes me.

When I get back to her she's still sleeping, so I nudge her on the shoulder to wake her. She is groggy and can't fully open her eyes to the light.

"Come on," I say. "You done enough sleeping for a while."

"I thought you left me."

"I set up camp over that way," I say. I help her walk over there— it's only about a mile off the trail—but it's down a slight embankment, below the line of rocks, and there are plenty of pine trees and bushes to shelter us and keep folks from stumbling in where they ain't wanted. She's such a little bitty thing, when she's walking next to me I have to lean down pretty far just to keep my arm under hers so I can keep her up. She don't say nothing, but I figure she knows by now I ain't gonna hurt her. When she sees the water in that stream she is happy to drop to her knees and settle herself again up against my saddle. I get her a cup of the water right away and she gulps it down. Like she ain't had no water in days. I think she's pretty happy to see the tent too.

"I was afraid you ran off," she says.

"I left Cricket tied right there so you could see her. You should of known I wasn't going nowhere."

"I didn't see the horse."

"Yeah, well. I ain't going nowhere now but to fetch her. I'll be back as soon as I can."

I walk back to the trail and untie Cricket and we start toward the camp, working our way around as much of the underbrush as we can. I want to keep her on grass too. There's thick mud in places. Even the places where we have grass to walk on the ground is slippery, and she keeps favoring that right front leg. I'm afraid she'll slip and make it worse, so I take it real slow. She is wet and tired and damn hungry. There's plenty of grass at the camp, so when we get back I don't bother to tether her. I let her roam and eat what she needs. With no saddle or bridle, she looks as wild as any bronco you might see on the plains, except she's sleek and well-groomed. I wish she didn't come up lame, though.

I get a pot from my pack and fill it with water from the stream. Then I take the sack full of beans and pour some into it. Ink looks at me, wondering.

"I'm gonna make us some supper," I say.

"And build a fire?"

"When the time comes. These got to soak for a while."

She don't look too happy, but I know she's hungry. She's been tearing at more of that sowbelly—chewing like a wolf.

"I'll kill us something," I say. "We'll eat fresh meat. If I don't get nothing, I got the hardtack. Or we can cook the sowbelly if we have to."

"But if you build a fire . . ."

"I'll use buffalo chips if I can find some. If not, then dry wood, and we'll have it out before dark. Don't worry."

She starts to say something else and I raise my hand to stop her. "I been where most folks never go. I seen what most folks never seen. I fought in battles and, God help me, I hope I never see another one. I foraged and roamed the countryside like a wild animal with other wild animals. I know what I'm doing."

She says nothing. But them dark eyes freeze me.

"Don't look at me like that," I say.

"I lived with the Sioux for many years," she says. "I know how to make a smokeless fire. So I am not worried."

"Well, don't be." But she's still glaring at me like I got both hands wrapped around her throat and I'm squeezing as hard as I can. "Stop staring at me, all right?"

She turns toward the stream.

"You're safe here," I say. "Nobody will find you." I hand her the pistol. "I know it's heavy, but you hold on to this in case you need it."

She tries to lift it with both hands and it bends her wrists, but finally she gets the barrel end of it up so it's level. She's got it pointed at the tent.

"There ain't no safety on that thing," I say. "You pull that hammer back until it clicks, then you squeeze that trigger there." I point it out for her, help her see how she has to have her hands and where to put her finger when she wants to pull the trigger. "It's got a kick," I tell her. "So lean back against something before you shoot it."

The whole time she studies it, then looks at me with a kind of wonder in her expression; the fierceness is gone now. It's just like she's a child discovering something mysterious and grand in the world. I like the way it feels to teach her about it. "Like this," I say as gently as I can. "Straighten your arms when you want to fire it."

When she's ready I tell her to let it rest in her lap, or somewhere that she can reach it. "I don't expect you'll need it," I say. "But just in case."

"If my husband is looking for me, I will need it."

"We went a long way on wet grass," I say. "He won't be able to follow it once the sun dries it out a little and straightens it. Don't worry."

"That will not stop him."

I pick up the carbine and sling the strap over my shoulder.

"Where are you going?"

"Hunting," I say.

"You going after him?"

"Who?"

She gets that furious look in her eyes again.

"Your husband?"

She nods.

"Hell no. I want to stay as far away from him as I can. I'm gonna find something to eat that's a lot more tender than that 'ere hardtack or sowbelly."

I start to leave, but then I stop and turn back to her. "I won't be gone long. You'll see me well before dark. Don't shoot at me."

"I will not shoot you."

"It'd serve me right," I say. "But I'd rather you didn't."

"I said I will not."

I leave her there and move on up the stream a ways, then deeper into the trees and underbrush, still keeping the stream to my right. I know I can find my way back to her that way, but also I figure if I'm going to find something to shoot, it will be near water.

CHAPTER 19

A FELLOW SHOULDN'T HUNT when he's hungry. It's hard to sit still, and as long as you're moving, not much in the way of animal life is going to present itself to you. Eventually I sit down by a fallen tree near a bend in the stream. Water runs down under the far end of the tree and a thicket on the other bank looks promising. There's a worn place in there—almost a path—where the underbrush is trampled, so I expect it's been well used and will be used again. Whatever stomped on that brush was pretty big. I know I can't wait long, but I sit as still as I can and watch that worn place in the thicket. Listening to the water trickle under the end of the dead tree makes me sleepy. I drift off for a while.

Then I ain't nowhere. I try to lift my head, to open my eyes and move again, get up and walk on my two feet and move, but I can't. Then I see Eveline a-standing over me. She looks surprised to see me. "I told you I'd come back," I say. But she don't speak. I'm dreaming and I know it. It seems like hours, days, I struggle against this feeling of being trapped behind my eyes, but then I open them and realize the sun ain't moved very far. I see a bird rise up in the distance and again hear the water rushing under the tree. There ain't nothing to shoot at yet. It's just me and a few birds and the newly bright sky. If it wasn't for the speed of the water in the stream, you'd have to dig down through the matted grass and leaf meal into the dirt to figure out that it had rained.

I wonder a little. Think about things. I don't like dreams. It's the way the war always comes back to me. I seen so many men die right before my eyes. I heard a bullet thwack into the breast of a fellow only inches away from me. He was saying that when you pick corn, the third ear on any stalk gets a little crazy looking.

"The first ear is tender and just beautiful," he said. We was standing in a copse of trees in the wilderness near Spotsylvania Courthouse, waiting for orders to move. It was a battalion—about a hundred and twenty of us and this fellow was right up against my shoulder and he was telling me about the corn he'd pick on his daddy's farm in Illinois. "The second ear is pretty good too. Still very tender, but maybe a little smaller. Maybe a little less milky. The third ear—that's when you know the corn knows what is happening to its seed; it's trying to survive. The kernels get fat and irregular. It looks almost inedible, like it might be poison, or—" and then the bullet hit him. I don't think I heard the report of the gun until that thwacking noise the bullet made in his breastbone. He just fell down next to me and it was like the world exploded, like hell come up out of the ground and scattered in all directions. The line closed up and we all started firing as fast as we could. All the air around us popped and sizzled with bullets. The whole line wavered, men falling all around me; then we started backing up pretty fast, still firing. By that time we had Henry repeaters, but they only fired seven bullets before you had to reload. In the noise and the confusion and the smoke, a lot of men just dropped their weapons and started running, which was almost impossible in all that underbrush. It was like we was trapped in a eight-foot-high hedge. I knelt down by a thick, moss-coated tree and fired until my gun was hot to touch. I shot into smoke and noise. Reloaded as quick as I could. I don't have no idea if I hit nobody, but eventually the firing stopped and we pretty much held our position. The thickets burned from the firing of the guns and wounded men caught fire where they lay. The screams was terrible. I remember I kept chewing on a small twig I picked out of one of the bushes. Just chewing as hard as I could, my stomach about to collapse from sickness and nausea.

Even now the screams keep echoing in my skull, like something plastered on the inside of it, like my skull's got the sound in a kind of fabric that peels off the bone and covers my brain sometimes. I wondered how anybody could scream so long without taking in air. After a while you try to figure out what they're saying. They call for their mothers, for somebody to shoot them, for mercy. And God. They shriek for God. And then I remember some never made a sound.

*   *   *

Now I'm hoping a deer or a elk wanders close by soon. The day wears on. I feel the empty hole in my stomach. Ain't nothing but birds in this place, and I start to figure how much longer I can stay before I have to race the sun to get back. I don't want it to get dark: Ink'll shoot me if I startle her.

Finally, just before I make up my mind to give up, I see something moving across the stream in the thicket. It scurries under the brush, along its roots, but it's spotted and furry. I aim for the head, but then it turns to face me. I don't want to send a bullet straight down its windpipe; it'll ruin the meat. Eventually it turns a little to the side and I aim for the head and fire. It whirls around with the impact and then lies still. Before I get to my feet, I smell it and know what it is. A damned skunk.

I crawl a ways toward the stream, then get up and walk around to where I can step across it without getting my boots wet. The skunk is flat still under the low branches of a bush, so I take the butt of the rifle and scoot it toward the stream. If I get it good and wet, wash off the musk, it won't smell so bad. I've eaten them before, and they're just as tender and tasty as a rabbit or a squirrel, except they can have a lot more meat on them. It will be enough for both Ink and me. I figure if she's been with the Sioux she's eaten worse. Still, I won't tell her what it is. I gut it and strip the skin off it.

She must of heard the shot I fired, and I guess she'll be expecting me to come back fairly soon, so I cinch the skunk to my belt and scoot pretty quick along the stream. Then I hear another shot. It's from up where she should be waiting for me, so I start running. I try to keep low, and the branches of small trees and bushes lash across my face and in my eyes. The ground is covered with leaf meal and pine needles and damp grass, so I don't make as much noise as you might think, but I slow down and begin to creep as quietly as I can when I think I'm near the camp. I stop for a few seconds, trying to listen for what might be ahead. Ink ain't making a sound. I think I hear Cricket nicker a little, or it's another horse. It's getting on toward dusk, but the sun still clings to a few dark clouds on the horizon, like it don't want to drop down completely. I can't hear nothing. I move again, real quiet now, with my rifle in front of me, ready. When I finally get to where I can see the tent, I don't see Ink. I ain't going to just come blundering in now. I figure it might be easier to see what's going on if I circle around and come at it from higher ground. So I cross the stream and move around the camp a ways, then cross again and climb up the embankment to where I can look down on everything. I get on my belly, feel the skunk there, so I move it around my belt so it's behind me. I put the carbine against my shoulder and move as slow and quiet as I can to the edge. I look down and there's Ink, skinning a jackrabbit.

"Well, I'll be damned," I say.

She don't even look up. She says, "You finished fooling around up there?"

"I thought somebody got you."

"You made so much noise coming back, if somebody did, they would get you too."

I slide my way down the embankment and right into the camp. When I give her the carcass she says, "Skunk."

"It's good eating," I say.

"Some have said so."

"You ever had one?"

"No. And I will keep it that way."

"You'll eat it if you get hungry enough."

She's finished skinning and cleaning the rabbit. A jackrabbit has long legs and good thighs, but there ain't enough meat on that thing to feed even one person. You pick between thin bones for everything else you get off one of them things.

When she sees the breast meat and the good leg and thigh meat on the skunk, she looks at me. "You eat this and I will eat the rabbit."

"There's enough meat anyway," I say.

I make a fire out of dry dead wood laying around. It don't smoke too much. To be safe, I round up Cricket and tie her to a tree nearby. She'll make a sound if she hears any new sound or smells something she don't recognize. We eat pretty much without saying nothing. I eat the skunk meat and she eats what she can off the rabbit. The stewed beans taste hot and fine. We watch the sun finally drop out of sight and

I let the fire die down to nothing. It's colder than I thought it would be, but then I figure the fire warmed us so much, we ain't ready for cold night air.

I make sure Ink has a blanket, then I say, "We'll stay here tonight and tomorrow so you can rest. Then we'll start out again." I lay down next to her in the tent. A little later she says, "You sure came running when you heard me shoot."

I don't say nothing to that.

"I guess you did," she says.

"You still hurtin'?"

"A little. Mostly it burns."

"That means it's infected," I say. "That's my main worry now."

I feel her move a little, then take in air deeply and let it out.

"I better pour some more whiskey on it," I say. She says nothing, so I crawl out of the tent and get the whiskey and a candle out of my pack. When I crawl back in, she has raised her leather blouse, lifted the linen wrap, and is looking down at the wound.

In the faint moonlight it looks like somebody wrote on her stomach with black ink. "Just a minute," I say. I light the candle and tell her to hold it so I can see. Then I open the whiskey and take a sip of it. I feel its fire all the way down to my belly. "You want a sip?"

She shakes her head without looking at me.

The wound where the bullet went in is doing fine. It's tightly puckered and got enough dried blood caked there, it will make a nice scab. The other wound, I see, is fiery red around where I sewed it and beginning to ooze pus. "That's a good sign," I say. "You got a fight going on there." When I pour some of the whiskey on it, she grabs my shoulder with the other hand and squeezes pretty hard. You'd think a little bitty thing like her wouldn't be able to snap a match with those fingers, but it feels like she might of could broke my shoulder if she squeezed just a little bit harder.

She puts her head down and takes in air, then holds it. I know it really hurts.

"That'll clean it," I say. "It will fight the infection too. Just like your body's trying to."

She puts her shirt down over it and lays down on her back. I put the blanket over her, lay back down, and blow out the candle.

"You sure did come running," she says.

In the morning I say, "So, what's your husband's name?"

"Hump."

"I heard a him."

"He is Sioux. Miniconjou. And he will kill you if he finds us."

"Guess we better not be traveling in the day, then."

We chew some of the hardtack, sitting by the tent. It's not a bad morning. I stayed just outside the tent, awake most of the night listening for any sound. I seen the whole voyage of the moon across the sky, wondered at the faint light of its passage and the soft wind in the leaves around us. When I got out of the army, I thought I'd never have to be that awake again. Some folks never know what it's like to lay like a predatory animal with all your senses so fired up, you feel like a fuse burning, like something that can strike faster than a shooting star and reach just as far. My eyes ached from the concentration.

"You set for a spell and watch," I say. "I have to shut my eyes awhile."

She nods and I crawl back into the tent.

I didn't think I was sleeping, but then Ink shoves my shoulder to wake me. "Stop it," she says.

"Stop what?"

"You were screaming."

I sit up on my elbows. Outside the tent I see Cricket eating grass by the stream. "What was I saying?"

"I could not determine it."

"I guess it was loud, though. Sometimes I dream about the war."

"Very loud."

She sits next to me, just inside the tent. She holds her hand over her abdomen.

"Let me see it," I say.

She lifts her shirt and I move the bandage to where I can see the wound in the sunlight. Her whole belly is swollen, and pus still oozes around the stitches. "Can you ride, do you think?"

At first she shakes her head. Her eyes fix me good. "We can wait another day," I say. "But I don't want to. That looks bad."

"If you can get me on the horse," she says.

"The horse is lame. Walking with that limp'll be awful bumpy."

She gets to her feet. "Let me look at it."

"I've studied the thing," I say. "It's something in the fetlock, or maybe a thin break in the cannon bone. Ain't nothing you can do."

"I want to look at it."

She walks toward Cricket and I follow her. The horse raises up a little when she gets up next to her. "Easy," she says. She knows what she is doing. She reaches down and lifts the front leg, then tilts the hoof up so she can see the bottom of it. She takes that hunting knife out of her belt and starts picking at something on the outer edge of the hoof. Cricket don't move.

"You're going to pull your stitches out," I say. "I tried that. The hoof's fine."

"Look at this," she says.

"What?"

She holds the tip of the knife up and there's a spiny piece of what looks like yellow bone on the end of it. It looks kind of sticky, and I know right away what it is. "Buffalo bur," I say. "I looked for that and couldn't find none."

"It was way up in between the hoof and the sole. It's bad medicine."

"Now you're talking like a Indian."

"There's more of it here." She starts back at it, more carefully now. She digs a little too far in against the side of the hoof and Cricket pulls away. I can see it really hurts Ink. She drops to her knees, doubled over.

Cricket moves toward the stream, still limping.

I kneel down next to Ink. "You all right?"

She sits back on her haunches and I can see the wound is bleeding again. She looks down at herself, then touches her shirt where the blood soaks through.

"That's probably a good thing," I say. "It will clean it out. But I should check the stitches."

Sure enough, the stitches have come loose on the bad end of the wound and blood seeps through the opening. It don't smell bad, and I think that is a real good sign. "I could probably put another stitch or two in there, but you know it ain't bleeding real bad."

"Leave it," she says.

"Let me tie a fresh bandage around you." I go to my pack and get the rest of my linen shirt. The sleeves, I realize, make a better bandage, so I use one and put the other one away for later. I don't tie it too tight. Then I round up Cricket and try to finish what Ink started. The bur is in pretty far between the hoof itself and the soft skin under it. There's another small spine in the frog at the back of the hoof. No wonder Cricket was limping. I dig it out gently with the knife. Then I dig a little more between the hoof wall and the sole. Cricket don't like it, but I get all of the thing out.

"Don't touch it," Ink says. "That is just as bad for you in your hand as it would be stuck into your skin."

"I didn't touch it."

"Take her down to the stream now and let her walk around in it."

"You don't have to tell me," I say. I let Cricket walk around in the water a bit. She is still limping, but now it ain't so bad. When we get back to the camp, Ink is laying down again, partway in the tent, to keep the sun out of her eyes.

"You okay?"

"How long was the horse limping?"

"A few days, maybe."

"The longer that bur stays in, the more damage it does. It can kill her."

"I know it."

"It is bad medicine."

"Well, she ain't limping so bad now."

She rises. "I will help you pack up."

"We'll wait until evening," I say. "Dusk. It's hard for most folks to see in the twilight and I don't want nobody to see us on the trail."

"We can't see anybody, either."

"I can," I say. "I can see at night better than a bat."

I leave her sitting by the tent and walk downstream to wash and take care of my morning business. When I come back, she's squatting in the stream herself, just below the camp. I don't want her to know I seen her, so I stop and crouch down, stare at the ground in front of me until she's done.

When I get back to the camp later she says, "Thank you."

"For what?"

"For not staring at me when I was making water in the stream."

I shake my head. "You sure are a Indian," I say. "I don't think your husband will be sneaking up on us."

"He is like a ghost."

"Folks used to say I could be pretty quiet."

"You make noise like a careless bear."

I look at her close to see if she's serious. "I can be just as quiet as a cat."

"Compared to Hump, a cat makes a lot of noise."

"Well, you let me know if you hear something. Maybe you should of stayed awake all night listening to the breathing of all the insects."

"I did stay awake. I listened with you the whole time."

"The hell you did. You inhaled and exhaled so loudly, I had to focus between each breath to hear."

She says nothing. I can see she don't think much of me, or that I can protect her. When I try to get the pistol back, she holds it against her chest and looks at me now with them dark eyes.

"You can keep it," I say. "If you can kill a jackrabbit with it, I reckon you can point it in the right direction and shoot."

This makes her happy. I let her sleep awhile and later in the afternoon we pack everything up and get ready to go.

"I figure we'll go straight back to the trail, then head north to the Missouri," I tell her. "We'll follow it east until we get to Fort Buford. It'll be safe to drop you there—nobody will know who I am—and if I'm lucky, I might stumble on a wagon train going back west to Bozeman."

It is almost impossible to get Ink up on Cricket without causing both of them pain. Cricket's leg is better but she holds it up off the ground, and when I lift Ink under her arms and try to throw her over the saddle without hitting her stomach on it, Cricket turns her head and looks at me like I must be crazy.

"Sorry, old girl," I say. I know she don't feel nothing more heavy than we do when a fly lands on our back.

Ink sets absolutely still, her fierce eyes staring at the ground in front of us, and I know she is quietly bearing great pain. "Okay," she says. "I am ready."

"I'll have to take it slow anyway," I say. "Cricket's hurtin' too."

I got my carbine slung over my shoulder, and Ink carries the pistol in a holster I tied to the saddle horn in front of her. She can reach for it and be ready to fire it pretty easy. What I want to do, though, is avoid seeing any folks at all.

We go for most of the night. Cricket don't limp as bad as before, but the ride is just awful for Ink. I walk alongside and try to keep to soft ground, but it's mostly stones and hard stubble where we're headed, hills we got to climb, and small ravines and gullies that get in the way and would be too far to go around.

Several times we have to stop so Ink can piss. I think she's glad we're traveling at night. When the sky turns pink in front of us, I start looking for flat ground near a stream. I don't want to be out in the open during the day, so I move us off the trail and we start down a long, sloping hill toward a stand of trees and what looks like a broad, level meadow. I don't see no water, but we've got both canteens full, and I don't want to keep going no longer.

"We'll stop down here," I say.

Ink leans forward in the saddle like she's sleeping. Her head droops a little and I know she's almost passed out if she ain't sleeping. When we get to the bottom of the hill, she wraps her arms around my neck and I haul her down off of Cricket.

"It'll be full daylight soon," I say.

"I'm very hungry."

"I know." Except for them bits of hardtack that we shared last night, neither of us eat nothing since the skunk and the rabbit, and that's almost nine hours. "When there's a little more daylight, I'll make a fire."

We didn't see no one along the trail, but lately I've had the feeling something is watching us. A couple of times during the long night, I noticed Cricket turn her head a little to the side and perk up her ears. So I decide not to set up the tent. I tie Cricket to a tree where there's plenty of grass, and then take down my pack roll and carry it back to where Ink lays on the ground. She don't say nothing. I unroll the pack and get a blanket for her and tell her to try and sleep. "I'll wake you when I got something to eat," I say.

"I think he is near," she says.

"Hump?"

"I think he is following us."

"You hear him?"

"No." She takes a deep breath, lets out a blast of foul-smelling air. "No, but I can feel him."

"Yeah, I got the same feeling. I think we're both just a bit nervous."

"I thought I saw your horse mark something."

"I seen it too."

"Hump will not make any noise at all," she says.

"I'm ready," I say. "Try and get some sleep."

The trees around us are high and almost full, and the sun makes long shafts of light and shadow through the branches and new leaves. It looks like one of them tall-windowed churches the way the light comes down through the trees. There is almost no breeze and I know it will be a warm day. A mist covers the ground so it looks like we're in the clouds—like we walked all night until we got to heaven—except we come a long way down a hill to get here. The air is moist and smells like horse sweat and wheatgrass. I think there must be water some-where nearby. I don't want to leave Ink by herself, though. I don't even think I will hunt any distance away from her. If Hump is around here, I don't want to run into him by myself.

The mist rises around mid-morning and I think it's safe enough to walk around and gather up windblown wood—dry branches and twigs that been on the ground a long time. I don't find no buffalo chips. I set the wood in the sun to dry out from the mist. I got Ink laying on a blanket with my pack roll under her head, just under the low branches of a big tree, out of the sunlight. She's got a fever now, and when I look at the wound again, I see a black line about as thick as a finger running away from the wound and up her abdomen. I don't like it at all. I've seen it before in a limb or two and it means that much flesh is dying and turning to gangrene poison. I have to lance it—cut the skin with a hot knife and get the poison out of there or she will die. I wish I had some maggots I could stuff into the wound.

I'm going to need something dead around here soon or I'll just have to cut on her. I really don't want to do that.

I take the driest wood from the pile and build a small fire so I can boil some beans. She don't move a bit the whole time. I set right at her feet and watch the fire and every place that I can see around us. I'm concentrating on sounds and movement. I never stop turning my head, even to look behind me. I wish now I had found a high bluff or cliff to camp up against; that way I wouldn't have to worry about my back. But I'm here now, got her laid out, and made the fire—I don't want to move. The wood's dry enough that the fire don't make a lot of smoke, just thin wisps that are almost clear the moment it leaves the heat of the fire. It's only wavy lines of heated air by the time it gets higher than a foot or two. If a body was to see that smoke, they'd have to be standing somewhere I can see them.

After a while I go ahead and heat some water and beans for her and then feed it to her.

She has a bit of the hardtack and some more of the sowbelly. I don't want her to eat too much of the bacon because it will make her thirsty. When she's done eating, I take up a position right next to her head and watch all the horizon I can get my eyes to scan.

The day wears on, warm and still. She starts to thrash a little. The sun creeps over her and I have to get up and pull her further under the trees. Her fever seems worse. I lay her down and then lift her shirt to look at the bandage. It's stopped bleeding again. I'm afraid to lift the bandage because blood may have dried on it and if I move it I might pull the wound open again. The black line on her abdomen looks a little thicker.

She opens her eyes and looks at me. "I don't feel so good."

"I think you got infection."

"It hurts."

"I may have to cut you," I say.

"I need water."

I get her one of the canteens and she holds it to her lips with trembling hands and drinks from it as though it's the last water she'll ever have. "Go easy," I say. I'll need a lot of water if I'm going to cut her and I don't think I can go looking for a stream.

She still holds the canteen, but now she's staring at me, listening. "You hear that?"

I pick up the carbine and kneel back down next to her. She scans the horizon around us. I think I can hear her heart beating. We set that way for what seems like a long time, but nothing happens. She finally puts her head back down and closes her eyes.

I check to be sure the carbine is fully loaded, then I get the pistol and lay it down next to her. "The pistol's right here," I say.

She opens her eyes again. "Where are you going?"

"I'm just going to scout around a bit. The day's almost over. It'll be dark in a couple of hours, and I want to get back on the trail pretty soon."

"I am hungry," she says.

"You can't be."

She looks away.

"Want some more of the beans?"

"No."

"You can't have the sowbelly."

"I don't want anything."

"I'm real sorry I shot you," I say.

"I wish you would just quit saying that." She turns herself a little further away from me, her eyes closed again.

I make a few circles around our little camp, each one further and further away from her. I don't see a thing moving, and I cover enough ground that I begin to feel like whatever we been hearing or sensing, it ain't Hump.

Except for a few birds, I don't even see a rabbit or a groundhog. I ain't hunting for something to shoot, but I wouldn't mind it none. I hate this feeling that I'm trapped in a space so big. I circle back to the camp and find Ink sitting up, holding on to herself.

"It burns like fire," she says.

"I got to cut you there," I say.

She gets this look of horror on her face and I have this feeling that she is prey and I'm here to finish her, but she don't say nothing. She can see it's got to be done.

"There ain't nothing for it," I say.

She lays back down and I take her hunting knife and start heating it over the fire. "You can't scream nor nothing," I tell her. "You want some whiskey?"

She don't make a move. Her eyes close again.

"By God, I'm sorry for it," I say. While the knife heats in the fire, I lift her shirt and then remove the bandage. The wound is as red as the wood in the fire, and it's oozing pus again. But I'm more interested in the black finger line that's growing up her belly. When the knife is hot enough, I sit across her hips to hold her down and cut real shallow, along the line of it, making as straight a cut as I can, then I use the knife to pry the skin open a little. She squirms to beat all. She bangs her fists into the ground but she don't try to stop me. The knife sears the skin all around and inside the wound, and it stinks pretty awful, but I keep at it, moving it around, reheating it some more and then moving it all in the slice I've made until the whole thing is a hell of a mess. But it's red now with blood, and blackened a bit from the hot knife, and I can see the infection is just under the skin. It is not in the muscle. When I'm pretty sure I've burned it enough, I cover it with another piece of clean linen. This time I pour whiskey on the bandage so it soaks into the wound. I don't do no sewing, neither. I tie the bandage tight around her.

"I hope that does it," I say. "I don't have no more shirt left."

The whole time I was cutting on her, she didn't make a sound. I watched her breathing and seen her heaving with the pain, felt her writhe under me, but in the end she just laid there and let it happen.

"You did that pretty wonderful," I say when it's all over. "I don't think I could take that kind of pain."

She don't look at me. She's still breathing like she just run for miles. Tears stream down the side of her face. If she ain't a full-blooded Indian, she's one hell of a half-breed. Dark as pitch, and strong and stubborn as a coyote.

I sure don't want her to suffer no more. It's like we're the last two people on earth, and I'm working like hell to keep it that way. At first all I wanted to do was get her to a place where I could leave her and she'd be okay. I owed that to her. But right now, after watching her while I carved up the better part of half her abdomen and she don't even whimper a little bit, it seems like we might end up owing each other something more than a happy farewell when it comes right down to it.

CHAPTER 20

INK'S BEEN ASLEEP about a hour or so now. I watch the sun fall out of the sky and think about how to get her up on a horse. It will be dark soon and we have to keep moving. After I cut on her I give her a little bit to eat and plenty of water. I think her fever is better, but I'm worried about how I'm going to get her up on Cricket. I want to ride all night. I can pretty much go right at the North Star. If Hump really is trailing her, we'd be walking right at him if we headed west even a little bit, but I have to do that to get back to the trail. I figure we'll cross the trail just about the time the moon rises on the horizon, and then I'll just follow it across the sky, staying out of the way of folks I might see. I'll keep my eyes wide open and walk in front of Cricket so I can see both ways.

I really can see in the dark. Everything looks bright to me—black and white—but bright anyway. Starlight is as good as moonlight to me. Even on a moonless, cloudy night, I can see better than most.

When the sun's final gleam sinks below the horizon, I feel the air getting colder. The rain brought clear, windless, cool air, and at night we're going to need to keep warm, so it's a good thing we'll be moving. I gently wake Ink. "We got to get going," I say. I help her up on her feet, then stand there looking into her eyes. "I think your fever's gone."

"I am thirsty again."

I give her the canteen. "We're going west, back to the trail," I say. "Do you remember what I told you about where we're going?"

She nods, but I can see she don't really know what I'm talking about. "When we get back to the trail, we're heading north, through the valley to the Missouri."

"It is not too dangerous?"

"It's the safest way to go."

"What happens when we get to the river?"

"I told you: we'll stay alongside of it, heading east until we get to Fort Buford."

I go over and get Cricket all packed up and then I hoist Ink up on her. It takes some doing. I lift her under her arms and she throws her legs up as best she can. I know the pain almost crushes the air out of her, but we get her situated.

"Where will you go then?" she says.

"I got to get back to Bozeman before June," I say. "So we have to move pretty steady and get where we're going."

She wants to know why it's so important for me to get back before June, so I tell her about Eveline.

"You are betrothed," she says. "And your woman will not wait for you?"

"Hell, I don't know," I say. "I just know I promised I'd be back there in June, and I don't want to lose her just because of all this business here."

She lets her head slump down a bit.

"I guess if that's what betrothment is, then I'm betrothed. So you're running away from your husband, and I'm trying to get back to a future wife."

"I am sorry to be a burden."

"You ain't no burden," I say. "To tell the truth, after what I seen you can take, I admire you. It ain't nothing to take you to Buford. I owe you that much. It ain't far once we get to the Missouri. Then I'll be on my way."

"I don't know about Buford now," she says. "When I was alone I wanted that. I know my father is not there."

"Well, that's where we're going. And then you'll be safe."

She studies the blood that's dried on her moccasins. I hand her the pistol again in its holster and attach it to the saddle horn in front of her so she can reach it. I don't know why, but her silent expectations make me kind of sad.

We move along pretty fast, traveling only at night. Within a week I know we are getting closer to the Missouri River. I think I can smell the grassland that drops down into the river valley. I'm still on foot, going as fast as I can walk. It ain't much of a trail going north, but we find our way in the dark. Cricket's still limping a bit, but she can clop along now without trying not to use her one foot. This part of the country is full of wide meadows and broad green pine forests. It rises and falls as we go along. We can see for miles in the starlight.

One night early in our second week, I see the sloping hills that lead to the long descent to the river valley. "We're getting close," I say. "Maybe a day or two more and we should be there—at the river anyway."

Ink says nothing.

About halfway through the night we come upon a herd of elk. I want so bad to shoot one of them.

"Are you sure Hump is after you?" I say.

Ink jumps awake. "What did you say?"

"Sorry," I say. "I didn't know you was sleeping."

"I was not sleeping."

"Well, maybe if you tried to look more awake, I'd believe that."

She don't say nothing. We start climbing a gentle slope. To our left is a great expanse of pine trees, and I worry about what might be in there watching us.

"We'll have plenty to eat tomorrow if I shoot one a them elk," I say.

"What if Hump is in those trees over there?"

"How'd he know we was a coming this way? How'd he get ahead of us? It ain't Hump I'm worried about in them trees."

We pass the elk. They stand there, gathered in the darkness like one beast, eating and watching us as we go by. Just looking at them makes me think of cooked meat and beer sloshing in a pail. I say, "What if he *is* in them trees. Why don't he just come out and kill me? Take you back?"

"You do not know him. You won't see him until he is ready."

"Well, what the hell, then. I ought to go on back and shoot me one of them elks." But I keep walking along in front of her, holding Cricket's reins. "What is he? A ghost?"

"He will want to kill you slow," she says.

"What would he do if I set you down right here and let him come take you back?"

"You are a wasichu," she says. "He'll want to kill you."

"Damn," I say. "What a place."

We go up the slope without saying no more. I listen to Cricket's hooves trampling dry grass and clip-clopping on the hard ground like it was cobblestone. It's the only sound in the still air. When the moon rises above the black trees to our left, I realize I can see my breath. We start down a long winding trail through dense trees into the valley. In the forest, on deep layers of pine needles, we don't make a sound. We go slow now so I can be sure what's around us. The moon is fractured and dances behind pine boughs. I don't know if I ever been in a forest so empty of noise. Then a owl lets out a screech that like to empty my bowels. Ink starts laughing, fighting against the noise.

"What?" I say.

"You jumped high."

I don't like her laughing. I think she shoulda kept that to herself, but I don't say nothing. She's tough, and she can speak English better than me, and even so, I think now maybe when we get to Fort Buford I'll be kind of sad to leave her there. But then I tell myself I don't need no judgment going with me everywhere I go.

The owl screeches again. I want to get out of these trees. Then up ahead I see something glowing. I stop, hold Cricket's head still and watch. Ink sees it too. "That's a campfire," I say.

The thing about this country out here is that you never know when you're going to have to go into battle. I roamed around enough to know anybody might want to kill you. Even folks that ain't in the fix I'm in got to be wary of strangers. It's one big, everlasting war—and the range of battles runs from man to man, all the way up to whole armies. The tribes want the wasichus to get out. The wasichus want to stay. The tribes want to ride and hunt wherever they please, and the wasichus want them to stay put. I met a guy at Fort Riley who called it "the War of the Northern Plains." I thought I was free and done with war, and I end up in the most spacious war of all. And in country like this, you don't know who your enemy might be. There ain't no real order except, if you can, you got to survive. And when you're in my kind of trouble you take no chances: you got to shoot first. It's that goddamn simple.

So I tie Cricket to a tree and lay Ink down in a little clearing with a soft pine needle floor. I leave her the pistol. Neither of us says a thing.

I cock the carbine so it's ready to fire, then start through the brush toward the glow in the distance. It seems far off, but as I creep toward it, the movement of the fire starts to make the shadows dance. It's closer than I thought. I move *real* slow now—I don't want to spook their animals if they've got them. I'm so keenly aware of everything around me, it feels like air is leaking from behind my eyes. If there ain't too many of them I'm gonna shoot them all. I ain't taking no chances.

Then I hear the owl again, only it ain't no owl. It's a man, and when I get close enough to their campfire, I see why he's screaming.

{ CHAPTER 21 }

I T'S THREE BRAVES. I think they might be Piegans or Flatheads. They got a Crow brave tied to the stump of a small pine tree. He's sitting down with his legs splayed out in front of him and he's naked. The three braves move around him like cats stalking a field mouse. They stop and start, crouch down, knives in their hands. In the firelight it looks like they are ghosts, dark shadows rising and falling out of the ground. The rope that binds the Crow brave is wrapped around his elbows and behind his back so that his forearms are free. He breathes really hard, his chest heaving, his abdomen sucking in and out. Then one of his captors moves down at him, lifts his forearm, and I see he's already missing all but two fingers on his hand. He stares up at the shadow, and waits. His face is contorted but only in the struggle for air, until the shadow slices off another finger. His scream goes through me like some sort of icy blast of fear. I don't know if I ever heard nothing so horrible, not even during the war. I heard men scream whose bowels was spread out in their laps, who was burning in a field that caught fire from all the shooting, and nobody made a noise like that poor Crow brave tied to that tree. And then I realize that his screaming ain't only from pain. Hell, it may not be from pain at all. It's from his warrior soul. A way of honoring his captors and showing his manhood. He stops just as suddenly as he started, then even in all his gasping for air, he closes his mouth, juts out his chin, and seems to say with his eyes, *Go ahead. Do it again.*

And I think, *My Lord, these folks are crazy.*

The dance continues in the firelight. I wait a while, waiting to see if there's any more of them to contend with. I watch this fellow lose the last one of his fingers and then one of his toes. Each time he lets out that scream and then stares back in defiance. He is making what the Crow call a "strong passing." I know I should just leave it, but I seen this kind of thing before, and now I ain't about to let it go on. When I am sure it's only them three, I kneel down real slow behind the trunk of a fallen tree and shoot the one closest to me. He drops into the fire, and the others whoop and scatter. I shoot the second one before he can get too far from the firelight, then turn and see that the third one is trying to get to the horses. I wait until I can get a good, clean shot at him. When he jumps up on one of the horses, I see his whole body like something painted on the night sky. He's only twenty yards or so to my left, and when he starts to turn his horse away from me, I shoot him in the middle and he drops to the ground.

The Crow tied to the tree sets there looking at me, waiting for his. I kick the one I shot first out of the fire. He's burning and it smells awful, but I leave him there smoldering. I look into the eyes of the Crow brave. "You speak English?"

He just stares at me. A lot of Crows can speak English, but the fact that this one can't don't make me think I'm dealing with any other kind of Indian. You can usually tell the difference between Indian tribes by the way they dress, but a Crow is defined for that near-perfect form. And they know they're perfect. They carry themselves proudly and wear their hair in a high pompadour in front to accent their height.

"English," I say. I know he's got a voice.

I sign to him, pointing to my mouth. "Speak?" I say.

He says, "Hin nay xaw eematchaw chik." His black hair is soaked from sweat, and his deep-set eyes glare at me as though I just come up out of the fire. "Hin nay."

"I don't know what you want."

"Xaw eem atchaw chik," he says. "Ischee lak, ihchee lak bakaalah."

I can't figure out what he wants. I sign that to him.

I walk over to the second one I shot. He's a Piegan Blackfoot. I got him in the side of the head, almost right through his ear. He's still got the knife in his hand. I pry it from his fingers, then walk over to the one by the horses. He's laying on his back, still alive, breathing fast, so I put the knife into him, just under the breastbone, and wait until the breathing stops.

The Crow brave sits there staring at his fingerless hands, then he looks up at me and I think I can tell what he wants. He ain't said no more. All I've heard from him is words I don't know and those screams, but now his eyes gleaming in the dying firelight tell me his whole future. I motion for him to put his head down. "I don't want you to see it coming," I say. But he don't understand me. He is so fiercely a man. He will face whatever might come, but I can't act under the light of them eyes. He says again, "Ischee lak, ihchee lak huhkaalah." He points to the dead one still smoldering by the fire. I think "huhkaalah" means "give me."

"I don't understand you." I say. I can't remember one single Crow sentence I ever learned. He gestures with those fingerless hands, holds them up for me to see, then points as best he can to the first fellow I shot. The look on his face implores me. He holds his hands up again, lets them hang limply, then gestures toward the body. "Ischee lak, ihchee lak huhkaalah." I wish I spoke his language. He is magnificent and I hate it that I can't do what he's asking me. I go to the body and lift one of its arms, and the Crow brave nods vigorously. He thinks I know what he's saying. He looks down at the ropes tying him, struggles to break free. I take the hunting knife and cut the ropes, and he moves on the ground, scooting on his haunches, bracing himself with bleeding hands, over to the body. He slides his lower arm under one of the arms and lifts it until it is out away from the body. Then he puts his palm on the fingers of the dead Indian and looks up at me. "Hinne beewiawaak," he says. He makes a cutting motion across the dead fingers with his hand. I kneel down and look into his eyes. I pick up the dead hand and point to the fingers. "This?" I say. He nods, relieved. I know what he wants. He crawls back to the tree and sits back against it. I kneel down and cut the fingers off the dead body. I do this to both hands. It's ghastly. The worst thing I ever done. When I place them in his lap, the Crow raises his foot and looks at me. "I ain't cutting off nobody's toes," I say. He will not look away from me and he don't know what I said. He's just waiting there for me to do what he wants. "All right," I say. "God damn it. All right." I go back to the body and cut off the toes. It takes me a few minutes to get through the joints. Twice I lean out of the light and puke into the bushes. When it's finally done, I put the toes on the ground next to the Crow brave.

"Beech-i-lack," he says.

"Don't mention it."

"Hilaake kammaashbimmaachik."

"I know 'Beech-i-lack,' " I say. "You're welcome."

"Hilaake kammaashbimmaachik."

"I don't know what else you want," I say.

He looks directly into my eyes and then I do know what he wants. I remember that 'bimmaachik' means to die. "I can't do it with you looking at me like that," I say. His face is blank. He is not afraid, not sad. I don't even think he's in pain no more. I take some beads off a necklace on the body and place them in the Crow brave's lap. He looks down at them, and I shoot him through the top of his skull. The shot lights his hair on fire and he twitches and writhes for a bit, then stops moving. Even with all the blood, his hair keeps burning. I take a scarf off the dead fellow that fell in the fire and swat at the flames in the Crow brave's hair and it finally goes out. White smoke curls up from his dangling head and I can't stand nothing no more. I'm sick knowing I will remember this forever.

When I get back to Ink, with four horses, another pistol, three hunting knives, and a bow with a quiver full of arrows, she looks at me with a kind of wonder.

"That wasn't no owl," I say. "It wasn't Hump, neither."

She just stares at me.

"I got you a pony you can ride that ain't limping."

Only one of the horses has a saddle on him, and it's a Indian saddle, but it don't matter. Ink's been a Indian for a long time, so she knows what to do. I take my gear and the pack off Cricket and load it on one of the other horses. I put my saddle on the biggest one—I wouldn't be surprised if this one isn't the one that belonged to the Crow brave. Crows need big horses. This one has had a white man's saddle on it before, which I might of guessed. The gullet don't fit like it should and I know I'm going to rub this nag's spine raw before long, but it's the best I can do for him.

When we're all set, the moon has commenced to sink to the horizon. "We're gonna stay clear of them woods," I say. So we turn a little to the left and head for a open meadow that rises steadily above the tree line. We're still headed north, but we're tilting to the east a little too. With both of us riding now, we make a little better time. Cricket brings up the rear, carrying nothing. She don't limp now hardly at all, since she ain't carrying no weight. A few times I pick it up a bit and get all of us galloping some, but then Ink points to the dust we're raising. Even in the dark it looms in the falling moonlight, so I slow down to a walk again. We go like that until the moon is gone and it's only starlight. We cross several streams, where the horses drink, and I fill the canteens; then we start out again, climbing and twisting through ravines and gullies, back up steep slopes to another meadow. It ain't no valley we're a-riding in, but I still think the river is near. Ink says nothing but she's awake. Every now and then, I catch her looking behind us.

All night I'm watching the trail ahead and behind us. That Crow brave's screams keep echoing in my head. I left all the bodies there for the birds and coyotes. I remember when I first come out here, and how it felt after I killed my first Indian. I remember the dreams, and then wonder at what I've got used to. There's a good reason the Indians call their warriors "braves," I can tell you. A couple of times during the night, I think I might get sick. It didn't bother me none to kill them other three. It was my survival.

Some Indians believe that if you dream about a dead person, he ain't dead. He's out there, wandering wherever your dreams put him, and you got to do something to make him die. A dance, or a shaman ritual, or maybe another killing. I've seen some fellows fairly crazy with it and that's how I'm getting. I realize once and finally for sure that I want to get out of this beautiful, dangerous, miserable killing ground. I want to find my way back to Eveline and go as far west as I can go. I want to get a hotel room and sleep with four walls and a ceiling around me. It might be damn nice to work in a print shop, or a candle factory, or a foundry. I don't care. It'll be civilization, and won't nobody be lurking behind a tree thinking to kill me.

{ CHAPTER 22 }

W E NOW HAVE five horses, counting Cricket, and three rifles, a bow, and some arrows. Just when the sun starts to glow beyond the horizon, we stop near a great stone that hangs out a little over the trail. Across the way is a small stand of trees. I get down and help Ink off her horse and settle her in the darkest place under the rock. I take a long rope and tie it to one of the trees, then tether each horse to it at about ten-foot intervals.

When I get back to Ink, she is sitting up on one elbow, watching me. "We'll camp here today," I say.

"I am hungry."

"I'll scout around a bit." I set the pistol down next to her. "See if you can sleep."

"I am hungry. I won't sleep."

"I don't like where I got the horses," I say. "They're too much in the open and ain't a lot of grass under them trees." I sit with Ink for a spell, but I don't say nothing more. The horses are a problem now. We got so many of them.

In a little while Ink nods off. She don't have much pain no more, but it still exhausts her. I get up as quietly as I can and start walking toward the rising sun.

Not far from where I left her sleeping in the shadow of the rock, I find a open meadow that runs down into a small valley and then bends back up again on the other side. In the morning light it's a sweet, green bowl in the landscape and it's behind the trees where I first tied the horses. So I go back to them, then walk them down into the meadow. They will have a wide range to eat and the meadow is far enough below the tree line a body would have to be in front of us and halfway up the mountain on the other side to see them. I walk back to the trees and then follow a small path down to my left where there is a blue and black stream scuttling over rocks and tree branches. I kneel down and drink the cold water. I don't know if I should go back and check on Ink or go in search of game. Then I remember the bow and arrow. Whatever I shoot, maybe I should do it silently. So I creep back up to the stone and this time I try as hard as I can not to make a sound. But halfway up the hill it occurs to me that she might not expect me back so soon, so she'd shoot whatever she heard coming her way. "I'm coming back," I say. "It's me." When she can see me she puts the pistol down.

"I was already awake," she says.

"Really."

"I heard you coming a long time before you said anything."

"I tried to be real quiet."

"Maybe next time you should try to make noise."

"I don't know how you could hear me coming when I couldn't hear myself."

"I can hear you breathing. It sounds like a buffalo."

"I didn't make a sound."

"Except for the breathing. I do not believe you can't hear it."

I get the bow and the quiver of arrows. I put it across my back and shoulder my carbine. I hold the bow out so she can look at it. "I'm going to kill something we can eat with this."

"You know how to use it?"

"It looks pretty simple."

She don't say nothing. She has been collecting buffalo chips for a smokeless fire. She nods slightly and goes back to what she was doing. She carries the pistol around her neck in a skunk-skin sling she made.

"Don't shoot me when I come back," I say.

A few hours later, about two miles up the stream, I shoot a otter with the bow and arrow. It's a clean shot, and hardly makes a sound except for the twang of the string and the whoosh of the arrow. I carry the thing back to Ink, then make a fire with the chips and a few pieces of the driest wood I can find. I boil coffee and make a pot of beans as well. I clean the otter in front of the fire, and we eat until we can't no more. It looks like Ink is getting her strength back.

"You heal fast," I say.

She nods.

I sleep for a bit in the afternoon while Ink keeps watch. It was a damn good retreat into blankness, I can tell you. It feels good to know that I have gotten to where I trust Ink enough to sleep good and not worry about her.

Near the end of the day I break up the fire and we clean off the bones of the otter. I give Ink the last of my hardtack, and I eat the last of the dried venison. As the day begins to wear out, the air becomes a bit cooler. There ain't much in the way of clouds overhead, and when the sun's light softens and begins to sink, the small breezes feel almost like somebody caressing you kindly; like the earth has your interests at heart. It is bright green and rock white and dirt brown under the shadows of the trees, and damn fine to look at. At dusk Ink says, "Well? Shouldn't we be going?"

"This is a great spot," I say. "I wonder how much it will hurt to stay here another day."

"Hump will catch up if we stay here," she says.

"You still worried about him?"

"I don't know how far ahead of him I was or how long it took him to find I was gone. He could be getting close."

"You think he knows we turned north? We crossed in front of him and I covered our way pretty good. He gone right past and is still headed east, probably."

"We should keep going," she says.

"But it's so warm and peaceful here."

I wonder what on earth Ink might be thinking. Lately I notice her eyes more, find myself studying them. They're bigger and darker than Eveline's—got a glitter to them, they're so dark. I wonder what she wants and what she thinks will happen when we get to where we're going. Out of the blue, sometimes, I feel bad all over again for shooting her and I'll say, "I really am sorry I shot you." She don't even answer me no more. Half the time she just smirks and sighs, like she's impatient with a mule that won't take a step.

She gets up and starts for the trees. "Where are the horses?"

"I got them in a meadow yonder. I'll fetch them. Pack us up while we still got some light."

Riding only at night, we cover a lot of ground. In six more days we finally begin to smell the Missouri River. We never was close as I thought, but ain't no doubt about that smell. Ink starts to move better, and the wound on her belly really is beginning to heal. When she ain't in pain, she rides that painted pony just like she ain't nothing but a Indian. She moves with it when it climbs up the side of a ravine or starts to trot down a small hill. We make good time and don't see nobody. Finally on the seventh day, near dusk, just about the time we're getting ready to start out again, I say, "You ain't looked over your shoulder lately. You think Hump is still after us?"

"I don't know. I am listening for him," she says. "But . . ."

"But what?"

She looks at me for a second. Then she says, "I am not so afraid of him as I was."

"Really."

"I have seen what you can do." She points to the other horses. "You killed many."

"I don't like to think about that," I say. I'm not going to think about it.

"And I have a gun now," Ink says.

"You ain't thinking of shooting *me*, are you?"

She don't answer me. She's putting that Indian saddle on her horse. It don't have no buckles. It cinches all the way around the horse's middle and loops over the top and ties to a ball of leather sewed into the top of the saddle. I don't like it that she just keeps working and says nothing.

"I wouldn't blame you," I say.

"I will not shoot you," she says. "I hope I never have to."

Cricket no longer limps, so I've put the saddle back on her. I climb up on her back and start looking for the other stirrup. Ink takes me by the ankle and places the stirrup on the end of my foot.

"What do you mean, you hope you never have to?" I say. She don't need my help no more to get up on her horse. She does it swiftly and easy.

"What do you mean, you hope you never have to?" I say again.

She looks at me with those dark, serious eyes. "I will defend myself," she says. "That is all you need to know."

"Yeah, well," I say. "I don't guess I'll be attacking you any time at all."

"That is just fine," she says, and then she kicks the side of her horse and trots off in front of me. I got the other animals tethered to a long line behind me. The other horses are used to the way we move along, so they don't take much hauling, but I still have to hold the rope in one hand or the other and it's a strain. I wish I had a pair of gloves.

The country is beginning to slope downward into a evening mist. It looks like clouds lay on the ground in front of us and I watch as Ink's horse's legs disappear in it. Now she looks like she's floating on the clouds. I trot a little to catch up.

And then, just like that, she's gone.

I don't holler at first. I slow down a bit, wondering if she fell off a edge or something. "Hey, where are you?" I say, not too loud. Then I shout, "Ink."

Her voice comes to me from way up to my right. "Over here." Then I see the hill that drops down to the bank of the river. Cricket manages to stay up but she almost keeps going into the river. The mud is thick here, and Ink has already turned her horse so that she can keep him up out of the soft ground. She heads east, more than a little bit in front of me. I notice a lot of horse prints in the mud by the river. I ride back up the embankment a little to find solid ground, and to keep the other horses from the mud, then gallop with them up to where Ink has stopped to wait for me. In the thick fog she is dark and ghostly. She looks like something painted on a white wall, dark with white eyes and teeth, her hair like jet-black smoke around her face.

"You see those tracks?" I say.

"It is a lot of horses. Unshod," she says.

Her horse don't want to stand still. She pulls on the reins, but he throws his head back and turns completely around, stomping his front hoofs.

"What's he scared of?" I say.

"I do not know."

"Well, ain't nobody can see us in this mist."

"I saw a lot of tracks," she says.

"Ain't none up this way. Maybe they crossed the river back there."

"I followed some tracks in the mud right by the river."

"Why would a body ride in the mud like that?"

"Maybe they want us to follow them."

"Well, we ain't. You know, if it ain't a pack of wild horses, it's likely Indians, and if it's Piegan or Sioux and they seen us, we won't have these horses long."

She keeps her eyes on me as her horse backs away, his nostrils wide with fear. He snorts and keeps throwing his head up and down, left and right.

"Maybe a bear around here," I say. "Or a cougar."

"We have to keep moving," she says. "It is getting to be light. If anyone is ahead of us, we won't see their fire."

"If they bother to make one."

"If it is a hunting party or a war party, they will make a fire."

"Maybe we should cross the river." It ain't really a suggestion. I turn Cricket and start east toward the rising sun. The ground this close to the river is just too uneven and thick with saw grass and swamp mud. I move on up further from the riverbank and start heading directly east. Ink comes up beside me and the other horses fall in behind us. We move along quickly now, feeling some of the anxiousness of Ink's horse. We have to watch for whatever folks made them tracks by the river.

"Fort Buford can't be more than a day or two ahead," I say. "But it's almost daylight. We should set up camp somewhere around here on high ground."

It's trouble coming, I can feel it. I'm pretty good at that too. Maybe it's a sixth sense, but I can feel trouble like some folks notice humidity. We're losing all the rest of the darkness. The ground is soft, so we don't make much noise—just the creak of my saddle and the breathing of the horses.

Toward dawn I hear something caterwauling ahead of us in the tall grass. It's a high-pitched sound, something like a trapped rodent or bird of some kind. It's loud. We're riding along another sloping hill, near the river. A hour ago we crossed a fairly swift stream that branched off and run south. I know Fort Buford sits at the place where the

Yellowstone River runs south from the Missouri, but I still don't know how much farther we have to go. When we come to the stream that run south, Ink stopped for only a second, then rode along it a ways until she seen where it could be crossed, and she led her horse right down in there and I went on behind her with the others. It was shallow enough that we didn't have to get much more than our feet wet and the horses stepped through it fine. It was a hard surface of stones underneath.

Now, when we hear the high-pitched screaming ahead of us, Ink stops her horse and looks at me.

"I'll go see," I say.

"It is a child."

"What?"

"That is a child's cry."

"I ain't never heard no child make a noise like that."

I ride on ahead a little, then stop and get off Cricket when I see something moving in the tall grass ahead of me. I hold my carbine at the ready and start moving toward it. The grass is wet, waist-high, and I'm getting soaked as I move through it. The sun ain't appeared full yet, but it lights the distant low clouds in red and gold. When I see what it is making the noise, I stop. I can't believe my sight. Lying in the grass, where it is trampled down and flat, is a great, bloated corpse, black-faced, with long black hair, leather shirt stretched and tattered. And running back and forth from one end of it to the other is a young thing—a boy or girl, I can't tell—crying and crying like it wants to wake its mother from this black sleep. There are flies everywhere, buzzing in the kid's hair, crowding into the eyes of its dead mother. I look up and notice vultures circling. They ain't ready to swoop down and begin to eat with all that movement and noise.

I think it might be a boy. He's small, the thin legs churning, his screams breathless and frantic; I realize he's been doing this long enough, his voice is ruined now. He sounds like a wild boar. His cries are strained and horrible. I move back to where Ink waits for me.

"It's a child," I say. "No more than eight or nine."

Ink dismounts.

"I hope you know what to do," I say. "The little thing's crying for its dead mother. She's right there in the grass. I don't know what killed her."

Ink moves through the path I made in the grass, and I follow her.

We both frighten the little guy. It *is* a boy, maybe Cheyenne. His mother is almost through delivering another one. Both she and the newborn are dead. It didn't find its way to the world right, and got all twisted up inside her.

"Where's their village?" I ask when we figure out what's happened.

Ink shrugs, then stands high to look all around where we stand. The little boy is whimpering at her feet. He ain't even five feet tall. He looks at me with eyes so wide with fear, it begins to make me feel like some sort of evil thing. "I won't hurt you," I say to him. "Neither will she."

Ink turns and stares at me. The boy won't let go of her legs. He's not screaming now, and I think his throat must be pretty sore. His eyes are so red and swollen, he looks near dead himself. When she tries to lift him he pulls away from her. I don't think he's afraid of her, but he's too old to be picked up. Ink says, "Look after him for a minute," and goes past me back toward the horses. The little fellow watches her go and then starts to cry again, only not so loud no more. I don't say nothing. I stand there looking at him, and he looks at me.

Now I realize I'm in real trouble. Everything I've tried for since I made up my mind I was going back to Bozeman has blown up in my face. I feel like I'm falling deeper and deeper down a dark mine shaft and I don't know where the bottom is. While Ink is gone, it occurs to me that I should just get on Cricket, say my good-byes, and get the hell out of there. I have been obliged for so long—most of the rest of March, all of April—trying to make up for a stupid mistake. It's going to cost me the life I thought I might have. I ain't going to get back to Eveline and now I'm in the middle of this giant, wide-open country with a little slip of a woman and a child crazy with grief. I ain't never been too comfortable around children. That realization works on me like a growing alarm. I felt it before in the battles I got caught in during the war. It's like death. Death whispers to me, I think. I can't get my mind to leave me be.

But then I remember how close to Fort Buford we are. "There ain't no need to panic," I say out loud to myself. I can still be shed of Ink and the boy. He stares at me with them dark Indian eyes when he hears me speak.

"Nope," I say. "I ain't gonna panic." I almost say to him that I won't be much use to him, but this little guy, when he finally gets quiet, I feel sorry for him. I can't imagine what he's been through. What horror he would always remember of it. Watching his mother die and swell up and turn black with death. The poor kid must of fought to keep the big birds from pecking her eyes out.

You got to admire that kind of natural, unwilling courage. Maybe it comes from anger, or even fear. But he would not leave his mother to the buzzards. His belly is swollen, and when Ink comes back with some of the salted otter meat, he gnaws on it furiously. Ink tries to keep him from eating it too fast. He drinks the water I give him, letting it run down his jaw. He's got some beads around his neck and he touches them with pride when he sees me looking at him. His little fingers make me sad. I don't know. I ain't used to seeing nothing so small and helpless and human all at once. After he's chewed on some meat, he lets Ink put her arms around him finally. He wraps his arms around her neck and puts his face deep into the crook of her neck and shoulder. She looks at me, then at the corpse.

"I know," I say. "I'll take care of it."

"I will set camp over close to the river."

"Stay in this grass," I say. "We shouldn't be out in the open like this." She still holds the little fellow against her, and when she tries to give him to me so she can mount her horse, he won't have it. Once she's mounted, he does let me help him up onto her horse. "We're getting to be quite a party," I say. I look beyond her and see a small rise that is thickly covered in pine trees, but it's on the other side of the river. "If you can find a place to cross, why don't you try to make it to them pines over yonder."

She sees it and turns back to me. "What will you dig with?"

I take out my sheath knife. "This is all I got."

"I will cross," she says. "You follow?"

"It's gonna take me some time," I say. "What about Hump?"

"He will not kill me."

"No, I expect not. He'll come after me."

"I do not fear for you."

"I got enough for both of us."

"You will follow when you are done here?"

"I'll be along," I say. She gallops off and the other horses start to stir and stomp and nicker. I know Cricket won't run off, so I tie the lariat that holds all the other horses to the horn of my saddle. Then I kneel down and start to dig in the dirt. Here, this close to the riverbed, the dirt is soft and gives easily. It don't take long and I got a shallow grave, maybe a foot and a half deep, but long enough for the body. I hate touching it. The smell of a human body is worse than any other dead thing; it's got a sweetness to it that makes me puke. The flies are thick and busy. Maggots already wriggle in her eyes and mouth. Without no consideration at all, I empty my tobacco pouch into my shirt pocket, then I take a handful of the maggots and put them in the pouch. There's no telling if the boy has wounds. I tie the tobacco pouch back on my belt. As I do, I know I ain't running from all this. I'm stuck like a bear in a steel trap.

The half-born baby is black and swollen. I get the body situated in the hole, then I pile grass on as thick as I can before I cover it with dirt. The grass will keep the odor deep and help the earth take it back to the ground. I pile the dirt; it makes a pretty high mound over the body. When I'm done, I stand up and puke again.

Cricket looks at me with what feels like a kind of disgust.

"There ain't nothing else to do about this," I say. Then I climb on her and, with the lariat still tied to the horn of the saddle, start after Ink. The sun is high now, above the far hills. The river glistens in the sunlight. I ride slow and keep watch all around. I feel like I got nothing inside me. Not even a soul. I think I know what it feels like to be a animal, breathing air and stalking under the sinking sun, with no idea of the past or future.

I don't hear the boy crying again until I've found where Ink went across the river. I know she is not far. Cricket has to begin to swim through as we cross. The other horses don't like it, and the tug on the lariat is considerable; I wrap it around my waist and hold on, and it squeezes my empty gut until I think I might just split in two. Even so, I get them all across. I'm soaked right up to my chest, but in the sunlight it feels kind of pleasant. I stand there for a while with the horses, letting them breathe a bit and eat some of the saw grass that grows on the riverbank. Then I start up the rise to the trees.

In a day or two—three at most—we will reach Fort Buford, and then I can say good-bye to Ink and the boy and be back on my way. It's the last day of April. I got time. I got time.

I can still hear the boy crying.

CHAPTER 23

WE SIT AROUND a fire Ink made and the boy stares at me without blinking. I was still feeling the sting of burying his mother when I come back from crossing the river. I may of had the stink of his mother's body on me still. I figured I should stay away from him for the rest of the trip, but now Ink don't want to go nowhere.

"He is not ready for the fort," she says.

"I think he don't like me," I say.

"More than likely his mother was killed by white men. You are white."

I don't say nothing at first. Then I whisper to her, "Plenty of Indians at Buford. We'll leave him with them."

"You don't have to whisper. He doesn't speak English."

"Can you speak to him?"

"I can understand him and speak a little of his tongue. He is Cheyenne."

"Well, what do you mean, he ain't ready for it?"

"He's in a state," she says. "A trance from grief. He needs to be away from white people, soldiers especially."

"Well, we can't stay here long," I say. "I got to be heading back to Bozeman before we get too far into May."

We stay in the trees for a few days. I hunt in the early morning. The boy sniffles and stays silent most of every day. The weather warms, and deep in the trees where we are there ain't much we have to fear except maybe a bear or a cougar. I don't worry none about Hump. As far as he knows, we already got to Fort Buford, and he won't follow us there. I rode a long way east along the river one evening just to see the terrain. When I told Ink about it, she didn't say nothing. I don't know why Ink wants to stay here, but when I make any motion toward packing things up, she stops me. She looks at me with them dark eyes, now serious and kind of menacing, and I know I don't have nothing to do but wait. I try not to think of Eveline, but I keep seeing her looking out the back of that covered wagon as she moves westward, wondering what happened to me. I know I am a disappointment and I don't like knowing it.

I don't want to be in the position of trying to force Ink to do nothing. But I worry about the horses. There ain't much for them to eat here. I wonder how much longer I can give Ink what she wants. I ain't completely stupid. I know she ain't got nothing but that little boy on her mind now, and she needs me if she's going to save him. So I am useful to her. I don't feel like she knows me no more, but I can't get through a damn day without wondering what's going on in her mind. I'm always watching her, waiting for some sign. Anything.

On our fourth day in camp the boy goes with me to hunt. I let him have the bow and arrow. This pleases Ink no end, but I keep him in front of me just in case he decides to point the thing back my way. I ain't yet ready to fully trust him. We hunt most of the morning, and just when I'm ready to call it quits, the little fellow shoots a arrow into a scurrying doe. It's a good shot, and I almost reach out and pat him on the back, but I think better of it. He can see I'm happy for him. "They teach you to shoot with one of them things right early," I say. I guess if his papa seen it, he'd be proud.

Later in the day, after we've eaten the deer, Ink gives the little fellow a name. He has a flat, round face; he's as dark as Ink, and only about four and a three quarters of a foot tall. We sit by a faltering camp fire in the afternoon and suddenly she says, "I will call him Little Fox."

"Little Fox?" I say. "Why Little Fox?"

"We found him running in the tall grass like a fox."

"Why give him a Indian name?"

"He is an Indian."

"But your daddy was white. If you're fixing to raise him, shouldn't he have a white man's name?"

She just looks at me. We set there staring at each other while she makes up her mind if she should pay attention to me at all. Then she says as she turns away. "Little Fox."

She don't say no more. I throw another small branch on the fire and wait for the moon to rise.

The boy's come to trust her enough that he let her clean his hair and put a new piece of leather on him. By now she's tanned the deerskin and made a shirt for herself and for him. His shirt is long enough, it hangs down to his knees. She made a head covering for him with the skin of a prairie dog I killed and he puts it on his head with pride. He almost smiles when I tell him how good it looks. He still ain't said nothing to me or her. But when she speaks bits of Cheyenne to him, he listens.

At night, when we should be traveling, we hunker down with no fire and try to sleep. I listen to the night sounds, the tree frogs and cicadas, and sometimes I hear a kind of rhythm that sounds like language, like voices chanting in the forest. One night all I hear is *This will be so, this will be so, this will be so,* and I try to get my mind to change it into something else, but I just can't. Every day that goes by is proof that I ain't going back to Bozeman and I ain't never gonna see Eveline again. *This will be so, this will be so.* The whole thing makes me right irritable. But I can't say nothing in the face of what Ink and that boy been through and what I got to do for them if I can.

In the daylight the boy looks at me sometimes and I know from the way his eyes go to my hands and then my face and then my hands again he still worries I might do him harm. It must of been white men that killed his momma, or at least chased her into that tall grass. One day near the end of that first week, around noon, sitting next to a small campfire, I say this to Ink and she says, "It is probably so. But that woman may have died trying to give birth to the other child." I know that ain't true. Or at least it ain't the whole truth. But I don't challenge her on the idea. I say, "I expect that's true." I try to meet her eyes, but she stares at the fire. She holds Little Fox's head in her lap. She don't say no more, and I sit there with a stick in the fire, wishing it would get dark enough so maybe I can sleep again.

I know what probably happened. Soldiers attacked the dead woman's village and took everybody with them, men and women all. No soldier would let a brave go off to find his wife and child. Ain't no tribe I know of would let a woman go off to give birth and then leave her there to die. And she wouldn't take her other child with her to give birth, neither. So they was probably hiding, and maybe the boy seen the white men taking his family away.

Now Little Fox curls up next to Ink and closes his eyes. I think he might sleep a bit. For a few days now he's slept without crying out and he don't weep no more. I think he is getting used to us. He still clings to Ink for all he's worth.

When his breathing gets to be regular, I whisper, "He's fallen asleep."

Ink says nothing.

"You been through one hell of a lot," I say.

She thinks I am talking to Little Fox. She puts her finger in front of her mouth to shush me.

"I'm sorry," I say.

"You say those words more than any others," she says.

This catches me by surprise. But then I remember what she's been through, and how useless them words are in the face of it. I say, "When you think we should go on to Buford?"

She does not answer me. I sit there awhile longer, then I get up and go a-hunting again, this time by myself. When I'm out in the forest, looking for game or moving up to the high ridges near the river, I feel sometimes like I'm on my own again. I remember what that feels like, and it don't seem possible I ever lived it. And if I think about it for even a little bit, a kind of sick feeling takes over my gut and I can't decide if that's because I want that solitary life again or if I don't; maybe I'm getting nervous about what I'm gonna do with Ink and the boy. Maybe I'm sick about having them with me, or worried about leaving them behind. The only thing I know for sure is that thinking about my future ruins the alone time something awful. It's only when I find a deer or a elk or even a rabbit or a groundhog to shoot that I feel pure again. But when I've done hunting and I'm getting ready to find my way back to them, Ink and the boy seem like a bad memory. I wish I could figure what's in her head.

It don't take long to lose track of time when you ain't moving. Sometime in the third or fourth week of May, we get hit with a storm of ice balls and then a driving rain. We huddle under the trees and the animals stomp and whinny. Ink looks at me. It's like we're both in some sort of white dream, dark against the whiteness. It's suddenly very cold.

"This ain't a regular thing," I say.

"It's a storm," she says. "It will pass."

I stand there watching the white balls on the ground rattled by the rain. I can hear the river roaring down below us.

When the rain stops and everything settles again, Ink says, "We should move."

"On to Buford?"

"The rain has stopped."

"You want to move now."

She looks at me.

"It ain't like I can make it back to Bozeman now. So what's the point?"

She says nothing while we pack up the horses. She tries to let Little Fox know what we're doing.

I climb up on Cricket, lead them back down to the riverbed, and we start heading east, following the river. I see a dead horse in the water, frozen stiff as a statue. Then I see a woman in a dress, a child gripping her arm as they go by in the current. I realize it is suddenly very cold and the water is like a wall of moving ice. Up ahead the darkening sky looks bruised.

"Big Ice," Ink says. "Great chunks of it. I have seen it before."

"My Lord," I say. "If we'd of been out in the open, it's likely them balls of ice would of killed us and the animals too." I don't want her to know how nervous this event has made me. I hope Little Fox and Ink didn't see the child and the woman. My voice shakes when I talk, but maybe she thinks I'm cold. It's easy thirty degrees colder than it was a hour ago. And I'm heading east with her. Getting farther away from Eveline. This makes my heart feel fat and heavy. But I don't know what I can do about it. We're riding along the Missouri, and soon we'll be to Fort Buford.

"We are getting to the weather of spring," she says.

"Maybe that big ice ain't done," I say.

Ink just rides on, looking back over her shoulder now and then. She's thinking again. Her eyes shine in the weak light like a snake's eyes, black and sparkling.

We ride along up the embankment a little and out of the mud, but next to the river for a while. The mist is still low to the ground, but now there's a general fog all around. We can barely see in front of us. When it's completely dark, I can't even tell if there's a moon. The air is drippy with the fog, so I start climbing to higher ground, trying to rise up out of the damp, swampy air. We get to more solid ground, but still no light nor clear air. I hear the breathing and chuffing of the horses, the sound of their hooves, and nothing else. Ink rides next to me, and Little Fox is behind her, holding her around the waist. When I look over at them I don't see nothing but a dark shadow a little lower than me and off to my left. I know she's there with him, but she ain't got nothing to say. We're just going steadily now, trying to get to morning.

When the sun begins to rise, it burns the fog until it turns into great columns of gray light that rise up to the top of the sky. There's a breeze now, and it sweeps the fog past us and the world is shadows again and dark places in front of us. Sometime in the middle of that night, one of the horses riding behind us got cut loose. I don't notice it until we're getting ready to stop.

When I tell Ink about it, she sets Little Fox on the ground gently and then rides back, jumps from her horse, and picks up the rope. She studies it in the weak light, then gets back on her horse and rides back to me.

"You shouldn't jump off your horse like that," I say. "You could open one of them wounds again."

"The rope was cut," she says. She looks so sad, it's almost a kind of purity—like she is innocent of everything in the world and don't know death and decay yet, like a damn child. She's been kidnapped and lived with the Indians for five years or more, she's afraid of her husband's fury, and she looks to me like a small, dark virgin child.

"You don't have to worry," I say. "If all he wants is horses, he can have them all."

She looks at me.

"Except for Cricket here."

"It is just his way of letting us know he is here," she says. "It is his way."

"He can't be nowhere near," I say. "Not through all we been through."

She's looking all around now, like some kind of wary animal in a streambed. Little Fox don't understand. We're still mounted, but he's on the ground and it's light enough he can see Ink's face.

"He thinks I'm threatening you," I say.

"No he doesn't. He trusts you now."

She speaks words to him that are soft and kind. It's a tone in her voice I ain't never heard before. He goes to her and she reaches down and helps him get back up behind her. I take the carbine off my shoulder and hold it ready in front of me. The sun's high enough to gleam over the trees in front of us. To my right I see mountains, high and green in the new light.

"Want to head for them hills?" I say.

"Hump is watching us right now."

Below us to our left is the river, wide and fast, deep with water that still steams with cold. All around us ain't nothing but tall grass and a few clumps of bushes and trees that look black now and like any one of them might move.

I turn Cricket toward the mountains. "Follow me," I say. Ink kicks her horse in the side and comes along, still looking behind her and all around in a kind of panicked, jerky movement, like a bird. Little Fox holds on for dear life.

"It ain't nothing to worry about," I say. We ain't running. I keep my eye on the mountains. Ahead I see a place where the ground rises up and curves enough at the bottom that I think we can camp there. I want to camp up against that hill so it's at my back, and I only have to keep watch of what's in front of me.

When we get to the bottom of the hill, though, I see it's really a pond there collecting water that runs over the crest and drops into it. I don't like the noise it makes. I won't be able to hear nothing else. So we go on up past the hill and the little waterfall into the trees at the foot of the mountain. By that time the sun has risen over the far trees on our left and we can almost see our shadow.

"It's by God daylight," I say. "We pretty much have to stop here."

We go far enough into the forest that it's still pretty dark. We're in a long stretch of flat land that rises very slowly ahead of us. There ain't nothing but tall black trees all around. The ground is covered with pine needles and not much else. It's like a brown, smooth carpet under the shadow of the high branches.

"This place is not good," Ink says.

"It'll have to do." I climb down off of Cricket and tie her to one of the thinner trees. I bring the rest of the horses around in front of us and tie the tether to the same tree. Ink sets Little Fox on the ground, then she rides a ways back from where we come and ties her horse to a tree down that way. She pulls the saddle off and then carries it back up to me and throws it down against a tree. "You sleep first," she says.

"What'd you put that animal all the way down there for? Think he'll make noise if Hump comes?"

She don't say nothing.

"That horse'll make noise like the other one did when he cut him loose," I say.

"If it is Hump, he will not take the horse," she says. "He took the first one to let us know he is here. If that one is taken, it is not Hump following us."

"That's right smart."

We set up camp in the clearing between three fairly large pine trees. The branches hang low enough that it feels like a kind of roof over our heads. Sunlight leaks in, of course, but it don't light up too much. It scatters so much around us, it looks a little like jewelry laying around.

I ask Ink if I can see her wounds again.

"They are fine," she says. "I am healed."

"Can't hurt to check."

She don't look at me. She's studying that horse she left down the hill a ways.

"Was you scared from all them balls of ice?" I say.

"No." She turns to Little Fox, who sits on the ground next to her and asks him something. He nods and then looks at me. She says, "He's seen it before too."

"I got to admit, I was scared."

She stays quiet. After a while I say, "You know, I got to where I think I can count on you."

Now she looks at me. The white parts of her eyes around the dark, gleaming lenses and the white teeth in that dark face are almost eerie. Like she come up out of some dark place of the earth to judge us all, but all she says is "How long do you think before we get to Fort Buford?"

"Maybe the day after tomorrow, if we travel all night both nights."

She nods and looks away again.

"You know," I say, "I been kind of protective of you."

"I know you have."

"I have." I feel kind of proud that I said it. I didn't know I would, but it seems to fix something soft in her. She looks right into my eyes now.

"I am grateful to you," she says.

When she says that, I think of Morning Breeze saying "Beech-i-lack" and suddenly I feel kind of sad that I'm going to take off and leave Ink in Fort Buford. I don't think it's anything but what she expects, but what if it ain't? What if she's starting to hope I don't? I don't want to shock her with it. "I really am sorry that I shot you," I say. "But maybe it will turn out to be a good thing."

She looks at me like I might of said something bad. "I would like to stop talking about it."

"It's enough that you know I wish I had not done it," I say.

"I know it. You have never stopped speaking of it."

I almost reach out to put my hand on her arm. We are in this bejeweled forest, bathed in dark and light, her black hair glistens and brightens with every movement of her head. I feel kind of close to her, but respectful too. I don't want nothing from her at all. I ain't going to get back to Eveline before she takes off without me. I know that now. It surprises me how it don't make me angry as it should. It's the damnedest thing: I don't want to just say farewell to Ink, at least not so soon. I can wait for that time now. I ain't in no all-fired hurry no more, and when it hits me that I ain't so trapped by time, I smile at Ink and say, "I think we will both remember this journey."

"You sleep," she says. "I will keep watch."

Little Fox stares at me. He does not know how to take this sudden calm talk between me and Ink. I reach out my hand toward him, and he leans back. "I won't hurt you," I say.

Ink leans close to him and says, "Nahveesay-eh. He is my friend."

Then, by God, Little Fox says, "Tosunny cheost?" His voice is still raspy and wore-out, but Ink understands him.

"I am from the Sioux," she says. "Nee-Se-Sioux. Nee-do-schi-vay?"

"O-dah, leeshee ey," he says.

Ink turns to me. "His name is Little Moon."

"Well, we got it half right," I say. "Should we call him that from now on?"

"No," she says. "When he can speak our language, we will let him decide."

I lay down under a pretty low-hanging branch, but I can't sleep. She sits a few feet away, holding the pistol in her lap. It's getting warmer, and the moisture from the river finds its way even up here. I sit up.

"I can't sleep right now," I say. "I'm going to do a little hunting first."

She nods her head.

"If I get something, you can sleep while I prepare it. Then, after we eat, I'll try sleeping again myself. I do better with a full belly."

It's the first time we've stopped where there ain't no water running next to us. We'll have to go back out of the woods and a ways down the side of the mountain to get back to that pond we passed. But we got water in the canteens, and enough food that even if I don't have no luck we won't starve. Still, I want to find fresh meat. I take my carbine and give the bow and arrow to Little Fox and we head off on foot into the forest. We leave Ink sitting at the base of a tree with the pistol in her hands. "Do not fret," she says. "I will not shoot you when you come back."

Little Fox stops and looks at her. She waves, and then he comes along with me.

We walk up the slight incline toward deeper and darker places in the forest ahead. It turns out to be a long climb up a hill that gets more and more steep. After a while I realize we are climbing up the low side of the mountain, getting higher and higher. I got that cold feeling behind my eyes again, thinking about Hump. Maybe he could be in these trees. Little Fox don't make no noise next to me. Even under ten years old, he moves like a cat, silent and ready. He's already got a arrow nocked into the bow.

Near the middle of the day, I watch him kill a small deer. Except for the plunk of the bowstring, there ain't no sound. I'm pretty well shocked to find out a deer makes a loud cry when it gets hit. That first one he shot, scuttling fast along the ground, didn't make no noise at all. This one's smaller. I roll it over and give Little Fox my hunting knife. He knows exactly what to do. He cuts from between the back legs up the belly to the soft white fur at the base of the throat. He cuts as shallow as he can, just under the skin, so he don't open the sac that contains all the organs. Just as he's about to reach inside the still-warm body for the windpipe so he can cut it free, I hear a pistol shot down the mountain and way back where we left Ink. It's so loud, it swallows a few beats of my heart. Like it come from deep in there and not the woods at all. I wonder if Ink shot something herself; another rabbit maybe. But then I hear another shot. And another.

Little Fox jumps to his feet. I take the knife from him and put it back in my belt, grab the carbine, and we leave the half-gutted deer right where it lays and start running back. I go fast for a long time. Little Fox can't keep up but he knows where I'm going. I race downhill headlong, working like hell to stay on my feet, dodging trees, holding the carbine at the ready, and I hear two more shots, loud and final. I stop for a second to listen, so out of breath I can't break out of the noise

I'm making. It's like the woods have no sound. I don't even hear Little Fox coming up behind me. I feel my heart hammering against my ribs. I think I can still hear the echo of them pistol shots moving through the trees and out into the sunlight. And then I don't even hear my breathing or the pounding of my heart. I stand in the light-scattered forest and listen. But there ain't no noise at all, and I know whatever happened is over now.

{ CHAPTER 24 }

WHEN WE GET back to camp, everything is gone except for two white men laying on the ground near the tree where Ink was sitting the last time I seen her. One has been shot right in the left eye and at the base of his neck. The only thing moving near him is a couple of flies that circle and drop over the gurgling wound. His other eye don't see nothing at all. The other fellow is still alive but holding on to his lower gut like it's on fire. He squirms and breathes, hisses like a big snake. He sees me and tries to slither away, but I go over to him and stop him with the barrel of my carbine right in the space between his shoulder and his jaw and he don't move a inch.

"I'm done for," he says. "He's killed me."

"Who's killed you?"

"The Injun that was a-settin' here."

"Really."

"Help me," he says.

"What Injun?"

"A little fellow," he grunts out. "We was trying to take the horses back."

"What do you mean take them back?"

"He stole our horses."

"The hell he did. Those was our horses."

He looks at me hard, like he can't really make me out. He gasps for air. I sling the carbine over my shoulder and squat down next to him. He ain't no more than twenty years old, if that. He'd have a hell of a time getting a beard to sprout. He's missing his front teeth and he ain't seen a bath in a long time. He's wearing a dirty buffalo-skin jacket and blue regular army trousers. Leather moccasins cover his feet. He's got thin, wispy blond hair and dark brown eyebrows. Right now pine needles and chips of wood cling to his hair. I can see he's sweating to beat all. Blood seeps through his shaking hands.

"Help me," he says.

"Ain't nothing for it," I say.

"Ohhh, Lordy, Lordy." He commences crying a little bit, and I feel embarrassed for him.

"Was you the ones that stole our horse yesterday?"

He don't say nothing.

"Cut it loose from the tether as we was moving up the path?"

He nods his head. "Help me."

"Where'd he go?"

"Who?" He looks at me.

"The Indian."

"They took him. They'll make him pay."

"Who took him?"

"Treat," he grunts it out. "Treat."

"Treat?" I say. "Treat. I'll be damned."

He looks at me.

"Treat's a young fellow, ain't he?"

He scrunches his face up a bit in pain. Then he gasps, "Near about my age."

"How many?" I say.

"There was five of us. We was in the militia and run together. That'n over there's my big brother."

"Well, he's done for."

Little Fox has put a arrow in the other fellow, and he stands over him now getting ready to do it again.

"Little Fox," I say.

He looks at me with them dark eyes.

"We're gonna need them arrows." I hold my hand out palm down and signal by cutting the air in front of me. "Stop it."

"Ohhh, God. Oh, God," the dying fellow says.

"Where was Treat headed?" I ask him.

"I can't feel nothing below my waist."

"It's probably a good thing. Tell me. Where was they headed?"

Suddenly he comes back to hisself a little bit and it hits him that he don't know who I am or what I might be up to. "I ain't telling you nothing."

"Suit yourself," I say, and stand up.

He starts to try and move away, and I put the barrel of the gun against his jaw again. "You ain't going nowhere."

He's crying some more, but not out loud. "I need water."

"I got no water."

"I sure could use some water. My canteen . . . my canteen . . ." He can't finish. He breathes so fast, he's turning red.

Neither one of us says nothing for a spell. It's going to take a very long time for him to die, and when it's finally over, he won't have vocal chords left because of all the screaming he's bound to do. The bullet has made a big hole in his lower stomach, and I can already smell it.

"You are bowel shot," I say. "If you're lucky you'll bleed to death. I seen it happen to some folks. Most die of the infection, though. That's a long time."

New terror bulges in his eyes. He's seen this kind of death before, even as young as he is.

"It could be real bad," I say.

"Finish me," he gasps.

"I'd be more than happy to," I say. "Just tell me where Treat was headed."

He thinks about it for a spell. I see his eyes staying fierce for just a little bit, but then something in them gives way. He don't see no point in suffering for folks that left him here to die. "It's Treat and two others. They was headed for the Yellowstone."

"Where they going from there?"

He shakes his head, like he needs to get fog out of it. "The Black Hills."

I lift the carbine up and let it hang over my shoulders. He lays there, staring at me, his mouth open a little, and dry as a sunbaked rock. Every time he breathes, it takes everything moist out of his mouth and eyes. When he tries to talk some more, his tongue seems to stick to the roof of his mouth and it makes a noise like something that's slapped into a bowl of molasses.

"Help me," he manages to say.

"You got a pistol?"

He nods.

I squat down again, lay the carbine next to me, and open his jacket. He's got a Schofield revolver tucked in his trousers. I pull it out, empty all the shells but one out of it, and give it back to him. "You do it," I say. "I don't want to."

I go back over to his brother and remove his pistol—it's a Colt dragoon, the exact same kind of pistol as the one I give Ink, except it's got a fancy pearl handle. I search him for ammunition and find a pouch of it tied to his belt. I give the pistol and the pouch to Little Fox. I can see the pistol is right heavy for him, but when I move to take it back, he looks at me and stuffs it into the waistband on his leather breeches. "Ne ah esh," he says.

I ain't even thought yet about the fact that I'm on foot now. I got no food. I got a little boy with me I don't understand, and we got to move fast to find Ink.

I hear a click behind me and turn to see the wounded fellow sitting up, holding the Schofield to his head. "Shit," he says. "It misfired."

I walk back over to him.

"I'm still here," he says, and he actually gives this little laugh. Like the joke is on him.

"Yes, you are." I take the gun away from him and put a few more shells in it, then I hold it next to his head, just above his ear. "Thank you," he says. "I would probably miss." He looks straight ahead, like a man waiting for the barber to make the first snips of his hair. I pull the trigger and it clicks a second time.

"Damn," he says.

I pull the trigger and it clicks again. "I hate these god-damn Confederate pistols," I say.

"One more time ought to . . ." he starts to say, but this time when I pull the trigger it goes off. His head snaps away from me, a splash of blood flying with it, and he falls over.

I drop the gun where he lays and start off down the hill, walking as fast as I can toward the clear ground away from the trees. I don't even look at Little Fox, but I know he's coming right behind me. I want to get away from these pine needles that leave no track where people or horses walk. I figure I'm following at least seven horses, and Cricket is one of them. I think Treat will want to be near water, so he'll lead them down to the river. The ground in the foothills, closer to the river, will be easier to track them in. I want Treat to have good sense—to want to stay near the river. I don't want him to be smart enough to wonder what that last shot was all about; I don't want him to know I am following him.

I try not to think of what they plan on doing with their "Injun" captive.

{ CHAPTER 25 }

We're on foot. I got nothing but my carbine and a sheath knife. Little Fox has that Colt pistol and the bow and arrow. I don't think he knows a thing about how to shoot the pistol, but he seen me fire the Schofield, so maybe he's a fast learner. He's got a skin hat on his head, and so do I. I have a canteen of water that I stole from that young fellow I shot. I am hunting in a kind of killing rage.

I find the track near the river, and it's headed west, and for some reason it hits me that I'm now going toward Eveline. It comes to my mind even though it's something I forgot. It feels like something I long ago give up on.

I think we're on the right track because I recognize the small place in Cricket's hoof where Ink scraped out the burr. I know for sure when Little Fox finds Ink's garments laying alongside the trail by the river. At first I think it's a dead rabbit or something, but when he picks it up I realize what it is. There's blood on the shirt up around the collar, and on the pants too. We spend the better part of half a day walking around that spot—all the way down to the river, and up and down it a good ways, too, looking for a body, but find none. I'm in such a panic, I start moving again, fast, almost running. We get to where the Yellowstone turns south from the Missouri and the track goes that way. They are on the eastern side of the river. I don't even think about Hump or nobody that may be following me. Half the time I don't even hear the breathless gasping of my little companion trying so desperately to keep up with me.

I try not to think nothing but how to keep going. I know with such a large party they'll stop soon, and I won't. I'll just keep on. Sometimes I find myself running, carrying my carbine in one hand, leaping over stones and small branches. I'm trying to be quiet, and I stay pretty much to the low side as I run. Then I remember Little Fox and I stop and wait for him, breathing hard, impatient. When I walk, I stay bent low and try to keep the small trees and bushes near the river

255

between me and what might be in front of me or to my left. I keep the river on my right as I move, and I'm always ready to fire my carbine.

But finally we do stop. We have to. I don't see how Little Fox can go on. He can't catch his breath. He stands next to me, waiting, and I realize if I wanted to go on, he would do it. I am amazed that he has kept up with me. Whoever his father was, he prepared him well for this kind of hunt. It's the middle of the night on the second day, and so cold I see our breath as we gasp for air. I'm exhausted, too, and sweat runs in my eyes; I think I might fall down unconscious if I don't eat something and drink some water.

We lay down in a thicket near the river. When I can finally breathe normal again, I roll down to the riverside and begin to drink. Little Fox crawls up next to me and does the same. It is ice-cold sweet water. I cover my face with it, wet my whole head. Then I lay there trying to sleep. Above me the moon seeks the cover of a dark curtain of clouds. I think I can see starlight but then I'm gone somewhere. When I wake up, the sun bakes my face and flies and mosquitoes buzz all around my head. Little Fox is shaking me. I don't know how long I been laying here, but I know I've lost some time. The sun is very high above the horizon, almost overhead. The air is warm again. I gather my things, refill the canteen with the cold water, and we both start running. This time I try to keep track of Little Fox. I pace myself. For a while I lose the trail and I stop and wander around a bit until Little Fox finds it. They're still on this side of the river.

Near dusk the third day, we come upon them. We're moving at a steady pace, Little Fox silent and right there with me, his bow in hand. I see the horses first. Then I see two heads way in front of me, on the other side of a line of brush. They got their backs to me. I hear the horses nickering some. I know Ink has heard me coming up, but the others don't know a thing. I motion to Little Fox to get down and he sinks to the ground with the bow ready. I flatten my palms on the ground and pat it twice to let him know I want him to stay put. He is not afraid. He takes a arrow out and nocks it in the bow. I crawl on my belly along a small ravine that runs next to the river and to the right of where they are camped out. It ain't dark yet, but they already got a fire. I see a thin wisp of smoke in front of me and I crawl slow up the embankment, at the base of the place where the brush ends. I feel the damp mud of the river-bed seeping through my shirt. In the waning light of day, the campfire starts to reflect on faces and limbs and I see Ink sitting exactly across from me, on the other side of the fire. She is staring right at me. She is naked, her dark hair covering her breasts. Her eyes are dark and fierce. The way she sits, I realize her hands are tied behind her back. They've put a stake in the ground behind her and tied her to it. The young one, Treat, holds his hunting knife up to the light, looking at the edge of it. He's got two others with him. One, I notice, is Joe Crane. He's crouched by the fire, poking it with a stick. He's still got Preston's hat.

I holler, "Joe Crane," and he gets up fast.

Treat puts the knife in the sheath on his belt and takes out his pistol.

"You better put that pistol down," I say.

"Who's there?" Joe says. He squints over the fire.

"It's me," I say. "Bobby Hale."

I hear him say something under his breath to Treat, and then Treat puts his gun away.

The other fellow, whose been standing there motionless, moves a little closer to the fire. I get up and walk toward them, holding my carbine at the end of my arm, but level and pointed in their direction. It ain't no walking stick, and they can see that I got it where it needs to be to do business.

"Jesus Christ," Joe Crane says. "If it ain't so. Bobby Hale." He seems glad to see me. The others are wary. I don't look at Ink, but I feel her eyes on me.

When I get up to him, Treat says, "Well, shit. I remember you from Fort Riley."

I nod.

"That was a long time ago," Joe Crane says. "I thought you was headed west with that train."

"I was."

"What happened?"

I now look directly at Ink. "What do you have here?"

"It ain't nothing," Treat says. "It belongs to me."

"It ain't just yours," Joe Crane says. "She belongs to all of us."

257

"That is what the Sioux call a warrior," the other fellow says, and they all laugh.

Joe Crane says, "We been having a bit of fun with her. She don't speak English nor Crow."

"We thought she was a brave," Treat says. "She sure knew how to fire that pistol she was holding."

"Killed two of ours before we got the gun from her," Joe Crane says.

"We been paying back," Treat says. The others laugh. "But she don't speak a damn word. Quiet as a skunk."

They all laugh at this too.

"Hell, she don't even moan," the other fellow says.

I notice blood dripping out of Ink's right nostril. She does not look at me now. "There ain't enough of her left for nobody but me," Treat says.

"Well, you're *all* done with her now," I say.

Joe Crane looks in my eyes, but he don't see it coming. I fire my carbine from the waist and hit him in the center, between the shoulders, then raise the gun, take aim, and shoot Treat in the throat before he can figure out what's going on. He drops to the ground still holding his pistol in the ready position. The other fellow just stands there looking at me. Joe Crane is sitting down, looking at the wound in his chest. His feet are crossed in front of him. "What'd you do that for?" he says.

"I done it for Preston, hanged in a tree," I say. "And for her. For what you done to her."

The other fellow starts to back away, but I point the gun at him. "You want to take one in the back, you go right ahead," I say. "For myself, I'd rather see it coming."

"Please, Christ, don't shoot me," he says. "I never touched her nor nobody else, I swear it."

"Was he with you when you hanged Preston?" I ask Joe Crane.

"I'm finished," he says. "You've killed me, you bastard. And I never seen no gold."

"I think I'm going to have to finish you too," I say to the other fellow. "What's your name?"

"Why?"

"Don't you want to be remembered?"

He turns and starts running. I raise the rifle and aim at him, then lower it and watch him for a spell. He disappears on the other side of the line of brush, then I see him get up on a spotted horse and take off away from the river. I don't feel like killing him. It's bad enough what I done to Joe Crane and Treat. They was white men, and except for whatever I done accidental in all the smoke and damnation of the war, and shooting that fellow the other day who was already dead, I ain't killed none of them before. At least not on purpose. I am killing my own people now and it don't feel right. But then I look over at Ink and see her sitting there in her own blood and with no clothes on, scratched and bloody as a skinned doe, and it really sets me off again.

Joe Crane tries to say something. I hear him gasping for air through blood-filled lungs. I must of missed his heart or he'd be dead by now, but air sucks into the wound and I know he ain't got long. I guess I feel sorry for him.

"You shouldn't of done what you done to her," I say. "Nor Preston, neither."

"Preston had it coming. I didn't like it much. But it was his trouble and his . . ." He coughs. Then he looks up at me.

"It don't matter," I say. "I shot you for what you done to her."

"It was bad about Preston," he whispers. "I did not like it one bit. But hell. It ain't nothing but what happens out here."

"Well, now it's happened to you," I say.

He makes a sound, almost like a stifled cough or sneeze. "Damned if it ain't," he says, and then I realize he is trying not to laugh. Blood spatters out of his mouth and nose when this happens. "Damned if it ain't. And killed by a old friend."

"I guess," I say.

He tries to hold his head up, but then it just drops down toward his feet. He dies a-setting there with his head between his knees, like he's looking for something in his limp hands.

"It's a damned shame," I say to nobody.

Treat was a small fellow, so I take off his vest and shirt, and when I cut Ink loose I hand them to her. "Go on and get dressed," I say.

259

She still don't look at me, but she takes the clothing. When she turns to get up, I see that she has messed herself. Her ass is cut and bleeding and it won't do to let her go like that. I help her up. "Come on," I say. "We'll go down to the river and you can take a bath."

She moves like something only half alive, like a sick dog being held up on its hind legs. Her head droops, and she slobbers. She smells of whiskey and urine, and shit. Sweat and blood, too, I guess. I don't want Little Fox to see her like this.

"I'm sorry," I say. "I wish this didn't happen to you."

"They were your friends?" she whispers.

"I known two of them. They wasn't no friends."

I leave her at the edge of the river with Treat's shirt and vest, and then I go back up and get his trousers too. I walk back to where I left Little Fox and point to all the horses. I motion for him to go there. I take the trousers back to Ink and notice she ain't moved from where I left her. "You got to clean up," I say. I help her move a little into the water. It's shallow where she stands, but as she moves further in, holding herself from the cold, it gets deep enough. "Just stay there," I say. "Wash yourself off. I'll turn the other way."

It's getting dark now, and I turn my back from her a little. In the fading light she cannot see what I'm up to. I watch her squat down and begin to wash. She splashes the water over herself, slowly at first—like it might burn her with the cold—but then she really gets into it. She sits down and scrubs and scrubs. She buries her face and hair in it, then throws it all back over her head. Some of the water splashes on me and I know it is ice-cold. Her hands tremble as she runs them over her face, the water dripping down under her eyes and off the tip of her nose. Her lips are swollen and torn. She pats them with the cold water, then sniffs back and looks at me. Without saying a thing, she starts crying silently. Even back when I put that bullet in her—back when I sewed the wound and then had to cut it again and burn it—she never cried like that.

When she comes up out of the water, I put my hands on either side of her face. We both stand there, and then I slowly kneel down with her. We face each other like that for a while, like we're praying or something, and then she puts her head on my shoulder and I sit back and she sort of rests on my legs and I hold her against me while she weeps. She's quiet with it. I hear nothing but her quick breathing and feel the motion of her shoulders. She's naked and wet against me and I just hold her in my lap like a small child. It's a long cry. The moon rises fairly high over the rippling river before she finally begins to get hold of herself. It don't matter to her that she's naked. I feel her dark wet hair against me and keep my arm wrapped around her neck and head and just hold her. She trembles so much it feels like she might break apart in my arms. I can't get her warm. But the crying stops. Now she just breathes deeply, in and out, and shudders in my arms.

"I'm sorry," I say again.

But she still don't speak.

"We got to get moving," I say. "You think you can ride a horse?"

I think I feel her nod her head a bit.

"We're a long way back south and west. They was taking you to the Black Hills."

Now she does nod.

"I'm sorry this happened," I say again. She raises her head and looks into my eyes. I can still see her tears, and in the moonlight I think she is the most handsome and sad creature I ever seen in the world. I lean down and kiss her gently on the forehead. She don't move or say a thing.

"Can you put them clothes on?" I say.

She keeps looking in my eyes for a while, but then she turns and gets up, trying to cover herself with her arms. I go back up to where the fire is beginning to die out and retrieve Joe Crane's Colt pistol, some canteens, and one bedroll. The horses are hobbled on the other side of the brush. When I get to them, I see Little Fox holding on to the tether, keeping them in place. "Good job," I say. Cricket is glad to see me, I think. Now we got eight horses, including Cricket and Ink's mount. They'll come in handy at Fort Ellis back in Bozeman and I'm wondering if we shouldn't just keep on west and head for there. In spite of the continued chill in the air, I know it's already near the end of May. Even making thirty or forty miles a day, we won't make it back to Bozeman by June. I know I've lost Eveline for sure. The idea of leaving Ink at Buford or anywhere else don't seem possible now. It don't seem like something I can even do. It's something I'm going to have to decide right away, and there ain't nobody to consult about it. I don't think I'll get Ink to even speak to me. She's been robbed of speech and ain't going to be much of help from now on.

I get up on Cricket and start back for the camp with the rest of the horses. Little Fox has taken one of the smaller horses—probably Treat's—for his own. I'm beginning to be glad what I done to Joe Crane. When we get back to the firelight, Ink is kneeling next to Joe Crane and she's pulling the rest of his scalp off. She's already mutilated Treat.

"Come on, now," I say. "There's no use in that."

But she finishes the job. Then sheathes the knife and climbs up on her horse. She struggles to do it, but when I reach out to help her, she brushes my hand away. I know it hurts her to be on that horse. She sits there for a spell looking at the fire, holding the scalps in her hand. Then she ties them to the side of her saddle.

"You'll just attract mosquitoes and flies," I say.

She turns and starts south and I follow along. I don't know where she thinks she's going nor why, but I don't have nothing to say now. Little Fox rides between us. She has not spoken to him, and he ain't said nothing, neither.

{ CHAPTER 26 }

I FOLLOW HER MOST of the night, then at dawn she turns up toward a long hillside. We're well south and west of where we first come to the Yellowstone, and now we've just crossed the Powder River. We're in dangerous country again—back where we might run into folks who will want to kill me. Ink still has not said a word. She won't look at me, neither.

I tried talking all along the trail, but in the dark I couldn't even tell if she was listening. Every now and then Little Fox would turn around and nod; I think he felt sorry for me. I made up my mind I'd leave her alone and let her work out when she might want to say something. For the last two or three hours of our night ride, I rode in silence, listening to the darkness and the rush of the river.

Now we ride up a long, sloping rise. We are headed for some trees again. The sky is almost full blue now, and white clouds crowd the horizon, like they might rise up and overtake the sun when the time comes. The sun ain't far from beneath the horizon. The land is powerful dark green. There's purple flowers everywhere on top of the green meadows. They seem to scurry from one end of the plains to the other. Cricket has developed the skill of dropping her head down and picking some of the greenery to eat while we walk along. We are making good time, but we'll have to stop soon, and it ain't looking like good country for a camp. I don't want to be in the open with all these horses.

"We got to stop soon," I say.

She looks down at the scalps on her saddle, but she don't change the way she's moving. She rides along, bending herself a bit with each step of her horse as we make our way up the slope. I can see it really hurts her to be a-setting in that saddle. I know what she's been through rendered her pretty tender and sore and I feel mighty sorrowful for her. It's full daylight before we get into the trees and the ground levels off a bit. I'm getting real hungry. I take up my canteen and drink some water. It has been a cold night and now the sun begins to warm things. I feel the heat and sweat of Cricket under me.

Finally Ink pulls up. I ride up next to her. All the horses stand around, breathing heavy.

"You want to camp here?" I say.

She studies the ground.

"This looks like the best spot," I say.

She gets down and walks a ways. I stay where I am. She ties her horse to a tree, then starts unpacking her bedroll. She's still wearing Treat's shirt, vest, and trousers. She's got the vest buttoned in the front, but it hangs on her loosely. The armholes dangle very low on her and there's blood on the front of the shirt near the collar on one side.

When we get camp set up, and I've got the horses tethered, I leave her with Little Fox and the Colt Dragoon, and ride off on Cricket a-hunting again. It's a bright, hot day, but the sun only breaks through the canopy of the trees in long, sweeping needles and curtains of light. It looks like I wandered into some kind of giant church—a great dome of heaven, maybe. I don't get far in the woods before I stumble on a bear with her cubs. She's huge and brown. You don't mess with grizzly bears, especially when there's a cub around, so I make a wide circle around her. She's moving in the other direction, further into the trees. I don't worry about Ink none. Not with the bear anyway. I wonder if she'll ever say another word.

About a mile or so north of where I left Ink, I see a doe. She's laying down until she hears me, and as I come through the brush she stands up and I raise my carbine and shoot her before she can bolt. She's small and light. Lighter than Ink, probably. But she'll do. I throw her over Cricket's back, across my saddle, then jump up behind her and hold on as we move along back toward camp.

On the way I see the grizzly again. This time she's coming down the trail, headed for our camp. Cricket don't like it much, but I force her to gallop toward the bear. I shout, then fire my carbine in the air, and the grizzly lets out a kind of grunt—like a big drunk growing sober—and then moves off in the other direction.

Ink is sleeping at the base of a tree with the Colt pistol in her lap. Little Fox is crouched next to her, ready, the bow in his hands with a arrow in it. "Don't shoot me," I say. When Ink wakes and sees me, her eyes change some, but I can't tell if she's happy to see me or the doe. She cleans it good and cuts up the meat and I make a campfire. In these woods it don't matter about the smoke. She cooks the meat over the fire and we eat in silence. I figure there's no point in trying to get her to talk to me and I don't have nothing to say. Little Fox watches both of us. When we finish eating, he moves over next to her and puts his hand up on the back of her neck, staring into her eyes. "Ha-ho," he whispers. "Ha-ho."

She starts crying again. She puts her arms around him and looks at me. " 'Friend,' " she says. "He just called me 'friend.' "

"Well, you are," I say. "He knows it."

She pats his head, fighting her tears.

"He stayed with me all through this," I said. "Running like hell, he stayed right with me. He's a young brave, is what he is."

She tries to tell him what I said in Cheyenne. He pulls back and looks up at her, but he don't say nothing.

She spends most of the day scraping the deerskin with her sheath knife and rubbing it with wood ash from the fire. Then she pours salt all over it and lays it out on the ground in a place where the sun breaks through.

"That won't be ready to wear for a long time," I say.

She's gotten all the hair off of it, and there ain't no flesh or blood I can see. It's a clean piece of leather now. When it dries out completely, she'll finish tanning it and then she can make a shirt and wear it. She's got enough for trousers, too, I think.

I sleep for a good long while in the afternoon, and when I wake she's got the deer meat packed in a kind of pouch she's crafted from a small portion of the skin. She's salted all of it to keep the flies away. She's draped the rest of the cleaned skin over one of the other horses and strapped it down. She ain't got the scalps on her saddle no more. Little Fox is already mounted, and she clambers up on her horse and waits for me.

"I'd like to wash my face," I say. I get my canteen and splash myself. The whole time they set there watching me.

When I get up on Cricket, I say, "I don't blame you if you want to kill me."

There's still sun, but it's well below the trees now and not breaking through much at all. I can barely see her face in the dim light, but I see her eyes glistening and I know she is frowning. Then she whispers, "No."

I say, "Well, I wouldn't blame you."

She turns her mount and I follow her again, headed south and west toward Bighorn country. We get to the Powder River and ride along next to it in the dark. It's hard to go with a person that you know must hate the sight of you for being a white man. I don't think she'll kill me but I can feel that hate coming off her like a odor or something.

We ride for a hour or so until the ground levels off again. We are very near the river. I can hear the water rushing over stones and through cuts along its way. What's left of the moon rises over the high ground, about half full but not strong enough to make a shadow. The sky is streaked white with stars that seem to run behind low, thin clouds.

Suddenly, out of the blue and not really looking at me, Ink says, "Why would I want to kill you?"

I am so surprised to hear her voice again, it takes me back a second. Then I say, "I know what they done. They was white men. I'm a white man. If I was you, I'd hate all men. All white men anyway."

"I hate those men."

"Yeah, well."

We find a good place to cross the Powder River, then we keep next to the Yellowstone as it goes south and west. I don't know why, but it feels like I want her to talk for her own good and mine. Finally I say, "You okay?"

"I am many sleeps away from okay."

"Many sleeps?"

"I am Indian," she says. "Right now I am Indian."

"I don't blame you."

"To me," she says, "you are Indian too."

"I've killed enough of Indians, I think they might not take kindly to it if I enlist among 'em."

"Are you an Indian fighter?"

"No. But I ended up fighting a lot of them anyway. If you want to call it fighting."

She looks at me.

"When I shot you, I was fighting Indians."

"That is how you fight?"

"It's how a lot of us fight. From a distance. The cavalry rides right in among 'em if they can catch 'em sleeping."

We get quiet again for a while. I wait for her to say something else, and when she don't, I say, "You ain't never gonna talk about what happened, are you?"

"No," she says. "No. I will not."

"I understand it," I say. "You mind if I ask where we're going? We must be near where your village was when you run off."

"I want to take Little Fox back to his people."

"So we're *looking* for Indians?"

"He has told me where to look—in the Bighorn country. That is where we're going."

"We can't go into that country," I say. "We should cross to the north side of this here river and go on west to Bozeman. We should not go further south."

"We go this way," Ink says. "We have been over this country and we know what is in front of us."

"What about Hump?"

"He is not here. I know it."

"You was waiting for him up in them trees near Buford all this time, wasn't you?"

She says nothing.

"You waited for him, and when you was sure he wasn't after you no more . . ."

She looks at me.

"You think you'll find his people back in that country? There's soldiers all over it. I know. I was among 'em."

"If we don't find his village, then we'll go to Indian country. No white men."

"I don't know where you think that is."

"We go to Idaho. To the land of the Nez Perce."

"Why we got to go through the same country we just left?"

"We know the trail. That is best and easiest," she says. "It is where Little Fox thinks his people are. We can travel at night."

It hits me that she's saying more words to me than at any time since she was taken. "Look," I say. "I *can't* go back there."

Now she looks at me.

"I want to go west real bad too," I say. And then when Ink looks at me, I realize I can't explain it to her. Anyway, it'll be well into July before we ever get to Bozeman. Eveline's probably halfway to Utah by now. "I ain't told you much of this, but I'm on the run too," I say. "It's one of the reasons I shot you."

She pulls back a little on her horse and stops. I stop too. Cricket nods her head up and down a bit, then starts eating the saw grass in front of her.

"What do you mean, you are on the run?"

"I got soldiers *and* Indians after me."

She wheels her horse around and faces me. It's just dark enough that I can see the whites of Ink's eyes and the shadows of the horses. Little Fox has gone on a little but now he stops too. He turns his horse and sets there waiting. There ain't a peep out of him. We stand there like that, Cricket facing her horse and Ink staring at me to beat all, then she motions for me to let go of the packhorses. I remove the lariat from the lead horse but leave them all tethered together, and they start feeding in the field around us and just off the trail. I ain't telling her nothing if I don't have to, but then she says, "What did you do?"

"It don't matter. If the wrong soldier or Indian finds me, I'm a dead man."

"Why?"

"I killed a peace party." I don't want to, but I tell her all about it. I let her have the whole story about Big Tree and White Dog. The anger I felt and how I seen White Dog and that red bandana and something in me snapped. "It was a accident," I say. "I didn't know it was a peace party. Hell, I didn't even know I'd do what I done." It sounds good to me. I don't know if I really believe it. What I done surprised me, I'll own up to that. But I can't half believe it was something I had no control of or didn't want.

"But how does any of them know it was you?"

"The trooper that left me there watching the trail knows, and them two braves that got away seen me too. They got a good look at me."

She shakes her head. "What about your betrothed? You will not get back to her sooner this way, knowing the trails as we do?"

"Hell, she ain't in Bozeman no more. She said she'd wait 'til June. We're well-nigh into that now."

"We will go south first," she says.

"A lot of them folks on both sides know me," I say. "I can't take the chance to be in any a their company."

"No one is chasing you," Ink says, and I think I sense a kind of contempt in her voice.

"I don't know that," I say. "I do know if the right fellow sees me, he'll chase me."

"We will travel at night," she says. "We have done just fine traveling at night."

She's right about that, I have to admit. She got taken in broad daylight, but we done pretty well in the dark.

We let the horses feed a bit longer, then start off again, almost directly south. I don't argue with her. All that night, it is one hell of a quiet ride. I only hear the water rippling in the river, the soft tread of the horses on meadow grass and mud, and the creak of my saddle. It is kind of creepy, to tell the truth: I'm riding alone under a pale sliver of moon with eight horses and this little thing next to me, and Ink that stares off in the starlight like a cat. And she will *be* like a cat to me. She will be with me as long as she needs, and when she is done she'll wander off by herself, a-looking at the world. From that moment I won't exist no more.

We follow the Yellowstone all the way to the Tongue River. We trail south along that river for a few days, then head directly west. Little Fox helps out when we set up camp. He's especially good with the horses. I leave most of that work to him now. It's nice some days to talk to him at least. He is amazed at my thick beard and long red hair.

He likes the stories I tell even though he don't understand a word. Ink sets there and listens. She's always got her ears perked up, and since I know she can hear better than a elk or a squirrel, I don't pay no attention to what's happening around us.

Some nights, riding in the dark, I realize as I listen to the creaking of my saddle and the soft clinking of metal in Cricket's bridle that I miss Ink a little. The woman she was before she got taken. She's all business now and don't pay me no attention at all except to tell me what to do. I think if I don't do what she wants she'll judge me in ways I can't abide. She might even be afraid of me and what I might eventually do and I don't want that. I think it's real important that she knows I will protect her. I know it don't make no sense, but I believe that's what keeps me going along behind her in the dark.

In another week we cross Rosebud Creek and I know we're near the Bighorn River. I get more and more nervous with every mile. In the dim light of early morning we cross a wide trail—horses and travois tracks through the countryside that are as broad as the tracks left by a wagon train. The next morning, just before we stop for the day, we cross several places where we see wagon tracks and the prints of hundreds of shod horses. I know Brisbin and Gibbon are in this area and probably by now Reno and Custer too. I never seen so many Indian tracks, though. We ride down into a coulee and stay next to a pretty big river. I think it must be the Bighorn. We camp at dawn near a small creek that runs off the river. I tell Ink this valley is thick with soldiers and Indians and it ain't safe no more to be moving around in it. As I tie the horses up close by, I notice a lot of tracks on the ground here too. Horse and travois tracks make a wide path along this side of the river. It's a damn miracle we ain't been run over in our sleep.

We stay completely still most of that day. I don't think I sleep more than a half hour or so, and when the sun begins to drop behind the high hills behind us, we start off again. We move slow and quiet most of the night. I watch for campfires, and around midnight we come upon a long slope and rising part of the country that runs up against scrub brush and small timber this side of the river. It's still pretty dark, but I see a glow just over the rise. And then I hear it. A kind of soft rumble that's too regular to be distant thunder. Ink comes up next to me and says, "It is a dance."

"You don't say."

Little Fox looks out at the light with wide, watchful eyes.

"I don't think it is a war dance," she says. "I think it is just celebration."

"How do you know that?"

"The drums," she says.

I listen but now I don't hear nothing but the tree frogs and crickets. "What drums? They stopped."

She says, "It is just a social time."

We start gently up the hill. When we get to the top I see a sight I never thought I'd ever see. Hundreds of fires light the sky, and there are lodges everywhere, all grouped together in a line of big half circles up that whole side of the river. All of them face east, and there must be a hundred of them, with thirty, forty, fifty tepees in each one. Ink stares down the hill in awe. I hear the drums again now, the voices of the dancers.

"It is all of them," she says. "Cheyenne, Sioux—Uncpapa, Ogalala, Arrows All Gone, Assiniboines."

"What is it, every Indian in the world?"

"I have never seen so many."

"Well, we gotta get away from here," I say. "I told you we shouldn't come back this way."

Little Fox pulls back on his horse and looks at us. Ink says, "If his people are here, he will know it."

"What do you mean?"

"He will recognize his family's lodge."

I say nothing. Little Fox stares down that hill now.

"I will take him there," Ink says. "Down there."

"You can't do that."

"I must."

"What if Hump is there?"

That stops her. She turns to Little Fox, points at the camp. He nods, and before either of us can say or do nothing, he kicks his horse and starts down the hill. We steady our horses, and then he stops and turns around to look at us—like he don't believe what he's doing and wants to remember us for all time. Then he raises his arm high, in a strong manly wave, and goes on down the hill.

"He don't want to go down there," I say.

Ink turns her mount and trots away and I follow.

We ought to put a lot of ground between us and that Indian camp, but with all the horses to manage and no help from Little Fox, we don't get too far, maybe two or three miles. I can see Ink don't want to get so far away Little Fox won't be able to find us. We go back toward Rosebud Creek and find a place deep in the trees there to camp. It takes me a while to get the horses tethered out of sight. There is not much grass here and I know we cannot stay long. By now the sun leaks through the trees and scatters misty light everywhere. If we don't make a fire, I don't think we can be seen. When I get back to Ink, she is sitting in the shadows of the trees with her arms wrapped around her knees and her head down.

"You should maybe have stopped him," I say. "You feel bad he's gone?"

She looks at me. "I would not take him."

"What do you mean?"

"I would not keep him if he didn't want to stay."

"But you're still sad."

"If it will make you happy, then I will say I'm sad."

This really takes me down. I don't know what to say. She puts her head back on her arms. I sit there for a minute looking at her, thinking about what I give up to stay with her and the boy all this time while the weather warmed and spring commenced. But all I say is "It wouldn't make me happy at all."

We don't hear no more movements or see no more Indians for a while. It is already well into June. Little Fox is not coming back, and I decide we got to go on back to Bozeman anyway. I know Eveline is gone but I got to see for myself. I can leave Ink in Bozeman. She can go to Fort Ellis herself and start the rest of her life without me. She said that first day I met her that she wanted to go to Fort Buford because that was the last place she lived with her father. Maybe she'll find some people at Fort Ellis that remember her.

I tell Ink we are leaving when the sun goes down and she says nothing. She starts packing everything up.

"I'll go get the horses," I say, but as I turn to do so, I hear horses coming. Ink stops what she's doing and looks at me. I get down low and she does the same. I got my carbine off my shoulder and she has her pistol pointing back toward the noise. She lets out a little girlish sound in the back of her throat when Little Fox comes into view through the trees. He is mounted, leading our horses behind him.

Ink almost runs to him. He dismounts and stands there looking up at her. She says something to him and he says, "Ha-ho."

Both of them look at me. "We got to get out of here," I say. But I guess I'm smiling.

"His family was not in the camp," Ink whispers later as we ride along in the dark. We are next to a creek that runs west from the Rosebud. The Bighorn River should be right in front of us if we keep going.

"So he's come back to us," I say.

"I am his family now," she says.

"Of course. That's what I meant."

Toward morning, Little Fox shoots a deer with his bow and we decide to camp for the day a little early.

Ink guts the deer and cuts it up good and we cook it over a small buffalo chip fire. It makes more smoke than I would like, but we are hid away in a gulch that runs next to the creek and I don't think no folks can see us unless they come down into the creek and ride up to us. After we eat the broiled meat, I settle back against my saddle and rest. I think to sleep soon. I watch Little Fox helping Ink tan the skin on the deer. He can creep through the brush as good as any Indian. It's in his blood. I watch him and it gives me a start to think he will one day creep through leaves and brush so he can get close enough to kill a man. A chill goes through me.

"He'll grow up and be a killer just like the rest of us," I say out loud. I do that now—just speak out at the air and all—and if Ink thinks to answer, she will.

"Listen," Ink says.

"What?"

"That sounded like a horn."

"I didn't hear nothing."

"I think it is soldiers," she says.

"I shouldn't of built that damned fire," I say. "We better put it out."

"Is it soldiers?" Ink says.

"If it's somebody I know," I say, "I'll probably have to shoot the son of a bitch."

{ CHAPTER 27 }

BEFORE WE KNOW it, we are surrounded by commotion and noise. Horses and I don't know how many folks move along on the ridge above the gorge in the creek where we are crouched. I can't see nobody, but I hear a lot of shooting and Indian yipping and hollering. We cover the fire with a soaked piece of the skin from the deer and then lay down against the bank of the creek, and Ink holds on to Little Fox. He ain't afraid, and he already knows not to make no movement that might give us away. We lay there listening and the water starts to rise at our feet. The horses are tethered downstream a ways, in a darkly shaded coulee surrounded by pine trees and thick brush. Anybody riding along the creek can see them, but the slope of the ground on our side of the creek, and the low-hanging branches of trees on the other bank, should conceal them from folks not trying to find them.

I got my carbine and the Colt pistol. I huddle up next to Ink and watch the other bank. I can see the bank above us in the reflection of the water at our feet. I look for anything that moves. It seems like hours go by, but maybe it's only a few minutes. The noise gradually moves away from us. Ink turns around and looks at me over the little guy's dark head. I see fear in her eyes.

"It's probably the soldiers rounding up Indians," I say. "They ain't seen us." The noise is in the distance now. There's as much yelling as shooting. The firing is irregular, but once it gets going, it goes very thick, each quick pop of hundreds of guns echoing in the hills.

"I ain't heard noise like that since the war," I say. "It's a battle."

Ink says, "We have to move."

"It ain't safe."

Little Fox looks up at me. His mouth is slightly open. He signs to me about going to get the horses. "We got to stay here for now," I say.

"Mo ache noch," he says.

"That means 'horse,'" Ink says.

"No," I say. "Tell him we have to stay put. The sun's got a long way to go before it's down."

I wish I could make him understand that we are safest here, in this near cave over the creek that keeps us pretty much out of sight. Only folks on the opposite side of the creek might see us if they cut through considerable underbrush to get to the edge of the stream.

And then I hear horses across from us on that other side behind the brush. A lot of horses. I turn and face whatever's coming through the trees on that side. To our right, coming down out of the hills on that side, trampling through the brush, riding along at a trot, is more Indians than I ever seen at one time in my life. They just keep coming. Cheyenne, Arapaho, Sioux, Blackfeet. They ride together, they got paint on, and they mean business. Most have bows and arrows. I see a few spears and every now and then one of them carries a rifle. The go right by us, only a few yards away, and it takes a long time for all of them to cross the stream and head up the other side of the bank. They are so intent on where they are going, they don't pay no attention to us at all.

"Something really big is going on," I say. "I have to see what it is."

"No," Ink says.

"Stay here," I say. "Nobody seen us." I give her the Colt pistol and sling the carbine over my shoulder. I'm wearing a leather vest, yellow leggings, and moccasins. I got long hair, and I realize even with red hair I might be mistaken for a Indian, so I use a piece of leather to tie my hair back. I'm wearing my army-issue hat. It's blue with a black visor and crossed rifles in the front of it, but it sits low on my head.

Ink says, "You look like a renegade."

"Well," I say, "I guess that's what I am." I take the hat off and hand it to her. I smile, but she only looks away. "Just stay here," I say. "I'll be right back." I start to move away and the little guy grabs my arm. His eyes freeze me for a second. Then he says, "Tosend aus tearth?"

Ink says, "He wants to know where you're going."

"I'll be back."

Little Fox says something else I can't hear. Ink says, "He told you to come back."

"I will," I say to him. "Don't fret." I pat his head and he almost smiles.

Ink puts her face against his head and watches me leave. The embankment is steeper than the one we come down to get here. I crawl up through wet clay, then prickly grass, until I reach the top. I lay on the ground at the base of a pine tree on the edge of a clearing and I see that the ground rises gradually in front of me. It's covered in brush and green grass as it rises farther and farther. To my left the Indians scurry up the hill, moving pretty fast now. There's a stand of trees over there, and I see lots of blue uniforms on foot, moving in the underbrush, firing on the Indians in front of them. Those fellows are cut off from the group on my right, where the hill slopes down a bit, then rises again toward the Little Bighorn River. There's another crest over there, and I realize it is beginning to thicken with blue uniforms. I'm close enough that I can aim my carbine and hit one or two of them. I see the flag, and their colors fall. Further over to my right, beginning to ascend the hill on horseback, more Indians ride, lunging and screaming, weapons held high over their heads. Then I see smoke in the air and hear more gunfire. Some of the soldiers move back and forth on horseback, waving bright weapons, and the ones on foot begin to form a circle at the crest of the hill across from me. Horses fall and more men dismount. Now the sound of the gunfire increases. I see puffs of smoke, then seconds later hear the report of the guns. The Indians on my left wheel to their right and ride in front of me toward the hill on the other side where the soldiers have gathered. They are yipping and hollering to beat all, and now they're riding in big circles at the bottom of the hill, around the group of soldiers who kneel on the crest, firing their guns.

I start to move back down toward the creek and Ink, but I see her coming up the other side of the coulee to my right. She's got Little Fox with her and he's got the horses. When she rides up to me she says, "We must go."

"Get back down there," I say. "What's got into you?"

She has a look of panic on her face, and I see the boy, too, is terrified.

I wanted her to go back, but now I think that is not such a good idea. I see more Indians coming from below us, running on foot from where the others had come. They will cross right next to us and on foot they won't miss us. I walk over and get up on Cricket. I reach out to Ink and take her by the arm. I holler into her ear, "The safest thing to do is go on down this stream toward that fight and wait in the trees down yonder until it's over."

She don't say nothing. She sets there watching me, and I realize she's going to do what I say. We ride along the creek and down the side of the hill until we reach the trees at the bottom. We have moved closer to what's going on at the top of the hill on the other side of the trees. When we get to a place where I think it's safe to tie the horses, I move on foot through the underbrush so I can get to where I can see everything. Ink and Little Fox follow me. His eyes are big and focused. In front of me I see a lot of horses and two young braves watching them. They ain't much older than Little Fox. I move around to the left of them, holding my carbine ready if I have to use it. We get to where we can make out most of the ground before us, even in the smoke, and what I see don't fully register right away. Near the bottom of the hill a horde of Indians on horseback ride back and forth shouting war cries and waving spears and rifles high over their heads. They're too far away from the soldiers, so they can't be hit with no bullets or do no business with their rifles or arrows. In front of them, though, further up, the hill is covered with Indians moving around mostly on foot, shooting toward a group of maybe two or three hundred blue-coated soldiers at the top. The fellows on foot, moving steadily up the hill, drop down in the sagebrush to put a arrow in their bow, stand up to shoot, run a few paces, and drop down again. Hundreds of them, all around the hill. The ground is littered with dead horses and dead soldiers and a few Indians. The noise is deafening and the smoke begins to thicken and makes it hard to see clearly. I don't know how long we watch. The fight goes on for at least a hour, maybe more. The Indians keep coming, more and more of them getting down off horses and starting up the hill. Most firing arrows. Some with pistols and some more with rifles. I'm just beginning to think we should run away from here when I realize the Indians have stopped firing arrows. I don't hear their guns, neither. A strange and eerie lull sweeps over the field like sudden weather, and through the blue smoke I see one of the soldiers put his pistol to his head and shoot hisself. The soldier next to him does the same. Then another one. The Indians watch in amazement.

FAR AS THE EYE CAN SEE

Their yipping quiets a little when they see what's going on. One soldier after another, some of them right at the same time, shoots hisself in the head. Some of them shoot the fellow next to them, then theirselves. It don't take long and they're all dead. I don't know how many of them was left before they started killing theirselves, but after fighting so long it was a wild thing to see.

Ink looks at me when she realizes what they done. She says something I can't hear in the noise of the Indian celebration, so I lean in close to her and put my ear in front of her mouth.

"White men are crazy," she says.

"I'm white," I say.

Them Indians killed maybe fifty or sixty of them soldiers on that hill before the bluecoats started killing their own selves with their own guns. It is the damnedest thing I ever seen in my whole life, and that includes Stone Mountain and Chickamauga. It give me the most empty feeling, like ain't nothing under my skin but air, and I can't get enough of that to keep on living.

Ink starts crying. Little Fox commences, too, but he don't want to show it. "You both shut up," I say. "We got to stay out of sight here and get the hell out when it's dark."

There's still a lot of smoke and the Indians carry on, doing a little scalping and celebrating up and down both sides of the hill. They ain't paying much attention to what's going on in the trees at the bottom of the hill. I get the horses and we start off on foot, leading them into a deep ravine that runs down into the Little Bighorn River. We tie the horses in the deepest part of the ravine, then hunker down under deep-green branches and underbrush that covers us pretty well. I let Little Fox keep watch first and try to get some sleep.

I don't know as I got much sleep, but Ink comes to me just as the dusk begins, and we start off again on foot, leading the horses. I'm in the lead with Ink behind me, and Little Fox in back with the horses behind him.

On the other side of the river we see hundreds of horses and a few more braves watching over them. I don't know if they see us or not. We head upstream toward the place where the Little Bighorn River meets the Bighorn River. We can hear more fighting on the other side of the hill, in the trees. We stay on foot most of that way until it is completely dark. When we get far enough north of the massacre, we mount up and ride along the Bighorn until we see the Yellowstone sparkling in the morning sun.

We camp near the river and I sleep most of that morning. It's early in the afternoon and strangely quiet when I wake up.

"We made forty miles or more, last night," I say.

Ink don't look at me. Little Fox sits facing her, eating what's left of the deer meat.

"We can travel in the daylight now, I expect."

"We can?"

"I think we've left every Indian and soldier back at the Little Bighorn. Ain't no army up this way. Nor Indians. They're all down in the valley, killing each other."

That afternoon we cross the Yellowstone River and head west over some rough terrain. Traveling in the daytime, it's easier to find the path, though. I don't even think no more about who we might run into. The country is empty in front of us.

When it starts to get dark, we stop. I let Ink set up camp, and I go off by myself to scout the territory and figure out what we might do in the morning.

{ CHAPTER 28 }

OW IT'S ME that don't have nothing to say. Every day we ride along in silence. We're headed for Bozeman. It's almost July now. I run through my mind all the things Eveline would say to me and what I might say back. All I promised was I'd try to get back to her, and I did do that. She would of done the same thing if she found herself in my predicament. Anyway, I never told her I loved her nor nothing like that. We understood the both of us what might happen if things didn't go like we planned. I expect she's happy, headed on to Oregon with a fellow a lot better than me, and after a while I don't feel so bad about all of it no more. I go through this progression of thinking most every day, and so by dusk, when we stop to camp, I feel like I done my best and it's okay. Only in the fresh evening sky, when light falls off the world, and we got to make camp and settle in for the night, I commence to get sad all over again.

And still we ride in silence. The boy don't know English, and when he speaks at all it's in a language even Ink don't fully understand, even though he has no trouble helping her figure out what he wants.

We fight hot weather and scorching winds on some days, and in the night we rest under dry trees or as close to stones and boulders as we can get. The country rises and gets more and more rocky. We are near the Musselshell when I finally kill something larger than a groundhog. It's a good-sized elk calf. And then one morning a week or so later a herd of buffalo wanders nearby and I kill one of them. They ain't easy to kill, neither, not with a rifle like my carbine. But I fell one and then put a bullet in his brain to finish him off. We have plenty of meat and skins to boot. Ink wraps what we don't eat in bloody bags of skin so it will keep. By the time we're back near Bozeman, I'm ready for some kind of talk.

"You know," I say, "them fellows on that hill was just doing what they was told."

She says nothing. We sit by a fire, late in the evening, just before dark. The sky ain't got much light left in it, and the moon gets brighter and higher. Little Fox is asleep on the ground next to Ink and she rubs his hair gently, staring at the fire. He sleeps most of the night now, and we both set our schedule from his waking and sleeping. We know when he wakes up we will start traveling again.

I clear my throat to let Ink know I'm about to say something. She don't look at me, but I go ahead anyway. "I remember when I went to work for the army, the talk was you didn't want to be caught by no Indian. Save the last bullet for yourself. Them fellows heard about the mutilations," I say. "Some may of seen it."

She lifts her hand from Little Fox's head and lets it rest on her thigh. She's got her legs crossed. She don't look so scrawny no more because we been eating pretty good since we left the Missouri. Now when I look at her I can see how one day she will be a heavy, low-riding squaw. I don't know, it's a image I get suddenly sometimes. She's half white, but she's got a jaw that will be fat and round someday, and arms that will be heavy, and she'll be worked to death from life on the plains. It ain't no wonder she wanted to run away. She looks at me now and I see she's thinking hard about something.

"What?" I say.

She shakes her head.

"You worrying again about Hump?"

"No." She slants her eyes away.

"What is it?"

"I saw Hump. Back there."

"Back where?"

"At the battle."

"You're gonna tell me you actually seen him in all that smoke and confusion."

"I know his horse. He always rode a big painted horse. And he wore a full headdress in battle. It was him."

"So he ain't after you no more."

"Maybe he never came after me." She says this kind of disappointed.

282

"You feel bad about that?"

"His horse got shot out from under him. I do not know if he was killed."

"Well, now he is for sure busy enough that he ain't concerned with you no more."

She looks at me like she's a-wondering something of a puzzle.

"Or maybe he wasn't never after you," I say.

Her eyes glitter, but she don't say nothing.

"You feel sorry about it, don't you," I say.

"I hope he was not killed."

"Well, that's a damn fine thing. You go on and hope like that."

"I knew him for a man," she says. "He was not cruel."

"But you run from him anyway."

"I ran from that life."

I don't bother to mention what Hump may of done to me and her if he was chasing after us and he caught up, but she knows it. All I say is, "Well, you got far from it, didn't you?"

"Now I want to go back," she says.

"Back to Hump?"

"No. Don't be so loud. You'll wake the boy." She pauses for a second, then she says, "I do not want to live with white men. Not now. Not with . . ." She don't finish, but she looks down at Little Fox and I know what she means.

"I'm a white man," I say.

"You are not like other white men."

"I'm just like other white men." She knows it too.

"You won't harm me or the boy. You will protect us."

"Well," I say. "You got me there."

She actually smiles a little. Then she says, "Not like any other white men."

"Maybe not." It's almost dark and we got to get some sleep, but this is the most she's talked since she got took. I take a deep breath and say, "I guess we'll be in Bozeman soon."

She don't say nothing.

"Probably tomorrow."

She looks at me and I think she's going to shush me, because the boy is sleeping next to her, but she bites her lower lip slightly, then she says, "You have done well."

I look away, kind of on the spot. "Well, I . . . You know . . ."

She gets up and comes over to me, stands there looking down on me, and in the firelight her face looks eerie and cold, like she's passed judgment and she's about to shoot me to put me out of my misery. Then, by God, she sinks to her knees and sort of falls into my arms. She rests her head on my breast and I hold her again, like I did that awful day she bathed in the river and washed off the horror of what Treat and his gang done to her. She is crying again, and I pat the hair on the back of her head and don't say nothing for fear she will move away. I know this must shame her somehow, because I'm a man and for what men have put her through. Still, it's right generous the way she holds on and lets me touch her hair and all. It don't occur to me what she might want, or what I want. We just stay that way for I don't know how long and then she gathers her breath back and stops crying, but she stays where she is, thinking again.

"What?" I say.

She moves back a little and looks at me. Her eyes are soft now, and dark, and they sparkle from the fire and the moon. "We should go around the town."

"Around it?"

"If we are going to the land of the Nez Perce, we can go around Bozeman."

"If that's what you want," I say. "We got plenty to eat."

She glances at the boy. "In Bozeman, they will not understand."

"I know."

It's quiet for a spell, then she says, "We travel at night again, leave the day for camping." Now she's all business, but she's still there in my arms, real close. It puts shame in my mind, and embarrassment. I start to move away, but she holds on.

"We don't need to do that," I say. "We'll go much faster if we can see the trail by sunlight. And ain't nobody interested in us no more."

"I am thinking of the heat," she says. "It may be hard on you."

"I ain't going to wilt in the sun."

She seems to nod. It strikes me that for the first time she thinks of me in a way caring and womanly, and I am grateful for it.

"You know," I say, "I should go into Bozeman by myself. I need some cartridges."

She thinks for a spell, then she says, "You will go to find your betrothed."

"No. She's gone. Ain't no way she waited this long."

"But the army. You said the army is going to be after you."

"I know. I got to take that chance. I don't expect there's many of them left at Fort Ellis, and anyway, maybe they don't know yet what went on in the Yellowstone valley."

"You should not take chances," she says. Her voice is a bit softer now, but still I think I should try to get her off me. Gently and all, but maybe to help her move away without awkwardness. I think she don't know how to disentangle herself. She don't want to set herself against me, but this ain't nothing carnal, neither. Carnal don't enter into it. But when I start to move under her a little, she puts her head back in the crook of my neck, sort of holds me back, then she scoots up a little and puts her mouth right up on mine and kisses me. It's a kiss that stirs me considerable. Morning Breeze never used her mouth that way, and Eveline never done it like that, neither. I feel my heart stutter and then it feels like it drops down a little in my chest. It's a good feeling and I hold Ink up against me now tight and realize this here's carnal as it can be.

She pulls back a little and looks me in the eye. "I must not lose you," she says.

I just set there a-holding her, and nodding my head, and then she kind of sets up and pushes her hair back and the boy rouses. I think to say: *As long as the boy's here you're safe. But don't ever kiss me like that again unless you want to incite me to considerable passion.* I don't say nothing, though. I only find a lot to swallow suddenly in my throat, and she sees me take a big gulp of air. Then finally I say, "Damn."

"When we can," she says. "The next time we stop and Little Fox is asleep."

I know what she means, and I feel that drop in the bottom half of my heart again. "Sure," I say. "Sure enough."

*   *   *

Even though she is dead set against it, I pack a few things and prepare to head into Bozeman. I have to find out what happened to Eveline. Besides, I'm gonna try and sell three of the horses and some buffalo robes. When I'm up on Cricket looking down at her and the boy, I say, "I won't be until this time tomorrow night."

She says, "We will be ready."

The boy comes over and stands next to Cricket. He touches my boot in the stirrup. He mumbles something I don't understand, and then he actually smiles a little. I think he might start crying again, but he's fighting it and being brave. Ink comes over and puts her arm around his shoulders. They really do look like a mother and son to me, and I feel like I ought to take care of them both. I reach down and touch the top of Little Fox's head. "You mind your ma," I say. He don't understand it, and she ain't his ma, but I say it anyway.

I ride along in the dark all the way to Bozeman and I can't think about nothing but the way she looked when I left the camp. There was a believing and hoping behind her eyes, a thing between us that was never there before, but now comes at me with the strength of some true fact about living and dying, like knowledge of the seasons and weather and the certain end of everything. I swear, it's amazing how much a thing can change in a single damn minute. Ink kisses me and now it ain't like nothing I can remember that claws at me the farther away from her I get. And not just her. The boy too.

{ CHAPTER 29 }

IT'S ALMOST DAWN when I get to Bozeman. I ride on in and avoid Fort Ellis. I go to the livery stable and leave Cricket there to be fed and brushed. I hand the other horses and the buffalo robes over to the fellow at the stable and tell him to see if he can sell it all to the army. "They're good animals," I say. "And them skins will make damn fine coats."

He looks everything over and agrees. "I'll get what I can for them."

"I'll give you ten percent of whatever you get."

"I'll take fifteen."

"Fine," I say.

Then I go to the bathhouse and buy a hot bath. When I'm done with it and coming to the street all clean and feeling more awake, I realize I'm getting ready to walk all the way to the end of the street and see if the wagon and Eveline and Christine are still there. I don't think it's in my heart to hope that they are but I got to know. That's what I tell myself anyway.

As I'm standing there in front of the bathhouse, a fellow I think to recognize but can't place walks up to me and stops. "Excuse me," he says. "You rented a room from me here a while ago."

"Here?"

"At Miss Pound's place."

I realize it's Robert. He's still got the long face, but now he's got a white beard clipped close to the jaw so it don't seem to lengthen the face none. His droopy eyes still look half awake. He takes my hand and starts shaking it. "I expect you'd be Bobby Hale?"

"I could be."

"Fellow at the stable told me you'd be here," he says. He lets go my hand.

"I won't be staying," I say. "I don't need no room."

"No, I have something for you."

287

"I forgot something?"

"You was staying with them sisters in the wagon."

"I was."

"They finally took off for the far west—just a fortnight ago. First week of July, I believe it was, but they left something for you."

He seems very pleased that he can deliver what they left for me. So I follow him over to Miss Pound's place. He hands me the Shakespeare book, two envelopes and a box. "They told me to be sure you got these things if you come back here." He stands there like a waiter expecting recompense. "They waited a long time. You just did miss them," he says. His face is gray and pitted like a tombstone, and the white beard looks icy even in August.

"You can keep the book," I say.

"Thank you kindly."

I got nowhere to sit down and open these things, so I ask him if'n he'd mind me on his front porch for a spell.

"Go right ahead," he says, and he walks out there with me. I can see he wants to know what's in the box, and he ain't going away until I open it. I sit down on a small wooden chair out there and set the box on my lap. I put the two envelopes in my shirt and open the box.

Robert says, "What's that? Undergarments or some such?"

It's the gowns I bought for them at Christmas. "I guess they kept the toilet water," I say.

"Pardon?"

"It ain't undergarments. It's linen. Like dressing gowns." They will be good for cloth but both are way too big for Ink.

I sit there with the gowns in my lap and wait and finally Robert gets the idea. "I guess I'll go on back inside, then," he says.

I nod.

"Much obliged for the Shakespeare. Any chance you might want to sell them gowns?"

"No," I say. "I think I'll keep them for myself."

He looks at me funny.

"To trade with the Indians," I say.

He goes on inside and I gather the gowns up and walk over to the stable. I stuff them in my pack, then set down against the post in front of the stable and take out the envelopes. It's a letter from each of them.

Christine's says:

Bobby Hale or whatever your name is—

I knew you would not come back. I do not blame you. I believe it was fate, and think I said so at the time. I knew it would not be. I hope you are alive and that you were not killed by the savages who attacked General Custer. Fate has intervened and we have met a very kind fellow who is big and strong and more than capable. He brought with him two oxen and his family. He has thrown in with a train of thirty wagons, and he promises to take us the rest of the way. My sister and I thank you for your kind help when you provided any. We are returning the articles of clothing you gave us at Christmas, as we believe it would be inappropriate for us to keep such intimate articles from a complete stranger. We buried General Cooney the 2nd of June, in the army cemetery at Fort Ellis. We both hope and pray that you are alive and that you fare well.

Cordially,
Christine Barkley

Eveline wrote:

Bobby Dearest,

I am horrified to hear of the battle and the heroic death of so many. I am hoping with all my heart that you have not been among those who bravely gave their lives on the Little Bighorn. I am crying as I write this. Christine has taken back the gown you got me at Christmas and intends to leave it here in case you are alive. I would not consent to such a thing but that I know it might bring a kind of luck that you may survive to see this letter. I would hate for you to be handed back such a fine gift as though I did not and Christine did not appreciate it. But, my love, I have such bad luck in things of that nature, perchance my bad luck will continue and you will be handed these gifts back, and in the

process prove to be alive and well. If you have survived, please come after us on the trail. I am yours, Bobby, if you wish it.
    Love,
    Eveline

I set there leaning against that post, with the smell of horse manure in my nostrils, and think about all I been through. I feel a sadness in my mind that leaks into something of my whole damn soul. Poor Eveline. She was true at heart and a fine woman for any man. I don't know if I wish I had made it back or not. It's a tragic kind of world we find ourselves in, all the time looking for some way to have what we want, hoping for nothing but a reason to hope. It ain't easy being on this earth for none of us—because we know about future things and what we want or don't want, or we can be pretty damn confused by both wanting and not wanting. And we don't know all the time what is taken away and what is given. Sometimes we know what we have been given only when it's been lost. I don't know why I am so sad. I got to take care of Ink and Little Fox, and I don't know what I would do if Eveline come back for me or if I run into her again. She is gone, and with her goes the life I'd of had with her. Maybe I am just sad because she cared for me and I let her down.

I put my head back and try to sleep, but it ain't easy with the sun climbing the sky and everything heating up. Even setting outside on the ground, the air is still and steaming. I might of drifted off a bit, but then I finally open my eyes to the bright day and decide to get moving. I walk over to the commissary store and buy two boxes of cartridges for my carbine. As I'm turning to leave, I see a newspaper tacked to the wall next to the counter. It reads:

EXTRA, EXTRA

DISPATCH FROM THE NEW YORK TIMES, JULY 6TH 1876
The dispatches giving an account of the slaughter of Gen. Custer's command, published by THE TIMES of yesterday, are confirmed and supplemented by official reports from Gen.

A. H. Terry, commanding the expedition. On June 25 Gen. Custer's command came upon the main camp of Sitting Bull, and at once attacked it, charging the thickest part of it with five companies, Major Reno, with seven companies attacking on the other side. The soldiers were repulsed and a wholesale slaughter ensued. Gen. Custer, his brother, his nephew, and his brother-in-law were killed, and not one of his detachment escaped. The Indians surrounded Major Reno's command and held them in the hills during a whole day, but Gibbon's command came up and the Indians left. The number of killed is stated at 300 and the wounded at 31. Two hundred and seven men are said to have been buried in one place. The list of killed includes seventeen commissioned officers.

Indians, who numbered in the thousands, led by Sitting Bull, made repeated and desperate charges, which were repulsed with great slaughter to the Indians. They gained higher ground than Custer occupied, and as their arms were longer range and better than the cavalry's, they kept up a galling fire until the last man of the cavalry fell.

While I'm reading the article, a fellow comes up next to me. I step to one side to make room, but he keeps crowding me. I look at him directly and he says, "It's a damn shame, ain't it?"

I realize it's Nate, the fellow I rescued along with Jake and Daniel. It gives me a start to recognize him. I wonder if he's talked to Daniel, if he knows what I done. I step back, a bit wary for the way he looks at me. He's in uniform and looking polished, although his cowcatcher teeth still jut out at me and his thick red hair bulges from under his hat.

"A damn shame," he says again.

"I guess it is," I say.

"What're you doing here?"

"I might ask the same of you."

"I ain't been sent nowhere. I been here all along."

"You got over your sickness?"

"I guess I did. How'd you get to know about it?"

I don't say nothing to that. We stand there for a spell, then he says, "Wasn't you with them scouts that went out with General Gibbon?"

"I was there," I say. "I seen this here battle they're talking about in this paper."

He puts his hands behind his back and seems to swagger a bit standing there. He don't say nothing, but I can see he's trying to figure what he should do now. "You was there."

"I was."

"There wasn't no survivors."

"You see me standing here, don't you? I was there."

"Well, we're all going now," he says. "The whole fort is heading east to have it out with them Injuns once and for all."

"I ain't in on it," I say.

"We're leaving this afternoon. We're gonna kill every single Injun between here and the Missouri River."

I think of where I left Ink and what might happen if I don't get going pretty quick. Nate stands too close to me and seems like he's waiting for me to say something. When I don't, he says, "You say you was there?"

"I was. It ain't nothing glorious about it. And them Indians did not have better arms. They hardly had any guns at all."

"You know that for a fact."

"It ain't what it says here, I can tell you that."

"How'd you get here?"

"I ain't no soldier in no man's army. I signed on to help them find Indians. They found them."

"I guess they did."

"And the Indians was none too happy to be found."

"They'll pay for what they done."

"They didn't do much," I say.

"What do you mean by that?" He's got his dander up a bit. He steps closer and I smell whiskey on him.

"You folks can go on killing each other all you want," I say. "I've had my stomach full."

"What do you mean, the Indians didn't do much? You on their side, renegade?"

"I ain't on nobody's side."

"A renegade," he says, happy with his conclusion.

"Them fellows in Custer's cavalry was green and young," I say. "Most ain't never seen a battle. They fought a long time, but the truth is, in the end, most of them went ahead and killed theirselves."

"Who done that?"

"Custer's men. On the hill. I seen it with my own eyes."

"You take that back," he says. Suddenly his face is red. I think if I ever got angry that fast, everybody I know would be dead.

"It ain't nothing against you," I say.

"You're a coward and a liar."

"Well," I say. "I ain't got time for this."

I turn to leave, but he grabs my arm. "You take it back, what you just said."

"Sure," I say. "I gladly take it back." He waits there, looking at me. "Now let me go."

"I think you skedaddled out of there the same way you done in the army during the war."

I don't know how he can know about that, but I see no reason to challenge him on it. Then I realize it's a accusation—that he thinks I will be insulted if he claims this is what I done in the war. He has no idea he guessed my true history. So I step up close to him. He don't back down much. I say, "I wasn't born in the woods to be scared by no owl." He's looking up at me because I'm a mite taller. I see something behind his eyes falter. Then I say, "I'm leaving this here place right now. You want to try and stop me?"

"You get out," he says, like it's his idea.

He watches me walk out of the place. I go back over to the stable to see what that fellow got for my horses and the robes. But when I get there, ain't nobody around. It's late in the afternoon and hot. I can hear bugles and then men and horses at Fort Ellis. It's a commotion that I know means I have to get out of this place and get back to Ink now. I can't wait around to talk to nobody, but I don't want to leave my horses there with them robes. So I get everything packed up again and ride out of there with everything I had when I rode in, and more. I got the two gowns from Eveline and Christine, and plenty of ammunition for my rifle.

CHAPTER 30

I DON'T WANT TO ride Cricket too hard, and the other horses can't really keep up if I go too fast, but I keep them moving along. It ain't far and in the daylight I can keep to good terrain. I know the army is behind me and we got to get our camp packed up and head north to miss them.

When I get back to her, Ink is laying on the ground with the boy behind her, and she's aiming the Colt Dragoon right at my throat. When she sees it's me, she gets up and lets the pistol drop to her side. The boy rushes up and grabs the reins of my horse.

"We got to hurry," I say.

"Are they after you?"

"No. They're coming though. I don't want to be here between them and where they're going."

"Who?"

"The army."

We get packed up and Ink cuts some tree branches and brushes the ground around our camp. She turns the stones away from where the fire was and buries some of them. In a few minutes you can't tell we was even there.

We head north up the Gallatin valley toward Fort Benton and the Missouri River. On both sides of us is high, white-tipped mountains and good timber in the foothills. We push hard up that valley, and we'll keep going until we get to the river, then we'll follow it north and west.

On the first day, when I think it is safe to stop, we go into the timber a ways from the trail and set up another camp. We are near the end of the Musselshell River. We don't build no fire yet; it's getting near dark and I don't know what's ahead of us. I give Ink and the boy a bit of dried venison, and I chew on a bit of it myself. We got plenty of water. I watch the sun disappearing behind the trees and the shadow of the mountain begin to rise up on the ridge at the other side. We are in paradise. The blue water of the river and the high white clouds over the top of the mountains sparkle in the evening light; most everywhere it ain't blue, it's green, and the few stones that poke through look like the gray rocks of heaven. We can hear the water rushing in the river and not much else. We are very far from the army, and Ink knows it. She says she wants a fire. Even in the middle of the summer it can get pretty cold at night, and this close to the river you can almost believe it's December, not July. I can see my breath.

"Nobody is following us this way," she says. "We can build a big fire if we want."

"I don't like it," I say. But I see the boy shivering.

"We are far enough in these trees, nobody is going to see us," Ink says.

"I guess it's okay," I say.

It ain't hard to find dry wood and brush to get a fire going. The smoke climbs high, though, and I know when it is dark anybody on the other side of this canyon will see the glow of it. The army went out east, though, I'm sure of that. Who would want to find us where we are?

I ain't thinking too much about what was promised yesterday. I am glad to be here, was glad to see Ink when I come upon her, even though she had that Colt Dragoon pointed at me. Little Fox don't seem near ready to bed down, and the three of us sit up against a fallen tree and watch the dark green climb the cliffs across from us while the light dies out.

"Where we going?" I say.

"To Indian country."

"Idaho?"

"The land of the Nez Perce," Ink says. In the weak firelight, with the sky turning gray, she appears almost ghostly. She looks at me, a half smile on her face. "They live in peace, and no white man is interested in their land."

"It's a long way to northern Idaho," I say.

"It is not that far," she says.

Little Fox tries to say "Idaho," but all he manages is "Waygo."

"Waygo?"

Ink says, "We go."

The boy nods his head. His skin is brown as Ink's and nobody will doubt he's her kin. Next to them, with my red hair and pale skin, I might be taken as their captor before a body'd think maybe they was with me of their own free will. This makes me think a little more on the subject of where we might be headed.

"Maybe you should go to Idaho without me," I say.

Both of them look at me with black, serious eyes.

"I'll help you get there," I say. "But I'm just as much a conversation piece among them Indians as you and the boy would be among the whites."

She don't say nothing. Little Fox, I see, don't have no idea what I said. But he knows something is going on.

"That's about the half of it and the whole of it," I say. "Any way we try to go, there's trouble."

"Not among the Nez Perce," she says. "They are friendly with everyone, even white men. You would be welcome around their fires."

"How do you know that?"

"My mother was Nez Perce."

"I thought you said she was Miniconjou."

She shakes her head. "I will have family there. They will know me."

"You speak the language?"

"Some. I will remember more when we are with them." She looks down at the boy now and begins to pat his head. He yawns, and I think of what she said the other day about the next time we was together and Little Fox was asleep.

"There is no gold in Idaho," Ink says. "The Nez Perce live in peace with the white man and all others."

"Okay," I say. "We'll go to Idaho." I smile at the little boy and rough the hair on his head. He knows me good enough now that he don't duck when I reach for him. He only looks at me with them needy eyes and I know I will take care of him. I think he may know it too. If he don't, someday I intend he will.

"We will be safe with the Nez Perce," Ink says. "We can live our lives there and raise this boy to manhood. We can teach him not to hate."

I don't believe it for a minute. But it sounds so fine. I wish it was true as the movements of earth. So much of what folks want in the world turns out to be just a thing they say. Words change the way you feel for a small time and that just about goes as far as it can go toward being a true thing. Everybody says they want to live in peace; everybody says they don't want to go to no war. Nobody wants to spend every waking moment looking to be killed or having to kill somebody to keep from getting killed. That's what you would think. But what humans do is just that. All the time. So no matter how it makes you feel, no matter what folks *say* about war and killing, we're all lying to ourselves and everybody else. It's all one big everlasting lie. When I know this, it don't feel right even thinking about a thing so far off as happiness. Something way down inside of me feels like it's dripping and damp and completely evil. I know I am a animal that can talk and there ain't nothing that will ever save me nor no one else. This is what we are, and until we die, it's all we are. A savage animal that can talk.

But then after more than just a little while the boy falls asleep and Ink wraps him up tight in a blanket. She comes to me and puts her arms around my neck and says again, "You have done very well," and it makes me feel like the whole world don't exist outside the rim of this here fire.

"I done well getting to be with you," I say, and I realize I mean it. Now something very different seems to take hold of my mind. It ain't desire, neither. It's a feeling of being saved from something dark and final.

"You shot me," she says. "And now I say to you I am grateful for it."

"We will travel in daylight from now on," I say.

She don't say much of nothing else the rest of that night. We lay in each other's arms and I don't understand words like "hate" nor "death" nor "killing" nor nothing at all nowhere but here, between us, in the blue night next to the curling fire and the white moon high over the silver tops of the dark mountains. Much later that night I say, "Diana. It's a beautiful name."

She laughs sweetly. "I am Ink now."

"Yes," I say. "I will take care of you and the boy. If that's what you want."

"With you," she says. "That is what I want."

"You won't run from me, then?"

"I will be with you and no other."

"I won't have to chase after you someday, like Hump?"

She moves even closer to me, her head on my shoulder, her cheek against mine. "No. Do not say it," she says. But she knows I don't mean the question.

"Maybe this is all we need," I say.

She is quiet. Sleep comes to me like a feeling of joyful remembering; like I ain't never lifted nothing heavy in my life; like I been a boy all my time and the world ain't at all what I come to fear it is. And in the bright, misty morning, we pack up silently, put out the fire, and load up for the long trek to the land of the Nez Perce—far away from all this trouble and slaughter—where Ink is certain we can be happy and live in peace.

{ A NOTE ON THE LANGUAGES } USED IN THIS BOOK

Aside from the dialect used on the part of the narrator, the language spoken by Ink and to some extent Eveline and her sister was the proper learned speaking language of the time. Speakers rarely used contractions in their speech, nor did they approve of double negatives or slang terminology.

In Indian languages, double consonants are almost always indications of the voice spending a longer time on that particular consonant than one would in English. In English we say a word like "normally" by pronouncing only one *l* sound. With double consonants in Indian languages, it would sound more like the sound we make when we say "will lie," or "still left." The same with the *s* sound. The *s* in "sentence" is shorter than the *s* sound in "yes seven" or "horse sense." The same is true of the vowels. "Aa" is the same as the "a" in "above." All of what I learned about Crow languages came from George Reed Jr. In the text of the novel, sometimes I tried to spell the language phonetically if I could. Most of the language is written the way it should be. Here I've listed the English phrases first and under them what George provided as the Crow equivalent:

This is a bad thing
Hinne xawiimmaatchaachik

Give me the hands and feet
Ischee lak ihchee lak bakaalah

Let me have his hands and feet
Ischee lak ihchee lak huhkaalah

I want this
Hinne beewiawaak

Now I must die
Hilaake kammaashbimmaachik

This is Chiischipaalia
Hinne chiischipaaliash kook

He is the leader of the River Crow
Biinneesappeele ishbacheettuua kook

We are your friends
Diilapaache biituuk

I make you a gift
Baamniawaawalakuk

I offer you a gift
Hinne baaniiummuak

I am grateful to you
Biiitchilaak (I spelled this phonetically in the book.)

The following are Sioux words and how they would be pronounced
phonetically:

Bad
Sica (shee-chah)

Big
Tanka (dahn-kah)

Chief
Wicasa Yata Pi (wee-chah-shah yah-dah-pee)

White man's world (in the)
Wasicula Eekta (wah-shee-chue-lah ay-kdah)

The following are Cheyenne words and how they would be pronounced phonetically:

Friend, usually only said by one female to another. (Ink gets this wrong.)
Navésé'e—Nahveesay-eh

Where did you come from?
Tósa'e nénexhé´óhtse—Tosunny cheost

What is your name?
Ni-don-sshi-vi—Nee don she eve

Horse
mo´éhno´ha—Mo ache noch

Where are you going?
Tósa´e nétao´sɛtsɛhe´ohtse—Tosend aus tearth

Thank you (This term is used among many tribes.)
Hahóo—Tda-ho

{ ACKNOWLEDGMENTS }

I AM GRATEFUL TO Thomas McGuane for his friendship and his suggestion of several books to read before I began to write this novel. Several books provided the kind of information that allowed me to imagine myself with these characters—to inhabit them—where and when they lived. I knew from experience what it was like to ride a horse into good country and camp under a night sky. In my youth I owned a horse I called Cricket and took her on trails in and around Rantoul, Illinois, for two years. I learned and felt all the sounds, the smell, the warm touch, of a breathing animal walking with you in black pine forests. But I needed to be in that time, wandering in the broad, beautiful, savage expanse that was the Great Plains and the country in Wyoming, Montana, and the Dakotas.

I am also grateful to George Reed, a Crow Indian who helped me with the Indian languages, especially Crow. Although many of the words I used in this book were phonetically spelled, they are the Crow and Sioux spoken languages as closely as I could approximate it. I have provided a list of the actual spellings of these words at the end of the narrative.

Most of the books I read were written by contemporaries, by folks who lived through those times. The best were two books suggested by Tom McGuane: *Wooden Leg: A Warrior Who Fought Custer*, by Wooden Leg, as translated by Thomas B. Marquis, and *Tough Trip Through Paradise, 1878–1879*, by Andrew Garcia.

Both of these books are memoirs by people who lived and breathed in the northern plains of the late nineteenth century. Both books are still available in paperback. *Wooden Leg* is the story of a Cheyenne brave who was among those who attacked Custer's command at the Little Bighorn. It is not only about that battle. It traces life on the plains, Indian family life and traditions, even some of the laws and the system of justice between couples and families. It tells the story of growing to young manhood among the Cheyenne, and methods of survival and war among the other Indians of the plains.

Tough Trip Through Paradise is detailed, personal, and especially enlightening about the country between Bozeman and the Musselshell, as well as Idaho and Montana. The manuscript was discovered in 1942 in a box among the effects of Mr. Garcia after he died. It is a remarkable memoir and impossible to put down. Although it covers the years 1878 to 1879—three years after my story concludes—it was an invaluable source of information for custom, language, ways of travel, and so on. It was also especially informative about the tragedy that befell the Nez Perce in the last lost battle to preserve the culture and life of the American Indian in the territories of the northwest. It was the destruction of the Nez Perce that ended the European conquest of the Great Plains.

Memoirs of a White Crow Indian by Thomas Laforge as told by Thomas B. Marquis gives a vivid picture of the daily lives of not only the Crow but many of the settlers when they were neighbors and pretty much allies in the ongoing, almost mischievous warfare with the Cheyenne and the Sioux.

Of the books I read that have been written in our time, Allen Wier's great novel *Tehano* is perhaps the most stirring work of all of them. In some ways it alone inspired me to write this book. So much has been written about this period in American history, and much of it tends toward a kind of praise of conquest; there are good guys and bad guys. The good guys are pioneers or cowboys and the bad guys are almost always Indians. This is what I like to call the "*How the West Was Won* syndrome." Other books romantically present this period with reverence for Native Americans and the tragedy of the loss of their land, their heritage, and their identity. They are the good guys. The bad guys are white interlopers carrying disease and industry and a lasting disrespect for all things natural and good. *Tehano* treats the subject only on the level of the persons in it: these events happened to people, and whatever "culture" or "race" attaches does so in the light of their human story. That is the only story I wanted to tell here.

Larry McMurtry's little book *Crazy Horse* is a fine source of information about life among the Sioux around the time of this story. In McMurtry's capable hands, in spite of a lack of real information on the life of Crazy Horse, that great Sioux warrior becomes a living man.

The Portable North American Indian Reader, edited by Frederick W. Turner, gave me the voices of the native Americans, their method of speech.

I read Nathaniel Philbrick's great book on the Puritans, *Mayflower,* to get a clear idea of the mind-set of the earliest Europeans to "settle" this land.

Finally I am grateful for James Donovan's recent book, *A Terrible Glory: Custer and the Little Bighorn, the Last Great Battle of the American West,* which provided crucial information about Indian military strategy and methods of warfare.

Among the Indians there were battles, and men were killed, but many times the conflict between these tribes was almost playful; they strove to steal horses from each other, mostly, and counted it as a great victory if they could do so without killing anyone—without, in fact, even being detected. The Plains Indians, for all their skill on horseback and in battle, rarely sought out an enemy to kill him. It was considered a weakness among the Cheyenne to have to kill a man, and it was not a way to demonstrate courage or valor. Courage was better demonstrated in the way you died, not in how many or how often you killed. Many of the books I read commented on this one fact: the American Indians were mostly appalled at the ease with which Europeans killed, and how many they were pleased to kill all at once. The first Puritan settlers, during the savage and costly Pequot War, trapped an entire Indian encampment inside a long thatch lodge. They set it on fire and shot those who tried to escape—men, women, and children. All the rest died in the fire. The Indian allies of these men of God were horrified. One said, "You kill too many," and they all walked away from it.

In the last analysis, what happened to the American Indian was a colossal tragedy that could not have been avoided. Even the most enlightened people of those times, Indian and European, were so completely different in their understanding of the world and man's place in it, no other outcome was possible. This was a holocaust that was not governed so much by unified hatred as it was by expansionist, nationalistic fervor coming face-to-face with tribal freedom and independence. The clash between the Native American cultures and the Europeans was inescapable because of a deeply psychic difference between the two cultures. The Indians lived *in* nature; they accepted nature as it is and thanked it every day for what they took from it. Their lives depended on the weal and woe of natural circumstances, of the movement of herds, the weather, the hunt. Almost no Indian tribe could conceive of ownership of land—any more than we can today conceive of ownership of air or space or light or weather. But one should not romanticize the American Indian. To a large degree they were so different in their practices and religious beliefs that it is easy to see why Europeans would see them as savages. Some of their rituals *were* savage—the mutilation of the dead by the women comes to mind—but they were still human beings. They had all of the many human vices and crimes: adultery, theft, murder, cruelty, and so on. They also had all of the virtues: love, faithfulness, charity, compassion, and family loyalty. They did not understand the world any more than the Europeans did. Nor did the Indians and the Europeans understand each other.

The Europeans came from a long history of mostly Christian thought—the Augustinian idea that the earth is not finished and it is man's duty to finish it. All of their literature and religion told them to "subdue" nature, to have "dominion over the fish of the sea, the birds of the air, and everything that crawls upon the ground." Their heroes lashed themselves to the mast in the midst of a stormy sea and strived *against* nature; the religious teaching exhorted men to strive against their *own* nature as well. These people had a "destiny." They were going somewhere. Their one true object was continued "progress," i.e., finishing creation. They believed God blessed them in their endeavors, and thus He approved of their actions in bringing about that progress. This meant "civilizing" and "saving" those who were not of the same beliefs, and eradicating those who could not accept it. So the struggle against the American Indian began as a struggle against *nature*. It was not a bald attempt to steal land. Stealing land was easy, since the Indians didn't believe a person could own such a thing. Thus, to the European it wasn't stealing at all. It was subduing nature, and the only way to do that was to get the Indian and all he believed, all he treasured and cherished, out of the way. Some have said the Indians never invented the wheel because they weren't going anywhere. That is historical rubbish.

They knew of the wheel—in fact, they used a kind of wheel to grind corn. The Indians didn't *need* the wheel because it *was* true they weren't going anywhere. Life was a holistic balancing act, not a linear progression to some destiny. The Europeans had a destiny from the start: from "sea to shining sea." We are now living in that destiny, and to some degree we are engaged in the same kind of struggle. Only time—a lot of time—will tell if that earlier tragedy was an unrepeatable misunderstanding between two widely diverse cultures or a prelude to a lasting human disaster.

{ A NOTE ON THE AUTHOR }

ROBERT BAUSCH is the author of six novels and one collection of short stories. They include *Almighty Me* (optioned for film and eventually adapted as *Bruce Almighty*), *A Hole in the Earth* (a *New York Times* Notable and *Washington Post* Favorite Book of the Year), and *Out of Season* (also a *Washington Post* Favorite). He was born in Georgia and raised around Washington, D.C. Educated at George Mason University (B.A., M.A., M.F.A.), he has taught at the University of Virginia, American University, George Mason University, Johns Hopkins University, and currently at Northern Virgina Community College. In 2005, Bausch won the Fellowship of Southern Writers' Hillsdale Award for Fiction for his body of work. In 2009, he was awarded the John Dos Passos Prize for Literature, also for sustained achievement. He lives in Virginia.